GERMAN LITERARY
FAIRY TALES

The German Library : Volume 30

Volkmar Sander, General Editor

GERMAN LITERARY FAIRY TALES

Edited by Frank G. Ryder
and Robert M. Browning

Introduction by Gordon Birrell

Foreword by John Gardner

CONTINUUM · NEW YORK

1992

The Continuum Publishing Company
370 Lexington Avenue
New York, NY 10017

Printed in the United States of America

Library of Congress Cataloging in Publication Data

Main entry under title:

German literary fairy tales.

(The German library; v. 30)
1. Fairy tales—Germany—Translations into
English.   2. Fairy tales—Translations from
German.   3. Short stories, German—Translations
into English.   4. Short stories, English—Trans-
lations from German.   I. Browning, Robert Marcellus,
1911–   .   II. Ryder, Frank Glessner, 1916–
III. Series.
PT1327.G38   1982   833'.01'08   82-12550
ISBN 0-8264-0276-3
ISBN 0-8264-0277-1 (pbk.)

Contents

Foreword *

E veryone knows perfectly well what fairy tales are, and I don't mean to say anything here that changes anyone's mind on the matter; but it has recently struck me that there is a way of talking about fairy tales that no one (so far as I know) has used before, a way that may possibly make clearer what we've known all along. Fairy tales are—literally, I think—the place where myth and reality meet.

Let me start with the observation that "myth" is one of those things everybody knows about and no one feels comfortable defining. I'm something of a specialist on this confusion. For years, partly because I specialize in classical and medieval literature, and partly because I once wrote a more or less "mythic" novel, *Grendel,* I've been invited to conferences or asked to deliver lectures on the subject of myth. I never used to admit until late in the conference or lecture that, to tell the truth, I hadn't the faintest idea what a myth is. (I would confess the truth only when it was clear that everyone present was as baffled as I was.) In fact the only reason I went to these conferences or delivered these lectures was my secret hope that somehow I might finally find out what myths are. I had about decided that no one would ever know, when, a week or so ago, I was suddenly given, in a conversation with poet/fiction-writer Liz Rosenberg, an answer so simple, complete, and satisfying that I will probably have trouble expressing it here.

Editors' note: Between the writing of this Foreword and its publication John Gardner died in a motorcycle accident. He was not yet 50, but he had distinguished himself both as writer and as scholar-critic. His stimulating reflections on the genre make it clear why so many modern writers, Gardner included, have found it no paradox to create their own folk tales, fairy tales, myths.

A character is "mythic," according to Liz Rosenberg, when you can use his name, without reference to any specific story about him, to describe a general type. One can say about one's neighbor, for instance, "He's a real Hercules," or, "The trouble with Elbert is, he thinks he's Jesus."

I admit that pedants can find fault with this definition, but let me pursue it a moment, begging pedants to listen and temporarily hold their fire. A mythic character is what he is in himself, by nature, not by virtue of his role in some large, important story. Though Homer's Achilles, in the *Iliad,* is a very great figure, one of the greatest characters in all Western literature, one does not feel quite right calling him mythic because his striking individuality is inextricably part of his particular story. He is not, simply, the greatest warrior who ever lived (if he were that, he would be mythic); he is a great warrior caught up in an imperfect war—partly just, partly unjust—and tortured by inner conflicts, forced to decisions he doesn't want to make, a brilliant spokesman for peace but also the greatest butcher in all literature. He is, in effect, too complicated for myth. The same is true of Shakespeare's Hamlet: a great and noble prince, but a figure inseparable from the story that makes him what he is—devious, cunning, histrionic, witty, and ultimately mad. If his story had gone otherwise he might be remembered only for his wit.

Mythic figures, on the other hand, are simply what they are. They may be literary creations or they may come from life. Medea, it seems to me, is mythic. Whether she's hypnotizing a giant serpent, arranging her brother's murder, digging herbs at midnight, setting a rival's dress on fire, or murdering her own children, she is essential; she is Medea. Helen of Troy is mythic. In the same way, though he comes from real life, Jesse James is mythic, as is Abraham Lincoln. Among comic book heroes—with the possible exception of Wonder Woman—only Superman feels mythic. One can say, "He's a real Superman"; one cannot so comfortably say, "He's a real Green Hornet" or "a real Batman."

Obviously the definition I'm accepting is not very precise, mainly because it depends heavily on intuition. I would say Paul Bunyan and his Blue Ox, Babe, are mythic; you, especially if you're a Canadian lumberjack, may object, finding him psychologically complex and inseparable from his story. And disagreement may deepen if I argue that Dan'l Boone, Davy Crockett, and Buffalo Bill are mythic. But as Aristotle said, one can ask of any science only as much precision as that science admits, and it seems to me clear that, at least in a general way, mythic heroes (and heroines) are absolute types—the Indian trickster, Old Coyote; god- or godlike-figures such as Zeus, Jehovah, and Buddha; and the classic witch, whatever story she appears in, or her counterpart, the Fairy Godmother. It might also be objected that this character-centered definition of myth does not account for stories universally acknowledged as myths but not focussed on characters, notably creation myths. I think that objection can be answered—creation myths always involve essential beings, whether they be gods or titans or the Seneca Indians' great turtle—but I need not develop that argument here.

What interests me is the fact—at least I think it's a fact—that in fairy tales we always get a conflict between mythic figures and one or more real-life characters, the person or persons who serve as surrogate for the child to whom the story is addressed. In Jack and the Beanstalk, the giant is mythic: he behaves and thinks in this story as he (or his replacement, the ogre) behaves in every other story. Jack, on the other hand, strikes us as, more or less, a real boy. Right from the start his problems are those real children must somehow deal with: he obeys his mother in a way that displeases her, taking beans instead of money for the family cow, and he must somehow redeem himself. It's true that the Welsh have many "Jack" tales, as they're called, and in each of them Jack comes out triumphant. But though all the Jacks have the same name, no one really supposes they're all the same boy. Each is defined by the necessities of his story. One kills numerous giants, jubilantly proving himself. Another—dreamy, poetic—gets lost in the woods and is carried home, asleep, by an owl.

Or think of Snow White. Her wicked stepmother is classic, both in her shape as wicked stepmother and in her shape as witch; and the seven dwarves, even when individualized by Walt Disney, are a permutation of the classic helper group, sometimes fairies, sometimes animals, but in any case always essential, defined by their nature. Snow White herself, on the other hand, is a person inseparable from her progressing story. One cannot easily say, "My neighbor Alice Fitzhugh is a real Snow White." No one would know quite what to make of the comparison. One can say, on the other hand, "Poor Alice! Her mother's a witch."

Fairy tales are neither myths nor realistic stories but a little of each. That is perhaps the secret of their lasting power. The old grandmother who makes up the story or passes it on knows the troubles of the real child in her lap and slyly encourages the child to confront and overcome them; that is, the storyteller presents a fictional character who represents the child (the beanstalk Jack who makes mistakes and feels humiliated, the Snow White whose father's second wife seems jealous of her) and, without oversimplifying or denying the seriousness of the problem, the storyteller vindicates the child. The storyteller could, if she or he wanted, tell a realistic story; but the choice not to do so is obviously a wise one. Using mythic opponents and mythic secret helpers (fairy godmothers, dwarves, animals, kindly woodsmen), the storyteller simultaneously avoids telling a story distractingly close to the child's own and manages to suggest that the child's problem is a common one.

It hardly needs saying that telling a story distractingly close to the child's own would do more harm than good, producing self-pity in the child or justifying the child's hostilities. The last thing one wants, when telling a fairy tale, is to make the child feel justified in running away from home! Archetypes—or mythic figures, as I'm calling them—distance the story, making it *like* but not *the same as* the child's real-life story. However angry the child may be, he cannot really think of his stepmother, however harsh she may be, as an actual witch. (These stories were invented, it should be mentioned in passing, at a time when women regularly died young and stepmothers were common, as they are now again, thanks to the prevalence of divorce. If the traditional fairy tales had been invented in our time, stepfathers would appear as frequently as stepmothers.) Since the child's stepmother is not actually a witch, the child's situation is not as bad as it might be, though the implied long-range result offers hope. Thus fairy tales, like our dreams (as such writers as Bruno Bettelheim have pointed out), help us solve or learn to live with deep psychological problems.

And at the same time, as I've suggested, the mythic figures in fairy tales—both opponents and helpers of the child-hero—help the child see his problem as common, not a result of his personal freakishness. We all feel, as children—and sometimes as adults— a little freakish. "No one is as ugly as I am," we think—or as dishonest, or cowardly, or misunderstood. The fairy tale gives the child someone as bad or unlucky as himself, if not worse, for whom everything nevertheless turned out splendidly, as indeed things often do, especially if one has faith to help one over the rough spots. Fairy tales present children with a universe of angels and devils in pagan disguise, a universe in which the angels almost always win, as long as the child-hero has what the fairy tales define as the normal virtues of childhood—innocence, good-heartedness, sensitivity, alert intelligence. Almost any single fairy tale carries this message (there are, admittedly, a few sick fairy tales); the child who hears dozens of fairy tales gets the message again and again: goodness will triumph eventually; life is ultimately benevolent. Younger brothers, stepchildren, princesslike girls cruelly forced to sweep cinders will in time win their rightful place. The suffering of childhood, the fairy tales say, is as old as the hills; childhood is a terrible time of life, but it passes.

In fairy tales the evils of the world are simplified to archetypal evils—witches, wolves, stepmothers, giants, ogres, dehumanizing spells—and the innumerable subtle forces that sustain us are simplified to magic-helper figures. The world of fairy tales is thus entirely the world of dreams and the so-called unconscious, a shifting, obscurely symbolic landscape outside time, peopled by archetypes; but the dreamer, represented by the child-hero, is like a character out of realistic fiction, defining himself in the process of the story, an individual, wide awake.

JOHN GARDNER

Introduction

O nce upon a time—a not so distant time—the fairy tale suf-
fered the same fate as its heroes and heroines, those neglected third sons and unwanted step-children. Folklorists were
inclined to dismiss the fairy tale as a late and degenerate form of
myth; parents, distressed by elements of violence and terror, presented their children with tasteful adaptations in which there was
no more talk of severed limbs, willfully abandoned children, or
blood-filled slippers.

The time I am referring to is not the late twentieth century—or,
more precisely, not *only* the late twentieth century—but the late
eighteenth century. Despite the efforts of men like Bruno Bettelheim or Max Lüthi, whose subtle and sympathetic studies of the
folk fairy tale are widely read and widely admired, we still find
ourselves much in the same situation as those parents and educa-
tors of the Enlightenment who regarded the folk tale as rather too
grisly material for sensitive young minds, and who felt more comfortable with the graceful literary versions of Charles Perrault or
Johann Karl August Musäus.

It was not until the end of the eighteenth and the beginning of
the nineteenth century, in the context of German Romanticism,
that the folk fairy tale was first acknowledged as oral literature of
the highest order. Significantly, the endorsement of the folk tale
went hand in hand with the creation of a new and far more am-
bitious variety of literary fairy tale, a narrative invention of such
extraordinary appeal that it became, for a brief period, the very
centerpiece of Romantic literary theory.

The retrieval of the folk fairy tale from its furtive existence in the chimney corner and the nursery was part of a larger Romantic reevaluation of the two age groups most closely connected with the fairy tale: the very young and the very old. The ancient grandmothers who narrated the tales and the spellbound children who listened to them shared a privileged view of reality, a view that was not at all analytical or practical or even remotely "reasonable." The fairy tale reflected a state of mind in which all things were possible; in which there was no important distinction between the real and the imaginary; in which such marvelous things as witches, glass mountains, and gingerbread houses were quite simply taken for granted. To the child's "extravagant gaze," as Novalis put it, the world presented itself as a state of disorganized harmony. While adults insisted on classifying and delimiting reality to fit the needs of their realistic and uninspired lives, children enjoyed a sense of chaotic well-being that was perfectly captured in the fairy tale. For the events and situations in the fairy tale were not governed by any sort of logic or causality that the Enlightenment would have cared to acknowledge; fairy-tale characters moved in a radiant, self-contained world that was so removed from everyday existence that any search for serviceable moral messages was utterly misguided. The grandparents who told the tales, grown beyond the concerns of responsible adulthood into a wise and wonderful second childhood, could once again participate in the childlike vision, bringing to it a lifetime of experience, a diffuse, unjudging comprehension that could perhaps begin to divine the profound and mysterious meanings contained in the fairy tale.

The Romantics understood that the folk fairy tale *does* make a coherent statement about the nature of things; they were the first to perceive that the images and situations of oral literature carry an archetypal significance. In fashioning their own literary fairy tales, they were determined not to trivialize the folk materials by turning them into the sort of rococo confections that had appealed to the early eighteenth century. The Romantic strategy was to maintain the naive harmony of the folk tale while at the same time suffusing the narrative with symbolic or allegorical associations. Simplicity of tone was to be combined with complexity of allusion. In the mathematical metaphor favored by the Romantics, the literary fairy tale represented an "exponential function" of the folk tale; it raised the folk tale to the second or third power of intellec-

tual depth and inclusiveness without sacrificing the original sense
of simpleheartedness and wonder.

The literary tale, then, has something important to say about
adult existence, but it says it in a prismatic way, through the language and situations of the folk tale. To borrow Blake's terminol-
ogy, the works in this collection are tales of experience told in the
idiom of innocence. For this reason, very few of the stories can
legitimately be termed children's literature. While certain tales, such
as Novalis's "Hyacinth and Rosebud" or Storm's "Hinzelmeier,"
are certainly accessible to a younger reader, they share with the
other tales an underlying complexity of vision that few children
can grasp: a nostalgia for lost innocence coupled with a knowing
eye for the evasive maneuvers that men and women use to circum-
vent the trials of self-realization and true adulthood.

For an American reader, it may come as something of a surprise
to see represented in this collection some of the most distinguished
names in German literature. We are accustomed to think of fairy-
tale writers as people like Lewis Carroll or J. R. R. Tolkien, who
have a genius for fantasy but little success in, or concern for, more
conventional forms of fiction. In German letters the situation was
quite different. Well into the twentieth century, the ability to turn
out a finely crafted fairy tale was considered a mark of the highest
literary accomplishment. It meant the ability to combine playfulness of form with seriousness of content; to bring to narrative
prose the tautness and luminosity of lyric poetry; to create a fully
imagined, self-contained fantasy world that expresses something
essential about the nature of the real world. The fairy tale is not
a mere trifle or a diversion from the important work of serious
fiction. Both Novalis's "Klingsohr's Tale" and Goethe's "Fairy
Tale" serve as the final chapters of otherwise realistic novels
(*Heinrich von Ofterdingen* and *Stories of German Emigrants*), to
which they provide a fantastic culmination, a technically stunning
finale not unlike the last movement of Beethoven's Ninth Sym-
phony.

The literary fairy tale always contains an element of self-con-
sciousness and ironic quotation, since it derives its materials and
its organization from another, older form of narrative. As a sec-
ondary or hybrid genre, the literary tale presents special problems
of classification. Clearly, any short piece of fiction that borrows

props (magic rings, poisoned apples), personnel (witches, enchanted princesses), or structural features (interdictions, magic curses) from the folk tale may style itself as a literary fairy tale. And the extent of borrowing may vary quite widely. Brentano's "Myrtle-Girl," for example, duplicates the tone and the themes of the folk fairy tale so faithfully that the story might be taken from Grimm. Hoffmann's "Krakatuk," on the other hand, combines the naive feeling of the folk tale with a number of arch references to contemporary life, such as the Queen's idea of placing an advertisement in domestic and foreign newspapers to help locate the young man who can crack the magic nut. The tale of Sleeping Beauty lies deeply imbedded, but still recognizable, within Novalis's "Klingsohr," while Goethe's "New Melusina," as the title suggests, takes considerable liberties with the old legend and reestablishes it in a setting that is unmistakably nineteenth century. At the far end of the spectrum are works such as Hofmannsthal's "Tale of the 672nd Night" or, to cite two examples from contemporary American literature, J. P. Donleavy's *A Fairy Tale of New York* and Donald Barthelme's *Snow White,* in which the ironic distance from folklore has been stretched to such an extent that authorial testimony (in the title itself) must be supplied in order to orient the reader to the presence of fairy-tale elements.

While there scarcely seems to be any limit to the ways in which writers can appropriate and adapt the materials of the folk tale, literary fairy tales nonetheless tend to fall into two broad categories. The first group is derived from the familiar tales of the Brothers Grimm, the tales of those young heroes or heroines who set out to make their fortune, aided by magical assistants and challenged by equally magical opponents, none of whom arouses even the slightest trace of supernatural dread or curiosity. This radiant world, in which real and marvelous figures exist on a common plane, becomes in the literary reworking an allegorical field of forces, a fantastic two-dimensional game board on which the vivid figures of the folk tale move as representatives of abstract ideas. Novalis's Hyacinth and Rosebud are not merely universal Boy and universal Girl, but questing Mind and passive Nature, Cognition and Reality, whose lost unity is recovered forever in the lovers' concluding embrace. Storm's Hinzelmeier is torn between a remote, infinitely receding vision of Knowledge (represented allegorically through his magical green glasses) and the restrictive but rejuvenating interior space of Love (represented by the Rose Maiden). The identification of figure and meaning is, of course, not always so straightforward; in "Klingsohr" and Goethe's "Fairy Tale" each of the characters is weighted with such an abundance of allegorical associations that the stories have a kaleidoscopic quality, their meanings aligning and realigning themselves differently with each new reading.

The second group of literary tales is not, strictly speaking, based on the folk fairy tale at all, but on a kind of folklore known in German as *Sagen,* local legends of the supernatural. In these narratives, marvelous events are emphatically experienced as marvelous; their extraordinary and unfathomable nature forms the very heart of the narrative, its reason for being told at all. The *Sage* records the terror, the fascination, the delight, or the outrage of ordinary mortals who stumble upon beings who have no right to exist in a rational universe. Demonic temptresses, vengeful ogres, helpful elves: the list is long and familiar. The literary fairy tales derived from the *Sage* go beyond this simple formula by exploring the psychological situation of the human beings who encounter the supernatural. Typically, the element of horror is heightened by the suggestion that a hidden and unsavory *affinity* exists between the subconscious needs or fears of the hero and the numinous creatures he comes across as soon as he strays beyond the secure territory of human society. The marble statue of Venus, in Eichendorff's tale, appeals to a dangerous inclination in the young hero, an unfocused, self-indulgent longing in which infatuation with love itself becomes more important than devotion to the human object of love. In Hofmannsthal's tale, the surrealistic scenes of squalor and despair that the merchant's son confronts reflect in a nightmarish way his relationship to the ersatz family of servants he has gathered around him. Tieck's "Fair-haired Eckbert" adds an ironic twist to the format: for the guilty, confused Eckbert it is, of all things, the innocent world of the folk fairy tale that arouses supernatural horror, as Eckbert finds himself unaccountably reentering the magical valley of birches once inhabited by his sister Bertha.

Whatever form the literary tale may take, certain themes recur in it so consistently that they may be considered central to the genre. One such theme is the quest. The heroes of the literary tale, like their counterparts in the folk tale, are either thrust out into the world to seek their fortune or feel too restless to stay at home passively awaiting what fate may bring. The stakes, however, are loftier (or in any event more cerebral) than the hand of a princess or the wealth of a kingdom. The hero of the literary tale strives for self-discovery, self-fulfillment, or, in some cases, nothing less than a totally integrated existence. In Goethe's "Fairy Tale," the goal is, among other things, the union of life (the youth) and art (the lily); in "Klingsohr" it is the fusion of mind (Eros) and nature (Freya). The fairy-tale travelers move through what might be termed expressive space: landscapes of the soul that mirror the mental or emotional changes in the heroes as they pursue their quest. For the narrator of "The New Melusina," the constraints of domestic life represent, figuratively and also quite literally, a terrifying diminution of his existence. In Tieck's "The Runenberg," the contradictory needs of the hero's soul are expressed in the divided terrain of mountains and plains, inorganic and organic nature. Indefinite space reflects a quest that has degenerated into disorientation or hopelessness: Kafka's eerie jackals roam forever through the desert in their desperate search for self-justification, while the merchant's son in Hofmannsthal's tale journeys toward death in the sordid labyrinth of his own psyche.

Another recurrent motif is that of transformation and enchantment. Here again the literary tale adapts the devices of the folk tale to demonstrate the dynamics of the mind. Physical changes reveal mental changes. When Eros and Ginnistan ("Klingsohr's Tale") make love, Eros awakens from the "forbidden intoxication" to find himself transformed from a strapping young man to a mischievous winged cupid: the union of love and fantasy has changed love into restless, irresponsible infatuation. ("The Marble Statue" makes much the same point, but without the trappings of allegory.) One of the central premises of the literary fairy tale is its belief in the volatility of the human mind. Mental and emotional states are capable of the most wondrous and unforeseen transformations—or of the most appalling fixations. Wackenroder's naked saint, whose sensitive soul is obsessed to the point of madness with the roaring noise of time, instantaneously changes into a luminous ethereal being, the spirit of music, when he beholds two young people floating by in the timeless harmony of love. The woman of the forest in "The Runenberg" appears variously as a splendid beauty, an ugly hag, and a strange man who passes through Christian's village; that Christian is able to identify her through all of her remarkable transformations testifies to the mysterious vision that he has acquired on the mountain, a vision that recognizes the illusoriness of surface reality and penetrates to the hidden essence of things. Transformations can also have a negative effect. Figures like Eckbert and the merchant's son are so fundamentally deluded or so torn by ambivalence that self-revelation is tantamount to self-annihilation. As the landscape around him is transformed into the scenery of Bertha's childhood and the old woman speaks the words that once might have saved him, Eckbert falls to the ground, insane and dying. The merchant's son is fatally wounded by the kick of a horse whose expression of haughty malevolence reflects the innermost nature of the young man himself (and his father as well); as death approaches, the handsome features of the merchant's son are in fact transformed by bitterness and despair into a hideous likeness of the horse's face.

The motif of enchantment takes a playful, humorous turn in Hoffmann's "Krakatuk," in which the princess Perlipat is metamorphosed into a giant ratlike creature by the vengeful Mrs. Mouserinks, matriarch of the palace mice. More serious is the enchantment of Donato in "The Marble Statue," whose surrender to the spell of Venus results in permanent desolation of the soul. Kafka's jackals are likewise bewitched creatures, suspended forever in a curious state of mind that combines arrogant self-assurance with a pathetic need for recognition, chaste otherworldliness with bloodthirsty appetite.

The literary fairy tale can no longer seriously be understood as the "paradigm of literature," as Novalis termed it. Fashions in narrative art change, and what once was considered an audacious experimental form has lost much of its vitality and freshness. Nevertheless, the concerns of the literary tale are still very much with us. In a world of chemical psychotherapy, behavioral modification, and paperbacks outlining the road to holistic happiness, the themes of enchantment, transformation, and cosmic quest have not been abandoned or superseded but, if anything, reconfirmed in their universal validity.

GORDON BIRRELL

Fairy Tale

Johann Wolfgang von Goethe

Wearied by the labors of the day, the old ferryman lay sleeping in his hut beside the great river, which, swollen by a recent heavy rain, had overflowed its banks. In the middle of the night loud voices awakened him: travelers wanted to be set across.

When he stepped out of his doorway he saw two large will-o'-the-wisps hovering above his moored boat. They assured him that they were in great haste and already wished to be on the farther shore. The old man wasted no time but shoved off and rowed with his accustomed skill diagonally across the stream, while the strangers rapidly hissed at each other in an unknown language and occasionally broke out in loud laughter, meanwhile skipping to and fro, now on the edge of the boat and the benches, now on the bottom.

"The boat's rocking!" cried the old man; "if you're so restless it may capsize; sit down, you wisps!"

At this unreasonable demand they broke out in a great laugh, made fun of the old man and were more flighty than ever. He bore their bad behavior with patience and soon landed on the opposite shore.

"Take this for your trouble!" cried the travelers. They shook themselves and many shining gold pieces fell into the damp boat.

"For heaven's sake, what are you doing!" cried the old man; "you'll bring me the greatest misfortune! If a gold piece had fallen into the water, the stream, which cannot abide this metal, would have risen in mighty waves and swallowed me and my craft, and who knows what might have happened to you. Take back your gold!"

1

"We can't take back anything we've shaken off," they replied.

"Then I shall be compelled," said the old man, bending down and collecting the gold pieces in his cap, "to find every last piece and take them ashore and bury them."

The will-o'-the-wisps had sprung out of the boat. "What about my fare?" said the ferryman.

"Whoever refuses to take gold can work for nothing!" cried the will-o'-the-wisps.

"One can pay me only with fruits of the earth."

"Fruits of the earth? We despise them and have never eaten them."

"Just the same, I can't let you go until you promise to deliver to me three heads of cabbage, three artichokes, and three large onions."

The will-o'-the-wisps were about to slip gaily away, but they felt themselves incomprehensibly fettered to the ground; it was the most unpleasant sensation they had ever experienced. They promised to satisfy the ferryman's request at the first opportunity. He released them and shoved off. He was already at some distance when they called after him, "Hey, old man! Listen! We forgot the most important thing!" But he was too far away to hear them. He had let himself drift downstream on the same bank of the river where he intended to bury the perilous gold in a rocky region the water could never reach. He found a tremendous cleft between great rocks, emptied the gold into it and rowed back to his hut.

In this cleft dwelt the beautiful green serpent, who was awakened from her sleep by the fall of the jingling coins. As soon as she caught sight of the luminous, radiant discs, she devoured them with great eagerness, diligently seeking out all the pieces that had fallen in the bushes or between crevices.

Scarcely had she swallowed them when she became most pleasantly aware that the gold was melting in her entrails and spreading through her whole body, and to her great joy she noticed that she had become transparent and luminescent. She had long been assured that this phenomenon was possible, but being doubtful whether this light would last for long, her curiosity and the wish to secure more for the future drove her out of her den to ascertain who could have strewn the beautiful gold into it. She found no one. But all the more pleasure did she take in admiring herself and the charming light she cast as she crawled through the green foliage between plants and bushes. All the leaves seemed made of emerald, all the flowers gloriously transfigured. In vain she searched the lonely wilderness, but her hope sprang anew when she reached a level piece of ground and glimpsed in the distance a brilliance similar to her own. "At last, someone like me!" she cried and hastened toward the spot. She was not deterred by the difficulty of having to creep through bog and morass, for though she much preferred to live on dry mountain meadows and in fissures high in the rocks, liked to eat spicy herbs and usually quenched her thirst with gentle dew and fresh spring water, still for the sake of the beloved gold and in hope of its glorious light she would have undertaken any task imposed upon her.

Very wearied, she at last reached the damp morass where our two will-o'-the-wisps were gamboling. She shot towards them, greeted them and rejoiced to find such charming gentlemen among her relations. The wisps played around her, jumped over her and laughed their own peculiar laugh. "Dear aunt," they said, "even though you are of the horizontal line, that makes no difference. To be sure, we're only related from the side of luminescence, but just look" (here the two flames, sacrificing their breadth, made themselves as long and pointed as possible), "how beautifully this slender length becomes us gentlemen of the vertical line. Don't be offended, dear friend, what family can make a like boast? As long as there have been will-o'-the-wisps, not a one has ever sat or lain down."

The serpent felt very uncomfortable in the presence of these relations, for as high as she might raise her head, she still felt compelled to lower it to the earth again in order to move from place to place, and though she had been extraordinarily pleased with herself in the dark woods, in the presence of these relations her brilliance seemed to be decreasing every second: indeed, she feared that it would finally be wholly extinguished.

In her perplexity she hastily inquired whether the gentlemen could tell her where the shining gold came from that had lately fallen into the rocky cleft. She imagined it must be a shower of gold dropping directly down from heaven. The will-o'-the-wisps laughed and shook themselves, and a great quantity of gold pieces sprang round about them. The serpent hastened to devour them.

"Enjoy your meal, dear aunt," the gentlemen said politely, "we can supply you with more." They shook themselves a few more times so briskly that the serpent could hardly swallow the precious food fast enough. Her brilliance began to increase visibly and she shone quite gloriously, whereas the will-o'-the-wisps had grown thin and small, though without losing their good humor in the slightest.

"I am eternally grateful to you," said the serpent upon regaining her breath after her meal. "Ask of me what you will; if it is in my power, I will do it for you."

"Very well!" cried the will-o'-the-wisps, "tell us where beauteous Lily lives. Take us to her palace and garden as swiftly as possible; we are dying of impatience to throw ourselves at her feet."

"This favor," replied the serpent with a deep sigh, "I can't bestow immediately. Beauteous Lily unfortunately dwells on the other shore."

"On the other shore! And we have ourselves ferried over on a stormy night like this! How cruel is the river that now separates us! Would it not be possible to call back the old ferryman?"

"Your efforts would be in vain," replied the serpent, "for even though you were to come across him on this shore, he wouldn't take you into his boat. He is permitted to bring everyone over, but no one back."

"That's a fine kettle of fish! Are there no other means of crossing the river?"

"There are, but not at this moment. I myself can take you across, but not until midday."

"That's an hour when we don't like to travel."

"Then you can ride across in the evening on the giant's shadow."

"How does one manage that?"

"The great giant, who lives near here, can accomplish nothing with his physical strength; his hands couldn't lift a straw, his shoulders wouldn't bear the weight of a bundle of twigs, but his shadow can do a great deal, in fact, everything. For that reason he is mightiest at sunrise and sunset, and in the evening one need only sit down on the back of his shadow and the giant will then slowly proceed to the shore of the river and the shadow will bear the passenger across. On the other hand, if you wish to go at midday to that patch of woods where the bushes are growing close to the water, then I can set you across and introduce you to beauteous Lily; but if you shrink from the midday heat, all you need do is look up the giant towards evening in that rocky cove—he will be happy to be of service."

With a slight bow, the young gentlemen took their leave, and the serpent was glad to be rid of them, partly in order to be able to rejoice in her own light, partly in order to satisfy her curiosity in regard to something that had been strangely tormenting her for a long time.

In the rocky clefts, in which she often crawled, she had made at a certain spot a strange discovery. For although she was obliged to crawl through these chasms without a light, she could still clearly distinguish objects by feeling. She was accustomed to find everywhere only irregular objects produced by nature; now she would wind between the points of great crystals, now she would feel the teeth and hairs of a vein of pure silver, and she had also brought a few precious stones with her to the light of day. But to her great astonishment she had also felt, in a cave closed on every side, objects that betrayed the forming hand of man: smooth walls, on which she could not crawl up, sharp, regular angles, well-formed columns, and, what astonished her most, human figures, about which she had wound herself a number of times, and which she was bound to think must be made of bronze or highly polished marble. All these experiences she wished to consolidate through the sense of sight and thus confirm what she only surmised. She now thought herself capable of illuminating this wondrous subterranean vault with her own light, and hoped finally to become fully acquainted with these strange objects. Hastening away, she soon found her accustomed path and the crevice by means of which she habitually crept into the sanctuary.

When she arrived at the spot, she looked around curiously, and although her light could not illuminate all the things in the rotunda, those nearest stood out clearly enough. With amazement and reverence she looked up into a shining niche, in which stood the statue of a venerable king cast in pure gold. The size of the statue exceeded human dimensions, but the figure was that of a small rather than a large man. The well-proportioned body was clothed in a simple robe and a wreath of oak leaves encircled the head.

Scarcely had the serpent beheld this venerable image when the king began to speak, asking, "Where do you come from?"

"From the clefts where the gold lives," answered the serpent.

"What is nobler than gold?" asked the king.

"Light," replied the serpent.

"What is more vivifying than light?" he asked.

"Speech," she answered.

While they were talking, the serpent had glanced to one side and seen another splendid image in the adjoining niche. There sat a silver king, tall and rather slight of figure. His body was covered with an adorned garment; crown, girdle and scepter were set with precious stones. He had the serenity of pride in his countenance and seemed about to speak when in the marble wall a dark-colored vein suddenly grew bright and spread a pleasant light throughout the whole temple. By this light the serpent saw the third king, a colossal seated figure made of bronze leaning on a club and adorned with a laurel wreath. He resembled a boulder rather than a man. She was just about to look around at the fourth king, who stood farthest from her, when the vein flashed like lightning, twitched and disappeared and the wall opened up.

A man of medium stature came through the opening and attracted the serpent's attention. He was dressed like a peasant and carried a small lamp, into whose quiet flame it was soothing to look and which marvelously illuminated the whole cathedral, without a trace of shadow.

"Why have you come?" asked the golden king. "We have light already."

"You know I am not permitted to light up the dark."

"Will my kingdom end?" asked the silver king.

"Late or never," replied the old man.

In a deep voice the brazen king asked: "When shall I arise?"

"Soon," returned the old man.

"With whom should I unite?" asked the brazen king.

"With your elder brothers," said the old man.

"What is to become of the youngest?" inquired the brazen king.

"He will seat himself," said the old man.

"I am not weary," cried the fourth king in a hoarse stutter.

While this exchange was taking place, the serpent had been slipping about the temple, observing everything, and was now examining the fourth king from close by.

He stood leaning on a column; his imposing figure was ponderous rather than handsome. The metal from which he was cast was not easy to identify. Actually, it was a mixture of the three metals of which his brothers were composed. But in casting these materials seemed not to have truly amalgamated; gold and silver veins ran irregularly through the brazen mass and lent the image an unpleasing appearance.

Meanwhile, the golden king was addressing the old man. "How many secrets do you know?"

"Three," the old man replied.

"Which is the most important?" asked the silver king.

"The one that is revealed," returned the old man.

"Will you also reveal it to us?" asked the brazen king.

"As soon as I know the fourth one," said the old man.

"What difference does it make to me!" muttered the composite king to himself.

"I know the fourth one," said the serpent. She approached the old man and sibilantly whispered something in his ear.

"The time has come!" cried the old man in a mighty voice.

The temple reverberated, the metal statues resounded, and in the same instant the old man sank away toward the west and the serpent toward the east and with great rapidity pursued separate ways through the clefts of the rock.

All the passages through which the old man took his way at once filled up with gold as he passed, for his lamp possessed the wondrous property of transforming all stones into gold, all wood into silver, dead animals into precious stones, and of destroying all metals; but in order to exercise this power it had to shine alone. If another light was near it, it only sent forth a lovely gleam, which refreshed every living thing.

The old man entered his hut, which was built against the mountainside, and found his wife in a very despondent mood. She was sitting beside the fire weeping disconsolately. "How unhappy I am," she lamented. "I knew I shouldn't have let you leave me today!"

"What's the matter?" asked the old man calmly.

"You had scarcely left," she said sobbing, "when two rude travelers came to the door. I was incautious enough to let them in; they seemed polite, decent people. They were dressed in transparent flames; one might have taken them for will-o'-the-wisps. But they had hardly entered the house when they began to flatter me shamelessly and became so importunate it makes me blush to think of it."

"Well now," her husband replied smiling, "the gentlemen were probably just joking. At your age, one can take such things as common courtesy."

"My age!" cried the woman. "Do I always have to hear about my age? How old am I anyway? Common courtesy! I know what I know. And just look around at what a sight the walls are. Look at those old stones—I haven't seen them in a hundred years. They licked all the gold off them, you can't imagine how quickly, and kept saying it tasted better than ordinary gold. When they had licked them clean, they seemed to be in fine fettle, and it's true that in a short time they had become taller, broader and more gleaming. Then they commenced their former wiles again, patting me and calling me their queen. They shook themselves and a rain of gold pieces sprang about the room; you can still see some shining there under the bench. But alack and alas! Our pug ate some of them, and look, there he is lying dead in front of the fire, poor beast! I didn't notice it until they had gone, otherwise I wouldn't have promised to pay their debt to the ferryman."

"What do they owe him?" asked the old man.

"Three heads of cabbage," said the woman, "three artichokes, and three onions. I've promised to carry them down to the river at daybreak."

"You can do that favor for them," said the old man; "they'll also do us a good turn when the time comes."

"Whether they will or not, I don't know, but they promised and vowed they would."

Meanwhile the fire had sunk low; the old man covered it with ashes and disposed of the shining gold pieces, and now his lamp shone with a beautiful light, the walls became covered with gold and the pug turned into the most beautiful onyx one can imagine. The alternation of brown and black in the veined gem transformed him into a rare work of art.

"Take your basket," he said, "and put the onyx in it; then take the three heads of cabbage, the three artichokes, and the three onions, lay them around it and carry them to the river. Around noon, have the serpent set you across and go visit beauteous Lily. Give her the onyx; her touch will bring it to life, just as her touch kills all living things. She will find a faithful companion in the dog. Tell her not to despair, her redemption is near, the greatest misfortune she can regard as the greatest fortune, for the time has come."

The old woman packed her basket and at daybreak started on her way. The rising sun shone brightly across the river that gleamed in the distance. The woman walked slowly, for the basket weighed on her head, and yet it wasn't the onyx that was so heavy. If she was carrying something dead, she did not feel it at all; on the contrary, then the basket would rise into the air and hover above her head. But it was extremely burdensome to her to carry a fresh vegetable or a small living animal. She had gone along ill-humoredly for a while, when she suddenly stopped, affrighted, for she had almost stepped on the giant's shadow, which stretched out toward her over the plain. Now she perceived his enormous bulk; he had been bathing in the river and was just climbing out of the water. She did not know how to avoid him. As soon as he became aware of her presence, he greeted her jestingly and at once thrust his shadow hands into her basket. Easily and skillfully they removed a cabbage, an artichoke, and an onion and conveyed them to the giant's mouth, who then walked on up the river, leaving the way free for the woman.

She considered whether she shouldn't return and supply the missing vegetables from her garden but went on ahead in spite of her doubts and soon reached the bank of the stream. She sat for a long time waiting for the ferryman, whom she finally saw crossing over with a mysterious passenger. A handsome young man of noble mien, whom she could not get her fill of gazing upon, stepped out of the boat.

"What have you brought with you?" cried the ferryman.

"The vegetables that the will-o'-the-wisps owe you," replied the woman, showing him her wares.

When the old man found only two of each kind, he became irritated and said he could not accept them. The woman pleaded with him, saying she couldn't go back home now, that the burden she was carrying was very heavy and she still had a long way to go. But he refused to yield, assuring her that his decision did not even depend on him.

"What is owing me, I have to leave together for nine hours, and I am not permitted to take my share until I have surrendered one-third to the river."

After a long argument, the old man finally said, "There is still a way out. If you will make a pledge to the river and recognize yourself as its debtor, I will accept the six articles, though there is some danger in it."

"If I keep my word, there can be no danger for me?"

"Not the slightest. Thrust your hand in the river," the old man continued, "and promise you will pay the debt within twenty-four hours."

The old woman complied, but great was her fright when she saw that the hand she withdrew from the water was black as coal. She angrily rebuked the ferryman, maintaining that her hands had always been the most beautiful thing about her and that, for all her hard work, she had always managed to keep these noble members white and dainty. She examined her hand with disgust and cried out in despair, "This is worse yet! I see that it has even shrunk, it's much smaller than the other one."

"It only seems so now," said the old man, "but if you don't keep your word it will become so in fact. The hand will gradually shrink and finally disappear altogether, though you won't lose the use of it. You will be able to do everything as usual, only no one will see it."

"I would prefer not to be able to use it and have people see it," said the old woman. "But no matter, I'll keep my word, if only to get rid of this black hand and my worry as soon as possible."

She quickly took up her basket, which rose of its own accord above her head and hovered freely in the air, then hastened after the young man, who was walking slowly and pensively along the shore. His noble figure and strange attire had deeply impressed the old woman.

His breast was covered by a gleaming cuirass, through which the movement of every part of his handsome torso was visible. About his shoulders hung a scarlet cloak, from his bare head brown hair flowed in beautiful curls; his kindly face was exposed to the rays of the sun, as were also his beautifully formed feet. He calmly trod barefoot over the hot sand; a deep sorrow seemed to make him insensible to all external impressions.

The garrulous old woman tried to draw him into a conversation, but he answered her so curtly that, in spite of his beautiful eyes, she finally grew tired of continually addressing him in vain and took leave of him, saying, "You walk too slowly for me, sir; I must arrive in time to cross the river on the green serpent and deliver my husband's fine gift to beauteous Lily." With these words she strode rapidly onwards, and just as quickly did the handsome youth collect himself and hurry after her.

"You're going to beauteous Lily!" he cried. "That's my way too. What kind of gift is that you're carrying?"

"Sir," replied the woman, "it is not seemly for you to inquire into my secrets so eagerly after having given my questions such brief answers. But if you'd like to make a bargain and tell me your history, then I'll tell you how it stands with me and my present." They soon agreed. The woman confided to him her circumstances, including the story of the dog, and let him look at the wonderful gift.

He at once lifted the natural work of art out of the basket and took the dog, which seemed to be softly slumbering, into his arms.

"Fortunate animal!" he cried; "you will be touched by her hands, she will bring you back to life, while what is living must flee her if it is not to suffer a sad fate. But why sad? Is it not much more grievous and troubling to be lamed by her presence than it would be to die by her hand!

"Look at me," he said, turning to the old woman, "see what a miserable state I must suffer. This armor, which I bore in war with honor, this scarlet cloak, which I sought to deserve by wise governance, is all that fate has left me; the armor is a useless burden, the cloak an insignificant adornment. My crown, scepter, and sword are gone, and I am as naked and needy as any other son of the earth; for the beautiful blue eyes have such a dire effect that they deprive every living creature of its strength and cause those not slain by the touch of her hand to feel themselves transformed into walking shadows."

He continued to lament in this vein, much to the dissatisfaction of the old woman, who was not so much interested in his internal as in his external circumstances. She learned neither the name of his father nor that of his kingdom. He stroked the petrified dog, and, warmed by the sun's rays and his own bosom, it seemed almost alive. He asked many questions about the man with the lamp and about the effect of the sacred light and seemed to expect from it much future benefit for his sad state.

As they conversed, they saw in the distance the majestic arc of the bridge extending from shore to shore begin to shimmer marvelously in the rays of the sun. Both gazed in astonishment, for they had never seen this structure so resplendent.

"What!" cried the prince, "was it not beautiful beyond compare when it stood there before our eyes, built of jasper and opal? Must we not fear to walk upon it, now that it seems composed of emerald, chalcedony, and chrysolite in such enchantingly varied beauty?"

Neither knew about the change that had taken place with the serpent, for it was she who every midday arched herself across the stream and formed the bold sweep of the bridge. The travelers crossed over in silent reverence.

They had scarcely reached the further shore when the bridge began to sway and shortly afterwards touched the surface of the water, whereupon the green serpent assumed her proper form and glided after the travelers. These had barely thanked her for permission to cross the river on her back when they noticed that, besides themselves, there must be other persons in their company, who were, however, invisible. Near them they heard a hissing sound, which the serpent answered in kind. They listened intently and were at last able to distinguish the following words:

"First," two voices were saying alternately, "we will look about incognito in the park of beauteous Lily and beg you at nightfall, when we are halfway presentable, to introduce us to her perfect beauty. You will find us down beside the large lake." "Agreed," answered the serpent, and the hissing sound faded away in the distance.

Our three travelers now discussed in what order they should present themselves to beauteous Lily, for no matter how many persons might be about her, they were only permitted to come and go singly, if they did not wish to suffer very sensible pain.

The woman, the transformed pug in her basket, approached the garden first. She easily located her patroness because she was just then singing and accompanying herself on a harp. The sweet tones appeared first as rings on the surface of the quiet lake, then, as a gentle breeze, swayed the grass and the bushes. She was sitting on an enclosed lawn in the shade of a splendid group of various trees and at first glance once again enchanted the woman's eyes, ears, and heart. She approached her with rapture and swore to herself that this beauteous maiden had grown even more beautiful during her absence.

Still at a distance, the good woman saluted her, saying, "What happiness to look upon you! With what a paradise does your presence surround you! How charmingly the harp rests in your lap, how gently do your arms enclose it, how it seems to long for your bosom and how tenderly it resounds at the touch of your slender fingers! Thrice fortunate the youth who could take its place!"

With these words, she came nearer; beauteous Lily raised her eyes, let her hands sink and replied, "Do not sadden me with untimely praise, it only makes me all the more sensible to my misfortune. Look, there at my feet the poor canary lies dead that used to accompany my song. It would sit on my harp and was carefully trained not to touch me. But today when I was raising my voice in a calm morning song and my little songster was pouring forth his sweet notes more joyously than ever, a hawk swooped down over my head. In its fright the poor little thing took refuge in my bosom and at the same instant I felt the last quiver of its expiring life. It is true that the murderous hawk, struck by my glance, is now drooping its powerless wings there beside the lake, but what good does its punishment do me: my darling is dead, and its grave will only increase the mournful shrubbery of my garden."

"Take courage, beauteous Lily!" said the woman, herself drying a tear that the narration of the unhappy maiden had brought to her eye; "take courage! My husband sends word that you should moderate your sorrow and regard your greatest unhappiness as the harbinger of greatest happiness, for the time has come. And truly," the old woman continued, "these are indeed strange times. Just look at my hand, how black it's become! And, sure enough, it's already smaller. I must hurry, before it disappears altogether! Why did I have to go and do a favor for the will-o'-the-wisps?

Why did I have to meet up with the giant and why did I have to dip my hand in the river? Can't you give me a head of cabbage, an artichoke, and an onion? I'll take them to the river and my hand will be as white as ever; I'll almost be able to compare it with yours."

"Cabbages and onions you might find," replied beauteous Lily, "but artichokes you'd look for in vain. The plants in my extensive garden bear neither blossoms nor fruit, but every twig that I break and plant upon the grave of one of my loved ones thrives and shoots up at once. All this stand of trees, these shrubs, these copses it has been my misfortune to see grow. These shading pines, these obelisk-like cypresses, these colossal oaks and beeches, were all small twigs planted by my hand as mournful monuments in this otherwise infertile soil."

The old woman had paid scant attention to this speech but only gazed at her hand, which, in the presence of beauteous Lily, seemed to be getting ever blacker and growing smaller by the minute. She was about to pick up her basket and hurry away when it occurred to her that she had forgotten the most important thing. She immediately took out the petrified dog and placed it in the grass near the beauteous maiden.

"My husband," she said, "sends you this memento. You know that you can animate this stone by your touch. The loyal, good-natured animal will surely be a great comfort to you, and my unhappiness at losing it will be lessened by the thought that it belongs to you."

Beauteous Lily looked at the pretty creature with pleasure and, as it seemed, with amazement. "Many signs that give me some hope are coinciding," she said, "but alas! are we not prone to the delusion that the best must be near when much misfortune befalls us?

These happy omens, what can they avail?
My poor bird's death, my dear friend's blackened hand?
This dog, a precious stone from head to tail,
Sent by the Lamp to me o'er flood and land?

Far from the human pleasures I esteem,
This grief alone is all that's known to me.

Oh, why does not the Temple stand beside the stream
Spanned by the Bridge, so wide and free?"

This song, which the beauteous Lily had accompanied by the
sweet notes of her harp and which would have charmed every ear,
the good woman had listened to with impatience. She was about
to take her leave when she was again detained by the arrival of
the green serpent. The latter had heard the final verses of the song
and for this reason at once confidently encouraged the beauteous
Lily.

"The prophecy of the bridge is fulfilled!" she cried. "Just ask
this good woman if the arch does not now stand in radiant splendor. What was formerly opaque jasper or opal, through which the
light shone only at the edges, has now become a transparent precious gem. No beryl is so clear and no emerald so beautifully colored."

"My congratulations," said Lily, "but pardon me if I doubt that
the prophecy is fulfilled. Only foot passengers can cross over the
high arch of your bridge, and we have received the promise that
horses and carriages and travelers of all sorts are to be able to
pass back and forth at the same time. Is it not prophesied that the
great pillars are to arise out of the river itself?"

The old woman, who had been keeping her eyes fastened on her
hand, now interrupted the conversation and took her leave.

"Wait just a moment," said beauteous Lily, "and take my poor
canary with you. Ask the lamp to transform it into a beautiful
topaz; then I will restore it to life through my touch, and it, together with your pug, shall be my best consolation. But hasten as
fast as you can, for with sunset a hideous putrefaction will attack
the poor thing and destroy its beautiful form forever."

The old woman laid the tiny corpse in her basket among some
fresh leaves and hurried away.

"However that may be," said the serpent, continuing the interrupted conversation, "the temple is built."

"Yes, but it still does not stand beside the river," replied Lily.

"It still rests in the depths of the earth," said the serpent; "I
have seen and spoken to the kings."

"But when will they arise?" asked Lily.

The serpent replied, "I heard these momentous words resounding through the temple: 'The time has come.'"

A bright and cheerful expression came over the countenance of the beautiful maiden. "That's the second time today I have heard those happy words," she said. "When will the day come when I hear them thrice?"

She rose, and immediately a charming girl stepped forth from the shrubbery and took her harp. This girl was followed by another who folded the carved ivory camp stool on which Lily had been sitting and took it and the silver pillow under her arm. A third girl carrying a large umbrella embroidered with pearls now appeared, waiting to see if Lily might want her to accompany her on a walk. These three maidens were inexpressibly beautiful and charming, and yet they only heightened Lily's beauty, for anyone would have had to admit that they could by no means be compared with her.

Meanwhile beauteous Lily had been admiring the wondrous pug. She bent down, touched him, and in the same instant he sprang up. He looked about him in a lively fashion, scampered back and forth and finally ran to give his mistress a friendly greeting. She took him in her arms and pressed him to her breast.

"As cold as you are," she said, "and even though only half a life is active within you, you are still most welcome to me. I will love you tenderly, play with you, pet you and press you firmly to my heart."

She then let him down, chased him from her, called him back, playing with him so gaily and innocently that one could not help observing her joy with rapture, just as shortly before her sadness had moved every heart to pity.

This joy and these merry games were interrupted by the arrival of the downcast young man. He entered in the state in which we have already seen him, except that the heat of the day had wearied him even more, and in the presence of his beloved he grew paler every second. He was carrying the hawk on his wrist, where it sat with drooping wings as peaceful as a dove.

"It is unkind of you," Lily called out, "to bring that hateful bird into my sight. The monster killed my little songster."

"Don't blame the unhappy bird!" replied the youth. "Blame rather yourself and your untoward fate, and allow me to keep company with the companion of my misery."

Meanwhile the pug had not ceased teasing his mistress, and she responded to the affection of her transparent darling with great pleasure. She clapped her hands to chase him away, then ran to make him follow her. The youth observed all this silently and with growing distaste, but finally, when she took the ugly beast, who seemed to him positively repulsive, in her arms, pressed him to her white bosom and kissed his black snout with her heavenly lips, he lost all patience and cried out in desperation, "Must I, who am compelled by a sad fate to lead my life in your presence, though separated from you, perhaps forever—must I, who have lost everything, even myself, on your account, be forced to behold how such an unnatural monster gives you joy, charms your affections and enjoys your embrace! Am I to continue to wander back and forth, tracing the mournful circle over the river and back again? No, there is still a spark of the old spirit alive in my breast; let it now burst forth in one final flame! If stones can rest on your bosom, then let me turn to stone; if your touch can kill, then let me die by your hand."

He made a violent gesture and the hawk flew from his wrist. He rushed towards the beautiful maiden; she extended her hands to ward him off and touched him all the sooner. He lost consciousness, and with horror she felt the dear burden lying on her bosom. She stepped back with a cry, and the fair youth sank lifeless out of her arms to the ground.

Now the misfortune had come to pass! Sweet Lily stood motionless, gazing fixedly at the lifeless body. Her heart seemed to stop beating and her blue eyes were tearless. In vain did the pug seek to entice her to play with him; life had gone out of all the world with her beloved. Her mute desperation did not cast about for help, for it knew no help.

The serpent, on the other hand, was all the more active. She seemed to be planning some kind of rescue, and in fact her strange movements did at least have the effect of preventing the immediate consequences of the misfortune. With her supple body she described a wide circle about the corpse, seized the end of her tail in her teeth, and then lay there quietly.

Before long one of Lily's beautiful attendants stepped forth, carrying the ivory stool, and gestured to the lovely maiden to seat herself. Soon afterwards the second servant girl appeared with a flame-colored veil and adorned rather than covered the head of her mistress with it. The third girl handed her the harp, and she had scarcely pressed the splendid instrument to herself and struck a few chords when the first attendant returned with a bright, round looking-glass and, taking her stand in front of beauteous Lily, caught her glances in the glass, thus presenting to her the most pleasurable image to be found in nature. Her sorrow heightened her beauty, the harp her grace, and as much as one hoped to see her sad situation changed, even so much did one wish to retain her image forever as it now appeared.

Silently gazing into the looking-glass, she drew melting tones from the harpstrings. Now her sorrow seemed to increase, and the strings responded mightily to her grief; a few times she parted her lips to sing, but her voice failed her and soon her grief found relief in tears. Two of her attendants took her in their arms, the harp slipped from her lap; an attentive girl was barely able to catch it and lay it aside.

"Who will fetch the man with the lamp before the sun goes down?" hissed the serpent softly but audibly. The attendants looked at each other, and Lily's tears flowed more abundantly. At this juncture the woman with the basket came back, all out of breath.

"I'm lost and maimed!" she cried. "Look how my hand has almost entirely disappeared! Neither the ferryman nor the giant was willing to set me across, because I am still in debt to the water. I tried to offer a hundred heads of cabbage and a hundred onions, but in vain; three of each is all they want, and no artichoke is to be found anywhere."

"Forget your own troubles," said the serpent, "and try to help us, then perhaps you too will be helped. Hurry as fast as you can and find the will-o'-the-wisps! It is still too light for you to see them, but maybe you'll hear them laughing and fluttering about. If they hurry, the giant will still set them over the river, and they can find the man with the lamp and send him to us."

The woman hastened away at full speed, and the serpent seemed just as anxious as Lily for the couple's return. Unfortunately the rays of the setting sun were already gilding the highest treetops and long shadows were falling over lake and meadow. The serpent stirred impatiently and Lily dissolved in tears.

In her distress, the serpent looked about everywhere, for she feared the sun might go down any minute, and then putrescence would penetrate the magic circle and irresistibly attack the handsome youth. At last she glimpsed the hawk high in the air, its feathers crimson in the last rays of the setting sun. She shook herself with joy at the good omen, and she was not deceived, for shortly afterwards they saw the man with the lamp gliding over the lake just as though on skates.

The serpent did not move, but Lily called out to him, "What good spirit sent you to us at this moment when we so longed for you and needed you?"

"The spirit of my lamp," replied the old man, "urged me hither and the hawk guided me. The lamp splutters when I am needed, and then I must only look up into the sky for a sign: some bird or meteor will show me the direction I have to take. Be calm, beauteous maiden! Whether I can help, I don't know; one person alone cannot help, but only he who joins together with many at the destined hour. We will try to postpone the crisis and hope for the best.

"Keep your circle closed," he continued, turning to the serpent, and, sitting down on a hillock beside her, he illuminated the dead body with his lamp. "Bring the dead canary here also and lay it in the circle!" The attendant maidens took the little body out of the basket the old woman had left standing and followed the old man's instructions.

The sun had now gone down, and, as the darkness closed in, not only did the serpent and the old man's lamp begin to glow in characteristic fashion, but Lily's veil also shed a soft light that colored with inexpressible grace her pale cheeks and white garment like a tender dawn. Those present looked at one another meditatively, their cares and sorrows alleviated by sure hope.

All were therefore happy to see the old woman accompanied by the two lively flames, who, to be sure, must have expended themselves quite extravagantly in the meantime, for they had again become very gaunt, though they only behaved all the more graciously toward the princess and the other young ladies. In tones of absolute certainty and with much expressiveness they said quite ordinary things, showing themselves especially sensitive to the charm that the radiant veil spread over Lily and her attendants. The young women modestly cast down their eyes, and the praise of their beauty made them all the more beautiful. Everyone was calm and contented except the old woman. Despite her husband's assurances that her hand could not shrink further as long as it was illumined by his lamp, she repeatedly declared that if things went on this way that noble member would disappear altogether before midnight.

The old man with the lamp had been listening attentively to the words of the will-o'-the-wisps, and was pleased that Lily was distracted and cheered by their conversation. And now midnight had already come without anyone realizing it. The old man looked up at the stars and then said, "We are gathered together at a propitious hour. Let each perform his office, each do his duty, and a common happiness will dissolve our individual woes, just as a common misfortune consumes individual joys."

After these words there arose a wondrous murmur: all present began talking aloud to themselves, saying what they had to do. Only the three attendant maidens were silent; one had fallen asleep beside the harp, another beside the umbrella, the third beside the ivory stool, and one could not blame them, for it was late. The flame-clad youths, after a few superficial expressions of courtesy directed to the maidens, had turned their attention exclusively to Lily as the most beautiful of all.

"Grasp the looking-glass," said the old man to the hawk, "and illumine the sleeping girls with the first rays of the sun; wake them with the reflected light from the depths of the sky."

The serpent now began to move: she broke the circle and glided slowly in great sinuous curves toward the river. The two will-o'-the-wisps followed her with great solemnity—one would have thought they were the most serious flames imaginable. The old woman and her husband grasped the basket, whose soft light had hardly been noticeable up to now, pulled on it from both sides, and it became ever larger and more radiant; they then lifted the body of the young man into it and laid the canary on his breast. The basket rose into the air and hovered over the head of the old woman, who then set off after the will-o'-the-wisps. Beauteous Lily took the pug in her arms and followed the old woman; the man with the lamp closed the procession, and the whole scene was marvelously illuminated by all these various lights.

But upon reaching the river they saw with astonishment that it was spanned by a magnificent arc: the benevolent serpent had prepared for them this lustrous passage. By day they had admired the transparent precious stones of which the bridge seemed to consist, and now at night they were astounded by its radiant splendor. Above, the brilliant arc stood out sharply against the night sky, while below vivid rays darted toward the midpoint and revealed the mobile solidity of the structure. The procession proceeded slowly across, and the ferryman, looking from afar out of his hut, gaped in amazement at the luminous arc and the strange lights moving across it.

As soon as they had reached the farther shore, the arc began to sway in characteristic fashion, approaching the water with a wavy motion. Soon the serpent was gliding along the ground, the basket descended to earth, and the serpent again described a circle about it; the old man bowed before her and asked, "What have you determined?"

"To sacrifice myself before I am sacrificed," replied the serpent. "Promise me you will leave no stone on land."

The old man promised and then said to beauteous Lily, "Touch the serpent with your left hand and your beloved with your right."

Lily knelt down and touched the serpent and the corpse. At the same instant the latter seemed to return to life. There was a movement in the basket: the youth sat up. Lily was about to embrace him, but the old man held her back, first helping the youth to get up out of the basket and leading him out of the circle.

He now stood erect, the canary fluttering on his shoulder. In both there was life again, but the spirit had not yet returned. The handsome young man had his eyes open, but he did not see, or at least seemed to look upon everything with indifference. The amazement at this event had scarcely lessened when they noticed how strangely the serpent had changed. Her beautiful, slender body had broken apart into thousands and thousands of lustrous gems. The old woman, in reaching for her basket, had incautiously disturbed the stones, and one could no longer distinguish the form of the serpent—only a beautiful circle of lustrous gems lay there on the ground.

With the help of the old woman, the old man immediately set about collecting the stones in the basket and both then carried it to a high bank of the river where the old man, much to the disapproval of Lily and his wife, who would have liked to choose something for themselves, emptied the whole load into the water. Like brilliant twinkling stars the gems drifted with the current, and one could not tell whether they were lost in the distance or sank to the bottom.

"Gentlemen," the old man then said respectfully to the will-o'-the-wisps, "I will now show you the path and lead the way, but you can do us a great service if you will open the portal of the sanctuary through which we must enter this time and which no one but you can unlock."

The will-o'-the-wisps bowed courteously and fell behind. The old man with the lamp went ahead into a great rock, which opened before him, the youth following him like an automaton; in silent uncertainty Lily walked behind him at a distance. The old woman did not want to be left alone and stretched forth her hand so that the light of her husband's lamp could fall upon it. The will-o'-the-wisps brought up the rear, nodding the points of their flames toward each other as though conversing.

They had not gone far when they found themselves before a great bronze portal whose wings were closed with a golden lock. The old man at once called up the will-o'-the-wisps, who did not need a second invitation, but zealously began to consume lock and bolt with their sharpest flames.

The bronze portal resounded mightily and the wings sprang open, revealing within the sanctuary the venerable statues of the kings illuminated by the entering lights. All bowed before these revered rulers, the will-o'-the-wisps being especially prodigal of their lambent salutations.

After a pause, the golden king asked, "Where do you come from?"

"From the world," answered the old man.

"Where are you going?" asked the silver king.

"Into the world," said the old man.

"What do you want with us?" asked the brazen king.

"To accompany you," said the old man.

The composite king was about to speak when the golden one said to the will-o'-the-wisps, who had come too near him, "Keep your distance, my gold is not for your palates."

They then sidled up to the silver king, whose garment shone resplendently in their yellow glow. "I bid you welcome," he said, "but I cannot nourish you; eat your fill elsewhere and then bring me your light."

They departed, slipping past the bronze king, who took no notice of them, and approached the composite one.

"Who will rule the world?" he cried in his stuttering voice.

"He who stands on his feet," answered the old man.

"That's me!" said the composite king.

"That remains to be seen," said the old man, "for the time has come."

Beauteous Lily fell about the old man's neck and kissed him cordially. "Holy father," she said, "I thank you from the bottom of my heart, for now I have heard those comforting words for the third time." She had scarcely spoken when she began to clasp the old man more tightly, for the ground was swaying beneath them; the old woman and the youth also held on to each other; only the airy will-o'-the-wisps felt nothing.

One could clearly perceive that the whole temple was moving like a ship gently putting to sea when anchor is weighed; the depths of the earth seemed to open up before it as it passed through. It struck no obstacle, no rock stood in its way.

For a few moments a fine rain seemed to be drizzling down through the opening in the cupola. The old man clasped beauteous Lily more firmly and said to her, "We are under the river and will soon reach our destination." Shortly afterwards they thought they had come to a standstill, but they were mistaken: the temple was ascending.

A strange rumbling noise now arose above their heads. Planks and beams began to crash pell-mell through the opening of the cupola. Lily and the old woman sprang to one side, the man with the lamp grasped the youth and stood stockstill. It was the ferryman's hut, which the ascending temple had sheared from the ground and engulfed, that was gradually sinking down and covering the youth and the old man.

The women raised a great outcry, the temple shook like a vessel that suddenly runs aground. The women anxiously ran hither and thither in the gloom about the hut. The door was bolted and no one answered their knocking. They knocked harder and were not a little surprised when at last the door began to give a metallic ring. Through the power of the lamp within, the hut had turned to silver from the inside out. It was not long before it even altered its shape, for the noble metal rejected the chance forms of the planks, posts and beams and expanded to a splendid structure of beaten silver. Now there stood a beautiful small temple in the midst of the large one, or, if one will, an altar worthy of the temple.

The noble youth ascended a staircase that mounted from the interior; the man with the lamp lighted his way, and another person wearing a short white garment and carrying a silver oar seemed to be supporting him. One easily recognized the ferryman, the former inhabitant of the transformed hut.

Beauteous Lily ascended the exterior stairs leading from the temple to the altar, but she still had to keep at a distance from her beloved. The old woman, whose hand, during the time the lamp had been hidden, had become smaller and smaller, called out, "Am I doomed to misfortune after all? Amid so many miracles is there none will restore my hand?"

Her husband pointed to the open portal and said, "Look, day is breaking, hurry and bathe in the river!"

"What advice!" she cried. "I suppose you want me to become black all over and disappear entirely; after all, I haven't paid my debt."

"Do what I say!" said the old man. "All debts have been paid."

The old woman hastened away, and at that moment the light of the rising sun struck the wreath of the cupola. The old man stepped between the youth and the maiden and called out in a loud voice, "Three are the things that rule the earth: wisdom, seeming, and power." At the first word the golden king stood up, at the second the silver king, and at the third the brazen king was slowly rising when the composite king suddenly sat down awkwardly.

Whoever saw him could hardly refrain from laughing in spite of the solemnity of the moment, for he neither sat, lay nor leaned, but had sunk down in a formless heap.

The will-o'-the-wisps, who had been fluttering about him, now stepped aside. Although they looked pale in the morning light, they again seemed well nourished and well inflamed. With their pointed tongues they had skillfully licked out the gold veins of the colossal statue like marrow. The irregular empty spaces that thus arose remained open for a time and the figure retained its original form. But when at last the finest veins were consumed, the statue suddenly collapsed, unfortunately, just at those places that must remain entire when a person sits down. On the other hand, the joints, which should have bent, remained stiff. If one could not laugh, one had to turn one's eyes aside; this intermediate thing, neither statue nor lump, was repulsive.

The man with the lamp now conducted the handsome youth, who was still staring vacantly into space, down from the altar straight to the brazen king. At the feet of this mighty prince lay a sword in a brazen sheath. The youth girded himself with it. "Sword on the left, right hand free!" cried the great king. They then proceeded to the silver king, who offered his scepter to the youth. The latter grasped it with the left hand and the king said approvingly, "Feed the sheep!" When they came to the golden king, he pressed, with a gesture of paternal blessing, his wreath of oak leaves on the youth's head and spoke: "Acknowledge the highest!"

The old man had closely observed the youth during this proceeding. After he had girded on the sword, his breast heaved, his arms moved and his step became firmer; when he took the scepter in his hand, his strength seemed to become gentler and yet through his inexpressible charm more powerful; but when the oaken garland adorned his locks, his features grew animated, his eyes shone with inexpressible spirit and his first word was "Lily."

"Dear Lily!" he cried, hastening toward her up the silver stairs, for she had observed his progress from the altar. "Dear Lily, what can a man, provided with everything, desire that is more precious than the innocence and quiet affection that your bosom offers mine? O my friend," he continued, turning to the old man and looking at the three sacred statues, "glorious and secure is the realm of our fathers, but you have forgotten the fourth power that rules the earth still earlier, more universally and more certainly: the power of love." With these words he fell about the neck of the beautiful maiden. She had cast her veil aside and her cheeks blushed like a rose in the most beautiful, imperishable color.

The old man then remarked with a smile, "Love does not rule, but it forms the disposition, and that is more."

Absorbed in these solemnities, this happiness, this rapture, the company had not noticed that it was already broad daylight, and now through the open portal a quite unexpected sight met their eyes. A spacious square surrounded by pillars formed a forecourt at the end of which one saw a long, splendid bridge spanning the river with many arches. It was built with broad, pillared walks on either side for foot passengers, and already many thousands of these were busily crossing back and forth. The wide roadway in the middle was animated by herds, mules, horsemen, and carriages, which were streaming across in both directions without hindering each other. They all seemed lost in admiration at this combination of splendor and convenience, and the new king and queen were as enraptured over the animation and activity of their multitudinous subjects as they were happy in their love for each other.

"Honor the serpent," said the man with the lamp; "you owe her your life, your people owe her the bridge by means of which these neighboring shores are now enlivened and united as countries. Those floating radiant gems, the remains of her sacrificed body, form the supporting pillars of this splendid bridge; on them she has erected herself and will preserve herself."

They were about to ask him for an explanation of this wondrous mystery when four beautiful maidens entered the portal of the temple. By the harp, the umbrella, and the ivory stool one immediately recognized Lily's attendants, but the fourth, even more beautiful than the other three, was a stranger. With sisterly playfulness she hastened with them through the temple and ascended the silver stairs.

"Will you credit my words more in the future, my dear wife?" said the man with the lamp to the beautiful maiden. "Happy you and every creature that bathes in the river this morning!"

The old woman, rejuvenated and transformed into such a beauty that no trace of her former appearance remained, embraced the man with the lamp with her vigorously youthful arms and he lovingly returned her caresses. "If I am too old for you," he said with a smile, "you may choose another husband today. From this day onward, no marriage vows are valid unless they are renewed."

"Don't you realize," she replied, "that you too have become younger?"

"I'm glad if I look to you like a young gallant. I accept your hand anew and shall be glad to live with you into the next millennium."

The queen welcomed her new friend and descended with her companions down into the altar, while the king stood between the old man and the ferryman, attentively observing the throng of people on the bridge.

But his satisfaction was short-lived, for he saw something that caused him a moment of vexation. The huge giant, who seemed not fully awakened from his morning sleep, was stumbling over the bridge and causing great disorder. As usual, he had got up still drunk with sleep and had intended to take a bath in his familiar cove, but had found instead firm ground and was now groping his way across the bridge. Although he trod very awkwardly among the people and livestock, and all gazed at him in amazement, no one *felt* him. But when the sun shone in his eyes and he raised his hands to rub them, the shadow of his enormous fists fell with such careless violence among the crowd that people and animals were hurled down in a confused mass, suffering injury and in danger of being flung into the river.

The king, when he beheld this misdeed, involuntarily reached for his sword; then he bethought himself and looked calmly first at his scepter, then at the lamp and the oar carried by his companions.

"I can guess your thoughts," said the man with the lamp, "but we and our strength are powerless against this powerless one. Be calm! He has caused harm for the last time, and luckily his shadow does not fall in our direction."

Meanwhile the giant had come nearer. In his astonishment at the scene before his eyes, he had let his hands sink, did no more harm, and stepped gaping into the forecourt.

He was heading straight for the door of the temple when he was suddenly immobilized on the spot in the middle of the courtyard. There he stood, a colossal statue of shining reddish stone, and his shadow showed the hours, which were inlaid about him in a circle, though not in numbers, but in noble, symbolic figures.

The king was more than a little pleased to see the monstrous giant's shadow put to good use; the queen was more than a little amazed when she caught sight of the strange statue, which almost blocked the view to the bridge, as she advanced, gloriously adorned and accompanied by her attendants, out of the altar.

In the meantime, the populace had pushed along behind the giant and, now that he had come to a standstill, was surrounding him and gazing in astonishment at his transformation. They soon turned to the temple, which they now seemed to become aware of for the first time, and pressed toward the door.

At this moment the hawk was hovering high above the cathedral with the looking-glass, which caught the light of the sun and reflected it over the group standing on the altar. The king, the queen, and their attendants appeared in the dusky vault of the temple illumined by a heavenly brilliance, and the populace fell prostrate before them. By the time the crowd had recovered and had risen again, the king and his train had descended into the altar, in order to enter the palace by a secret passage, and the people dispersed through the temple to satisfy their curiosity. With awe and reverence they beheld the three kings who stood erect, but were very curious to learn what sort of lump might be concealed beneath the carpet in the fourth niche, for someone or other had spread with well-meaning modesty over the collapsed king a splendid covering that no eye could penetrate and no hand dared raise.

There would have been no end to the gazing and admiration of the people, and the dense throng would have crushed itself in the temple, had their attention not been again attracted to the courtyard.

To their great surprise, a ringing rain of gold pieces began to fall, as though from the air, down on the marble paving stones. Those nearest pounced upon them; the miracle was repeated a number of times, first here, then there. It is not difficult to infer that the departing will-o'-the-wisps were allowing themselves a final jest and expending the gold from the limbs of the collapsed king in this merry fashion. The covetous crowd ran hither and thither for some time longer, pushing and tearing at each other's clothing, though the shower of gold pieces had ceased. Finally, they gradually dispersed, each went his way, and to this day the bridge is teeming with travelers, and the temple is the most frequented in the whole world.

Translated by Robert M. Browning

Translator's note: A number of phrases in this translation have been adapted from R. D. Boylan's inaccurate but resourceful rendering in *Novels and Tales, by Goethe* (London: Bell & Daldy, 1872), pp. 431–460.

Fair-haired Eckbert

Ludwig Tieck

In a district of the Harz dwelt a knight, whose common designation in that quarter was Fair-haired Eckbert. He was about forty years of age, scarcely of middle stature, and short light-colored locks lay close and sleek round his pale and sunken countenance. He led a retired life, had never interfered in the feuds of his neighbors; indeed, beyond the outer wall of his castle he was seldom to be seen. His wife loved solitude as much as he; both seemed heartily attached to one another; only now and then they would lament that heaven had not blessed their marriage with children.

Few came to visit Eckbert, and when guests did happen to be with him, their presence made but little alteration in his customary way of life. Temperance abode in his household, and Frugality herself appeared to be the mistress of the entertainment. On these occasions Eckbert was always cheerful and lively; but when he was alone, you might observe in him a certain mild reserve, a still, retiring melancholy.

His most frequent guest was Philip Walther, a man to whom he had attached himself after finding in him a way of thinking like his own. Walther's residence was in Franconia, but he would often stay for half a year in Eckbert's neighborhood, gathering plants and minerals, and then sorting and arranging them. He lived on a small independency, and was connected with no one. Eckbert frequently attended him in his sequestered walks; year after year a closer friendship grew between them.

There are hours in which a man feels grieved that he should have a secret from his friend, which, till then, he may have kept with niggard anxiety; some irresistible desire lays hold of our heart to open itself wholly, to disclose its inmost recesses to our friend, that he may become our friend still more. It is in such moments that tender souls unveil themselves, and stand face to face; and at times it will happen, that the one recoils affrighted from the countenance of the other.

It was late in autumn, when Eckbert, one cloudy evening, was sitting, with his friend and his wife Bertha, by the parlor fire. The flame cast a red glimmer through the room, and sported on the ceiling; the night looked sullenly in through the windows, and the trees without rustled in wet coldness. Walther complained of the long road he had to travel; and Eckbert proposed to him to stay where he was, to while away half of the night in friendly talk, and then to take a bed in the house till morning. Walther agreed, and the whole was speedily arranged: by and by wine and supper were brought in; fresh wood was laid upon the fire; the talk grew livelier and more confidential.

The cloth being removed, and the servants gone, Eckbert took his friend's hand, and said to him, "Now you must let my wife tell you the history of her youth; it is curious enough, and you should know it."

"With all my heart," said Walther; and the party again drew round the hearth.

It was now midnight; the moon looked fitfully through the breaks of the driving clouds. "You must not reckon me a babbler," began the lady. "My husband says you have so generous a mind, that it is not right in us to hide aught from you. Only do not take my narrative for a fairy tale, however strangely it may sound.

"I was born in a little village; my father was a poor herdsman. Our circumstances were not of the best; often we knew not where to find our daily bread. But what grieved me far more than this, were the quarrels that my father and mother often had about their poverty, and the bitter reproaches they cast on one another. Of myself too, I heard nothing said but ill; they were forever telling me that I was a silly, stupid child, that I could not do the simplest turn of work; and in truth I was extremely inexpert and helpless. I let things fall; I neither learned to sew nor spin; I could be of no use to my parents; only their straits I understood too well. Often

I would sit in a corner, and fill my little heart with dreams of how I would help them, if I should all at once grow rich; how I would overflow them with silver and gold, and feast myself on their amazement. Or sometimes spirits came hovering up, and showed me buried treasures, or gave me little pebbles that changed into precious stones. In short, the strangest fancies occupied me, and when I had to rise and help with anything, my inexpertness was still greater, as my head was giddy with these motley visions.

"My father in particular was always very cross to me; he scolded me for being such a burden to the house; indeed he often used me rather cruelly, and it was very seldom that I got a friendly word from him. In this way I had struggled on to near the end of my eighth year; and now it was seriously fixed that I should begin to do or learn something. My father still maintained that it was nothing but caprice in me, or a lazy wish to pass my days in idleness: accordingly he set upon me with furious threats; and as these made no improvement, he one day gave me a most cruel chastisement, and added that the same should be repeated day after day, since I was nothing but a useless sluggard.

"That whole night I wept abundantly; I felt myself so utterly forsaken, I had such a sympathy with myself that I even longed to die. I dreaded the break of day; I knew not on earth what I was to do or try. I wished from my very heart to be clever, and could not understand how I should be worse than the other children of the place. I was on the borders of despair.

"At the dawn of day I arose, and scarcely knowing what I did, unfastened the door of our little hut. I stepped upon the open field; next minute I was in a wood, where the light of the morning had yet hardly penetrated. I ran along, not looking round; for I felt no fatigue, and I still thought my father would catch me, and in his anger at my flight would beat me worse than ever.

"I had reached the other side of the forest, and the sun was risen a considerable way; I saw something dim lying before me, and a thick fog resting over it. Before long my path began to mount, at one time I was climbing hills, at another winding among rocks; and I now guessed that I must be among the neighboring mountains, a thought that made me shudder in my loneliness. For, living in the plain country, I had never seen a hill; and the very word mountains, when I heard talk of them, had been a sound of terror to my young ear. I had not the heart to go back, my fear itself drove me on; often I looked round affrighted when the breezes rustled over me among the trees, or the stroke of some distant woodman sounded far through the still morning. And when I began to meet with charcoal-men and miners, and heard their foreign way of speech, I nearly fainted for terror.

"I passed through several villages, begging now and then, for I felt hungry and thirsty, and fashioning my answers as I best could when questions were put to me. In this manner I had wandered on some four days, when I came upon a little footpath, which led me farther and farther from the highway. The rocks about me now assumed a different and far stranger form. They were cliffs so piled on one another, that it looked as if the first gust of wind would hurl them all this way and that. I knew not whether to go on or stop. Till now I had slept by night in the woods, for it was the finest season of the year, or in some remote shepherd's hut; but here I saw no human dwelling at all, and could not hope to find one in this wilderness; the crags grew more and more frightful: I had many a time to glide along by the very edge of dreadful abysses. By degrees, my footpath became fainter, and at last all traces of it vanished from beneath me. I was utterly comfortless; I wept and screamed; and my voice came echoing back from the rocky valleys with a sound that terrified me. The night now came on, and I sought out a mossy nook to lie down in. I could not sleep for in the darkness I heard the strangest noises. Sometimes I took them to come from wild beasts, sometimes from wind moaning through the rocks, sometimes from unknown birds. I prayed, and did not sleep till towards morning.

"When the light came upon my face, I awoke. Before me was a steep rock; I climbed up, in the hope of discovering some outlet from the waste, perhaps of seeing houses or men. But when I reached the top, there was nothing still, so far as my eye could reach, but a wilderness of crags and precipices. All was covered with a dim haze; the day was grey and troubled, and no tree, no meadow, not even a bush could I find, only a few shrubs shooting up stunted and solitary in the narrow clefts of the rocks. I cannot utter what a longing I felt but to see one human creature, any living mortal, even though I had been afraid of hurt from him. At the same time I was tortured by a gnawing hunger. I sat down, and made up my mind to die. After a while, however, the desire of living gained the mastery; I roused myself, and wandered forward amid tears and broken sobs all day. In the end, I hardly knew what I was doing. I was tired and spent, I scarcely wished to live, and yet I feared to die.

"Towards night the country seemed to grow a little kindlier; my thoughts, my desires revived, the wish for life awoke in all my veins. I thought I heard the rushing of a mill afar off; I redoubled my steps, and how glad, how light of heart was I, when at last I actually gained the limits of the barren rocks, and saw woods and meadows lying before me, with soft green hills in the distance! I felt as if I had stepped out of hell into a paradise; my loneliness and helplessness no longer frightened me.

"Instead of the hoped-for mill, I came upon a waterfall, which, in truth, considerably dampened my joy. I was lifting a drink from it in the hollow of my hand, when all at once I thought I heard a slight cough some little way from me. Never in my life was I so joyfully surprised as at this moment: I went near, and at the border of the wood saw an old woman sitting on the ground. She was dressed almost wholly in black; a black hood covered her head, and the greater part of her face; in her hand she held a crutch.

"I came up to her, and begged for help; she made me sit by her, and gave me bread, and a little wine. While I ate, she sang in a screeching tone some kind of spiritual song. When she had done, she told me I might follow her.

"The offer charmed me, strange as the old woman's voice and look appeared. With her crutch she limped away pretty fast, and at every step she twisted her face so oddly, that at first I was like to laugh. The wild rocks retired behind us more and more; we crossed a pleasant meadow, then passed through a considerable stretch of woods. The sun was just going down when we stepped out of the woods, and I never shall forget the aspect and the feeling of that evening. All things were as molten into the softest golden red; the trees were standing with their tops in the glow of the sunset; on the fields lay a mild brightness; the woods and the leaves of the trees were standing motionless; the pure sky looked like an open paradise, and the gushing of the brooks, and, from time to time, the rustling of the trees, resounded through the serene stillness, as in pensive joy. My young soul was here first taken with a forethought of the world and its vicissitudes. I forgot myself and my conductress; my spirit and my eyes were wandering among the shining clouds.

"We now mounted an eminence planted with birch-trees; from the top we looked into a green valley, likewise full of birches; and down below, in the middle of them, was a little hut. A glad barking reached us, and immediately a little, nimble dog came springing round the old woman, fawned on her, and wagged its tail; it next came to me, viewed me on all sides, and then turned back with a friendly look to its old mistress.

"On reaching the bottom of the hill, I heard the strangest song, as if coming from the hut, and sung by some bird. It ran thus:

> Alone in wood so gay
> 'Tis good to stay,
> Morrow like today,
> Forever and aye:
> O, I do love to stay
> Alone in wood so gay.

"These few words were continually repeated, and to describe the sound, it was as if you heard forest-horns and shawms sounded together from a far distance.

"My curiosity was wonderfully on the stretch; without waiting for the old woman's permission, I stepped into the hut. It was already dusk. Here all was neatly swept and orderly; some bowls were standing in a cupboard, some strange-looking casks or pots on a table; in a glittering cage, hanging by the window, was a bird, and this in fact proved to be the singer. The old woman coughed and panted: it seemed as if she never would get over her fatigue. She patted the little dog, she talked with the bird, which only answered her with its accustomed song; and as for me, she did not seem to recollect that I was there at all. Looking at her so, many qualms and fears came over me; for her face was in perpetual motion; and, besides, her head shook from old age, so that, for my life, I could not make out what sort of countenance she had.

"Having gathered strength again, she lit a candle, covered a very small table, and brought out supper. She now looked round for me, and bade me take a little cane chair. I was thus sitting close facing her, with the light between us. She folded her bony hands, and prayed aloud, still twisting her countenance, so that I was once more on the point of laughing; but I took strict care that I might not make her angry.

"After supper she again prayed, then showed me a bed in a low narrow closet; she herself slept in the room. I did not remain awake long, for I was half stupefied; but in the night I now and then awoke, and heard the old woman coughing, and betweenwhiles talking with her dog and her bird, which last seemed dreaming, and replied with only one or two words of its rhyme. This, with the birches rustling before the window, and the song of a distant nightingale, made such a wondrous combination, that I never fairly thought I was awake, but only falling out of one dream into another still stranger.

"The old woman awoke me in the morning, and soon after gave me work. I was put to spin, which I now learned very easily; I had likewise to take charge of the dog and the bird. I soon learned my business in the house and now felt as if it all must be so. I never once remembered that the old woman had so many singularities, that her dwelling was mysterious, and lay apart from all men, and that the bird must be a very strange creature. Its beauty, indeed, always struck me, for its feathers glittered with all possible colors: the fairest deep blue, and the most burning red alternated about his neck and body; and when singing, he blew himself proudly out, so that his feathers looked still finer.

"My old mistress often went abroad, and did not come again till night; on these occasions I went out to meet her with the dog, and she used to call me child and daughter. In the end I grew to like her heartily, as our mind, especially in childhood, will become accustomed and attached to anything. In the evenings she taught me to read; and this was afterwards a source of boundless satisfaction to me in my solitude, for she had several ancient handwritten books, that contained the strangest stories.

"The recollection of the life I then led is still singular to me: visited by no human creature, secluded in the circle of so small a family; for the dog and the bird made the same impression on me that in other cases long-known friends produce. I am surprised that I have never since been able to recall the dog's name, a very odd one, often as I then pronounced it.

"Four years I had passed in this way (I must now have been nearly twelve), when my old dame began to put more trust in me, and at length told me a secret. The bird, I found, laid every day an egg, in which there was a pearl or a jewel. I had already noticed that she often tended to the cage in private, but I had never troubled myself farther on the subject. She now gave me charge of gathering these eggs in her absence, and carefully storing them up in the strange looking pots. She would leave me food, and sometimes stay away longer, for weeks, for months. My little wheel kept humming round, the dog barked, the bird sang; and withal there was such a stillness in the neighborhood, that I do not recollect of any storm or foul weather all the time I stayed there. No one wandered thither; no wild beast came near our dwelling. I was satisfied, and worked along in peace from day to day. One would perhaps be very happy, could he pass his life so undisturbedly to the end.

"From the little that I read, I formed quite marvelous notions of the world and its people, all taken from myself and my society. When I read of witty persons, I could not figure them but like the little dog; great ladies, I conceived, were like the bird; all old women like my mistress. I had read somewhat of love, too; and often, in fancy, I would tell myself strange stories. I thought up the fairest knight on earth, adorned him with all perfections, without knowing rightly, after all my labor, how he looked; but I could feel a hearty pity for myself when he ceased to love me. I would then, in thought, make long, melting speeches, or perhaps aloud, to try if I could win him back. You smile! These young days are, in truth, far away from us all.

"I now liked better to be left alone, for I was then sole mistress of the house. The dog loved me, and did all I wanted; the bird replied to all my questions with his rhyme; my wheel kept briskly turning, and at bottom I had never any wish for change. When my dame returned from her long wanderings, she would praise my diligence; she said her house, since I belonged to it, was managed far more perfectly. She took a pleasure in my growth and healthy looks. In short, she treated me in all points like her daughter.

" 'Thou art a good girl, child,' said she once to me, in her creaking tone; 'if thou continuest so, it will be well with thee: but none ever prospers when he leaves the straight path; punishment will overtake him, though it may be late.' I gave little heed to this remark of hers at the time, for in my temper and movements I was very lively; but by night it occurred to me again, and I could not understand what she meant by it. I considered all the words attentively. I had read of riches, and at last it struck me that her pearls and jewels might perhaps be something precious. Ere long this thought grew clearer to me. But the straight path, and leaving it? What could she mean by this?

"I was now fourteen; it is the misery of man that he arrives at understanding through the loss of innocence. I now saw well enough that it lay with me to take the jewels and the bird in the old woman's absence, and go forth with them and see the world of which I had read. Perhaps, too, it would then be possible that I might meet that fairest of all knights, who forever dwelt in my memory.

"At first this thought was nothing more than any other thought; but when I used to be sitting at my wheel, it still returned to me, against my will. I sometimes followed it so far, that I already saw myself adorned in splendid attire, with princes and knights around me. On awakening from these dreams, I would feel a sadness when I looked up, and found myself still in the little cottage. For the rest, if I went through my duties, the old woman troubled herself little about what I thought or felt.

"One day she went out again, telling me that she should be away on this occasion longer than usual; that I must take strict charge of everything, and not let the time hang heavy on my hands. I had a sort of fear on taking leave of her, for I felt as if I should not see her anymore. I looked long after her, and knew not why I felt so sad; it was almost as if my purpose had already stood before me, without myself being conscious of it.

"Never did I tend the dog and the bird with such diligence as now; they were nearer to my heart than formerly. The old woman had been gone some days, when I rose one morning in the firm mind to leave the cottage, and set out with the bird to see this world they talked so much of. I felt pressed and hampered in my heart: I wished to stay where I was, and yet the thought of that afflicted me. There was a strange contention in my soul, as if between two discordant spirits. One moment my peaceful solitude would seem to me so beautiful; the next the image of a new world, with its many wonders, would again enchant me.

"I knew not what to make of it. The dog leaped up continually about me, the sunshine spread abroad over the fields, the green birch-trees glittered. I always felt as if I had something I must do in haste; so I caught the little dog, tied him up in the room, and took the cage with the bird under my arm. The dog writhed and whined at this unusual treatment; he looked at me with begging eyes, but I feared to have him with me. I also took one pot of jewels, and concealed it by me; the rest I left.

"The bird turned its head very strangely when I crossed the threshold; the dog tugged at his cord to follow me, but he was forced to stay.

"I did not take the road to the wild rocks, but went in the opposite direction. The dog still whined and barked, and it touched me to the heart to hear him; the bird tried once or twice to sing; but as I was carrying him, the shaking put him out.

"The farther I went, the fainter grew the barking, and at last it altogether ceased. I wept, and had almost turned back, but the longing to see something new still hindered me.

"I had got across the hills, and through some forests, when the night came on, and I was forced to turn aside into a village. I was very shy on entering the inn; they showed me to a room and bed, and I slept pretty quietly, except that I dreamed of the old woman, and her threatening me.

"My journey had not much variety; the farther I went, the more was I afflicted by the recollection of my old mistress and the little dog. I considered that in all likelihood the poor thing would die of hunger, and often in the woods I thought my dame would suddenly meet me. Thus amid tears and sobs I went along; when I stopped to rest, and put the cage on the ground, the bird struck up his song, and brought but too keenly to my mind the fair habitation I had left. As human nature is forgetful, I imagined that my former journey, in my childhood, had not been so sad and woeful as the present. I wished to be as I was then.

"I had sold some jewels, and now, after wandering on for several days, I reached a village. At the very entrance I was struck with something strange; I felt terrified and knew not why, but I soon bethought myself, for it was the village where I was born! How amazed was I! How the tears ran down my cheeks for gladness, for a thousand singular remembrances! Many things were changed: new houses had been built, some just raised when I went away were now fallen, apparently destroyed by fires; everything was far smaller and more confined than I had fancied. It rejoiced my very heart that I should see my parents once more after such an absence. I found their little cottage, the well-known threshold; the door-latch was standing as of old, and it seemed to me as if I had shut it only yesternight. My heart beat violently, I hastily lifted that latch, but faces I had never seen before looked up and gazed at me. I asked for the shepherd Martin; they told me that his wife and he were dead three years ago. I drew back quickly, and left the village weeping aloud.

"I had figured out so beautifully how I would surprise them with my riches; by the strangest chance, what I had only dreamed in childhood was become reality, and now it was all in vain, they could not rejoice with me, and that which had been my first hope in life was lost forever.

"In a pleasant town I rented a small house and garden, and took to myself a maid. The world, in truth, proved not so wonderful as I had painted it, but I forgot the old woman and my former way of life rather more, and on the whole I was contented.

"For a long while the bird had ceased to sing; I was therefore not a little frightened, when one night he suddenly began again, and with a different rhyme. He sang:

> Alone in wood so gay,
> Ah, far away!
> But thou wilt say
> Some other day,
> 'Twere best to stay
> Alone in wood so gay.

"Throughout the night I could not close an eye; all things again occurred to my remembrance, and I felt, more than ever, that I had not acted rightly. When I rose, the sight of the bird distressed me greatly; he looked at me continually, and his presence did me ill. There was now no end to his song; he sang it louder and more shrilly than he had been wont. The more I looked at him, the more he pained and frightened me; at last I opened the cage, put in my hand, and grasped his neck. I squeezed my fingers hard together, he looked at me pleadingly, I slackened them; but he was dead. I buried him in the garden.

"After this, there often came a fear over me of my maid; I looked back upon myself, and fancied she might rob me or even murder me. For a long while I had been acquainted with a young knight, whom I altogether liked. I bestowed on him my hand; and with this, Sir Walther, ends my story."

Ay, you should have seen her then," said Eckbert warmly; "seen her youth, her loveliness, and what a charm her lonely way of life had given her. She seemed to me a miracle and I loved her beyond all measure. I had no fortune; it was through her love these riches came to me. We moved hither, and our marriage has at no time caused us any regret."

"But with our tattling," added Bertha, "it is growing very late; we must go to sleep."

She rose, and proceeded to her chamber; Walther, with a kiss of her hand, wished her good-night, saying, "Many thanks, noble lady; I can well imagine you beside your strange bird, and how you fed poor little *Strohmian*."

Walther likewise went to sleep; Eckbert alone still walked in a restless humor up and down the room. "Are not men fools?" said he at last. "I myself occasioned this recital of my wife's history, and now such confidence appears to me improper! Will he not abuse it? Will he not communicate the secret to others? Will he not, for such is human nature, cast unblessed thoughts on our jewels, and form pretexts and lay plans to get possession of them?"

It now occurred to him that Walther had not taken leave of him so cordially as might have been expected after such a mark of trust: the soul once set upon suspicion finds in every trifle something to confirm it. Eckbert, on the other hand, reproached himself for such ignoble feelings toward his worthy friend; yet still he could not cast them out. All night he plagued himself with such uneasy thoughts, and got very little sleep.

Bertha was unwell next day, and could not come to breakfast. Walther did not seem to trouble himself much about her illness and left her husband also rather coolly. Eckbert could not comprehend such conduct; he went to see his wife, and found her in a feverish state; she said last night's story must have agitated her.

From that day, Walther visited the castle of his friend but seldom, and when he did appear, it was but to say a few trivial words and then depart. Eckbert was exceedingly distressed by this demeanor. To Bertha or Walther he indeed said nothing of it; but to any person his internal disquietude was visible enough.

Bertha's sickness wore an aspect more and more serious; the doctor grew alarmed—the red had vanished from his patient's cheeks, and her eyes were becoming more and more inflamed. One morning she summoned her husband to her bedside; the nurses were ordered to withdraw.

"Dear Eckbert," she began, "I must disclose a secret to you, which has almost taken away my senses, which is ruining my health, unimportant trifle as it may appear. You may remember, often as I talked of my childhood, I could never call to mind the name of the dog that was so long beside me. Now, that night on taking leave, Walther all at once said to me, 'I can well imagine you, and how you fed poor little *Strohmian*.' Is it chance? Did he guess the name; did he know it, and speak it on purpose? If so, how stands this man connected with my destiny? At times I struggle with myself as if I but imagined this mysterious business; but, alas! it is certain, too certain. I felt a shudder that a stranger should help me to recall the memory of my secrets. What do you think, Eckbert?"

Eckbert looked at his sick and agitated wife with deep emotion; he stood silent and thoughtful, then spoke some words of comfort to her, and went out. In a distant chamber, he walked to and fro in indescribable disquiet. Walther, for many years, had been his sole companion; and now this person was the only mortal in the world whose existence pained and oppressed him. It seemed as if he should be gay and light of heart, were that one thing removed. He took his crossbow, to dissipate these thoughts, and went to hunt.

It was a rough stormy winter day; the snow was lying deep on the hills, and bending down the branches of the trees. He roved about; the sweat was standing on his brow. He found no game, and this embittered his ill humor. All at once he saw an object moving in the distance; it was Walther gathering moss from the trunks of trees. Scarce knowing what he did, he cocked his bow; Walther looked round, and made a threatening gesture, but the bolt was already flying, and he sank transfixed by it.

Eckbert felt relieved and calmed, yet a certain horror drove him home to his castle. It was a good way distant; he had wandered far into the woods. On arriving, he found Bertha dead; before her death, she had spoken much of Walther and the old woman.

For a great while after this occurrence, Eckbert lived in the deepest solitude; he had all along been melancholy, for the strange history of his wife disturbed him, and he had dreaded some unlucky incident or other, but at present he was utterly at variance with himself. The murder of his friend arose incessantly before his mind; he lived in the anguish of continual remorse.

To dissipate his feelings, he occasionally visited the neighboring town, where he mingled in society and its amusements. He longed for a friend to fill the void in his soul; and yet, when he remembered Walther, he would shudder at the thought of meeting with a friend, for he felt convinced that, with any friend, he must be unhappy. He had lived so long with his Bertha in lovely calmness; the friendship of Walther had cheered him through so many years; and now both of them were suddenly swept away. As he thought of these things, there were many moments when his life appeared to him some fabulous tale, rather than the actual history of a living man.

A young knight named Hugo made advances to the silent, melancholy Eckbert and appeared to have a true affection for him. Eckbert felt exceedingly surprised, but he met the knight's friendship with great readiness, because he had so little anticipated it. The two were now frequently together. Hugo showed his friend all possible attentions. One scarcely ever went to ride without the other; in all companies they got together. In a word, they seemed inseparable.

Eckbert was never happy longer than a few transitory moments, for he felt too clearly that Hugo loved him only by mistake, that he knew him not and was unacquainted with his history. He was seized again with the same old longing to unbosom himself wholly, that he might be sure whether Hugo was his friend or not. But again his apprehensions, and the fear of being hated and abhorred, withheld him. There were many hours in which he felt so much impressed with his entire worthlessness that he believed no mortal not a stranger to his history could entertain regard for him. Yet still he was unable to withstand his urge; on a solitary ride, he disclosed his whole history to Hugo, and asked if he could love a murderer. Hugo seemed touched, and tried to comfort him. Eckbert returned to town with a lighter heart.

But it seemed to be his doom that, in the very hour of confidence, he should always find materials for suspicion. Scarcely had they entered the public hall, when, in the glitter of the many lights, Hugo's looks had ceased to satisfy him. He thought he noticed a malicious smile. He remarked that Hugo did not speak to him as usual, that he talked with the rest, and seemed to pay no heed to him. In the party was an old knight, who had always shown himself the enemy of Eckbert, had often asked about his riches and his wife in a peculiar style. With this man Hugo was conversing; they were speaking privately, and casting looks at Eckbert. The suspicions of the latter seemed confirmed; he thought himself betrayed, and a tremendous rage took hold of him. As he continued gazing, suddenly he discerned the countenance of Walther, all his features, all the form so well known to him. He gazed, and looked, and felt convinced that it was none but Walther who was talking to the knight. His horror cannot be described; in a state of frenzy he rushed out of the hall, left the town overnight, and after many wanderings, returned to his castle.

Here, like an unquiet spirit, he hurried to and fro from room to room. No thought would stay with him; out of one frightful idea he fell into another still more frightful, and sleep never visited his eyes. Often he believed that he was mad, that a disturbed imagination was the origin of all this terror; then, again, he recollected Walther's features, and the whole grew more and more a riddle to him. He resolved to take a journey, that he might reduce his thoughts to order; the hope of friendship, the desire of social intercourse, he had now forever given up.

He set out, without prescribing to himself any certain route; indeed, he took small heed of the country he was passing through. Having hastened on some days at the quickest pace of his horse, he, on a sudden, found himself entangled in a labyrinth of rocks, from which he could discover no outlet. At length he met an old peasant, who took him by a path leading past a waterfall: he offered him some coins for his guidance, but the peasant would not have them. "What do you think of that?" said Eckbert to himself. "I could believe that this man, too, was none but Walther." He looked round once more, and it was Walther. Eckbert spurred his horse as fast as it could gallop, over meads and forests, till it sank exhausted to the earth. Regardless of this, he hastened forward on foot.

In a dreamy mood he mounted a hill. He fancied he caught the sound of lively barking at a little distance; the birch-trees whispered in the intervals, and in the strangest notes he heard this song:

> Alone in wood so gay,
> Once more I stay;
> None dare me slay,
> The evil far away:
> Ah, here I stay,
> Alone in wood so gay.

Now it was all over with Eckbert's senses, with his consciousness; it was all a riddle that he could not solve, whether he was dreaming now, or had before dreamed of a woman named Bertha. The marvelous was mingled with the common: the world around him seemed enchanted, and he himself was incapable of thought or recollection.

A crooked, bent old woman crawled coughing up the hill with a crutch. "Art thou bringing me my bird, my pearls, my dog?" cried she to him. "See how injustice punishes itself! No one but I was Walther, was Hugo."

"God of heaven!" said Eckbert, muttering to himself, "in what frightful solitude have I passed my life?"

"And Bertha was thy sister."

Eckbert sank to the ground.

"Why did she leave me deceitfully? All would have been fair and well; her time of trial was already finished. She was the daughter of a knight, who had her nursed in a shepherd's house; the daughter of thy father."

"Why have I always had a forecast of this dreadful thought?" cried Eckbert.

"Because in early youth thy father told thee: he could not keep this daughter by him because she was the child of another woman."

Eckbert lay distracted and dying on the ground. In dull, hollow confusion he heard the old woman speaking, the dog barking, and the bird repeating its song.

Translated by Thomas Carlyle
and revised by the editors

A Wondrous Oriental
Fairy Tale of a Naked Saint

Wilhelm Heinrich Wackenroder

The Orient is the home of all that is marvelous. In the ancient, childlike views prevailing there one finds strange signs and riddles still unsolved by Reason, which considers itself so much more clever. Thus, for example, one often finds living in the desert strange creatures whom we would call mad, but who are there revered as supernatural beings. The oriental mind regards these naked saints as the wayward vessels of a higher intelligence or genius that has strayed from the realm of the firmament and come to dwell in human form and now does not know how to behave in human fashion. But all the things of this world are this way or that according to whether we look at them this way or that— human understanding is a magic tincture whose contact transforms everything that exists to conform with our desires.

It so happened that one of these naked saints lived in a remote cave in a cliff beside a small river. No one knew how he had got there; for some years his presence had been known—a caravan first discovered him, and since that time people had been making frequent pilgrimages to his solitary dwelling.

In his place of sojourn this queer creature had no rest by day or night. It seemed to him he always heard drumming in his ears the unceasing, swiftly rushing revolution of the wheel of time. Because of this din he could do nothing, plan nothing—the overwhelming anxiety that kept him in constant, strenuous activity prevented him from perceiving anything except the way this dreadful wheel, which reached to the stars and beyond them, turned and turned, roaring like a mighty storm. Like a waterfall made up of thousands and thousands of raging rivers plunging down from the sky, pouring on forever and forever without a moment's pause, an instant's intermission, it dinned in his ears, forcing all his senses to heed it alone. His incessant anxiety was gripped and torn more and more into the maelstrom of this wild confusion; ever more monstrously did the monotonous tones intermingle with each other. He could not rest; day and night one saw him in violent, ardent exertion, like a person straining to turn a gigantic wheel.

From his wild, broken utterances it was evident that he felt himself pulled along by the wheel and that he was striving with all his might to assist it in its swift, raging revolutions, so that Time should not run the risk of coming to a standstill even for an instant. If people asked him what he was doing, he would scream at them, as though stricken by a seizure, "You miserable creatures! Don't you hear the rushing wheel of time?" Then he would again fall to his turning, exerting himself even more strenuously, so that his sweat flowed to the ground in rivulets, and with distorted features would lay his hand on his pounding heart, as though he wanted to assure himself that the great clockworks were still in eternal motion. He was enraged when he saw those who had made a pilgrimage to see him standing idly by watching or strolling up and down engaged in conversation. Then he trembled with agitation and pointed out to them the incessant rotation of the eternal wheel, the monotonous, metronomic, unceasing onrush of Time. He gnashed his teeth when he saw that the bystanders were totally unaware of the machinery in which they too were involved and by which they too were pulled along. He hurled them from him enraged when they ventured too close. If they did not wish to suffer bodily harm, they had to give a lively imitation of his own straining movements. But his raving grew much wilder and more dangerous if some physical labor was performed in his vicinity, if someone who did not know him happened to be collecting herbs or chopping wood near his cave. Then he would burst out in a wild laugh to see that anyone, while time was rolling on with horrible inexorability, could turn his thoughts to such petty, mundane occupations; leaping from his cave like a tiger, he would, if he could lay hold of the poor wretch, knock him dead with a single blow. Then he would rush back into his cave and turn at the wheel of time even more furiously than ever. But he would continue to rave for a long time afterwards, muttering brokenly about how it could be possible for human beings to busy themselves with any other task, how they could undertake a tactless occupation.

He was incapable of stretching out his arm towards any object or of grasping anything with his hand; he could not walk a step like other men. Trembling anxiety flowed through his every nerve if he once attempted to interrupt the dizzying whirl in which he was caught. Only now and then, on serene nights, when the moon suddenly appeared before the mouth of his dark cave, did he abruptly stop, sink to the ground, cast himself about, and whine with despair. He would weep bitterly, like a child, because the rotation of the mighty wheel of time granted him no peace to do anything on earth, to act, to be of influence, to create. He felt a consuming longing for unknown beautiful things; he struggled to rise, to move his hands and feet calmly and harmoniously, but in vain! He was seeking something *definite,* something *unknown* that he could grasp and attach himself to; he was trying to save himself from himself, within himself or without, but in vain! When his weeping and his despair had reached a climax, he would spring from the ground with a loud roar and begin once more to turn at the gigantic, humming wheel of time. This went on for several years, day and night.

Once, on a wondrously beautiful moonlit summer night, the saint was again lying on the floor of his cave, weeping and wringing his hands. The night was enchanting: on the dark blue firmament the stars sparkled like golden ornaments on a farspread shield and the moon beamed from its bright cheeks a soft light in which the green earth bathed. The trees hung on their trunks in this magical light like moving clouds, and the dwellings of men were transfigured into dark cliff-like masses and dusky spirit palaces. Human beings, no longer blinded by the rays of the sun, lived with their gaze on the firmament, and their souls threw a lovely reflection in the heavenly shimmer of the moonlit night.

Two lovers, who wanted to yield themselves wholly to the marvels of nocturnal solitude, were sailing in a frail craft up the river that flowed past the saint's cave. The pervasive moonlight had illuminated and released the innermost, darkest depths of their

souls; their subtlest feelings melted and undulated onward, united
on shoreless streams. From the vessel there rose an ethereal music
into skyey space: sweet horns, and I know not what other enchanting instruments brought forth a floating world of tones, and
in these undulating tones one heard this song:

> Thrill of future joy comes spreading
> Sweetly over flood and lea,
> Moonbeams too are gently bedding
> Cots where lovedrunk senses flee.
> Hear the waves roll, their whispering cry,
> See how they mirror the arch of the sky!
>
> Love dwells in the firmament,
> Under us in silvery flood,
> Sparks the stars, not one would sparkle,
> Gave not Love its own heart's blood.
> But, by heaven's breath ever fanned,
> Smiles sky and water and all the land.
>
> Moonlight lies on every blossom,
> All the palms are fast asleep,
> In the woodland's sacred places
> Ringing rules the tone Love keeps.
> Even in sleeping all tones proclaim,
> Palmtrees and blossoms, Love's sweet domain.

With the first strains of the music and the singing the rushing
wheel of time disappeared from the saint's sight. These were the
first notes of music that had ever fallen in this desert; his unknown
longing was stilled, he was released from his enchantment, the
strayed intelligence freed from its terrestrial husk. The saint's
earthly form had vanished, and an angelically beautiful spirit form,
woven of delicate mist, came floating out of the cave, stretched its
slender arms longingly to heaven, and rose with a dancing movement from the ground into the air to the measure of the music.
Higher and higher the bright aerial form swayed, carried by the
softly swelling tones of the horns and the song. With heavenly
joyfulness the form danced, now here, now there, on the white

clouds floating in the atmosphere; with dancing feet the saint raised himself into the heavens and flew at last among the stars, sinuously weaving. Then all the stars resounded, reverberating with a clear, vibrant tone, until the saint, the heavenly genius, was lost in the endless firmament.

Caravans making their way across the desert gazed up at the nocturnal marvel in amazement, and the lovers thought they beheld the Genius of Love and Music.

Translated by Robert M. Browning

Klingsohr's Tale

Novalis

The long night had just come on. The ancient hero struck against his shield so that the sound echoed far and wide in the desolate streets of the city. Three times he repeated the sign. Then the high windows of the palace began to brighten from within, and the figures in the stained glass stirred. They moved more and more quickly, as the reddish light grew more intense and began to illuminate the streets. Gradually even the mighty pillars and walls were seen to brighten; at last they stood in a pure, pale blue radiance, in which the softest colors played. The entire region was now visible, and the reflection of the figures in the windows, with their tumult of spears, swords, shields, and helmets, which bowed down on all sides to crowns that appeared now here, now there, and which finally, as the crowns disappeared to make room for a simple green wreath, enclosed the wreath in a wide circle: all this was reflected in the frozen sea that surrounded the mountain on which the city was built, and even the distant mountain belt that ran around the shores of the sea was bathed in a mild glow. Nothing there could be distinguished clearly; but one heard a strange cacophony from over the sea, as if from a distant, monstrous workshop. The city, by contrast, was bright and clear. Its smooth, transparent walls reflected the beautiful rays of light, and the fine symmetry, the noble style, and the beautiful grouping of all the buildings came into view. Before all the windows stood ornamental clay vessels full of the most diverse ice-flowers and snow-flowers, which sparkled in the loveliest way.

Most splendid of all was the garden on the great square before the palace, which was composed of metal trees and crystal flowers and planted all around with colorful flowers and fruits made of jewels. The diversity and exquisiteness of forms and the vividness of lights and colors provided the most magnificent spectacle, whose splendor was crowned by a lofty fountain frozen to ice in the center of the garden.

The ancient hero was walking slowly past the gates of the palace. A voice within called out his name. He pushed against the gate, which opened with a soft ringing sound, and stepped into the great hall. He held up his shield before his eyes. "Have you discovered nothing yet?" said the beautiful daughter of Arcturus in a lamenting voice. She was lying against silken cushions on a throne artfully made of a large sulfur crystal, and several maidens were energetically rubbing her delicate limbs, which seemed to be blended of milk and crimson. Under the hands of the maidens there streamed out from her in all directions the lovely light that was the source of the wondrous illumination of the palace. A fragrant breeze wafted through the hall.

The hero was silent. "Let me touch your shield," she said softly. He approached the throne and stepped onto the exquisite carpet. She grasped his hand, pressed it tenderly to her heavenly bosom, and touched his shield. His armor rang, and a pervasive force animated his entire body. His eyes flashed, and his heart pounded audibly against his armor. The beautiful Freya seemed more cheerful, and the light streaming from her blazed like fire.

"The King is coming!" cried a splendid bird that was sitting at the back of the throne. The serving maids laid a sky-blue coverlet over the Princess, covering her to the neck. The hero lowered his shield and looked up toward the cupola, to which two broad staircases wound their way on either side of the great hall. Soft music preceded the King, who soon appeared in the cupola and descended with a sizable retinue.

The beautiful bird unfolded its gleaming wings, moved them softly, and, as if with a thousand voices, sang to the King:

> The handsome stranger will not long delay.
> The warmth is near, eternity at hand.
> The Queen will waken from her dreams one day
> When Love's enraptured glow melts sea and land.
> The cold and hopeless night will end its reign

When Fable's ancient right is won again.
In Freya's womb the world will soon ignite,
And each desire its true desire requite.

The King tenderly embraced his daughter. The spirits of the constellations arranged themselves around the throne, and the hero took his appointed place among them. A countless throng of stars filled the hall in ornamental groups. The serving maids brought a table and a casket that contained a number of cards bearing profound and sacred signs that were composed solely of stellar constellations. The King kissed these cards reverently, shuffled them with care, and passed several to his daughter. The others he retained for himself. The Princess drew her cards forth one by one and laid them on the table. Then the King considered his own carefully and pondered at great length each time he selected one and placed it with the others. At times he seemed constrained to pick this card or that. But often one could see his joy when he hit on a suitable card and could lay down a pleasing harmony of signs and figures. As the game began, all of the onlookers displayed signs of the liveliest interest, as well as the strangest expressions and gestures, as if each were working an invisible instrument in his hands. At the same time there could be heard in the air soft but deeply moving music, which seemed to originate from the stars that were wondrously interweaving in the hall, and from other strange movements. The stars moved about, now slowly, now swiftly, in constantly changing lines, and following the progressions of the music, they imitated the configurations of the cards in the most artful way. The music, like the pictures on the table, kept changing incessantly, and as strange and as dissonant as the transitions frequently were, at the same time one simple theme seemed to link everything together. With unbelievable lightness the stars flew around in imitation of the pictures. They would pull together now into a single great concentration, then again individual clusters would form beautiful arrangements; now the long train of stars would disintegrate like a beam of light into countless sparks, then again the smaller circles and designs would grow to reveal a single large and astonishing figure. During this time the forms in the stained glass windows stood motionless. The bird kept moving its coat of precious feathers in the most varied ways. The ancient hero had also been busily engaged in his invisible activity, when suddenly the King cried out in great joy, "Everything will go well. Iron, throw your sword into the world, so that they may learn where Peace is resting." The hero tore the sword from his hip, placed it with its point toward the sky, then seized and hurled it out of the open window over the city and across the sea of ice. Like a comet it flew through the air and seemed to burst asunder with a bright ringing sound as it hit the mountain belt, for it fell to the ground in a shower of sparks.

At that time the beautiful boy Eros was lying in his cradle sleeping peacefully, while Ginnistan, his nurse, rocked the cradle and nursed little Fable, his foster sister. She had spread her colorful scarf out over the cradle, so that the light from the glaring lamp that the Scribe had standing before him would not upset the child. The Scribe was writing tirelessly, glancing around from time to time with a sullen look at the children and a scowl for the nurse, who smiled good-naturedly at him and said nothing.

The children's father kept coming in and out, each time looking intently at the children and saying a few friendly words to Ginnistan. He incessantly had something to tell the Scribe. The latter listened with painstaking precision to what the Father said, and when he had written it all down, he would pass the pages to a noble, godlike woman who stood leaning against an altar on which there stood a dark basin with clear water, which she gazed into with a serene smile. Each time she would dip the pages into the basin, and, if upon drawing them out she perceived that some of the writing held fast and had become lustrous, she gave the page back to the Scribe, who bound it into a great book. Often he seemed vexed when his effort had been in vain and everything was obliterated. The woman turned occasionally to Ginnistan and the children, dipped her finger in the basin, and sprinkled several drops onto them, and as soon as they touched the nurse, the child, or the cradle, the drops would dissolve into a blue mist that produced a thousand strange images, constantly flowing around them and changing shape. If one of the drops happened to land on the Scribe, a great many numbers and geometrical figures would fall down, which he quickly strung onto a thread and hung around his scrawny neck for decoration. The boy's mother, who was the very picture of gracefulness and charm, would often come into the room. She seemed constantly busy, and would always carry some household utensil out with her. If this was noticed by the suspicious Scribe, who kept following her movements with squinting eyes, he would launch into a long reprimand. No one paid any attention to him. Everyone seemed accustomed to his useless objections.

The Mother nursed little Fable for a few minutes; but soon she was called away again, and then Ginnistan took back the child, who seemed to prefer to nurse from her. Suddenly the Father brought in a delicate sliver of iron that he had found in the courtyard. The Scribe examined it, turned it around with great liveliness, and soon discovered that if one suspended it in the middle from a string, it would turn by itself to the north. Ginnistan also took it in her hand, bent it, breathed on it, and presently gave it the form of a snake, which then suddenly took its tail into its mouth. The Scribe soon had his fill of looking at it. He wrote down everything precisely and ran on at great length about the uses that this discovery could yield. How angry he was, however, when his entire manuscript failed the test and emerged white from the basin. The nurse continued to play with the iron snake. From time to time she touched it to the cradle, and now the boy began to waken, threw back the covers, held one hand against the light, and reached with the other for the snake. As soon as he had taken hold of it, he leapt with a bound from his cradle, frightening Ginnistan and nearly causing the Scribe to fall from his stool in terror. Clad only in his long blond hair, Eros stood in the midst of the room and gazed with indescribable joy at the treasure, which strained in his hands toward the north and seemed to stir him to the depths of his being. Visibly he grew.

"Sophia," he said with a touching voice to the woman, "let me drink from the basin." She passed it to him without hesitation, and he could not get his fill of drinking, while the basin seemed to remain as full as ever. At last he gave it back, fervently embracing the noble woman. He pressed Ginnistan to his heart and asked her for the colorful scarf, which he bound around his waist for the sake of modesty. Little Fable he picked up and held in his arms. She seemed to take infinite pleasure in him and began to talk about all kinds of things. Ginnistan fawned on him. She looked extremely charming and frivolous and clasped him to her with the ardor of a bride. With furtive words she drew him toward the chamber door, but Sophia beckoned gravely and pointed to the snake; at that moment the Mother entered, and Eros flew to her immediately and welcomed her with a burst of tears. The Scribe had gone off in a fury. The Father entered, and when he saw Mother and Son quietly embracing, he crossed in back of them to the alluring Ginnistan and caressed her. Sophia went upstairs. Little Fable took the Scribe's pen and began to write. Mother and Son engaged in soft conversation, and the Father slipped off to the chamber with Ginnistan to refresh himself in her arms after the day's business.

After a considerable time Sophia returned. The Scribe entered. The Father came out of the chamber and went back to work. Ginnistan returned with flushed cheeks. With a string of abusive words the Scribe drove little Fable from his stool and found that it took some time to put his things back in order. He handed Sophia the pages that Fable had covered with writing, with the expectation of receiving them back clean and white; to his great indignation, the writing was luminously intact as Sophia drew it from the basin and laid it before him. Fable nestled close to her Mother, who took her in her arms, tidied up the room, opened the windows, let fresh air in, and made preparations for a delicious meal. Through the windows one could see the most splendid views and a cloudless sky that stretched over the earth. In the courtyard the Father was working to capacity. Whenever he grew weary he would look up to the window where Ginnistan was standing and throwing down to him all sorts of little things to eat. The Mother and Son went out to help wherever they could and to make preparations in keeping with the decision that had been reached. The Scribe kept writing, and would scowl terribly whenever he found it necessary to ask something of Ginnistan, who had a very good memory and retained everything that happened. Eros soon came back in a beautiful suit of armor, around which the colorful scarf was tied like a sash, and asked Sophia to advise him when and how he should set out on his journey. The Scribe was quick to speak up and immediately offered a detailed itinerary, but his suggestions went unheeded.

"You can begin your journey now; Ginnistan shall accompany you," said Sophia. "She is familiar with the roads, and she is well known everywhere. She will assume the form of your mother so that you will not be led into temptation. If you find the King, think of me: then I will come to help you."

Ginnistan exchanged forms with the Mother, which seemed to give the Father great satisfaction. The Scribe was glad that the two were going away, particularly since Ginnistan made him a farewell gift of her personal notebook, in which the chronicle of the house was recorded in detail; now only little Fable remained as a thorn in his side, and for the sake of his peace and satisfaction he couldn't have wished anything more than seeing her included among the departing travelers. Sophia blessed them as they knelt down before her and gave them a receptacle full of water from the basin to take along. The Mother was very distressed. Little Fable would have liked to go too, while the Father was too busy outside the house to take an active part in the preparations. It was night when they set off, and the moon was high in the heavens.

"Dear Eros," said Ginnistan, "we must hurry if we are to get to my father. He has not seen me in such a long time and has searched for me so longingly all over the earth. Can't you see his pale, grieving face? You will be my witness and make me known to him in my strange form."

Love went on a darkened path,
Glimpsed by the moon alone,
The realm of shadows lay revealed,
Its rare adornment shown.

A blue mist hovered all around
Edged with a golden band,
While Fantasy drew him swiftly on
Over stream and land.

His heart was full and soaring
With bold heroic fire,
A foresense of the future joy
Soothed his wild desire.

Yearning pined and did not know
That Love was drawing near;

His face was ever deeper lined
From mournful sigh and tear.

The little snake was faithful still:
Its loveliness shone forth,
And led the carefree couple
Straight onward to the north.

Love went through the wilderness,
The moon's child his escort,
They passed the kingdom of the clouds
And came to her father's court.

The moon sat on his silver throne,
With grief he shared the place,
At last he heard his daughter's voice
And sank in her embrace.

Eros stood by, touched at their tender embraces. At last the old
man, deeply shaken, collected himself and welcomed his guest. He
seized his great horn and blew on it with all his might. An awesome summons thundered through the ancient castle. The spiky
towers with their gleaming knobs shook and the steep black roofs
trembled. The castle stood still, for it had landed on the mountains beyond the sea. From all directions his servants came streaming in, whose strange shapes and costumes were of endless delight
to Ginnistan and did not daunt the brave Eros. Ginnistan greeted
her old acquaintances, and all of them appeared before her in renewed strength and the full splendor of their being. The turbulent
spirit of the Floodtide followed the gentle Ebbtide. The ancient
Hurricanes laid themselves on the pounding breast of the vehement, impassioned Earthquakes. The tender Rainshowers looked
around for the colorful Rainbow, who stood there pale, remote
from the sun with its greater attraction. Harsh Thunder scolded
at the foolishness of the Lightning Bolts, who kept flashing out
from behind the innumerable Clouds, who in turn stood about
with a thousand charms and kept enticing the fiery youths. The
two winsome sisters, Morning and Evening, were especially happy
about the arrival of Eros and Ginnistan and wept gentle tears in

their embrace. The sight of this wondrous retinue was indescribable. The old King could not get his fill of looking at his daughter. She felt happy ten times over in her ancestral castle and never tired of beholding the familiar wonders and curiosities. Her joy was quite inexpressible when the King gave her the key to the treasure chamber and permission to arrange a drama for Eros there, which could entertain him until the signal was given for departure. The treasure chamber was a large garden whose diversity and richness surpassed all description. Among the immense trees formed by stormclouds were innumerable castles in the air, all of astonishing construction, each more exquisite than the last. Great herds of sheep with silvery, golden, and rose colored fleeces wandered about, and the strangest animals filled the grove with movement and life. Remarkable statues stood here and there, and the festive parades and strange chariots that appeared from every direction constantly engaged one's attention. The flower beds overflowed with colorful blossoms. The buildings were piled high with weapons of every kind, with the most beautiful carpets, tapestries, curtains, drinking vessels, and all sorts of tools and instruments, arranged as far as the eye could see. Upon an elevation they looked out over a romantic land strewn with cities and castles, temples and burial sites, combining all the refinement of inhabited plains with the fearful beauty of the wilderness and craggy cliffs. The loveliest colors were to be found in the happiest combinations. The mountain peaks gleamed like fire balls in their coats of snow and ice. The plain rejoiced in the freshest green. The distance was adorned with all shades of blue, and from the darkness of the sea the pennants of untold fleets waved colorfully. Here a shipwreck was visible in the background, and close in was a merry rustic feast of country folk; there one saw the awesome beauty of an erupting volcano and the desolation of an earthquake, and in the foreground a pair of lovers in the sweetest caresses beneath shade trees. Down below a terrifying battle, and beyond it a theater full of the most comic masks. To the other side, in the foreground, a youthful corpse upon a bier clasped by an inconsolable lover, the weeping parents alongside; in the background, a lovely mother with her child on her breast, angels sitting at her feet and gazing down from the branches above her head. The scenes changed unceasingly and flowed together at last into a mysterious spectacle.

Heaven and earth were in complete uproar. All terrors had broken loose. A mighty voice cried "To arms!" An appalling army of skeletons with black flags descended like a storm from dark mountains and attacked Life, which with its youthful troops was cavorting and celebrating on the bright plains and had not foreseen an attack. A terrible tumult arose, and the earth trembled; storms raged, and the night was illuminated by frightful meteors. With unheard-of atrocities, the army of phantoms tore the tender limbs of the living to pieces. A towering funeral pyre rose up, and amidst the most gruesome howling the children of Life were consumed by the flames. Suddenly from the dark heap of ashes a milk-blue stream burst forth in all directions. The ghosts attempted to take flight, but the flood swelled visibly and engulfed the hideous rabble. Soon all the horrors were annihilated. Heaven and earth flowed together, transformed into sweet music. A flower of wondrous beauty floated radiant on the gentle waves. A brilliant arch formed over the flood, and upon it, down both sides, sat godlike figures on resplendent thrones. At the top sat Sophia, the basin in her hand, beside a lordly man with an oak wreath about his locks and a palm of peace in his right hand instead of a scepter. A lily leaf bent over the chalice of the floating flower, and upon it sat little Fable, singing the sweetest songs to the accompaniment of a harp. In the chalice lay Eros himself, bent over a beautiful sleeping maiden who clung tightly to him. A smaller blossom enclosed the two of them, so that from the hips down they seemed to be transformed into a single flower.

Eros thanked Ginnistan with a thousand expressions of rapture. He embraced her tenderly, and she returned his caresses. Weary from the ordeal of the journey and the great variety of things he had seen, he yearned for comfort and rest. Ginnistan, who felt herself keenly attracted to the handsome youth, took good care not to mention the drink that Sophia had given him to take along. She led him to a remote bath, removed his armor, and herself put on a nightgown in which she looked exotic and seductive. Eros submerged himself in the dangerous waves, and climbed out again intoxicated. Ginnistan dried him and rubbed his limbs, which were taut with the strength of youth. With ardent longing he recalled his beloved and embraced the enticing Ginnistan in sweet illusion. Heedlessly he succumbed to his tender and impetuous feelings, and at last, after the most sensuous pleasures, fell asleep on the lovely breast of his companion.

In the meantime, things had taken a turn for the worse at home. The Scribe had involved the servants in a dangerous conspiracy. His hostile soul had long been seeking an opportunity to usurp control of the household and shake off his yoke, and at last he had found it. First his followers seized the mother and put her in iron fetters. The Father was likewise arrested and restricted to bread and water. Little Fable heard the uproar in the room. She crept off and hid behind the altar, and, noticing that a door was concealed at the back of the altar, she opened it with a nimble touch and found that a stairway descended inside. She pulled the door closed after her and went down the stairway in darkness. The Scribe came storming in to take his revenge on little Fable and to take Sophia captive. Neither was to be found. The basin was also missing, and in his rage he smashed the altar into a thousand pieces, without, however, discovering the secret staircase.

Little Fable descended for a considerable time. At length she came out onto an open square that was graced round about with a magnificent colonnade and closed by a great gate. All forms here were dark. The air was like a monstrous shadow. In the sky was a black, luminous body. It was impossible to distinguish anything quite precisely, since every figure displayed a different shade of black and cast a light glow behind it. Light and shadow seemed here to have reversed their roles. Fable was happy to be in a new world. She examined everything with childish curiosity. Finally she came to the gate, in front of which a beautiful Sphinx was reclining on a massive pedestal.

"What are you seeking?" asked the Sphinx. "That which is my own," responded Fable. "Whence do you come?" "From ancient times." "You are still a child." "And shall forever be a child." "Who will stand by you?" "I stand for myself. Where are the sisters?" asked Fable. "Everywhere and nowhere," answered the Sphinx. "Do you know me?" "Not yet." "Where is Love?" "In the imagination." "And Sophia?" The Sphinx muttered inaudibly to herself and rustled her wings. "Sophia and Love," cried Fable triumphantly and passed through the gate. She stepped into the immense cavern and walked cheerfully up to the ancient sisters, who were engaged in their strange trade by the stingy light of a black-burning lamp. They pretended not to notice the little guest, who went out of her way to be polite to them and caress them. Finally one of them croaked, with rasping words and squinting eyes, "What business do you have here, idle girl? Who let you in? Your childish skipping around is disturbing the quiet flame. The oil is burning to no use. Can't you sit down and make yourself busy?"

"Pretty cousin," said Fable, "I have no interest in idleness. I must say I had to laugh at your doorkeeper. She would have liked to take me on her breast, but she must have eaten too much: she couldn't get up. Let me sit outside the door, and give me something to spin; for I cannot see very well here, and when I spin I must be able to sing and chatter away, and that might disturb you in your solemn thoughts."

"You are not to go outside, but in the adjoining room a ray of light from the upper world breaks through the crevices in the rocks; there you may spin if you are so good at it. Great piles of old pieces of thread are lying here. Wind them together, but be careful: if you make a mistake while spinning, or the thread breaks, the strands will twist around you and choke you to death." The old woman laughed hatefully and went on spinning. Fable caught up an armful of threads, took the distaff and spindle, and skipped singing into the other room. She looked out through the opening and caught sight of the constellation of the Phoenix. Happy at the lucky sign, she began to spin merrily, and, leaving the door slightly ajar, sang softly:

> Awaken in your traces,
> You children of the past,
> And leave your resting places,
> The morning comes at last.
>
> From your threads I'll spin now
> A strand of unity.
> Days of peace begin now,
> And *one* life you shall be.
>
> Each one shall live in all,
> And all in each as well.

With one breath's rise and fall
One heart shall in you swell.

You still are spectral vapors,
Mere dream and sorcery.
With wild and frightful capers
Go taunt the holy three.

The spindle swung with unbelievable swiftness between her little feet, while she used both hands to turn the delicate thread.
During the song countless little lights became visible, which slipped
out through the crack in the door and swarmed through the cavern as hideous ghouls. The crones, meanwhile, had gone on sullenly spinning, waiting for little Fable to cry out in anguish. How
horrified they were, however, when suddenly a frightful nose
peeped over their shoulders, and when they looked about them,
the entire cavern was full of the most ghastly figures who were up
to a thousand kinds of mischief. The crones rushed at each other
for protection, howled in a dreadful voice, and would have turned
to stone from fright if the Scribe had not this very moment stepped
into the cavern carrying a mandrake root. The little lights crept
away into crevices in the rocks and the cavern became quite dim,
since the black lamp had fallen over in the confusion and gone
out. The crones were delighted when they heard the Scribe coming, but they were full of wrath toward little Fable. They called to
her to come out, snarled and hissed at her frightfully, and forbade
her to spin any more. The Scribe smirked contemptuously, thinking he now had little Fable in his power, and said, "It's a good
thing that you are here and can be put to work. I hope there will
be no lack of opportunities to discipline you. Your good spirit led
you here. I wish you a long life and much pleasure."

"Thank you for your good will," said Fable; "one can see that
you are in your prime; all you need now is the hourglass and the
scythe, and you would look exactly like the brother of my pretty
cousins. If you need any goose quills, just pluck a handful of soft
down from their cheeks." The Scribe showed signs of pouncing
upon her. She smiled and said, "If you value your beautiful growth
of hair and your clever eyes, take care! Consider my fingernails.
You don't have much more to lose."

Grim with rage he turned to the crones, who were wiping their eyes and groping around for their distaffs. They were unable to find anything, since the lamp had gone out, and they burst into a stream of abuse at Fable. "Just let her go," the Scribe said cunningly, "and catch tarantulas for the preparation of your oil. I wish to say for your consolation that Eros is flying around without a moment's rest and will keep your scissors busily occupied. His mother, who often compelled you to spin the threads longer, will fall prey to the flames tomorrow." He tickled himself to make himself laugh when he saw tears in Fable's eyes at this news. He gave a piece of the mandrake root to the crones and went away, wrinkling up his nose. In an angry tone of voice the sisters ordered Fable to go looking for tarantulas, despite the fact that they still had oil on hand, and Fable hurried off. She pretended to open the gate, slammed it shut again with a bang, and crept softly back to the recesses of the cavern, where a ladder hung down. She quickly scrambled up and soon came to a trap door that opened into Arcturus's chamber.

The King was sitting surrounded by his councilors when Fable appeared. The Northern Crown adorned his head. In his left hand he held the Lily; in his right, the Scales. The Eagle and Lion were sitting at his feet. "Monarch," said Fable, bowing respectfully before him, "hail to your firmly founded throne! Glad tidings for your wounded heart! Imminent return for Wisdom! Eternal awakening for Peace! Rest for restless Love! Transfiguration of the Heart! Life for Antiquity and form for the Future!"

The King touched her guileless brow with the Lily. "Whatever you wish, it shall be granted you." "Three times I will ask; when I come for the fourth time, Love will be at the door. Give me now the Lyre."

"Eridanus! bring it to us," cried the King. With a roaring sound Eridanus streamed down from the ceiling, and Fable drew the Lyre from his glittering waters.

Fable struck several prophetic chords. The King ordered the goblet passed to her, from which she sipped; then with many expressions of gratitude she hurried away. She glided in lovely arcs across the sea of ice, while she drew lighthearted music from the strings of the Lyre.

Beneath her steps the ice gave forth the most magnificent tones.

The cliff of Sorrow took them for the voices of his returning children looking for their way and answered in an echo that resounded thousandfold.

Fable had soon reached the shore. She met her mother, who looked wasted and pale and had become slender and grave. Her noble features showed signs of hopeless grief and touching loyalty.

"What has become of you, dear Mother?" said Fable. "You seem completely changed to me; without an inner sign I would not have recognized you. I hoped to revive myself on your breast again; I have yearned for you for a long time."

Ginnistan caressed her tenderly and looked cheerful and amiable. "I thought at once," she said, "that the Scribe probably would not catch you. It revives me to look at you. I am in bad enough straits, but I will have some consolation soon. Perhaps I may have a moment of rest. Eros is close by, and if he sees you and you chatter about this and that with him, perhaps he will linger for a while. In the meantime you can lie on my breast; I will give you what I have." She took Fable on her lap, gave her her breast, and went on speaking while she smiled down at the little one, who was nursing with great relish. "I myself am the cause for Eros's having become so wild and erratic. But I do not regret it, for those hours I spent in his arms have made me immortal. I thought I might melt away beneath his fiery caresses. Like a heavenly marauder he seemed to want to destroy me cruelly and to exult in the defeat of his trembling victim. We awakened late from the forbidden intoxication, and in a strangely transformed condition. Long silvery wings had grown over his white shoulders, covering the enchanting fullness and curves of his figure. The force that had sprung up in him and so suddenly made a young man out of a boy seemed to have withdrawn entirely into the shining wings, and he was once again a boy. The restrained passion in his countenance had changed to the flirtatious fire of a will-o'-the-wisp, his solemn and serious air had changed to impish deceitfulness, his expressive quietness to childish instability, his noble bearing to a droll sort of animation. I felt myself drawn irresistibly and with grim passion to the willful boy, and I painfully felt his smiling mockery, his indifference to my most moving entreaties. I saw my own form changed. My carefree cheerfulness had disappeared and yielded to a sorrowful sense of affliction and delicate shyness. I would have liked to conceal myself, and Eros too, from everyone's sight. I did not have the courage to look into his hurtful eyes, and I felt terribly ashamed and debased. I had no other thought than of him and would have given my life to free him from his bizarre behavior. As deeply as he offended all my sensibilities, I could not help adoring him.

"He rose and fled from me, though I begged him as movingly as I could, and with the most ardent tears, to remain with me, and since that time I have followed him everywhere. He actually seems to make a point of teasing me. I hardly catch up with him when he maliciously flies off again. His bow and arrow are causing devastation everywhere. There is nothing I can do except to comfort the unhappy, and yet I have need of comfort myself. Their voices calling out to me show me where he has been, and their mournful laments when I must leave them again move me to the depths of my heart. The Scribe is pursuing us in a horrible rage and taking his vengeance on the poor stricken ones. The fruit of that mysterious night was a great host of strange children who resemble their grandfather and are named for him. Winged like their father, they accompany him everywhere he goes and torment the poor creatures who have been hit by his arrows. But here comes the light-hearted procession now. I must go. Farewell, dear child. His presence arouses my passion. May you have good fortune in your undertaking." Eros passed by without granting a single tender look to Ginnistan, who had hurried up to him. But he turned amiably to Fable, and his little attendants danced around her gaily. Fable was happy to see her foster brother again and sang a lively song to the accompaniment of her lyre. Eros seemed at the point of remembering something and dropped his bow. The little ones fell asleep on the grass. Ginnistan was able to take hold of him, and he endured her tender caresses. At length Eros also began to nod, nestled himself in Ginnistan's lap, and fell asleep with his wings spread out over her. The weary Ginnistan was infinitely happy and would not avert her gaze from the sweet slumberer. During the song, tarantulas had appeared from every direction, drawing a shimmering net over the blades of grass and following the beat of the music with lively movements on their threads. Now Fable consoled her mother and promised soon to help her. From the cliff resounded the soft echo of the music, cradling the slumberers as they nodded off. From her carefully guarded receptacle Ginnistan sprinkled a few drops into the air, and the loveliest dreams descended upon them. Fable took the receptacle along and continued her journey. The strings of her lyre were never at rest, and the tarantulas swiftly spun out their threads as they followed the enchanting sounds.

Presently she saw from afar the high flame of the funeral pyre rising above the green forest. Sadly she gazed up into the heavens and was gladdened to see Sophia's blue veil, which hovered rippling over the earth, covering the monstrous grave for all eternity. The sun stood fiery red with anger in the sky; the intense flame was sucking away its stolen light, and as violently as it tried to keep the light to itself, the sun grew more and more pale and spotty. The flame became whiter and more powerful as the sun faded. Ever more powerfully the flame drew the light to itself, and soon the radiant halo of the daystar was consumed and it stood there only as a dull gleaming disc, while every fresh impulse of envy and rage only increased the outbreak of escaping light waves. At last nothing was left of the sun but a black burnt-out slag, which fell into the sea. The flame had become brilliant beyond all powers of description. The funeral pyre was consumed. The flame rose slowly aloft and moved toward the north. Fable entered the courtyard, which looked desolate; the house had become dilapidated in the meantime. Thorn bushes grew in the crevices of the windowsills and vermin of all sorts swarmed on the broken staircases. She heard a dreadful noise in the room; the Scribe and his cohorts had been gloating over the immolation of the Mother, but were seized with terror when they beheld the collapse of the sun.

They had struggled in vain to extinguish the flame, and had not come away from the matter unharmed. Their pain and fear wrung frightful curses and moans from them. They were even more horrified when Fable entered the room, and they stormed down on her with a scream of rage, intending to vent their fury on her. Fable slipped behind the cradle, and her pursuers rushed headlong into the web of the tarantulas, which took revenge on them with countless stings. The whole lot of them now began to dance wildly, while Fable accompanied them by playing a merry song. Laughing heartily at their foolish antics, she went up to the ruins of the altar and cleared away the rubble to find the hidden staircase, which she then descended with her retinue of tarantulas.

The Sphinx asked, "What comes more suddenly than lightning?" "Revenge," said Fable. "What is most transitory?" "Unrightful possession." "Who knows the world?" "He who knows himself." "What is the eternal mystery?" "Love." "With whom does the mystery rest?" "With Sophia."

The Sphinx writhed in misery, and Fable entered the cavern. "I have brought you some tarantulas," she said to the old women, who had relit their lamp and were working very busily. They started up in fright, and one of them ran at her with scissors to stab her to death. Inadvertently she stepped on a tarantula, which stung her in the foot. She screamed pitifully. The others started to come to her aid and were likewise stung by the enraged tarantulas. Unable now to lay their hands on Fable, they jumped wildly around and about. "Spin us some light dancing clothes immediately," they cried out in fury to the little girl. "We cannot move in these stiff skirts, and we are about to perish from the heat; but you must soften the thread with spider juice so that it doesn't break, and flowers that have grown in fire must be worked into the design, otherwise you will never leave here alive."

"At your service," said Fable, and went into the adjoining room.

"I intend to produce three nice big flies for you," she said to the garden spiders that had fastened their airy cobwebs around the ceiling and the walls, "but you must at once spin me three light, pretty gowns. I will return immediately with the flowers that are to be worked into them." The spiders were ready to help and swiftly began weaving. Fable slipped over to the ladder and proceeded to Arcturus.

"Monarch," she said, "the wicked are dancing, the good are at rest. Has the flame arrived?"

"It has arrived," said the King. "The night is over and the ice is melting. My spouse is visible from afar. My enemy is burned out. Everything is beginning to live. I still may not reveal myself, for alone I am not king. Request whatever you want."

"I need," said Fable, "flowers that have grown in fire. I know you have a skillful gardener who understands how to grow them."

"Zinc," cried the King, "give us some flowers." The flower gardener stepped forth from the ranks, fetched a pot full of fire, and sowed gleaming pollen into it. It was not long before the flowers shot up. Fable collected them in her apron and set out on her return journey. The spiders had been industrious, and there was nothing left but to fasten the flowers on, which they immediately began to do with much taste and adroitness. Fable took care not to tear off the ends of the threads, which still clung to the weavers.

She carried the gowns to the exhausted dancers, who had sunk to the ground dripping with sweat and were resting a few minutes from the unaccustomed exertion. With great dexterity she undressed the haggard beauties, who had no lack of insults for their little servant, and dressed them in the new gowns, which were very prettily made and fit them splendidly. During this task she extolled the charms and the lovable character of her mistresses, and the old women seemed delighted indeed at the flattering words and the exquisiteness of their outfits. In the meantime they had recovered, and, enlivened by a fresh impulse to dance, began once again to whirl about briskly, promising in their treacherous way a long life and great rewards for the little girl. Fable went back into the room and said to the garden spiders, "You can go ahead now and eat the flies that I put in your webs." As it was, the spiders were already impatient at being tossed back and forth, since the thread ends were still inside them and the crones kept leaping about crazily; without further ado they rushed out and pounced on the dancers. The latter looked for their scissors to defend themselves, but Fable had stolen away with them. The crones thus succumbed to their hungry fellow craftsmen, who had not tasted such delicious morsels in a long time and proceeded to suck them clean to the marrow. Fable looked out through the crevice in the rocks and caught sight of Perseus with his great iron shield. The scissors flew on their own to the shield, and Fable asked him to use them to clip Eros's wings, and then to immortalize the sisters with his shield and thus to complete the great work.

She now left the subterranean realm and cheerfully ascended to Arcturus's palace.

"The flax is completely spun. The lifeless is again dead. The living will reign, forming and using the lifeless. The inward is revealed and the outward is hidden. The curtain will soon rise and the drama will begin. Once again I will make a request, then I will spin days of eternity."

"Blessed child," said the Monarch, touched, "you are our liberator." "I am nothing more than Sophia's godchild," said the little one. "Permit Tourmaline, Zinc the flower gardener, and Gold to accompany me. I must gather the ashes of my foster mother, and the ancient giant must rise again and carry the world, so that it will float and not lie upon chaos."

The King summoned all three and ordered them to accompany the little one. The city was bright, and in the streets there was lively traffic. The sea crashed and roared against the coves in the cliff, and Fable traveled across in the King's carriage with her companions. Tourmaline carefully gathered the flying ashes. They went around the earth until they came to the ancient giant and climbed down his shoulders. He seemed paralyzed by a stroke and could not move a single limb. Gold laid a coin in his mouth, and the flower gardener pushed a bowl beneath his loins. Fable touched his eyes and poured the contents of the receptacle over his brow. As soon as the water flowed over his eyes, into his mouth, and down over his body into the bowl, a lightning bolt of life flashed through all his muscles. He opened his eyes and vigorously rose to his feet. Fable leapt up to her companions on the ascending earth and cordially wished him good morning.

"Are you there again, dear child?" said the old man; "and you see, all this time I have been dreaming of you. I always thought you would appear before the earth and my eyes became too heavy for me. I must have been sleeping for a long time."

"The earth is light again, as it always was for the good," said Fable. "The ancient times are returning. Before long you will be among old acquaintances. I will spin happy days for you, and you won't want for a helper either, so that you can now and then share our joys and breathe youth and strength in the arms of your beloved. Where are our old friends and guests, the Hesperides?"

"At Sophia's side. Soon their garden will blossom again, and the golden fruit will fill the air with its fragrance. They are going about and gathering the wilted plants."

Fable departed and hurried to the house. It had fallen into total ruin. Ivy covered the walls. High bushes shaded the former court-yard, and soft moss cushioned the old stairways. She stepped into the room. Sophia stood at the altar, which had been rebuilt. Eros lay at her feet in full armor, more solemn and noble than ever. A magnificent chandelier hung from the ceiling. Around the altar the floor of variegated inlaid stones described a great circle, which consisted solely of noble, significant figures. Ginnistan was bending over a bier on which the Father lay, seemingly in deep slumber, and she was weeping. Her bloom of loveliness was endlessly heightened by a quality of reverence and love. Fable presented the urn in which the ashes were gathered to the sacred figure of Sophia, who embraced her tenderly.

"Dear child," she said, "your zeal and your loyalty have won you a place among the eternal stars. You have chosen the immortal within you. The Phoenix is yours. You will be the soul of our lives. Awaken the bridegroom now. The herald calls, and Eros shall seek out Freya and awaken her."

Fable was delighted beyond description at these words. She called to her companions Gold and Zinc and approached the bier. Ginnistan watched expectantly as they set to work. Gold melted the coin and poured the gleaming liquid up to the brim of the casket in which the father lay. Zinc wound a chain around Ginnistan's bosom. The body floated on the quivering waves. "Bend forward, dear Mother," said Fable, "and lay your hand on the heart of your beloved."

Ginnistan leaned forward. She saw her multiple reflection. The chain touched the liquid, and her hand touched his heart. He awoke and drew his enraptured bride into his arms. The metal hardened and turned into a bright mirror. The Father rose up, his eyes flashed, and as beautiful and significant as his figure was, at the same time his entire body seemed to be an endlessly responsive fluid that revealed every impression in the finest and most varied movements.

The happy pair approached Sophia, who spoke words of consecration over them and admonished them to consult the mirror assiduously, since it reflected everything in its true form, destroyed every illusion, and eternally retained the original image. She now grasped the urn and emptied the ashes into the basin on the altar. A soft roaring and bubbling was to be heard as the ashes dissolved, and a gentle wind blew through the raiments and hair of those standing by.

Sophia presented the basin to Eros, and he passed it on to the others. All tasted of the divine draught and perceived with inexpressible joy the friendly greeting of the Mother within them. She was present in each, and her sacred and mysterious presence seemed to transfigure them all.

The expectation was fulfilled and surpassed. All perceived what they had lacked, and the room had become an abode of the blessed. Sophia said, "The great mystery has been revealed to all, and remains eternally unfathomable. Out of pain the new world is born, and in tears the ashes are dissolved to become the drink of eternal life. In each one dwells the heavenly Mother, to bear each child eternally. Do you feel the sweet birth in the throbbing of your breast?" She poured what remained in the basin down into the altar. The earth shook in its depths. Then she said, "Eros, hasten with your sister to your beloved. Soon you will see me again."

Fable and Eros hurried off with their retinue. A vast and vigorous springtime was spread over the earth. Everything was rising and stirring. The earth floated closer under the veil. Amidst cheerful commotion the moon and clouds were moving north. The King's castle shone out over the sea in magnificent radiance, and on its battlements stood the King in full splendor with his court. Everywhere Eros and Fable saw whirlwinds of dust, in which familiar figures seemed to form. They encountered numerous crowds of youths and maidens, who were streaming toward the castle, and welcomed them with cheers. Here and there on a gravemound sat a happy couple just awakened, holding each other after long privation, taking the new world for a dream, and unable to stop assuring each other of the beautiful truth.

The flowers and trees were growing and leafing out in full force. Everything seemed enlivened and inspired. Everything was speaking and singing. Fable greeted old acquaintances everywhere. The animals approached the awakened human beings with a friendly welcome. Plants treated them to fruits and fragrances and adorned them in the loveliest way. No stone lay any longer on anyone's heart, and all burdens had collapsed to form a solid floor underfoot. Eros and Fable came to the sea. A boat of polished steel was tied fast at the shore. They stepped into it and loosened the rope. The bow turned to the north, and the boat cut through the caressing waves as if it were in flight. Whispering reeds slowed its impetuous speed, and it pushed gently against the shore. They hurried up the broad steps. They both marveled at the regal city and its riches. In the courtyard the fountain had come to life and was leaping into the air. The grove was astir with the sweetest sounds, and a wondrous life seemed to swell and push there, in its ardent stems and leaves and its glittering flowers and fruits. The ancient hero met them at the gates of the palace. "Venerable and ancient man," said Fable, "Eros has need of your sword. Gold gave him a chain that reaches down into the sea at one end, and which is wound around his chest at the other end. Take hold of it with me and lead us to the great hall where the Princess rests." Eros took the sword from the hand of the ancient, set the pommel against his breast, and leaned the point forward. The double doors of the hall flew open and Eros, enraptured, approached the slumbering Freya. Suddenly there was a mighty report like a thunderclap. A bright spark leaped from the Princess to the sword; the sword and the chain flashed. The hero held little Fable, who had nearly collapsed. Eros's helmet crest rose waving into the air. "Throw the sword away," cried Fable, "and awaken your beloved." Eros dropped the sword, flew to the Princess, and passionately kissed her sweet lips. She opened her great dark eyes and recognized her beloved. A long kiss sealed the eternal union.

Down from the cupola came the King with Sophia by the hand. The constellations and the spirits of Nature followed in dazzling rows. An inexpressibly serene daylight filled the great hall, the palace, the city, and the sky. A countless throng poured into the vast royal hall and beheld the lovers kneeling in quiet devotion before the King and the Queen, who solemnly blessed them. The King took his diadem from his head and placed it upon Eros's golden locks. The ancient hero drew off his armor, and the King cast his cloak around him. Then he placed the lily in his left hand, and Sophia clasped an exquisite bracelet around the entwined hands of the lovers, while at the same time placing her own crown on Freya's brown hair.

"Hail to our ancient rulers!" cried the people. "They have always lived among us, and we did not recognize them. Hail to us! They shall rule us eternally! Bless us also!" Sophia said to the new Queen, "Cast the bracelet of your union into the air, so that the people and the world will ever be united with you." The bracelet melted in the air, and soon luminous rings were visible around every head, and a brilliant band of light formed over the city and the sea and the entire earth, which was celebrating an eternal festival of spring.

Perseus entered, carrying a spindle and a small basket. He

brought the basket to the new King. "Here," he said, "are the remains of your enemies." Inside it lay a stone board with black and white fields, and next to the board were a number of figures made of alabaster and black marble. "It is a chess game," said Sophia. "All war is banished onto this board and into these figures. It is a monument to the old and gloomy times." Perseus turned to Fable and gave her the spindle. "In your hands this spindle will delight us forever, and out of yourself you will spin us a golden thread that will never break." With a melodious rustling of his wings, the Phoenix flew to her feet, spread his wings out in front of her for her to sit on, and then rose to hover over the throne without alighting again. She sang a heavenly song and began to spin, while the thread seemed to wind forth out of her breast. The people were seized with new rapture, and all eyes were raised to the lovely child. The sound of new rejoicing came from the door. The old Moon entered with his strange and whimsical court, and behind him the people carried in Ginnistan and her bridegroom, as if in a triumphal procession.

They were wreathed with garlands of flowers. The royal family received them with the most cordial tenderness, and the new regal couple proclaimed them their regents on earth.

"Grant me," said the Moon, "the realm of the Fates, whose curious buildings have just risen out of the earth in the courtyard of the palace. I plan to stage delightful dramas for you there, with which little Fable will be of help to me."

The King assented to the request, little Fable nodded friendly agreement, and the people looked forward with pleasure to the strange and diverting pastime. The Hesperides expressed their best wishes upon Eros's accession to the throne and asked for protection for their gardens. The King extended his welcome to them, and in this fashion there followed countless joyous envoys. In the meantime the throne had imperceptibly changed shape and had turned into a magnificent wedding bed; above its canopy hovered the Phoenix with little Fable. Three caryatids of dark porphyry supported it at the back, and the front rested on a sphinx of basalt. The King put his arms around his blushing beloved, and the people followed his example with mutual embraces and caresses. Nothing was to be heard but tender words and a whispering of kisses. At length Sophia said, "The Mother is among us; her presence will make us happy eternally. Follow us to our dwelling. In the temple there we will reside forever and guard the mystery of the world." Fable went on spinning energetically and sang in full voice:

Founded is the kingdom of eternity,
In love and peace is ended all hostility.
The long and troubled dream of mortal pain departs,
Sophia is forever priestess of our hearts.

Translated by Gordon Birrell

Hyacinth and Rosebud

Novalis

A long time ago, far to the west, there lived a youth. He was good and kindhearted, but at the same time he was strange beyond all measure. He moped and pined about nothing at all, went around lonely and silent, and sat down all by himself and brooded over strange things when the others were playing and were full of high spirits. He preferred most of all to spend his time in caves and forests, and then he would talk on and on with animals and birds, with trees and rocks, and of course he didn't say one reasonable word, but just such foolish stuff that you would die laughing if you heard it. But he stayed sullen and serious as ever, even though the squirrel, the monkey, the parrot, and the finch made every effort to divert him and to put him on the right track. The goose told fairy tales, the brook strummed along with a ballad, a big, fat boulder made silly somersaults, the friendly rose crept around behind him and twined itself through his hair, and the ivy plant stroked his troubled brow. But the dissatisfaction and gloom were stubborn. His parents were very aggrieved; they had no idea what they should do about him. He was healthy and ate well, they had never treated him badly, and up to a few years ago he had been as happy and lighthearted as anyone; the best at all the games, admired by all the girls. He was so handsome that he might have just stepped right out of a painting, and he danced like an angel. Among the girls there was one, an exquisite child, pretty as a picture, skin like the finest wax, hair like golden silk, lips like red cherries, the body of a little doll, raven-black eyes. Anyone who saw her would nearly have swooned, she was so lovely. At that time Rosebud (that was her name) loved

77

the handsome Hyacinth (that was *his* name) with all her heart, and he loved her to death, too. The other children didn't know anything about it at first. It was a violet that told them; the house cats had noticed; the houses of the two children were close together. Now when Hyacinth stood at night at his window and Rosebud stood at hers, the cats would run by hunting mice, and when they saw the two of them standing there, they laughed and giggled so loudly that Hyacinth and Rosebud heard them and became angry. The violet had mentioned it to the strawberry in confidence, and the strawberry told her friend the gooseberry, who from then on would simply not stop prickling Hyacinth when he came strolling by; and so it wasn't long before the whole garden and the woods heard about it, and when Hyacinth went out walking, voices called from every side, "Rosebud is my sweetheart!" Hyacinth was annoyed at all this, but still he had to laugh from the bottom of his heart when the lizard came creeping up, sat down on a warm stone, wagged its little tail, and sang:

> Dear little Rosebud, good as can be,
> Lost her sight and couldn't see.
> Thinks Hyacinth is her mother dear,
> Gives him a hug and holds him near;
> When she discovers the mistake she's made,
> She isn't flustered, isn't afraid,
> Acts as if there were nothing wrong,
> Just keeps kissing him all day long.

Alas! how soon these splendid times were gone. There came a man from foreign lands, who had traveled to an astonishing number of places; he had a long beard, deep eyes, horrifying eyebrows, and a wondrous garment with many folds and strange figures woven into it. He seated himself in front of the house that belonged to Hyacinth's parents. Now Hyacinth became very curious, and sat down next to him and fetched him bread and wine. The old man then parted his white beard and told stories until deep in the night, and Hyacinth didn't move an inch and never tired of listening. As much as one could tell later, the old man spoke at length of foreign lands, unknown regions, and amazingly wonderful things; he stayed for three days, and took Hyacinth with him down into deep shafts in the earth. Rosebud often enough cursed the old warlock, for Hyacinth was simply spellbound at his conversations and didn't care about anything else; he hardly took a bite of food. Finally the old man went on his way, but he left behind for Hyacinth a little book that nobody could read. Hyacinth gave the old man fruit, bread, and wine, and accompanied him until he was far away. And then he came back pensive and melancholy, and began a whole new way of life. Rosebud worried pitifully because of him, for from that time on he had little interest in her and always kept to himself.

Now it happened one day that he came home and seemed as if reborn. He threw his arms around his parents and wept. "I must go away into foreign lands," he said; "the strange old woman in the wood has told me how to get well, she threw the book into the fire and made me come to you and ask for your blessing. Perhaps I will come back soon, perhaps never again. Say goodbye to Rosebud for me. I would like to have spoken with her. I don't know what's wrong with me, something is driving me away. When I think back on the old times, more powerful thoughts immediately get in the way; my peace of mind is gone, my heart and love with it. I must go looking for them. I wish I could tell you where I'm going, but I don't know myself. I only know it is where the mother of all things lives, the Veiled Maiden. It is for her that my soul burns. Goodbye." He tore himself from them and went away.

His parents lamented and grieved; Rosebud stayed in her chamber and wept bitterly. Hyacinth, for his part, pushed on as fast as he could, through valley and wilderness, across mountains and streams, toward the mysterious land. Everywhere he went, he asked men and animals, rocks and trees about the sacred goddess Isis. Some laughed, some were silent, no one was able to tell him anything. In the beginning he came through rough, wild country; fog and clouds threw themselves in his path, and the weather was forever stormy. Then he encountered boundless deserts with glowing sand, and, as he continued to wander, his state of mind gradually changed, too; the hours became long for him and his restlessness settled. He became gentler and the violent longing in him slowly changed to a strong but tranquil stream in which his whole soul dissolved. It was as if many years had passed. Now the country became richer and more varied, the air mild and blue, the path more level. Green bushes enticed him with their refreshing shade, but he did not understand their language, indeed they seemed not to speak, and yet they filled his heart with green colors and cool stillness. Ever higher grew that sweet longing in him, broader and lusher became the leaves, louder and merrier the birds and animals, more fragrant the fruits, darker the sky, warmer the air, and more ardent his love; the time went faster and faster, as if it too were approaching its goal. One day he met a crystal spring and a crowd of flowers coming down into a valley between black pillars that rose far into the sky. They greeted him with friendly, familiar words. "Dear countrymen," he said, "do you know where I may find the sacred dwelling of Isis? It must be nearby, and perhaps you know this region better than I."

"We too are only passing through," answered the flowers; "a family of spirits is on a journey and we are preparing their way and their lodging for them, but a short time ago we came through a region where we heard her name spoken. Just keep going upwards, where we have come from, and you are sure to learn more." The flowers and the spring smiled as they said this, offered him a refreshing drink, and went on. Hyacinth followed their advice, asked again and again and finally came to that long-sought dwelling, which lay hidden beneath palms and other exquisite plants. His heart pounded in endless yearning, and the sweetest trepidation coursed through him in this abode of the eternal seasons. Amid heavenly scents he fell asleep, for only a dream could lead him into the holiest of regions. The strange dream led him through endless chambers full of curious things floating on harmonious sounds and with changing chords. Everything seemed to him so familiar and yet in such splendor as he had never seen. Then the last trace of earth disappeared, as if dissolved in air, and he stood before the heavenly maiden; he lifted the light, shimmering veil, and Rosebud sank into his arms. A distant music surrounded the mystery of the lovers' reunion, the outpourings of yearning, and excluded all that was foreign from this rapturous place. Hyacinth lived for a long time afterwards with Rosebud among his happy parents and playmates, and countless grandchildren thanked the strange old woman for her advice and her fire, for in those days people could have as many children as they wanted.

Translated by Gordon Birrell

The Runenberg

Ludwig Tieck

A young hunter sat lost in thought deep in the mountains beside his fowling nets while the rushing of waters and the rustle of the forest resounded in the solitude. He was musing on his destiny, thinking how, still so young, he had left his father and mother, his familiar home, and all the friends he had known in his native village to seek new surroundings, to escape from the round of the ever-recurrent commonplace, and he now looked up with a kind of amazement to find himself in this valley and engaged in such an occupation. Great clouds moving across the sky lost themselves behind the mountains, birds sang from the bushes and an echo answered them. He slowly descended the mountain and sat down on the bank of a brook that flowed foaming and murmuring over projecting rocks. He listened to the fitful melody of the water and it seemed as though it were telling him in language he could not understand a thousand things that were of great importance to him, and he became deeply downcast that he could not comprehend this speech. Again he looked about and it seemed to him that he was cheerful and happy; he plucked up new courage and sang in a ringing voice a hunter's song.

> Gaily 'mongst the crags now climbing
> Goes the huntsman to the chase,
> And his game he's sure of finding
> In these green and living windings,
> Though he seek till it grows late.

> How his faithful dogs bark, bounding
> Through the lovely solitude,

81

Through the woods the horns resounding,
Making hearts swell up redounding,
Hail thee, hunter brotherhood!

In these ravines his homeland dear,
All trees greet him as they sway;
Blow the winds of autumn sere,
Then he finds the stag and deer,
Shouting loud pursues his way.

Leave the husbandman his gleanings,
To the sailor leave the sea;
None there is at morning's gleaming
Sees Aurora's eyes more beaming
When the dew begems the lea

Than he who knows the chase, the forest,
Whom Diana smiles to see;
Her to whom his love's addressed
Form of fire shall manifest:
Who is happier than he!

While he was singing, the sun had sunk deeper in the west and broad shadows fell through the narrow valley. A cooling dusk stole over the ground and only the tops of the trees and mountain peaks still lay in the golden light of evening. Christian's spirits grew ever more despondent; he had no desire to return to his fowling nets and yet he did not want to stay where he was. Everything seemed to him so lonely and he longed for human companionship. Now he wished he had the old books he had seen in his father's possession, which he had never cared to read, as often as his father had urged him to do so. He recalled the scenes of his childhood, the games with the village children, those among them who had been his special companions, the school, which had been so oppressive to him, and he longed to return to all these surroundings, which he had left of his own accord when he went to seek his fortune in unknown regions, among strange people, in a new occupation. As it grew darker and the brook rushed on more loudly and nocturnal winged creatures began their erratic wandering flight, he was still sitting there disconsolate and sunk in thought; he felt like weeping and was wholly undecided as to what he should do or undertake. Unthinkingly, he pulled a projecting root from the earth and started in sudden fright to hear in the ground a dull moaning, protracted subterraneously in piteous tones, which died mournfully away in the far distance. This tone penetrated his inmost heart, it seized him as though he had unwittingly touched the wound of which the moribund body of nature was painfully expiring. He sprang up and was about to flee, for he had of course heard of the mysterious mandrake root that utters piercing shrieks when it is pulled up, and drives one mad by its ceaseless moaning. As he started to leave, a strange man was suddenly standing behind him; he looked at Christian in a friendly manner and asked where he was going. Christian had wanted company; nonetheless, he was startled by this friendly presence. "Where to in such haste?" the stranger asked again. The young huntsman tried to collect himself and told him how the solitude had suddenly seemed so frightening that he had wanted to flee; the evening, he said, was so dark, the green shades of the forest so sad, the brook so resounding with plaints, the clouds in the sky were drawing his longing with them over beyond the mountains.

"You are still young," the stranger said, "and probably cannot endure the rigors of solitude; I will accompany you, for you will find no house or settlement within a league of here. On the way, we can talk and tell each other stories; that way you will rid yourself of your dismal fancies. In an hour the moon will rise behind the mountains; its light will make your heart lighter, too."

They started on their way and the stranger soon seemed to the youth an old acquaintance. "How did you happen to come to these mountains?" the stranger asked. "From your speech you're not a native of this place."

"Oh, that's a long story," the young man answered, "and yet it's hardly worth repeating. It was as though some unknown power took me away from the circle of my parents and relatives; I was not master of myself; like a bird that has been caught in a net and flutters in vain, my soul was entangled in imaginings and desires. We lived far from here in the midst of a plain, where one saw no mountains, hardly even a hill, far and wide; a few trees adorned the green level ground; meadows, fertile fields of grain, and gardens stretched as far as the eye could see; a great river flowed gleaming like a mighty spirit past the fields and meadows. My father was a gardener at the castle and intended to bring me up in the same occupation. He loved plants and flowers above all else and could tirelessly spend his days tending them. He went so far as to maintain that he could almost converse with them; he drew instruction, he said, from the way they grew and prospered, as well as from the various forms and colors of their leaves and petals. But gardening was distasteful to me, and all the more when my father tried to persuade me to take it up, or even force me to it with threats. I wanted to become a fisherman and made a trial of it, but life on the water did not agree with me. I was apprenticed to a merchant in the city and soon left him to return to my father's house. Then suddenly I heard my father tell of the mountains, where he had traveled in his youth, of mines and miners, hunters, and the way they live, and there immediately awakened in me an overpowering urge, a feeling that I had now found the way of life meant for me. Day and night I pictured to myself mighty mountains, ravines, and fir forests; my imagination created towering cliffs. In my mind I heard the tumult of the hunt, the horns, the cry of the dogs and the game; all my dreams were filled with these things and I could not rest for thinking of them. The plain, the castle, my father's limited garden with its orderly flower beds, our narrow dwelling, the wide expanse of sky that spread around us and embraced no height, no sublime mountain, all this depressed me and I grew to hate it more and more. It seemed to me as though all those about me were living in the most deplorable ignorance and that all would think and feel as I did, if only they once became aware of their misery. Thus I continued restlessly until one morning I came to the decision to leave my parental home forever. In a book I had found an account of the nearest large range of mountains, together with illustrations depicting certain regions, and I laid my travel plans accordingly. It was early spring and I felt very cheerful and light of heart. I made haste to leave the plain as soon as possible, and one evening I beheld the dark outlines of the mountains lying before me. At my inn I was hardly able to sleep, I was so impatient to enter the region I looked upon as my homeland. At earliest dawn I was awake and stirring and soon on my way. That afternoon I found myself already among my beloved mountains, and like a drunken man I walked on, then stopped for a bit, looked back, and intoxicated myself anew with the sight of all these things, so strange and yet so familiar. Soon the plain was lost to sight, mountain torrents rushed down to meet me, beeches and oaks streamed downward with agitated leaves from steep slopes; my path led me past dizzy chasms, blue mountains stood vast and venerable in the background. A new world was opened up to me, I knew no weariness. Thus it came about that some days later, after I had wandered through a good part of these mountains, I met an old forester who, at my fervent request, took me in and instructed me in the hunter's art. I have been with him for three months now. I took possession of the region of my sojourn like a kingdom to which I had fallen heir. I got to know every cliff, every ravine of this mountain range, and I was supremely happy in my occupation when early in the morning we would set out for the forest, when we felled trees, when I sharpened my eye at target practice or trained my faithful companions, the dogs, in their skills. Now I've been sitting for a week up at my fowling nets, in the mountain solitude, and this evening I grew sadder than ever in my life; I felt so lost, so terribly unhappy, and I still cannot recover from this dismal mood."

The stranger had listened attentively while they were passing through a dark part of the forest. Now they stepped out into the open and the light of the moon, whose horns stood in the sky above a peak, greeted them like a friend. In unrecognizable shapes and many separate masses, which the pale moonlight again mysteriously united into one, the cleft range lay before them. In the distance rose a steep mountain on whose top age-old weather-beaten ruins awesomely revealed themselves in the white light. "Our paths part here," said the stranger. "I go down into this gorge, there beside that old mine shaft is my dwelling; the ores are my neighbors, the waters trickling in the mine tell me wondrous things in the night. To that place you cannot follow me. But see the Runenberg there with its precipitous walls, how beautiful and tempting the ancient masonry looks! Have you ever been there?"

"Never," said young Christian, "but I once heard the forester tell strange things about that mountain, things that I have foolishly forgotten; but I do remember that on the evening he told them to me I was full of dread. I'd like to climb that height, for there the light is more beautiful than elsewhere, the grass there must be green as an emerald, the world that lies about most strange, and one might also chance to find up there some wonder from times gone by."

"Almost beyond a doubt," the man replied, "if one only knows how to seek, if one's heart is inwardly drawn there, he will find age-old friends and great splendors, everything he most fervently desires."

With these words the stranger descended rapidly into the gorge without bidding his companion farewell. Soon he was lost to sight in the thicket and shortly afterwards the sound of his footfall also faded away. The young hunter was not surprised, he merely re-doubled his pace toward the Runenberg. Everything beckoned him thither: the stars seemed to cast their light that way, the moonlight made a bright road towards the ruins, light clouds rose toward them, and out of the depths the streams and the rustling woods spoke to him, inspiring him with courage. His feet were as though winged, his heart pounded, he felt such deep inward joy that it became anguish.

He came into regions where he had never been before; the cliffs grew steeper, the verdure disappeared, the bare mountainsides called to him as though in angry tones, and a wind drove him before it with a lonely moan. Thus he hastened onward without pause and came late after midnight upon a narrow footpath that ran close beside a chasm. He paid no attention to the depths that yawned beneath him, threatening to swallow him, so ardently was he spurred on by confused imaginings and incomprehensible de-sires. The perilous path now led him beside a lofty wall that seemed to lose itself in the clouds. The ledge grew narrower with every step and the youth had to cling to projecting rocks to keep from plunging downward. At last he could go no farther; the path ended beneath a window. He had to come to a standstill and was at a loss whether to turn back or remain where he was. Suddenly he saw a light that seemed to be moving behind the ancient masonry. He followed the beam and discovered that he could see into a spacious ancient hall which, strangely adorned with various min-erals and crystals, sparkled with manifold rays that shot mysteri-ously through each other when crossed by a wandering light carried by a tall female figure who was walking pensively back and forth within the room. She did not seem to belong to mortal kind, so tall was she, so mighty of limb, so severe her features, and yet it seemed to the enraptured youth that he had never seen such beauty or even dreamt of it. He trembled, but secretly wished that she would step to the window and notice him. Finally she ceased her wandering, set the light down on a crystal table, and gazing upward sang in a penetrating voice:

> Where do the ancients tarry,
> Why do they not appear?
> Crystals all are weeping,
> From the diamond columns
> Flow downward streams of tears;
> Plangent tones resound;
> In the waters bright
> Form of moving light
> Leading souls its way
> Bends hearts to its sway.
> Come, you spirits all,
> To the golden hall,
> Heads that give forth sparks
> Raise from out the dark!
> Make yourselves the masters
> Of the hearts and spirits
> Thirsting in their yearning
> With their gleaming, streaming tears!

When she had ended her song, she began to undress and to lay her garments in a costly wardrobe. First, she took a golden veil from her head, and long black hair flowed in curly abundance down over her loins; then she loosened the garment covering her bosom, and the youth forgot himself and everything around him at the sight of her supernal beauty. He hardly dared breathe as she removed one garment after another; finally she strode naked up and down the room, and her thick, flowing locks formed about her a dark swelling sea out of which the gleaming limbs of her pure body shone at intervals like marble. After a while she approached another golden chest, took from it a tablet blazing with inlaid stones, rubies, diamonds, and all kinds of jewels, and gazed at it critically for a long time. With its various lines and colors the tablet seemed to form some strange, incomprehensible pattern; now and then, when the gleam was reflected toward him, the youth was painfully blinded, then colors that played in green and blue would again soothe his eyes. He stood consuming the sight with his gaze and at the same time was deeply abstracted. Within him an abyss of figures and harmonies, of yearning and voluptuousness had opened up, multitudes of winged tones and nostalgic and joyful melodies passed through his heart and mind and he was moved to the depths of his being. He saw a world of pain and hope unfold within him, wondrous mighty crags of trust and defiant confidence, great rivers, flowing as though brimming with nostalgia. He knew himself no longer, and was startled when the beauteous female figure opened the window, handed him the magical stone tablet and said, "Take this in memory of me!" He grasped the tablet and ran his fingers over the pattern, which at once passed over invisibly into him, and the light and the overpowering beauty and the mysterious hall were gone. A dark night with lowering clouds seemed to descend over his inward being; he searched for his former feelings, for that exaltation and unutterable love, he gazed upon the precious tablet, in which the setting moon was reflected with a weak, bluish light.

He was still holding the tablet pressed tightly in his hands when the gray dawn came, and he rushed down the steep height, exhausted, dizzy, and only half awake.——

The sun was shining in the face of the benumbed sleeper, who found himself lying on a pleasant hill when he awoke. He looked about and saw far behind him, hardly recognizable on the distant horizon, the ruins of the Runenberg. He looked for his tablet but could find it nowhere. Astounded and confused, he tried to collect his thoughts and recall what had happened, but his memory was as though filled with a murky fog in which unrecognizable amorphous shapes stirred in wild confusion.

His whole former life seemed a great distance behind him; the strange and the ordinary were so inextricably mingled that he could not distinguish them. After a long inward struggle he was finally ready to believe that a dream or sudden madness had come over him during the night, but he still could not understand how he could have wandered so far astray into a remote, unknown region.

Still drunk with sleep, he descended the hill and came upon a well-traveled road that led from the mountains into the plain. Everything was strange to him; at first he thought he would reach his native village, but he saw about him a quite different region and at last decided that he must be beyond the southern edge of the mountain range he had entered in spring from the north. Towards noon he was standing above a village from whose cottages peaceful plumes of smoke arose; children in their Sunday best were playing in a grassy square and from the small church resounded the tones of an organ and the singing of the congregation. All this seized him with indescribably sweet nostalgia and touched his heart to weeping. The narrow gardens, the tiny cottages with their smoking chimneys, the neatly divided fields of grain—all reminded him of human needs, of man's dependence upon the kindly soil, in whose generosity he must put his trust. At the same time, the hymn and the sound of the organ filled his heart with a piety he had never before felt. The sensations and desires of the night past now seemed to him wicked and sacrilegious. Recognizing his own needs, he wanted once more to join his fellows in a humble, child-like, and needful way, to call other men his brothers and cast out his godless feelings and ambitions. The plain, with its little river embracing the meadows and gardens in its twistings and turnings, seemed to him charming and inviting; with fear he recalled his sojourn in the lonely mountains among the cliffs and rocks. He longed to be allowed to live in this peaceful village, and with these feelings he entered the crowded church.

The singing was just over and the pastor had begun his sermon on the Lord's bounty in the harvest: how His kindness feeds and appeases the hunger of all living things, how miraculously He provides for the preservation of mankind in the grain, how divine love is ceaselessly imparted in the bread we eat, and how the humble believer can thus celebrate an imperishable communion. The congregation was edified, and while the huntsman's gaze rested on the pious speaker, he noticed close by the pulpit a young girl, who appeared more reverent and attentive than all the rest. She was slender and blond, her blue eyes shone with the most pervasive gentleness, her face was as though transparent and blooming in the tenderest colors. The stranger had never before been so aware of himself and his heart as he was at this moment, so full of love, so given over to the calmest and most comforting feelings. He bowed his head in tears when the pastor finally pronounced the blessing; at the sacred words he felt himself pervaded by an invisible power and the shadowy vision of the night retreated into the deepest distance, like a ghost. He left the church, tarrying under the great linden tree to thank God in a fervent prayer for freeing him by His grace from the toils of the evil spirit.

On this day the village was celebrating its harvest festival and all were in a joyous mood. The children in their finery were looking forward to the cakes and dancing; on the village green, which was surrounded by young trees, young lads were busy arranging everything for their autumnal festivities: the musicians were already seated and tuning their instruments. Christian walked out into the fields once more to collect his thoughts and ponder his situation, then returned to the village, where everyone was already assembled for the merrymaking. Blonde-haired Elizabeth was also present, together with her parents, and the stranger mingled with the joyful crowd. While Elizabeth was dancing, Christian began a conversation with her father, who was a landowner and one of the richest persons in the community. The latter seemed to find pleasure in conversing with the foreign guest and so it was that they had shortly agreed that Christian should move into his house as gardener. The youth ventured to undertake this, for he hoped that now the skills and knowledge he had so despised at home would stand him in good stead.

A new life now began for him. He moved in with the rich landowner and was accounted one of the family. With his occupation, he also changed his style of dress. He was so kind, so helpful, and always so friendly, he worked with such a will, that soon the whole household, but especially the daughter, was fond of him. Whenever he saw her set out for church on Sunday, he always had a fine bouquet ready for her, for which she thanked him with blushing friendliness. He missed her if a day went by without his seeing her. In the evenings she would tell him fairy tales and amusing stories. They grew to be more and more necessary to each other, and the parents, who were well aware of this, seemed to have no objections, for Christian was the most diligent and handsomest lad in the village; they themselves had felt kindly disposed toward him from the very first. After half a year Elizabeth became his wife. Spring had come again, the swallows and songbirds had returned, the garden shone like a jewel. The wedding was celebrated with great joy; bride and groom seemed drunk with happiness. Late in the evening, when they retired to their bedchamber, the young husband said to his beloved, "No, you are not that vision that once enraptured me in a dream and that I can never wholly forget; but still I am happy when I am near you and blessed in your arms."

How delighted was the family when within a year it was increased by the birth of a little daughter, who was baptized Leonora. Christian, it is true, sometimes became rather solemn when he gazed on the child, but his youthful serenity always returned. He hardly thought any more of his former way of life, for he felt himself thoroughly at home and content. After some months, however, his parents came to his mind again and he thought how much his father, in particular, would rejoice at his calm happiness, his position as gardener and husbandman; it perturbed him that he had been capable of completely forgetting his father and mother for so long. His own child reminded him what a joy children are to their parents, and so he finally determined to undertake a journey to visit his old home again.

Unwillingly he took leave of his wife; everyone wished him luck, and in fine fall weather he set out on his way on foot. In a few hours, he already felt how this leavetaking pained him. For the first time in his life, he knew the pangs of separation; strange sights seemed to him almost wild, and he felt as though he were lost in a hostile solitude. Then the thought came to him that his youth was over, that he had found a place where he belonged, where his heart had taken root. He was almost beginning to regret the lost lightheartedness of his earlier years, and was extremely downcast when the time came to turn in for the night at a village inn. He could not understand why he had left his loving wife and her cherished parents, and set out again the next morning depressed and ill-humored.

His anxiety increased as he neared the mountains; the distant ruins were already becoming visible and gradually appeared more and more recognizable, round peaks rose up defined and clear out of the bluish mists. His step became hesitant; he often stopped, surprised at the fear and horror that, with every step, came over him ever more penetratingly.

"Madness, I know you well," he cried out, "you and your perilous temptations, but I will resist you manfully! Elizabeth is no empty dream, I know she is thinking of me now, that she is waiting for me and lovingly counting the hours until my return. Do I not already see the forest like a head of black hair before me? Do not shining eyes gaze up at me out of the stream? Do not great limbs stride toward me out of the mountain?"

With these words he was about to lie down to rest under a tree, when in its shade he saw an old man sitting and examining a flower with utmost attention, holding it now against the light, now shading it with his hand, counting the petals, and taking all pains to impress it exactly in his memory. When he came nearer, the figure seemed familiar to him and soon there was no doubt that the old man with the flower was his father. He threw himself in his arms with a cry of passionate joy; the former was pleased but not surprised to see him again so suddenly.

"Did you come to meet me, my son?" the old man asked. "I knew that I would soon find you, but I did not think I would have that pleasure this very day."

"How did you know, father, that you would find me?"

"By this flower," returned the old gardener. "All my life I have wanted to see it one day, but never had such good fortune, for it is very rare and grows only in the mountains. I set out to seek you, because your mother has died and the loneliness at home was oppressive and dismal. I did not know in what direction I should turn my steps, but finally I took my way through the mountains, sad as such a journey seemed to me. I kept a lookout for this flower, but could discover it nowhere, and now I've found it quite unexpectedly, where the fair plain extends. That is how I knew that I would soon find you, and look how justly this sweet flower has prophesied!"

They embraced each other again and Christian shed tears for his dead mother; the old man grasped his hand and said, "Let us go, so that we may soon lose sight of the shadows of these mountains; their steep, wild shapes, the horrible ravines, the sobbing streams always distress my soul. Let us return to the good, God-fearing flatland."

They began the return journey and Christian became more cheerful again. He told his father of his new-found happiness, of his child and his home; he himself grew as though drunk with the telling, and as he talked he felt how truly contented he was. Conversing thus sadly and cheerfully, they reached the village. All were pleased at the early conclusion of the journey, Elizabeth most of all. Christian's old father moved in with them and contributed his modest wealth to their household; they formed a contented, harmonious circle. The crops prospered, the livestock increased, and in a few years Christian's family was one of the most notable in the community. In addition, he soon found himself the father of several more children.

Five years had passed in this fashion when a stranger in his travels appeared in their village and took lodging at Christian's house because it was the most imposing. He was a friendly, talkative man who liked to tell about his travels, who played with the children and gave them presents, and who soon won everyone's good will. He liked the region so well that he decided to stay for several days; but the days became weeks and, finally, months. No one was surprised at his delay, for everyone had already grown accustomed to regard him as one of the family. Only Christian sometimes sat lost in thought; it seemed to him he had known the traveler somewhere before, and yet he could not recall any occasion when he might have seen him. After three months, the stranger at last took his leave and said, "My dear friends, a wondrous fate and strange expectations drive me into the nearby mountains; an enchanting vision, which I cannot resist, is luring me. I leave you now and I do not know whether I shall return. I have a sum of money with me, which is safer in your hands than mine, and therefore beg you to keep it for me. If I am not back in a year's time, keep it, and consider it my thanks for the kindness you have shown me."

The stranger departed and Christian took the money in keeping. He carefully locked it away and out of exaggerated solicitude looked at it from time to time, counting it to be sure that none was missing, and busied himself with it a great deal.

"This sum could make us very happy," he said once to his father. "If the stranger shouldn't return, we and our children would be taken care of for the rest of our lives."

"Don't worry about the gold," the old man replied; "happiness does not lie in that. Up to now, thank goodness, we have not wanted for anything; dismiss all such ideas from your mind."

Christian often rose at night to awaken the servants for work and to look after everything himself. His father was concerned that he might harm his youthful health through such excess, and it was for that reason he too got up one night to warn him to limit such intemperate activity and found him, to his astonishment, sitting at a table with a small lamp counting the gold pieces with utmost zeal.

"My son," the old man said sadly, "is this what is to become of you? Has this accursed metal been brought under our roof only for our misfortune? Bethink yourself, my boy, for in this way Satan is bound to consume you leg and limb."

"Yes," said Christian, "I don't understand myself any more. I have no rest by day or night. See how it is looking at me again, till the red sheen enters deep into my heart! Hear how it rings, this golden blood! It calls me when I'm asleep, I hear it when music plays, when the wind blows, when people are talking in the street. If the sun shines, I see only its yellow eyes, how it winks at me and tries to whisper words of love in my ear. That is why I have to get up in the night and satisfy its urgent desire; then I feel myself inwardly shouting and exulting. When I touch it with my fingers, it grows redder and more splendid for joy. See for yourself its glow of rapture!"

Shuddering and weeping, the old man took his son in his arms, prayed, and then said, "Christian, my boy, you must turn again to the word of God, you must go to church oftener and pray more devoutly, otherwise you will languish and consume yourself in misery."

The money was locked away again, Christian promised to take thought and change his ways, and his father felt easier. A year and more had already passed and they had not been able to find out anything further about the stranger. The old man finally yielded to the pleas of his son, and the money the stranger had left behind was invested in land and other properties. In the village there was soon talk of the wealth of the young landowner, and Christian seemed extraordinarily contented and happy, so that his father considered himself fortunate to see him so cheerful and well; all anxiety had now vanished from his mind.

He was therefore much astonished when one evening Elizabeth took him aside and tearfully told him how she no longer understood her husband, that he talked wildly, especially at night, that he had bad dreams, often walked up and down in the bedchamber in his sleep, and spoke of uncanny things that often made her shudder. The most frightening part was his gaiety during the day: his laughter was so wild and insolent, his look so lunatic and strange. Her father-in-law was much taken aback, and the sorrowing wife continued.

"He constantly talks about the traveler and claims that he knew him before, for this stranger was really a marvelously beautiful woman. He also does not want to go out to the fields any more or work in the garden, for he says he hears a fearful groaning in the ground whenever he pulls out a root; he starts back and seems horrified in the presence of plants and herbs, as though they were ghosts."

"Merciful God!" cried the father, "has that frightful hunger already taken such a hold of him that it has reached this pass? Then his bewitched heart is no longer human, but cold metal; he who cannot love a flower, has lost all love and the fear of God."

The following day, the father went for a walk with his son and repeated to him a number of the things he had heard from Elizabeth; he exhorted him to piety and religious contemplation.

Christian said, "Gladly, father, and oftentimes I do feel at peace, everything goes well for me; I am able for long periods of time, for years, to forget the true form of my inward being and easily live a life that is, as it were, foreign to me. But suddenly the ruling constellation, that is myself, rises like a new moon in my heart and conquers the foreign power. I could be quite happy, were it not that once, in a strange night, a mysterious sign passed through my hand and imprinted itself in my mind and heart; this magical figure often lies in calm sleep, and I think it has passed away, but then it suddenly revives again, like a poison, and all its lines begin to move. Then I can think and feel nothing but it, and everything about me is transformed, or rather, swallowed up by this constellation. Like the victim of hydrophobia, who is terrified by the sight of water and feels the poison in his body grow more venomous, so it is with me at the sight of any angular figure, any line, any ray or beam; everything then strives to deliver the form that lives within me and aid its birth, and my spirit and body feel fear. Since my mind conceived it from an external sensation, so does it torturously struggle to again make it an external sensation, in order to be rid of it and find peace."

"It was an evil star," said the old man, "that drew you away from us. You were born for a peaceful life, your disposition was inclined to quietude and to the care of plants, but your impatience led you in another direction, into the society of savage stones; the rocks, the wild cliffs with their rugged forms have deranged your mind and planted in you this devastating hunger for metals. You should always have been on your guard before the sight of mountains, and it was thus that I meant to raise you up, but it was not to be. Your humility, your calm, your childlike disposition has been overwhelmed by defiance, savagery and arrogance."

"No," said the son, "I remember quite clearly that it was a plant that first revealed to me the misery of all the earth; only since then do I understand the sighs and moans to be heard everywhere in nature, if one will only listen; in the plants, herbs, flowers, and trees there moves and stirs in pain *one* great wound. They are the living corpses of earlier magnificent worlds of stone, they offer to our sight the most shocking putrefaction. Now I understand that this is what that root wanted to tell me with its deep groans; in its pain it forgot itself and betrayed everything to me. That is why all green growths are so angry with me and seek my life; they want to erase that beloved form in my heart, and every springtime seek to win back my soul with their distorted corpselike look. Shocking and malicious is the way they have deceived you, old man, for they have completely taken possession of your soul. Just ask the stones, you will be astonished when you hear them speak."

The father gave him a long look and was incapable of answer. They returned home in silence, and now the old man was also frightened at his son's gaiety, for it seemed to him very odd and as though another being were playing from within his son, clumsily and unskillfully, as through a machine.

The harvest festival was to be celebrated again, the people were going to church, and Elizabeth had dressed herself and her children to attend divine service; her husband also seemed to be preparing to accompany her, but in front of the church door he turned around and walked out of the village, lost in thought. He sat down on a hill and saw again the smoking chimneys beneath him; the children, dressed for Sunday, were playing on the green.

"How I have frittered away my life in a dream!" he said to

himself. "Years have passed since I descended this hill and mingled with the children; those who were playing there then are today sitting solemnly in church. I also entered that building, but Elizabeth is no longer a childlike creature in the bloom of youth, her youth is fled, I cannot seek her glance with yearning as in those days. Thus I have wantonly neglected a high eternal happiness for sake of one that is temporal and transitory."

Full of longing, he took his way into the nearby woods and entered deep into its thickest shadows. An awesome silence surrounded him, not a breeze stirred in the leaves. Then he saw approaching him from afar a man whom he recognized as the stranger. He was startled, and his first thought was that he would demand the return of his money. When the figure came somewhat closer, he saw how mistaken he had been, for the outlines he had thought he perceived dissolved as though into themselves. An old woman of the utmost hideousness came towards him, dressed in dirty rags. A torn kerchief kept her few straggling grey hairs in place, and she was limping along on a crutch. She addressed Christian in a terrifying voice and asked his name and station.

He gave a detailed answer and then said, "But who are you?"

"They call me the Woman of the Woods," she replied. "Every child knows who I am; didn't you ever know me?" With these words, she turned around, and Christian thought he recognized between the trees the golden veil, the majestic gait, the mighty limbs. He was about to hasten after her, but she had disappeared from his sight.

Meanwhile, some gleaming object drew his glance down into the grass. He picked it up and beheld again the magic tablet with the bright gems, with the strange design, that he had lost so many years before. The figure and the gay gleams pressed in upon his senses with instant power. He grasped the tablet firmly in order to convince himself that he again held it in his hands, then hastened with it back to the village. His father met him.

"Look," he called out to him, "that which I have so often told you about, what I thought I saw only in a dream, is now really and truly mine."

The old man contemplated the tablet for a long time and said, "My son, I shudder in my very heart when I gaze upon the contours of these stones and guess with foreboding what the sense of the words written here may be. Only see how coldly they sparkle, what dreadful glances they cast, bloodthirsty as the red eye of a tiger. Throw this writing away, it makes you cold and cruel, it is bound to petrify your heart:

> See the tender blossoms gleaming,
> How from out themselves they waken,
> And like children roused from dreaming
> Smile at us until we're taken.
>
> In their play they turn their faces
> Ever toward the sun so golden,
> To its kisses' heated traces
> Is their highest bliss beholden.
>
> From its kisses quickly fading,
> Soon they die in love and longing;
> Thus they stand who smiled persuading,
> Stand now wilted, feel no wronging.
>
> And this is their highest pleasure:
> Love's destruction their salvation,
> Death for them transfiguration,
> Vanishing their sweetest treasure.
>
> Then they issue forth their fragrance,
> Send forth spirits filled with rapture,
> Ambient airs are all entranced,
> Yielding to such fragrant capture.
>
> Love may come to human heart,
> Stir the golden lyre to zeal,
> And the soul then says, "I feel
> What's most beautiful, know my seal
> Must be longing, sadness, and love's smart."

"Marvelous, immeasurable treasures," the son replied, "there must be in the depths of the earth. O, to find them, raise them, take them for oneself! O, to press the earth to one's bosom like a beloved bride until she gladly yields her most precious possessions in love and trembling! The Woman of the Woods has summoned me. I go to seek her. Nearby is an old abandoned mine shaft, dug centuries ago by some miner; perhaps I shall find her there!"

He hastened away. In vain the old man strove to detain him; he had soon disappeared from view. After a number of hours and great effort the father succeeded in reaching the abandoned shaft; he saw footprints impressed in the sand at the entrance and turned back weeping, convinced that his son in his madness had entered here and drowned in the ancient waters accumulated in the depths.

Since that hour his heart seemed broken; he was incessantly in tears. The whole village mourned the young landowner, Elizabeth was inconsolable, the children wailed loudly. After half a year the old father died, Elizabeth's parents soon followed him, and she was forced to look after the large undertaking alone. Her numerous duties distracted her somewhat from her sorrow; the education of her children, the management of the estate left her no time for grief and worry. So it was that after two years she decided to enter upon a second marriage; she gave her hand to a cheerful young man who had loved her from youth. But soon everything in the household began to take on a different aspect. The cattle died, the servants proved dishonest, barns full of hay and grain burned down, persons in the city who had borrowed money left without repaying. Soon the young husbandman saw himself forced to sell several fields and meadows; but bad crops and drought only brought him new misfortune. It was just as though the money that had been so strangely acquired were rapidly seeking to make its escape by every possible route. Meanwhile, the children were growing more numerous, and Elizabeth as well as her husband became careless and indifferent in their despair. He sought to distract himself, and drank a great deal of heavy wine, which made him ill-humored and choleric, so that Elizabeth in her misery often wept hot tears. As their fortunes declined, the people in the village began to avoid them, and in a few years they found themselves wholly friendless, barely eking out a meager living from one week to the next.

A cow and a few sheep, which Elizabeth and the children tended themselves, were all they had left. As she was sitting with her knitting one day in the pasture, Leonora at her side, and a nursing infant at her breast, she saw in the distance a bizarre figure approaching. It was a man in a tattered coat, barefoot, his face blackened by the sun and disfigured still more by a long, matted beard; he wore nothing on his head, but had twined a wreath of green foliage through his hair, which rendered his wild look even stranger and more outlandish. On his back he bore in a sack closed with a cord some heavy burden. As he walked, he supported himself on a young spruce.

When he came nearer, he put down his load, breathing heavily. He bade the woman, who was terrified at the sight of him, good day. The girl crept closer to her mother's skirts.

When he had rested a bit, he said, "I come from a very arduous journey out of the most rugged mountains on earth, but I have at last brought with me the most precious treasures the imagination can conceive or the heart wish. Behold and wonder!"

Hereupon he opened his sack and emptied the contents on the ground. Among the pile of pebbles lay large chunks of quartz and other stones. "It is only that these jewels are not yet cut and polished," he continued; "that's why they have no eyes and no fiery look. The outward fire that causes them to gleam is still buried in their inward hearts, but one only has to knock it out of them, then they will be afraid and realize that no dissembling can avail. Then one sees what their true nature is!"

With these words, he picked up one stone and struck it violently against another, so that red sparks sprang forth. "Did you see the flash?" he cried; "they are all that way, full of fire and light, they light up the dark with their laughter, but they still won't do it of their own accord."

He then carefully packed everything again into his sack and tied it securely. "I know you right well," he said in a melancholy tone, "you are Elizabeth."

The woman started. "How do you know my name?" she asked, trembling with foreboding.

"O, dear God!" said the unhappy man. "I am Christian, who once came to you as a huntsman; don't you know me any more?"

In her horror and compassion, she was at a loss what to say. He fell about her neck and kissed her. Elizabeth cried, "O God, my husband will come!"

"Be calm," he said, "I am as good as dead so far as you are concerned; there in the forest my beauteous one is already waiting for me, she of the mighty limbs, adorned with a golden veil. This is my favorite child, Leonora. Come here, my sweet, and give me a kiss too, only one, that I may once more feel your mouth upon my lips, then I will leave you."

Leonora wept; she crept close to her mother, who, with sobs and tears, half pushed her toward the wanderer, while he half drew her to himself. He took her in his arms and pressed her to his breast. Then he quietly departed, and in the forest they saw him speaking with the terrifying Woman of the Woods.

"What is the matter with the two of you?" asked Elizabeth's husband when he found mother and daughter pale and dissolved in tears. Neither would give him an answer.

The unhappy wanderer was never seen again.

Translated by Robert M. Browning

The New Melusina

Johann Wolfgang von Goethe

Honored gentlemen: Since I know you care very little for introductory remarks or preambles, I shall at once assure you that this time I hope to meet with your wholehearted approval. I admit that in the past I have given out many true stories that have proved highly satisfactory to everyone; but today I boldly assert that I have one to relate that far surpasses all previous tales, one which, although it happened to me several years ago, still makes me uneasy whenever I remember it, awakening the hope for some final resolution. It would be hard for you to match it.

Before all, it must be confessed that I have not always so planned my life as to insure my immediate future, or even my next day. In my youth I was not a good manager, and often found myself in various straits. Once I set out upon a journey that should have been highly profitable; but I cut my cloth too big, and after starting out in a private post chaise had to continue in the public stagecoach, till at last I was obliged to face the rest of the way on foot.

Being a quick-witted fellow, I had made a custom of seeking out the landlady, or even the cook, as soon as I came to an inn, and by treating them to a little flattery I usually succeeded in reducing my expenses. One evening as I was entering the post-tavern of a small town, intent on pursuing my usual practice, a handsome, two-seated carriage, drawn by four horses, rattled up to the door behind me. I turned and saw a solitary young woman, unattended by a maid or servants. I made haste to open the carriage door for her and to ask if I could be of service. As she stepped out she disclosed a beautiful figure and, on closer inspection, an amiable countenance marked by faint though not unpleasant traces of sadness. Again I inquired if I could in any way serve her. "Oh, yes," she said, "if you will lift out the little casket that lies on the seat and carry it in for me; but, I entreat you, hold it level and do not shift or shake it in the slightest." I took up the casket cautiously, she closed the carriage door, we ascended the steps together, and she told the servants that she would remain overnight.

Now we were alone in the room; she directed me to place the casket on the table that stood near the wall, and inferring from certain of her movements that she wished to be alone, I took my leave, kissing her hand respectfully but ardently.

At that she said, "Order supper for us both," and I leave you to imagine with what satisfaction I carried out her bidding, so exalted that I scarcely deigned to glance at the landlady or the servants. Impatiently I waited for the moment that would bring me to her once more. Supper was served, we sat facing each other. For the first time in quite a while I regaled myself with a good meal and at the same time with a charming sight: indeed, it seemed to me that she became more beautiful with every minute.

Her conversation was engaging, yet she sought to reject everything pertaining to attraction or love. The table was cleared; I tarried, I tried every dodge to approach her—but in vain. She held me off with a certain dignity I could not withstand; indeed, against my will I was forced to leave her rather early.

After a night spent mostly in wakefulness, or filled with restless dreams, I arose early and asked whether the horses had been ordered. Upon being told "No," I walked into the garden, where I saw her standing dressed at her window. I hastened to go up to her. As she came toward me, as beautiful, no, more beautiful than yesterday, I was suddenly overcome by desire, cunning and audacity; I rushed toward her and clasped her in my arms. "Heavenly, enchanting creature," I cried, "forgive me, but it is impossible to resist you!"

With unbelievable agility she released herself before I had the chance even to press a kiss upon her cheek. "Restrain yourself from such sudden and passionate outbreaks, unless you want to forego a bit of good fortune that lies near you, but which can be obtained only after certain tests."

"Exact of me what you will, angelic spirit," I exclaimed, "but do not drive me to despair."

She smiled as she answered, "If you wish to devote your services to me, hear the conditions. I came here to visit a woman friend and to spend a few days with her; meanwhile I would like my carriage and this little case to be brought further along the road. Would you care to undertake this? You will have nothing to do but to lift the case in and out of the carriage, to sit beside it and to be responsible for it. When you come to an inn you are to place it in a room by itself, in which you will neither sit nor sleep. You will lock the room each time with this key, which opens and closes every lock, and has the power of making it impossible for the lock to be opened by anyone in the meantime."

I looked at her, overcome by a feeling of strangeness; I promised her I would do everything if only I might hope to see her soon again, and if she would seal this hope with a kiss. She did so, and from that moment I became wholly her own. She told me that now I should order the horses. We discussed the road I should take as well as the places where I was to stop and await her. Finally she pressed a purse of gold into my hand, and I a kiss upon hers. At parting she seemed to be moved, and I was past knowing what I was doing or was about to do.

After I had given the order, I came back and found the door of the room locked. I tested my master key and it performed perfectly. The door sprang open; the room was empty save for the casket, which stood on the table where I had placed it.

The carriage had drawn up to the door; I took the casket down solicitously and placed it beside me. The innkeeper asked, "But where is the lady?" and a child answered, "She went into town." I took leave of the servants and drove off, as it were, in triumph, from the place where but last evening I had arrived with dust-covered leggings. You may take it for granted that now, completely at leisure, I reviewed the whole matter, counted the money, made all sorts of plans and occasionally glanced over at the casket. I kept straight on, passing several posthouses, and did not halt until I reached the fair-sized town where she had directed me to meet her. Her commands were scrupulously obeyed; the casket was placed in a room by itself and a couple of unlighted wax candles near it, just as she had ordered. I locked the room, got settled in mine, and made myself fairly comfortable.

For a while I was engrossed in thoughts of her, but very soon time hung heavy on my hands. I was unaccustomed to living without companionship and presently I found some to my taste at the inn tables and in public places. Under these circumstances my money began to melt away, and one evening when I had recklessly yielded to a passionate fit of gambling it vanished completely from my purse. On coming back to my room I was beside myself. Without funds, while to all appearances a rich man, with the prospect of a heavy debt, uncertain as to whether or when my lovely one would show up, I was in the greatest dilemma. Now my longing for her was doubled, and I was convinced I could no longer live without her and her money.

After supper, for which I had little appetite, since now I was forced to eat alone, I paced quickly to and fro in my room, talking aloud to myself, upbraiding myself, throwing myself on the floor, tearing my hair and behaving in a most unruly fashion. Of a sudden I hear a soft movement in the locked room adjoining, and shortly after a knock on the well-guarded door. I pull myself together, and reach for the master key; but the folding doors spring open of themselves, and in the gleam from the now lighted tapers my lovely one approaches. I throw myself at her feet, kissing her dress, her hands; she raises me, but I lack courage to embrace her, almost to look at her, yet frankly though ruefully I confess my fault.

"It is pardonable," she said, "only, alas, you delay your own good fortune as well as mine. Now you must once more cover some ground in the world before we meet again. Here is more gold, and it will suffice if you are disposed to be the least bit prudent. But if wine and gambling have proved your undoing this time, protect yourself henceforth from wine and women, and let me hope for a happier reunion."

She stepped back through the doorway, the folding doors closed. I knocked, I entreated, but nothing more could be heard. Next morning when I asked for my account, the waiter smiled and said, "We know all right why you lock your doors in so artful and baffling a way that no master key is able to open them. Our guess was that you had a lot of money and valuables; but now your treasure has been seen coming down the stairs, and from all accounts it appeared worth being well guarded."

To this I made no answer, but settling my account I entered the carriage with my casket. Once again I drove into the wide world, firmly resolved that in future I would heed the warning of my mysterious friend. Yet, almost as soon as I arrived at a large town I made the acquaintance of some affable young women from whom I was utterly unable to tear myself away. They, it seemed, wished me to pay dearly for their favor, for although they constantly kept me at a distance, they led me from one expense to the other. And as I sought only to advance their pleasure, I never gave a second thought to my purse, but continued to give out and to spend whenever occasion arose. Consequently, I was astonished and overjoyed when, after a few weeks, I noticed that my purse showed no signs of shrinkage but was as bulky and bulging as at first. Since I wanted to make sure of this charming trait, I sat down to count up what I had, made a note of the precise amount, and continued to live with my companions as gaily as before.

There were plenty of excursions by land and water, also dancing and other pleasures, but now no great attention was called for to perceive that the purse was indeed dwindling, as if, through my deuced counting, I had filched from it the virtue of being uncountable. Meanwhile, the life of pleasure being in full swing I could not back out, even though I was soon at the end of my cash. I cursed my state, calling out upon my friend for having led me into temptation, taking it ill of her that she failed to put in an appearance; angrily I declared myself free of all duties toward her and considered opening the casket on the chance that some help might be found in it. For, although it was not quite heavy enough to contain coins, yet it might hold jewels, and these too would be welcome. I was about to carry out my intention but decided to postpone it until the night, in order to undertake the operation in utter quiet, and ran off to a banquet that was just beginning. Things there were going full tilt and we were stirred up by the wine and the blaring of the trumpets when a stroke of ill luck befell me: at dessert, a former friend of my favorite beauty returned unexpectedly from a journey, and, sitting down beside her, attempted with very little formality to claim his old privileges. This gave rise to ill humor, disputes, and brawling. We drew our swords, and I was carried home half dead from several wounds.

The surgeon had bandaged me and left; it was already late in the night and my attendant asleep, when the door of the next room opened and my mysterious friend entered and seated herself beside my bed. She asked how I was; I did not answer, for I was worn and vexed. She went on speaking with much sympathy and rubbed my temples with a certain balsam, so that soon I felt decidedly stronger—so strong that I was able to arouse my anger and to chide her. Speaking impetuously, I threw all the blame for my misfortune upon her, on the passion she had awakened in me, on her appearance and her disappearance, on the tedium and on the longing that had been my portion. I became more and more violent, as though attacked by fever, and finally I swore to her that if she would not be mine, that if this time she refused to belong to me and be united with me, I had no further desire to live. And what is more, I demanded a decisive answer. As she hesitated, searching for an explanation, I grew quite beside myself, and tore the double and triple bandages from my wounds with the fixed intention of bleeding to death. But how astonished I was when I found my wounds entirely healed, my body spruce and shining, and her in my arms!

We were now the happiest couple in the world. We asked each other's pardon without rightly knowing why. She promised now to travel with me, and soon we were sitting side by side in the carriage with the casket opposite in the place of a third person. I had never made any allusion to it, and even now it did not occur to me to speak of it to her, although there it stood, right before our eyes, and both of us, as occasion required, took charge of it as by an unspoken agreement, save that it was I who always lifted it in and out of the carriage and, as before, attended to locking the doors.

As long as something still remained in the purse I continued to do the paying; when my cash gave out I let her know it. "That is easy to provide," she said, and pointed to a pair of small pockets attached at both sides to the top of the carriage, which I had undoubtedly noticed before, but had never used. She reached into one and drew out a few gold pieces, and from the other several silver coins, thus showing me it was possible for us to continue spending as much as we liked. In this way we journeyed from town to town, from country to country, happy either to be by ourselves or with others, and it never occurred to me that she could leave me again, all the less so since for some time she had definitely known she was pregnant, a circumstance that only increased our happiness and our love. But, alas, there came a morning when I found she was not there, and, since a sojourn without her was irksome to me, I took the casket and started to travel, tried out the powers of both pockets and found that they still held good.

The journey prospered, and if until now I had not reflected much on my adventure, since I expected these strange happenings to unravel themselves quite naturally, yet now something occurred that cast me into a state of astonishment, yes, even of fear. In order to get far away from a place it was my habit to travel day and night, and so it happened that often I drove in the dark, and if accidentally the lamps gave out, my carriage was in total blackness. Once on such a murky night I fell asleep, and on awakening saw the glimmer of a light on the ceiling of my carriage. I observed it and found that it came out of the casket which, because of the hot, dry weather of advancing summer, seemed to have sprung a rift. Again I started to speculate about the jewels; I fancied a carbuncle lying in the box and wished to make sure of it. Twisting myself around as well as I was able, I brought my eye in direct contact with the opening. But how great was my astonishment when I looked into a room brightly lit with candles and furnished with much taste, even magnificence, exactly as if I were looking down from an aperture in the ceiling into a drawing room of royalty. It is true that I could see only a part of the room, but from that I could surmise the rest. An open fire seemed to be burning on the hearth and near it stood an armchair. I held my breath and continued looking. Meanwhile a young woman with a book in her hand approached from the other side of the room, and immediately I recognized her as my wife, although her figure had shrunk to the smallest proportions. The beautiful creature seated herself in the chair near the fireplace to read, and as she arranged the logs with the daintiest pair of tongs I could plainly see that this most adorable of little beings was also about to become a mother. Now, however, I found it necessary to move slightly from my uncomfortable position, and immediately after, just as I was on the point of looking in again to convince myself that it had not been a dream, the light went out and I peered into blank darkness.

My amazement and terror can easily be imagined. I formed a

thousand theories about this discovery, and yet I could come to no definite conclusion. In this turmoil I fell asleep, and when I awoke I believed I had only dreamed it all. Yet I felt somewhat estranged from my lovely one, and although I carried the casket with ever greater care, I knew not whether her reappearance in full human dimensions was more to be dreaded or desired.

After a while, toward evening, my lovely one actually came to me, dressed in white, and as the room was just getting dark she seemed taller to me than she usually appeared, and I remembered having heard that all from the race of nixies and gnomes noticeably increase in stature with the coming of night. She rushed into my arms as she always did, but I was unable to clasp her to my uneasy breast with complete joy.

"My dearest," she said, "the way you receive me confirms me in feeling what I, alas, already know. You have seen me in the interval; you have learned of the state in which at certain times I find myself. This causes a break in your happiness and also in mine, which indeed is on the point of being utterly destroyed. I must leave you, and I do not know if I shall ever see you again." Her presence, the charm with which she spoke, at once removed nearly all recollection of the sight that even before had appeared in my mind's eye like a dream. Impulsively I embraced her, convinced her of my passion, assured her of my innocence, and told her the accidental nature of my discovery; in short, I apparently succeeded in allaying her apprehensions and she in turn sought to calm me.

"Test yourself thoroughly," she said, "to see whether this discovery has not marred your love, whether you can forget that I live with you in two forms, and whether the diminution in my person will not diminish your affection as well."

I looked at her; she was more beautiful than ever, and I thought to myself, "Is it then such a great misfortune to possess a wife who from time to time becomes an elf, so that one can carry her around in a box? Would it not be far worse were she to become a giantess and clap her husband into the box?" My serenity returned. Not for anything in the world would I have let her go. "Dear heart," I answered, "let us remain and continue to be as we have been. Could we find anything more delightful? Consult your own comfort, and I promise to carry the casket all the more carefully. How could I retain a bad impression from the prettiest spectacle I have ever seen in my whole life? How happy would all lovers be, could they possess such miniatures! And after all it was merely a picture, a little conjuring trick. You are just sounding me, teasing me; however, you shall see how I shall acquit myself."

"The matter is graver than you think," said the lovely creature; "meanwhile I am quite content that you take it so lightly; for it may still turn out quite happily for us both. I shall trust you, and for my part I shall do whatever is possible; only promise me never to think back on this discovery with reproach. In addition, I earnestly beg you to beware more than ever of wine and of anger."

I promised what she desired; I would have gone on promising anything and everything; but she herself changed the subject, and everything ran smoothly as before. There was no reason for us to move from the place where we were staying; the town was large, the society varied, the season favorable for country jaunts and garden parties.

At all such festivities my wife was greatly in demand, much sought after by both men and women. A kind and ingratiating manner together with a certain nobility made her loved and respected by everyone. Moreover, she played brilliantly on the lute, accompanying her own singing, and there was never a social evening but must be graced with her talent.

I may as well admit I have never derived a great deal from music; on the contrary, its effect upon me was often unpleasant. Therefore my lovely one, who had observed my reactions in this respect, never tried so to entertain me when we were alone; however, she seemed to find compensation for this when in company, where she usually found a host of adorers.

And now—why should I deny it?—our last conversation had not sufficed entirely to dispel the matter, notwithstanding my best intentions; rather had it induced in me an unwonted sensitivity of feeling of which I was not wholly aware. So one evening at a large gathering my repressed ill humor burst forth, which redounded to my great disadvantage.

Looking back upon the matter dispassionately, I acknowledge that I loved my charmer far less after that unhappy discovery, and now I was becoming jealous of her, a feeling that was new to me. This particular evening as we sat at the table, diagonally across though fairly far from one another, I found myself quite content with both my supper partners, a couple of young women whom for some time past I had found most attractive. What with jesting and sentimental sallies, we were not sparing of the wine. Meanwhile, at the other side of the table, a pair of music lovers had managed to persuade my wife, and to encourage and lead on the guests to participate in singing, both solo and in chorus. The two amateurs seemed importunate; the singing made me irritable, and when they demanded that even I should sing a solo stanza, I became really enraged, drained my glass and banged it on the table.

Although the charms of my neighbors soon calmed me again, still it is a bad thing for anger to get out of control. I boiled inwardly, although everything was conducive to pleasure and relaxation. In fact, I grew still more petulant when, a lute having been brought, my lovely one accompanied her song to every one else's admiration. Unfortunately, a general silence was requested. So I was not supposed to talk either, and the music was setting my teeth on edge. Was it any wonder then that the smallest spark set off the mine?

The singer had barely finished a song amid the greatest applause when she looked over to me most lovingly. Unhappily, her glance did not reach my heart. She observed that I gulped down my glass of wine and filled it up again. She warned me affectionately by wagging the forefinger of her right hand. "Remember it is wine!" she said, just loud enough for me to hear. "Water is for nixies!" I exclaimed. "Ladies," she called to my supper partners, "encircle the goblet with every enchantment, so that it is not emptied so often." "Surely you will not let yourself be dictated to!" whispered one of them in my ear. "What's the dwarf after?" I called out, with an impetuous movement that overturned my glass. "A great deal is being wasted here!" cried the exquisite creature, plucking the strings of her lute as if to distract the attention of the company from this disturbance and draw it once more to herself. She actually succeeded in doing so, all the more as she stood up, but only as if to play with more comfort, and continued her prelude.

When I saw the red wine flowing over the tablecloth I came to my senses. I realized the great mistake I had made, and was inwardly repentant. For the first time music spoke to me. Her opening stanza was a friendly leave-taking from the company while they could still feel themselves together; with the next one the gathering seemed on the point of flowing apart. Everyone felt himself alone, cut off; no one believed himself to be any longer present. But then, what should I say of the last stanza? It was addressed to me alone: the voice of offended love, bidding good-bye to ill humor and presumption.

I led her home without a word, expecting nothing pleasant for myself. Yet, scarcely were we in our room when she proved herself most kind and charming, yes, even arch, making me the happiest of men.

The following morning, wholly solaced and full of love, I said, "Many a time you have sung, invited to do so by good company, as for instance last night when you sang that touching song of farewell; now, once, for my sake, sing a pretty and joyful song of welcome in this morning hour, so that it may seem as if we were learning to know each other for the first time."

"That, my friend, I may not do," she answered gravely. "Last night's song made allusion to our parting, which must take place at once; for I can only tell you that the way you have violated your promise and your oath will result in calamity for us both: you lightly spurn a great gift of fortune, and even I must renounce my dearest wishes."

When, at this, I pressed her and pleaded with her to explain herself more clearly, she replied, "Unhappily, that is easy for me to do, since in any case the possibility of my remaining with you is over. Hear, then, what I would have preferred to conceal from you until our last moments together. The form in which you espied me in the little casket is really congenial and natural to me; for I am a lineal descendant of King Eckwald, the mighty prince of elves, of whom authentic history has so much to tell. As of old, our people are still active and industrious, and therefore easy to govern as well. But do not assume that the elves have remained backward in respect to their labors. Were this so their most famous products would still be swords that are able to pursue the enemy after whom they are thrown, chains that bind invisibly, mysteriously impenetrable shields, and things of this sort. Instead their principal occupation now is making articles of convenience and adornment, in which they surpass all other people on earth.

You would be amazed were you to pass through our workshops and warehouses. All of this would be highly satisfactory, had not a strange circumstance arisen that affected the whole nation, but above all the royal family."

When she paused for a moment, I requested her to tell me more of these prodigious secrets, to which she complied.

"It is well known," she said, "that directly after God had created the world, when the soil was still dry and the mountains stood there mighty and majestic, that God, I say, proceeded before all things to create the elves, so that there might exist reasonable beings to gaze in their clefts and burrows with wonder and reverence at His marvels within the earth. Furthermore, it is known that at a later time this little race undertook to exalt itself and to assume dominion over the earth. Wherefore God then created the dragons in order to drive the elves back into the mountains. But since the dragons themselves took care to settle down in the great caves and fissures and to live there, many of them spitting fire and working havoc in many other ways, the elves thus found themselves so hard-pressed and afflicted that they no longer knew what to do. Therefore they turned in humility and supplication to God, the Lord, calling out to Him and praying to Him to exterminate this unclean breed of dragons. Yet, if in His wisdom He did not decide to destroy His own creatures, still the great plight of the poor elves so touched His heart that He at once created the giants who were to fight the dragons and, if not to root them out, at least to reduce their number.

"But scarcely had the giants almost disposed of the dragons than their pride and presumption mounted, in consequence of which they too committed many atrocities, especially against the good little elves. These in their extremity turned again to the Lord. Then He in the might of His power created the knights who were to fight the giants and the dragons and live harmoniously with the elves. With this the work of creation was ended upon earth, and it came to pass thereafter that giants and dragons as well as knights and elves were able to coexist and bear one with another. From which you may infer, my friend, that ours is the oldest race in the world—an honor, no doubt, but one that brings us great disadvantages too.

"For since, as you know, nothing persists forever on this earth but, on the contrary, everything that has once been great must become small and less than it was, so it was in our case; since the beginning of the world we have continued to grow smaller and to fall away, and the royal family, because of the purity of its blood, was first and foremost to be subjected to this fate. Therefore, many years back, our wise men conceived of a plan to extricate us from our difficulty: from time to time a princess of the royal house was to be sent out into the world to take in marriage some honorable knight so that the race of elves might be rejuvenated and saved from complete decline."

As my lovely one spoke these words with complete candor, I looked at her uncertainly, because it seemed to me that she wished to play a little on my credulity. Concerning her dainty ancestry I had no further doubt; but it caused me some misgivings that she had seized on me instead of a knight, for I knew myself too well to be able to believe that my forebears had been directly created by God.

Concealing my amazement and doubt, I asked her kindly, "But tell me, my dear child, how do you come to have this tall and imposing form? For I know few women to compare with you in fineness of figure!"

"That you shall learn," said my beauty. "From olden times we have been advised through the council of the elf-king to beware of taking this extraordinary step as long as possible, which to me seems natural and right. In all probability there would still have been much reluctance to sending a princess out into the world again, had not my younger brother been born so tiny that the nurses actually let him slip through his swaddling clothes and he was lost, and nobody knows what became of him. In this emergency, hitherto quite unheard of in the annals of the elf-kingdom, our wise men were called together, and to make a long story short, they took a resolution to send me out to look for a husband."

"A resolution!" I cried. "That is all well and good. One may decide something for oneself, one may decree something for another, but to give a tiny dwarf the stature of a goddess! How did your wise men accomplish that?"

"It was already provided for by our ancestors," she said. "In the royal treasury lay an enormous gold ring. I speak of it now as it appeared in the past when it was shown me as a child, in its natural surroundings; for it is the very same one that I have here on my finger. At this point they went to work in the following manner: I was informed of everything that awaited me and was instructed what to do and what not to do.

"A magnificent palace, patterned after my parents' favorite summer residence, was constructed—a main building with side wings and everything one could wish for. It stood at the entrance to a large rocky ravine, adding greatly to its beauty. On the appointed day the court assembled there together with my parents and myself. The army was on parade, and twenty-four priests with no little difficulty bore the wonderful ring upon a precious barrow. It was placed upon the threshold of the building, just inside where one would step over it. Many ceremonies were performed and, after an affectionate leavetaking, I set to work. I stepped forward, laid my hand upon the ring, and at once began noticeably to increase in size. In a few moments I had attained my present height, whereupon I put the ring upon my finger. Now, in a trice, windows, doors, and gates closed up, the wings at either side drew back into the main building, and near me, instead of a palace, stood a small casket, which I at once picked up and took along with me, not without an agreeable sensation in being so large and strong. While yet a pygmy, to be sure, in comparison with trees and mountains, with streams and stretches of land, I was, however, a giant in comparison with grass and herbs, but especially with the ants who, since we elves were not always on good terms with them, took frequent occasion to plague us.

"How I fared on my pilgrimage before I met you, of this I might have much to tell. It will suffice to say that I put many to the test, but no one except yourself seemed to me worthy of renewing and perpetuating the line of the sovereign Eckwald."

This recital gave some occasion for headshaking, although I forebore to shake mine. I put various questions, to which, however, I received no direct answers, but instead I learned to my great distress that after what had happened it was necessary for her to return to her parents. Certainly, she hoped to come back to me, but for the moment it was unavoidable that she present herself, otherwise all would be lost for her as well as for me. Soon the purses would cease paying, and all sorts of other consequences might follow.

Upon hearing that our money might give out, I made no further inquiries as to what else might happen. I shrugged my shoulders and said nothing, as she seemed to understand me.

Together we packed up and seated ourselves in the carriage, and opposite to us was the casket in which I could still not discern anything resembling a palace. And so we went on, passing many places. Money for lodging and gratuities was easily and generously paid from the pockets to right and left, till at last we arrived at a mountainous region, where scarcely had we alighted than my lovely one went on ahead and I, at her behest, followed with the casket. She guided me up a rather steep footpath to a narrow strip of meadow through which a clear stream, now leaping, now loitering, wound its way. There she called my attention to a flat elevation, directed me to set down the case, and said, "Fare you well; you will easily find the way back; think of me, I hope to see you again."

At this moment it seemed to me impossible to leave her. She was just having one of her good days again, or, if you like, her good hours. To be alone with so lovable a creature on the greensward, amid grass and flowers, hemmed in by rocks, soothed by the sounds of water: what heart could have remained unmoved? I wished to take her hand, to clasp her in my arms, but she pushed me back, although most affectionately, threatening me with great peril if I did not leave at once.

"Is there not the remotest chance of my remaining," I cried; "of your keeping me with you?" I accompanied these words with such gestures and sounds of lamentation that she seemed touched, and after some reflection admitted that it was not entirely impossible for our union to continue. Who was happier than I? My importunity, which became more and more pressing, obliged her to speak out and tell me that, if I could decide to join her in being as small as I had already seen her, it was still not too late for me to remain with her, and pass over into her dwelling, her kingdom, and her family. This prospect was not altogether pleasing to me; yet at this moment I could not quite tear myself away from her, and since for a considerable time I had been accustomed to the marvelous, and committed to hasty decisions, I assented, telling her she could do with me what she wished.

Thereupon I had to stretch out the little finger of my right hand;

she placed her own against it, and drawing off the gold ring very gently with her left hand let it slip onto my finger. Scarcely had she done so when I felt a sharp pain in the finger; the ring contracted, torturing me horribly. I let out a scream and groped around involuntarily for my lovely one, but she had vanished. My feelings in the meantime were inexpressible, and nothing more remains to be said than that very soon I found myself in a small, compact body near my charmer in a forest of grass blades. The joy of reunion after so short and yet so strange a parting or, if you prefer, a reunion without parting, passes all comprehension. I fell upon her neck, she returned my embraces, and the little couple felt as happy as the big one.

With some discomfort we set out to climb a hill; for the grassy meadow had become for us an almost impenetrable forest. But finally we reached a clearing, and how astonished I was to see there a large, symmetrical mass, which I was soon forced to recognize as the casket, in the same condition in which I had set it down.

"Go, my friend, and merely knock on it with the ring," said my sweetheart. "You will behold wonders." I walked up to it, and scarcely had I knocked before I witnessed the greatest marvel. Two side wings jutted out, and at the same time, like a shower of scales and shingles, various portions fell into place, revealing a complete palace, equipped with doors, windows, and arcades.

A person who has seen one of Röntgen's ingenious writing tables, so made that a slight tug brings into play a number of ratchets and springs, whereby desk, writing materials, drawers for letters and money come to view either simultaneously or one right after the other, will be able to picture to himself the unfolding of this palace into which my sweet companion now drew me. In the main hall I at once recognized the hearth that I had formerly glimpsed from above, and the chair on which she had sat. And when I looked overhead I thought I could still detect something of the rift in the dome through which I had looked in. I spare you a description of the rest; it is enough to say that all was spacious, costly, and in good taste. Scarcely had I recovered from my amazement when I heard from afar the strains of martial music. My lovely half sprang up for joy and rapturously announced to me the approach of her royal father. We went and stood in the doorway and watched while a brilliant procession filed out of a high, rocky cleft. Soldiers, servants, household officials, and a shining array of courtiers followed one behind the other. At last we saw a gleaming galaxy and in its midst the king himself. When the whole procession had drawn up before the palace, the king advanced with his personal retainers. His affectionate daughter ran to meet him, dragging me along; we threw ourselves at his feet. He raised me most graciously, and it was only when I came to stand before him that I noticed that in this miniature world I was the most imposing in stature. Together we went toward the palace, where the king in the presence of his whole court addressed us in a well-prepared speech; expressing his astonishment at finding us here, he bade us welcome, acknowledged me as his son-in-law, and set the following day for the marriage rites.

How terribly depressed I felt at the mention of marriage! For hitherto I had dreaded this almost more than music itself, which otherwise seemed to me the most hateful thing on earth. "Those people who make music," I was wont to say, "at least remain under the illusion of being at one with each other, and of working in unison: for when they have been tuning up long enough, rending our ears with all manner of discords, they are firm and fast in the conviction that their difficulties have been solved, and that one instrument is exactly in tune with the other. Even the director shares this happy delusion, and delightedly they start off, while the rest of us feel our ears buzzing from the constant din. In the wedded state, on the other hand, even this is not the case: for although it is only a duet, which would lead one to assume that two voices, or rather two instruments, are bound to be brought into some degree of harmony, yet this seldom comes to pass. For if the man leads off with one tone, his wife at once takes a higher one; in this way they pass from chamber to choral pitch, on and on, getting higher and higher, until even the wind instruments cannot follow. Therefore, since even harmonic music remains so offensive to me, it is still less surprising that I can't suffer the inharmonic."

Of the many festivities to which the day was given there is not much of which I would or can speak; for I paid them scant attention. The sumptuous food, the delicious wines, nothing of this was to my taste. I speculated and pondered on what I should do. Yet

I could think of little. I resolved that when night came I would make short work of getting up and going off to hide somewhere. I succeeded in reaching a crevice in the rock, into which I squirmed, concealing myself as well as I was able. My next care was to get the unlucky ring off my finger, in which I was not at all successful. On the contrary, it was as if whenever I thought to take it off the ring became tighter, giving me acute twinges of pain, which subsided as soon as I desisted from my purpose.

I awoke in the early morning—for my little body had slept very well—and was on the point of looking around a bit further when it seemed as if it had begun to rain. For something like sand or grit fell in large quantities through the grass, leaves and flowers; but how terrified I was when everything about me came alive, and an endless swarm of ants rushed down upon me. No sooner had they become aware of me than they attacked me from all sides, and though I defended myself well and courageously, yet finally they so overwhelmed, pinched, and pricked me that I was glad when I heard myself called on to surrender. In truth, I did surrender at once, at which an ant of unusual size approached me with politeness, not to say reverence, and even commended himself to my favor. I found that the ants had become allies of my father-in-law, and that he had called upon them for aid in the present crisis, and pledged them to bring me back. Small though I was, I was now in the hands of those still smaller. I had to face the wedding and even to thank God if my father-in-law were not in a rage and my lovely one aggrieved with me.

Permit me to pass over the ceremonies in silence; it is enough to say that we were married; yet though we were gay and lively as the days passed, there were, despite this, some lonely hours in which, being led to reflection, I encountered something I had never encountered before. What it was and how it came about you shall hear.

Everything around me conformed fully to my present shape and needs; the bottle and glasses were well-proportioned to a small drinker, indeed, much better on the whole than those in our world. To my small gums delicate morsels had an unparalleled flavor; a kiss from my wife's dainty mouth was too enchanting for words, and I do not deny that novelty made all these associations highly pleasurable. However, I had unhappily not forgotten my previous state of existence. I felt within myself a measure of my former size, which made me unhappy and restless. Now, for the first time, I grasped what philosophers mean by their ideals, with which man is said to be so afflicted. I had an ideal of myself, and often in dreams I appeared to myself as a giant. In short, the wife, the ring, the dwarfed figure, and many other bonds made me so thoroughly and completely wretched that I began to give earnest thought to my deliverance.

As I was convinced that the whole magic lay in the ring, I determined to file it off. For this purpose I took several files from the court jeweler. Fortunately, I am left-handed and have never in my life done anything right-handedly. I held myself resolutely to my task, which was not slight: for the golden circlet, although it appeared so thin, had grown thicker in contracting from its former size. I gave all my leisure hours, unobserved, to this business, and when the metal was nearly filed through I was clever enough to step outside the door. This was well-advised; for all at once the golden circle sprang forcibly from my finger and my body shot up into the air with such vehemence that I really thought I had struck the sky, and in any case I should have broken through the dome of our summer palace, indeed should have wrecked the entire pavilion with my sudden clumsiness.

There I stood again, certainly much bigger, but also, it seemed to me, far more bewildered and ungainly. When I had recovered from my dizziness, I saw lying near me the casket, which felt rather heavy as I lifted it and trudged with it down the footpath toward the post-tavern, where I immediately called for the horses and set forth. On the way, I was not long in trying the pockets on either side. In place of the money, which seemed to have given out, I found a small key that fit the casket, in which I found a fair compensation. As long as this lasted I used the carriage; afterwards I sold it in order to be able to go on by the stagecoach. The casket was the last to be disposed of, for I kept thinking it ought to fill itself once more. And so I came at last, though by a somewhat devious way, back to the hearth and the cook, where first you came to know me.

Translated by Jean Starr Untermeyer
and revised by the editors

The History of Krakatuk *

E. T. A. Hoffmann

Perlipat's mother was the wife of a king—that is, a queen; and, in consequence, Perlipat, the moment she was born, was a princess by birth. The king was beside himself for joy as he saw his beautiful little daughter lying in her cradle; he danced about, and hopped on one leg, and sang out, "Was anything ever so beautiful as my Perlipatkin?" And all the ministers, presidents, generals, and staff officers hopped likewise on one leg, and cried out, "No, never!" Indeed, the real fact is, that it is quite impossible, as long as the world lasts, that a princess should be born more beautiful than Perlipat. Her little face looked like a web of the most beautiful lilies and roses, her eyes were the brightest blue, and her hair was like curling threads of shining gold. Besides all this, Perlipat came into the world with two rows of pearly teeth, with which, two hours after her birth, she bit the lord chancellor's thumb so hard that he cried out, "Oh gemini!" Some say he cried out, "O dear!" but on this subject people's opinions are very much divided, even to the present day. In short, Perlipat bit the lord chancellor on the thumb, and all the kingdom immediately declared that she was the wittiest, sharpest, cleverest little girl, as well as the most beautiful. Now, everybody was delighted except the queen—she was anxious and dispirited, and nobody knew the reason. Everybody was puzzled to know why she caused Perlipat's cradle to be so strictly guarded. Besides having guards at the door, two nurses always sat close to the cradle, and six other nurses sat

* Thackeray's title for Hoffmann's "Märchen von der harten Nuß," part of *Nußknacker und Mausekönig*.

every night round the room; and, what was most extraordinary, each of these six nurses was obliged to sit with a great tomcat in her lap, and keep stroking him all night, to amuse him, and keep him awake and purring.

Now, my dear little children, it is quite impossible that *you* should know why Perlipat's mother took all these precautions; but *I* know, and will tell you all about it. It happened that, once upon a time, a great many excellent kings and agreeable princes were assembled at the court of Perlipat's father, and their arrival was celebrated by all sorts of tournaments, and plays, and balls. The king, in order to show how rich he was, determined to treat them with a feast that should astonish them. So he privately sent for the upper court cook master, and ordered him to order the upper court astronomer to fix the time for a general pig killing, and a universal sausage making; then he jumped into his carriage, and called, himself, on all the kings and queens; but he only asked them to eat a bit of mutton with him, in order to enjoy their surprise at the delightful entertainment he had prepared for them. Then he went to the queen, and said, "You already know, my love, the partiality I entertain for sausages." Now the queen knew perfectly well what he was going to say, which was that she herself (as indeed she had often done before) should undertake to superintend the sausage making. So the first lord of the treasury was obliged to hand out the golden sausage pot and the silver saucepans; and a large fire was made of sandalwood. The queen put on her damask kitchen pinafore; and soon after the sausage soup was steaming and boiling in the kettle. The delicious smell penetrated as far as the privy council chamber. The king was seized with such extreme delight, that he could not stand it any longer. "With your leave," said he, "my lords and gentlemen"—jumped over the table, ran down into the kitchen, gave the queen a kiss, stirred about the sausage brew with his golden scepter, and then returned back to the privy council chamber in an easy and contented state of mind. The queen had now come to the point in the sausage making, when the bacon was cut into little bits and roasted on little silver spits. The ladies of honor retired from the kitchen, for the queen, with proper confidence in herself, and consideration for her royal husband, performed *alone* this important operation. But just when the bacon began to roast, a little whispering voice was heard. "Sister, I

am a queen as well as you, give me some roasted bacon, too";
then the queen knew it was Mrs. Mouserinks who was talking.
Mrs. Mouserinks had lived a long time in the palace; she declared
she was a relation of the king's, and a queen into the bargain, and
she had a great number of attendants and courtiers underground.
The queen was a mild, good-natured woman; and although she
neither acknowledged Mrs. Mouserinks for a queen nor for a relation, yet she could not, on such a holiday as this, begrudge her
a little bit of bacon. So she said, "Come out, Mrs. Mouserinks,
and eat as much as you please of my bacon." Out hopped Mrs.
Mouserinks, as merry as you please, jumped on the table, stretched
out her pretty little paw, and ate one piece of bacon after the
other, as the queen handed them to her. But then out came all
Mrs. Mouserinks's friends and relations, and even her seven sons,
ugly little fellows, and nibbled all over the bacon; while the poor
queen was so frightened that she could not drive them away.
Luckily, however, when there still remained a little bacon, the first
lady of the bedchamber happened to come in; she drove all the
mice away, and sent for the court mathematician, who divided the
little that was left as equally as possible among all the sausages.
Now sounded the drums and the trumpets; the princes and poten-
tates who were invited rode forth in glittering garments, some under white canopies, others in magnificent coaches, to the sausage
feast. The king received them with hearty friendship and elegant
politeness; then, as master of the land, with scepter and crown,
sat down at the head of the table. The first course was polonies.
Even then it was remarked that the king grew paler and paler; his
eyes were raised to heaven, his breast heaved with sighs; in fact,
he seemed to be agitated by some deep and inward sorrow. But
when the blood-puddings came on, he fell back in his chair,
groaning and moaning, sighing and crying. Everybody rose from
table; the physicians in ordinary in vain endeavored to feel the
king's pulse. A deep and unknown grief had taken possession of
him.

At last—at last, after several attempts had been made, several
violent remedies applied, such as burning feathers under his nose
and the like, the king came to himself, and almost inaudibly gasped
out the words, "Too little bacon!" Then the queen threw herself
in despair at his feet. "Oh, my poor unlucky royal husband," said

she, "what sorrows have you had to endure! but see here the guilty one at your feet; strike—strike—and spare not. Mrs. Mouserinks and her seven sons, and all her relations, ate up the bacon, and—and—" Here the queen tumbled backwards in a fainting fit! But the king arose in a violent passion, and said, "My lady of the bedchamber, explain this matter." The lady of the bedchamber explained as far as she knew, and the king swore vengeance on Mrs. Mouserinks and her family for having eaten up the bacon which was destined for the sausages.

The lord chancellor was called upon to institute a suit against Mrs. Mouserinks and to confiscate the whole of her property; but as the king thought that this would not prevent her from eating his bacon, the whole affair was entrusted to the court machine- and watchmaker. This man promised, by a peculiar and extraordinary operation, to expel Mrs. Mouserinks and her family from the palace forever. He invented curious machines, in which pieces of roasted bacon were hung on little threads, and which he set round about the dwelling of Mrs. Mouserinks. But Mrs. Mouserinks was far too cunning not to see the artifices of the court watch and machine maker; still all her warnings, all her cautions, were in vain. Her seven sons, and a great number of her relations, deluded by the sweet smell of the bacon, entered the watchmaker's machines, where, as soon as they bit at the bacon, a trap fell on them, and then they were quickly sent to judgment and execution in the kitchen. Mrs. Mouserinks, with the small remnants of her court, left the place of sorrow, doubt, and astonishment. The court rejoiced; but the queen alone was sorrowful, for she knew well Mrs. Mouserinks's disposition, and that she would never allow the murder of her sons and relations to go unrevenged. It happened as she expected. One day, whilst she was cooking some tripe for the king, a dish to which he was particularly partial, appeared Mrs. Mouserinks and said, "You have murdered my sons, you have killed my cousins and relations, take good care that the mouse-queen does not bite your little princess in two. Take care." After saying this, she disappeared; but the queen was so frightened, that she dropped the tripe into the fire, and thus for the second time Mrs. Mouserinks spoiled the dish the king liked best; and of course he was very angry. And now you know why the queen took such extraordinary care of Princess Perlipatkin: was not she right to fear that Mrs. Mouserinks would fulfill her threat, come back, and bite the princess to death?

The machines of the machinemaker were not of the slightest use against the clever and cunning Mrs. Mouserinks; but the court astronomer, who was also upper astrologer and stargazer, discovered that only the Tomcat family could keep Mrs. Mouserinks from the princess's cradle; for this reason each of the nurses carried one of the sons of this family on her lap, and, by continually stroking him down the back, managed to render the otherwise unpleasant court service less intolerable.

It was midnight when one of the two chief nurses, who sat close by the cradle, awoke as it were from a deep sleep. Everything around lay in profound repose; no purring, but the stillness of death; but how astonished was the chief nurse when she saw close before her a great ugly mouse, who stood upon his hind legs, and already had laid his hideous head on the face of the princess. With a shriek of anguish, she sprung up. Everybody awoke; but Mrs. Mouserinks (for she it was who had been in Perlipat's cradle), jumped down, and ran into the corner of the room. The tomcats went after, but too late; she had escaped through a hole in the floor. Perlipat awoke with the noise, and wept. "Thank heaven," said the nurses, "she lives!" But what was their horror, when, on looking at the once beautiful child, they saw the change that had taken place! Instead of the lovely white and red cheeks she had had before, and the shining golden hair, there was now a great deformed head on a little withered body; the blue eyes had changed into a pair of great green gogglers, and the mouth had stretched from ear to ear. The queen was almost mad with grief and vexation, and the walls of the king's study were obliged to be wadded, because he was always dashing his head against them for sorrow, and crying out, "O luckless monarch!" He might have seen how it would have been better to have eaten the sausage without bacon, and to have allowed Mrs. Mouserinks quietly to stay underground. Upon this subject, however, Perlipat's royal father did not think at all, but he laid all the blame on the court watchmaker, Christian Elias Drosselmeier, of Nuremberg. He therefore issued this wise order, that Drosselmeier should before four weeks restore the princess to her former state, or at least find out a certain and infallible means for so doing; or, in failure thereof, should suffer a shameful death under the ax of the executioner.

Drosselmeier was terribly frightened; but, trusting to his learning and good fortune, he immediately performed the first operation that seemed necessary to him. He carefully took Princess Perlipat to pieces, took off her hands and feet, and thus was able to see the inward structure; but there, alas! he found that the princess would grow uglier as she grew older, and he had no remedy for it. He put the princess neatly together again, and sunk down in despair at her cradle, which he never was permitted to leave.

The fourth week had begun—yes, it was Wednesday! when the king, eyes flashing with indignation, entered the room of the princess; and waving his scepter, he cried out, "Christian Elias Drosselmeier, cure the princess, or die!" Drosselmeier began to cry bitterly, but little Princess Perlipat went on cracking her nuts. Then first was the court watchmaker struck with the princess's extraordinary partiality for nuts, and the circumstance of her having come into the world with teeth. In fact, she had cried incessantly since her metamorphosis, until some one by chance gave her a nut; she immediately cracked it, ate the kernel, and was quiet.

From that time the nurses found nothing so effective as bringing her nuts. "O holy instinct of natural, eternal, and unchangeable sympathy of all beings; thou showest me the door to the secret. I will knock, and thou wilt open it." He then asked permission to speak to the court astronomer, and was led out to him under strong guard. These two gentlemen embraced with many tears, for they were great friends; they then entered into a secret cabinet, where they looked over a great number of books that treated of instincts, sympathies, and antipathies, and other deep subjects. The night came; the court astronomer looked to the stars, and made the horoscope of the princess, with the assistance of Drosselmeier, who was also very clever in this science. It was a troublesome business, for the lines were always wandering this way and that; at last, however, what was their joy to find that Princess Perlipat, in order to be freed from the enchantment that made her so ugly, and to become beautiful again, had only to eat the sweet kernel of the nut Krakatuk.

Now the nut Krakatuk had such a hard shell that an eight-and-forty-pound cannon could drive over without breaking it. But this nut was only to be cracked by a man who had never shaved, and never worn boots; he was to break it in the princess's presence, and then to present the kernel to her with his eyes shut; nor was he to open his eyes until he had walked seven steps backwards without stumbling. Drosselmeier and the astronomer worked without stopping three days and three nights; and, as the king was at dinner on Saturday, Drosselmeier (who was to have had his head off early Sunday morning), rushed into the room, and declared he had found the means of restoring Princess Perlipat to her former beauty. The king embraced him with fervent affection, promised him a diamond sword, four orders, and two new coats for Sundays. "We will go to work immediately after dinner," said the king in the most friendly manner, "and thou, dear watchmaker, must see that the young unshaven gentleman in shoes be ready with the nut Krakatuk. Take care, too, that he drink no wine before, that he may not stumble as he walks his seven steps backwards like a crab; afterwards he may get as tipsy as he pleases." Drosselmeier was very much frightened at this speech of the king's; and it was not without fear and trembling that he stammered out that it was true that the means were known, but that both the nut Krakatuk, and the young man to crack it, were yet to be sought for; so that it was not impossible that nut and cracker would never be found at all. In tremendous fury the king swung his scepter over his crowned head, and cried, with a lion's voice, "Then you must be beheaded, as I said before."

It was a lucky thing for the anxious and unfortunate Drosselmeier that the king had found his dinner very good that day, and so was in a disposition to listen to any reasonable suggestions, which the magnanimous queen, who deplored Drosselmeier's fate, did not fail to bring forward. Drosselmeier took courage to plead that, as he had found out the remedy and the means whereby the princess might be cured, he was entitled to his life. The king said this was all stupid nonsense; but, after he had drunk a glass of cherry brandy, concluded that both the watchmaker and the astronomer should immediately set off on their journey, and never return, except with the nut Krakatuk in their pocket. The man who was to crack the same was, at the queen's suggestion, to be advertised for in all the newspapers, in the country and out of it.

Drosselmeier and the court astronomer had been fifteen years on their journey without finding any traces of the nut Krakatuk. The countries in which they were, and the wonderful sights they saw, would take me at least a month to tell of. This, however, I shall not do: all I shall say is, that at last the miserable Drosselmeier felt an irresistible longing to see his native town, Nuremberg. This longing came upon him most particularly as he and his friend were sitting together smoking a pipe in the middle of a wood in Asia. "O Nuremberg, delightful city! Who's not seen thee, him I pity! All that beautiful is in London, Petersburg, or Paris, are nothing when compared to thee! Nuremberg, my own city!" As Drosselmeier deplored his fate in this melancholy manner, the astronomer, struck with pity for his friend, began to howl so loudly that it was heard all over Asia. But at last he stopped crying, wiped his eyes, and said, "Why do we sit here and howl, my worthy colleague? Why don't we set off at once for Nuremberg? Is it not perfectly the same where and how we seek this horrid nut Krakatuk?" "You are right," said Drosselmeier; so they both got up, emptied their pipes, and walked from the wood in the middle of Asia to Nuremberg at a stretch.

As soon as they had arrived in Nuremberg, Drosselmeier hastened to the house of a cousin of his, called Christopher Zachariah Drosselmeier, who was a carver and gilder, and whom he had not seen for a long, long time. To him the watchmaker related the whole history of Princess Perlipat, Mrs. Mouserinks, and the nut Krakatuk, so that Christopher Zachariah clapped his hands for wonder, and said, "O, cousin, cousin, what extraordinary stories are these!" Drosselmeier then told his cousin of the adventures that befell him on his travels: how he had visited the grand duke of Almonds, and the king of Walnuts; how he had inquired of the Horticultural Society of Acornshausen—in short, how he had sought everywhere, but in vain, to find some traces of the nut Krakatuk. During this recital Christopher Zachariah had been snapping his fingers, and opening his eyes, calling out hum! and ha! and oh! and ah! At last, he threw his cap and wig up to the ceiling, embraced his cousin, and said, "Cousin, I'm very much mistaken, *very* much mistaken, I say, if I don't myself possess this nut Krakatuk!" He then fetched a little box, out of which he took a gilded nut, of a middling size. "Now," said he, as he showed his cousin the nut, "the history of this nut is this: Several years ago, a man came here on Christmas Eve with a sackful of nuts, which he offered to sell cheap. He put the sack just before my booth, to guard it against the nut sellers of the town, who could not bear that a foreigner should sell nuts in their native city. At that moment a heavy wagon passed over his sack, and cracked every nut in it except one, which the man, laughing in an extraordinary way, offered to sell me for a silver half-crown of the year 1720. This seemed odd to me. I found just such a half-crown in my pocket, bought the nut, and gilded it, not knowing myself why I bought it so dear and valued it so much." Every doubt with respect to its being the nut they sought was removed by the astronomer, who, after removing the gilding, found written on the shell, in Chinese characters, the word Krakatuk.

The joy of the travelers was excessive, and Drosselmeier's cousin, the gilder, the happiest man under the sun, on being promised a handsome pension and the gilding of all the gold in the treasury into the bargain. The two gentlemen, the watchmaker and the astronomer, had put on their nightcaps and were going to bed, when the latter (that is, the astronomer) said, "My worthy friend and colleague, you know one piece of luck follows another, and I believe that we have not only found the nut Krakatuk, but also the young man who shall crack it, and present the kernel of beauty to the princess; this person I conceive to be the son of your cousin! Yes," continued he, "I am determined not to sleep until I have cast the youth's horoscope." With these words he took his nightcap from his head, and instantly commenced his observations. In fact, the gilder's son was a handsome well-grown lad, who had never shaved, and never worn boots.

At Christmas he used to wear an elegant red coat embroidered with gold, a sword, and a hat under his arm, besides having his hair beautifully powdered and curled. In this way he used to stand before his father's booth, and with a natural gallantry, crack the nuts for the young ladies, who, from this peculiar quality of his, had already called him "Nutcrackerkin."

Next morning the astronomer fell delighted on the neck of the watchmaker, and cried, "We have him, he is found! But there are two things, of which, my dear friend and colleague, we must take particular care: first, we must strengthen the underjaw of your excellent nephew by braiding a tough piece of wood into his pig-tail and connecting this to his jawbone to give it leverage, and then, on returning home, we must carefully conceal having brought with us the young man who is to bite the nut; for I read by the horoscope that the king, after several people have broken their teeth in vainly attempting to crack the nut, will promise to him who shall crack it, and restore the princess to her former beauty— will promise, I say, to this man the princess for a wife, and his kingdom after his death." Of course the gilder was delighted with the idea of his son marrying Princess Perlipat and becoming a prince and king; and delivered him over to the two deputies. The wooden jaw lever that Drosselmeier had fixed in his young and hopeful nephew answered to admiration, so that in cracking the hardest peach stones he came off with distinguished success.

As soon as Drosselmeier and his comrade had made known the discovery of the nut, the requisite advertisements were immedi-ately issued; but as the travelers had returned with the means of restoring the princess's beauty, many hundred young men, among whom several princes might be found, trusting to the soundness of their teeth, attempted to remove the enchantment of the prin-cess in vain. The ambassadors were not a little frightened when they saw the princess again. The little body with the wee hands and feet could scarcely support the immense, deformed head! The hideousness of the countenance was increased by a woolly beard, which spread over mouth and chin. Everything happened as the astronomer had foretold. One dandy in shoes after another broke teeth and jaws upon the nut Krakatuk, without in the slightest degree helping the princess, and as they were carried away half-dead to the dentist (who was always ready), groaned out, "That was a hard nut!"

When now the king in the anguish of his heart had promised his daughter and kingdom to the man who would break the en-chantment, the gentle Drosselmeier made himself known, and begged to be allowed the trial. No one had pleased the princess so much as this young man; she laid her little hand on her heart, and sighed inwardly, "Ah! if he were the person destined to crack Krakatuk, and be my husband!" Young Drosselmeier, approach-ing the queen, the king, and Princess Perlipat in the most elegant manner, received from the hands of the chief master of ceremonies the nut Krakatuk, which he immediately put into his mouth, and crack! crack! broke the shell in a dozen pieces. He neatly removed the bits of shell that yet remained on the kernel, and then with a most profound bow presented it to the princess, shut his eyes, and proceeded to step backwards. The princess swallowed the kernel; and oh! wonderful wonder! her ugliness disappeared, and, instead, was seen a form of angel beauty, with a countenance like lilies and roses mixed, the eyes of glancing azure, and the full locks curling like threads of gold. Drums and trumpets mingled with the rejoicings of the people. The king and the whole court danced upon one leg, as before at Perlipat's birth, and the queen was obliged to be sprinkled all over with eau de cologne, since she had fainted with excessive joy. This great tumult did not a little disturb young Drosselmeier, who had yet his seven steps to accomplish: however, he recollected himself, and had just put his right foot back for the seventh step, when Mrs. Mouserinks, squeaking in a most hideous manner, came up through the floor, so that Drosselmeier, as he put his foot backwards, trod on her, and stumbled— nay, almost fell down. What a misfortune! The young man became at that moment just as ugly as ever was Princess Perlipat. The body was squeezed together, and could scarcely support the thick, deformed head, with the great goggling eyes and wide, gaping mouth. Instead of the pigtail, a little wooden collar hung out from behind his back to make his lower jaw move. The watchmaker and astronomer were beside themselves with horror and astonishment; but they saw how Mrs. Mouserinks was creeping along the floor all bloody. Her wickedness, however, was not unavenged, for Drosselmeier had struck her so hard on the neck with the sharp heel of his shoe, that she was at the point of death. But just as she was in her last agonies, she squeaked out in the most piteous manner, "O Krakatuk, from thee I die! but Nutcracker dies as well as I; and thou, my son, with the seven crowns, revenge thy mother's horrid wounds! Kill the man who did attack her, that naughty, ugly wicked Nutcracker!" Quick with this cry died Mrs. Mouserinks, and was carried off by the royal housemaid. Nobody had taken the least notice of young Drosselmeier. The princess, however, reminded the king of his promise, and he immediately ordered the young hero to be brought before him. But when that unhappy young man appeared in his deformed state, the princess put her hands before her and cried out, "Away with that nasty Nutcracker!" So the court marshal took him by his little shoulder and pushed him out of the door.

The king was in a terrible fury that anybody should ever think of making a nutcracker his son-in-law: he laid all the blame on the watchmaker and astronomer, and banished them both from his court and kingdom. This had not been seen by the astronomer in casting his horoscope; however, he found, on reading the stars a second time, that young Drosselmeier would so well behave himself in his new station, that, in spite of his ugliness, he would become prince and king. In the meantime, but with the fervent hope of soon seeing the end of these things, Drosselmeier remains as ugly as ever; so much so, that the nutcrackers in Nuremberg have always been made after the exact model of his countenance and figure.

Translated by William Makepeace Thackeray
and revised by the editors

The Marble Statue

Joseph, Freiherr von Eichendorff

It was a beautiful summer evening when Florio, a young noble-man, rode slowly toward the gates of Lucca. The delicate haze that shimmered over the beautiful landscape and over the towers and roofs of the city, the colorful groups of handsome gentlemen and ladies, full of gaiety and animation as they strolled under the tall chestnut trees—all this filled him with happiness.

Another rider, mounted on a handsome gaited horse and headed in the same direction, joined Florio. He wore a colorful costume, a golden chain around his neck, and over his dark brown hair a velvet beret with plumes. After a friendly exchange of greetings they rode along close together in the deepening twilight and soon struck up a conversation. Young Florio was so completely charmed by the stranger, his slender figure, his proud and open manner, yes, even his happy voice, that he could not take his eyes off him.

"What business brings you to Lucca?" said the stranger finally. "I really have no business at all," answered Florio, a bit bashfully. "No business at all? Well, then you must be a poet," replied the other, laughing in amusement. "Not exactly," replied Florio, blushing deeply. "True, I have tried my hand a few times at the gentle art of song. But then sometimes I'd reread the great old masters and there I'd find, big as life, the very things I'd only secretly wished or dimly felt. At times like that I'd seem to myself like the faint, small voice of a lark blown by the wind under the immeasurable dome of heaven." "Everyone praises God in his own way," said the stranger, "and it takes all voices together to make the spring." With that his great expressive eyes rested with visible pleasure on the handsome youth, who gazed so innocently into the darkening world before him.

"For the present," Florio continued with increasing boldness and intimacy, "I have chosen a life of travel, and I feel as if I were released from a prison; all my old wishes and delights are now suddenly set free. I was raised quietly in the country, but for many years I used to gaze with longing on the far-off blue mountains, whenever Spring, like a magic minstrel, passed through our gardens, and sang enticingly of distant beauty and of great, immeasurable desire." These last words left the stranger deep in thought. "Have you," he said abstractedly but with great seriousness, "ever heard of that strange minstrel whose music lures young people into a magic mountain from which no one has ever returned? Be on your guard."

Florio did not know what to make of the stranger's words. However, he had no chance to question him further, for just then, as they were riding along unobserved behind the strolling company, they came not to the city gates, but to a broad, green square. Here, in the last glow of evening, a joyously noisy world of music, colorful tents, and people on foot and horseback shimmered in the changing light.

"Here's a good place to spend some time," said the stranger merrily, leaping from his horse. "May we meet again soon!" and with that he vanished quickly into the bustling crowd.

Florio stood still for a moment in joyful astonishment at this unexpected sight. Then he followed the example of his companion, turned his horse over to his servant, and mixed with the happy throng.

Music from hidden groups of singers echoed from the flowering bushes on every side. Under the tall trees dignified ladies strolled up and down, and their beautiful eyes surveyed the shining expanse of meadow. They laughed and chatted, and their brightly colored plumes nodded in the pale gold of evening like a bed of flowers swayed by the wind. Beyond them on a bright green lawn several girls were happily engaged in a game of ball. The balls, with their brightly colored feathers, fluttered like butterflies and described gleaming arcs back and forth through the blue air; on the green space beneath, the figures of the young women rose and fell gently, a charming sight. One girl in particular attracted Florio's attention, with her pretty yet almost childish figure and the grace of her movements. She had a full, brightly colored wreath of flowers in her hair, and it was like looking at a happy image of spring to see the great verve with which she flew over the lawn, or bent down, or reached her pretty arms into the bright air. A bad shot by her opponent caused the shuttlecock to fly off in the wrong direction; it came fluttering down directly in front of Florio. He picked it up and handed it to the girl with the garland as she ran to retrieve it. She stood before him, almost as if frightened, and looked at him silently with her beautiful big eyes. Then she curtsied, blushing, and returned quickly to her fellow players.

The main procession of glittering carriages and riders, moving slowly and splendidly through the central avenue, had in the meanwhile swept Florio away from the entrancing game, and for fully an hour he roamed alone through the ever-changing scene.

Then all at once he heard several knights and ladies near him cry out, "There's Fortunato, the singer!" He turned, looked quickly where they were pointing, and saw, to his great astonishment, the charming stranger who had accompanied him here shortly before. He was standing off at the edge of the meadow, leaning against a tree, surrounded by a circle of handsome knights and ladies who were listening to his singing; at times a number of voices from the circle would respond enchantingly. Among them Florio also noticed again the beautiful girl of the badminton game, gazing, eyes wide in silent delight, into this world of music.

Florio, taken aback, recalled how he had recently chatted so confidentially with the famous singer, whom he knew by reputation and had long admired. He lingered shyly, some distance away, to hear such a lovely contest of voices. He would have been happy to stand there the whole night, so much were his spirits lifted by the notes that floated toward him, and he was distressed when Fortunato ended so soon and the whole group rose from the lawn.

The singer caught sight of the young man in the distance and came over to him at once. In a gesture of friendship he took both of Florio's hands, and, disregarding all protest, led the shy youth like a charming captive to an open tent pitched nearby, where the whole group had gathered and prepared a festive supper. They all greeted him like old acquaintances; beautiful eyes rested in delight and amazement on his young, radiant figure.

After much good-humored talk, they soon took their places about the round table in the middle of the tent. Refreshing fruit and wine in brightly polished glasses sparkled on the gleaming white tablecloth; great fragrant bouquets of flowers stood in silver vases, and among them shone the pretty faces of young women. Outside, the last rays of evening played like gold on the lawn and on the river, which, smooth as a mirror, glided by in front of their tent. Florio had almost involuntarily joined the pretty ballplayer. She recognized him at once and sat there quiet and shy; but her long, timid lashes could scarcely conceal the dark fire of her glances.

It had been agreed that everyone in turn should improvise a little song as a toast to his sweetheart. Their lighthearted singing barely touched the surface of life, playfully, like a spring wind, without being drawn into its depths, animating the carefree faces of the company around the table. Florio was delighted to the depths of his heart; his spirit was freed of all bashfulness and apprehension. In almost silent, dreamlike communion with his thoughts, he gazed out through the lights and the flowers onto the beautiful landscape as it slowly faded into the glow of evening. And now when his turn came to pledge his toast, he lifted his glass and sang:

> Each happy fellow names his own,
> Only I stand here alone;
> Who cares what person all unknown
> Has set which lady on his throne?
> So I must pass unheard, like waves
> on yonder stream,
> On springtime's very threshold vanish
> like a dream.

As she listened to these words his pretty neighbor looked up at him almost roguishly and quickly lowered her head again when she met his glance. But he had sung with such heartfelt emotion and bent over her now with such pleading in his beautiful, imploring eyes that she did not resist when he kissed her quickly on her warm, red lips. "Bravo, bravo!" cried several gentlemen; and innocent, high-spirited laughter echoed around the table. In haste and confusion Florio emptied his glass. The fair recipient of his kiss, blushing deeply and gazing down at her lap, looked lovely beyond words, under her full wreath of flowers.

So each of the fortunate young men in the circle had gaily chosen his sweetheart. Fortunato alone belonged to every girl or to none and seemed almost lonely in all this charming confusion. His exuberance was unrestrained; he abandoned himself so completely to wildly alternating moods of wit, gravity, and jest that some might perhaps have called him overbearing, except that all the while he had such a clear and honest, almost magic look about his eyes. Florio had firmly resolved once and for all to confess to Fortunato at supper the love and respect he had so long cherished for him. But he had no luck this evening; all his subtle attempts to do so glanced off and were lost in the singer's lighthearted merriment. Florio could not understand him at all.

The world outside was quieter and solemn now; isolated stars came out among the crowns of the darkening trees; the river murmured louder through the refreshing coolness. Then at last it was Fortunato's turn to sing. He rose quickly, touched the strings of his guitar, and sang:

> What heavenly sound
> In my heart and my head!
> To clouds and beyond—
> Oh, where am I led?
>
> On mountain top lonely
> Still my heart sings
> To praise the world only
> And all lovely things.
>
> I see Bacchus' vision
> And who sees him knows
> The godhead, the passion,
> The dreamlike repose.
>
> In garlands of roses,
> O image of youth,
> Sweet fire encloses
> Your bright eyes in truth.

Is it love, is it reverence,
That makes your mood bright?
Spring smiles its deliverance,
You dream in delight.

Sing, Venus, in yearning,
How joyous to yield;
In morning light burning
Your realm is revealed.

On sunny hills ringed,
A magic surround;
Swift cherubs, all winged,
Attend you around.

They fly off to gather
All beauties that seem
Fit for their queen-mother
To put in a dream.

Knights, ladies-in-waiting
Stroll everywhere on
The green fields, creating
A flowershow lawn.

And everyone carries
His sweetheart along
And hustles and hurries—
A fortunate throng.

Here he suddenly changed mode and melody, and continued:

The music has faded
And gone is the green.
The ladies are pensive
The knights bold of mien.

A heavenly yearning
Sings out through the blue.

The land around shimmers
With teardrops of dew.

In midst of the party,
One silent, apart—
How soothing to see him!
Your home, lonely heart?

Bright poppies in blossom,
All dreamlike and red,
And garlands of lilies:
A crown for his head.

His lips invite kissing,
They're pale, and so fair,
He must have brought greetings
From heaven somewhere.

He carries a lantern,
Mysteriously bright.
"Is someone here longing
To go home tonight?"

But sometimes by twisting
His torch full around
He makes the world tremble
And die without sound.

What here were once flowers
Of joy, when they die,
You'll see up there sparkling:
Cool stars in the sky.

O young man from heaven,
Indeed you are fair.
I'd leave all the turmoil
And go with you there.

What more can I hope for?
Up, up, and be free!

For heaven is open
O Father, take me!

Fortunato was silent, as were the rest, for in fact the sounds outside had faded away now, and the music, the bustle of the crowd, and all the magic and illusion had little by little subsided, giving way before the immeasurable starry heavens and the mighty nocturne of rivers and woods. At this moment there stepped into the tent a tall, slender knight, wearing rich jewelry that cast a greenish gold luster among the lights flickering in the wind. The look of his eyes, in their deep sockets, was fiery and agitated, his face handsome, but pale and wild. At his sudden appearance everyone thought with an involuntary shudder of the silent stranger in Fortunato's song. However, after a passing bow to the company, he went to the buffet set up by the keeper of the tent and quickly downed long draughts of the dark red wine through pale lips.

Florio was completely startled when the strange fellow now singled him out and welcomed him to Lucca as an old acquaintance. Astonished and pensive, he regarded the man from head to heel, for he could not remember ever having seen him before. But the knight was exceptionally loquacious and talked a great deal about various events in Florio's earlier life. Also he had such precise knowledge of the young man's native region, his home and garden, and every old familiar spot dear to his heart that Florio soon became reconciled to the sombre figure.

Donati, for so the knight was called, did not seem to fit in with the rest of the company at all. An anxious feeling of unrest, to which no one could assign a cause, became obvious everywhere. And since in the meantime night had fallen, the party soon broke up.

Now there began a remarkable hustle and bustle of carriages, horses, servants, and of tall lanterns casting their strange light on the nearby water, among the trees and the beautiful figures milling about. In this wild illumination Donati took on an even paler and more frightening aspect than before. The beautiful young lady with the garland had constantly been looking at him out of the corner of her eye, in secret fear. Now, when he came up to her to help her chivalrously onto her horse, she drew back timidly against

Florio, who was standing behind her. His heart beating, he lifted the lovely girl into her saddle. By this time everyone was ready for departure. She gave him one last friendly nod from her graceful seat, and soon the whole glittering apparition had vanished into the night.

Florio had a most peculiar sensation, finding himself suddenly alone with Donati and the singer on the broad empty grounds. With his guitar on his arm, Fortunato walked up and down along the riverbank in front of the tent and seemed to be thinking of new melodies; for he was plucking isolated chords, which floated soothingly over the quiet meadow. Then suddenly he stopped. A strange feeling of displeasure seemed to pass fleetingly over his otherwise clear features. He was anxious to be off.

So all three mounted their horses and rode together to the nearby city. Fortunato did not speak a word the whole way; all the more amiably Donati poured forth his well-turned, elaborate phrases. Florio, still in the afterglow of delight, rode between the two as silent as a young girl in a dream.

When they came to the city gate, Donati's horse, which had already shied at several passers-by, suddenly reared almost straight in the air, and refused to enter. Across the rider's face, almost distorting it, there shot a bright flash of anger, and from his trembling lips a wild, only half-articulated curse, at which Florio was not a little astonished. For such conduct seemed to him not at all consistent with the knight's otherwise refined and reasonable manner. But the stranger soon regained his composure. "I meant to accompany you to the inn," he said, smiling and turning to Florio with his accustomed charm, "but my horse, as you see, has other plans. I live just outside the city in a country house, where I hope very soon to have you visit me." With that he bowed, and the horse, scarcely to be restrained in its incomprehensible haste and anxiety, flew off swift as an arrow, into the darkness, the wind whistling behind him.

"Thank God!" cried Fortunato, "the night has swallowed him up again! I tell you, he looked to me like one of those sallow, misshapen night moths that seem to come flying out of some fantastic dream, whir through the twilight, and with their long bearded antennae and horrible great eyes almost appear to have a real face." Florio, who had already become rather friendly with Donati, expressed his astonishment at so harsh a judgment. But the singer, only the more annoyed by such surprising charity, went blithely on with his abuse, and, to Florio's secret vexation, called the knight a chaser of moonbeams, a languishing fool, a vaunter of his own melancholy.

In the course of such conversation they finally arrived at the inn, and each one went promptly to the room assigned him.

Florio threw himself on his bed, fully dressed, but for a long time he could not get to sleep. His heart, excited by the recollected images of the day, incessantly rose and fell, echoed and sang. The doors of the inn opened and closed less frequently now; only an occasional voice rang out. House, city, and field at last sank into deep silence. It seemed to him as if he were sailing alone with swan-white sails on a moonlit sea. The waves beat softly against the ship; sirens rose from the water and all of them looked like the beautiful girl with the garland from earlier in the evening. They sang without end, so magically, so sadly, that he thought he would die of melancholy. Its bow dipping imperceptibly, the boat sank slowly deeper and deeper. He woke with a start.

He sprang from his bed and opened the window. The house lay near the outer gate of the city; he looked out over a great silent circle of hills, gardens, and valleys, brightly lit by the moon. Out there as well, among the trees and streams, everywhere, there came, answering or fading, echoes of past happiness, as if the whole landscape were softly singing like the sirens he had heard in his slumber. He could not resist the temptation. He seized the guitar, which Fortunato had left with him, went from the room and softly down the stairs through the peaceful house. The door below was ajar; a servant lay fast asleep on the threshold. He slipped unnoticed into the open air and strolled happily between vineyards, through empty avenues, past sleeping cottages, walking farther and farther.

From the vineyards he could see the river in the valley; scattered here and there were numerous castles, gleaming white, resting like slumbering swans in the ocean of stillness below. He sang with a happy voice:

> How cool it is at night to wander,
> My faithful zither in my hand,

Saluting from the hilltop yonder
The sky and all the silent land.

The things I loved are here, but each is
Changed from the happy vale I knew.
How still the wood—through halls of beeches
Only the moon now gliding through.

The vintners' joy is still, just listen;
Life's merry pulse, it beats no more.
Only the winding rivers glisten,
Silvery along the valley floor.

Often a nightingale awakens
As from a dream and sweetly sings.
The treetops stir as memory beckons;
A secret whisper fills all things.

Still, there's no sudden end to pleasure.
The shining joys of day depart
But leave behind a deeper treasure,
A secret singing, in my heart.

Far away, across the water,
In joy, my love, I'll touch these strings.
Listening, you'll hear the words I utter,
And by the message know who sings.

He could not help laughing at himself, for in the end he did not
really know who it was he was serenading. It was no longer the
charming young girl with the garland that he was thinking of. The
music among the tents, the dream he had dreamed in his room,
the reverie of his own heart as it relived the sounds and the dream
and the lovely vision of the girl—all this had imperceptibly and
magically changed her image into something much more beautiful,
greater, more splendid than anything he had ever seen.

For a long time he walked on, deep in thought, until he came
unexpectedly upon a little lake surrounded by tall trees. The moon,
just rising over the treetops, illumined in sharp, clear outlines a

marble statue of Venus set on a stone close to the bank. It was as if the goddess had at that very moment risen from the waves and were now watching in enchantment the image of her own loveliness reflected from the quivering mirror of the surface of the water, among the stars softly rising from its depths. A few swans silently described their monotonous circles around the statue; a soft whisper passed among the surrounding trees.

Florio stood and gazed as if he had taken root there. The statue seemed to him like a long-sought lover, suddenly found and recognized, like a magic flower sprung from the dawning light of spring and from the dreamlike stillness of his earliest youth. The longer he stared, the more it seemed to him as if those soulful eyes were slowly opening, as if the lips were about to move in greeting, as if life were surging up with vital warmth through those beautiful limbs, like a lovely song. He kept his eyes closed for a long time, dazzled, sad, and enraptured.

When he looked up again, everything seemed suddenly transformed. The moon looked out mysteriously between the clouds; a fairly strong wind ruffled the pond into turbid waves; the statue of Venus, fearfully white and motionless, stared at him from the marble sockets of its eyes, out of the infinite stillness, almost like a phantom. A sense of horror such as he had never before felt took possession of the young man. He left the place quickly; walking faster and faster, without pausing for rest, he hurried back through the gardens and vineyards toward the peaceful city. For now even the rustling of the trees seemed to him like a clearly audible, intelligible whispering, and the tall, ghostly poplars seemed to reach out after him with their great, long shadows.

He arrived at the inn visibly shaken. The sleeping servant still lay there on the threshold and started up in fright as he brushed by him. Florio quickly closed the house door behind him; he did not draw a free breath until he was upstairs and in his room. Here he paced back and forth for a long time before he calmed down. Then he threw himself on his bed and finally fell asleep, dreaming the strangest dreams.

The following morning Florio and Fortunato sat together at breakfast in front of the inn, with the morning sun sparkling through the tall trees overhead. Florio looked paler than usual, with the unpleasant pallor of a wakeful night. "Morning," said Fortunato merrily, "is a strapping, madly handsome fellow, the way he comes down from the highest mountains into the sleeping world shouting with joy and shaking the tears from the flowers and trees, swelling and blustering and singing. He doesn't have much sympathy with the gentler emotions; he lays his cool hands on all our limbs and laughs in our solemn faces when we walk out to meet him, tense and still under the spell of the moonlight." Florio was now ashamed to tell the singer anything about the beautiful statue of Venus, as he had originally intended, and he maintained an embarrassed silence. His nocturnal outing had, however, been noticed by the servant at the house door and the secret apparently revealed, for Fortunato continued with a laugh, "Well, if you don't believe me, just try; just stand over here and say, for example, 'Oh fair and gracious spirit, oh light of the moon, pollen of tender hearts,' and so on, and see how ridiculous that would be. But I'll bet you said things like that often enough this very night and I dare say looked perfectly serious as you said them."

Florio had always thought of Fortunato as quiet and gentle; now he was deeply hurt by the impertinence and lightheartedness of his beloved singer. He spoke quickly, with tears welling in his soulful eyes. "I'm sure you're talking very differently from the way you feel, and you should never do that. But I'm not going to let myself be confused and misled by you; there are such things as pure and gentle emotions, shamefaced no doubt, but with no cause for shame, or quiet happiness that shuns the noisy day and opens its sacred petals only to the starlit sky, like a flower in which an angel dwells." Fortunato looked at the youth in surprise and then cried out, "I swear you've fallen head over heels in love."

In the meantime Fortunato's horse had been led out for him since he planned to go riding. He gave the pretty, well-groomed pony a friendly pat on his arched neck, as the animal, in his happy impatience, pawed the grass. Then he turned once more to Florio and, smiling pleasantly, held out his hand to him. "You know, I'm really sorry for you," he said. "There are too many nice, gentle young people, particularly ones in love, who are absolutely determined to be unhappy. Forget it, all that rubbish about moonlight and melancholy. And even if things really go wrong at times, just pull yourself together, get out into God's fresh morning air, shake off your troubles, pray from the bottom of your heart, and if that doesn't make you regain your strength and good spirits completely, it must really be the devil's work." And with that he quickly swung himself up on his horse and rode off between vineyards and flowering gardens into the colorful, echoing countryside, as bright and cheery a sight as the morning itself.

For a long time Florio followed him with his eyes until the waves of brilliant light closed over the distant sea. Then he paced rapidly back and forth under the trees. The experiences of the night before had left a deep, vague yearning in his soul. Fortunato, on the other hand, had strangely disturbed and confused him by what he said. Like a sleepwalker suddenly called by his name, he no longer knew what it was he wanted to do. Several times he stopped, lost in contemplation, before the rich and marvelous prospect of the land below, as if he meant to ask the advice of the mighty forces joyously at work out there. But morning answered only with a play of isolated magic lights that seemed to shine through the trees above him into his dreamily sparkling heart, a heart that lay under quite a different spell. For there the stars still described their magic circles, in the midst of which the marvelous marble statue gazed up at him with a new and irresistible power.

So he decided finally to seek out the little lake once again, and quickly set off down the same path he had taken the night before.

But now—how different it all looked! Happy people walked busily here and there through the vineyards, gardens, and walkways. Children were playing quietly on the sunny lawns before the same cottages that in the night and in the dream landscape of the trees had so startled him, appearing like sleeping sphinxes. The moon stood far off and pale in the clear sky. Countless birds sang their happy medley of songs through the forest. He was quite unable to comprehend the strange fear that had come over him before in this same place.

Soon, however, he noticed that, lost in thought, he had strayed from his path. He surveyed attentively all the clearings he came to and in his uncertainty first retraced his steps, then walked ahead again, but all to no avail. The more persistent his search, the more unfamiliar and completely different everything seemed.

He wandered about in this fashion for a long time. The birds

were already still, the encircling hills fell gradually silent, the rays of the noonday sun covered the whole surrounding region with their shimmering heat, so that it seemed to slumber and dream in a veil of sultry haze. Then, to his surprise, he came to a wrought iron gate, through the ornately gilded bars of which one could see the wide expanse of a splendid park. A current of air, cool and fragrant, wafted forth from it to refresh his weariness. The gate was not locked; he opened it softly and walked in.

Avenues of tall birches welcomed him with their solemn shadows; golden birds fluttered among them here and there like blossoms blown by the wind, while great strange flowers, such as Florio had never seen, waved their red and yellow cups dreamily back and forth in the gentle breeze. Innumerable fountains splashed monotonously in the great solitude, with gilded balls playing on their waters. Between the trees one could see in the distance the shimmer of a splendid palace with tall, slender columns. No human being was in sight anywhere; deep silence reigned all around. Now and then a nightingale would stir and sing in its sleep, almost sobbing. Florio gazed in awe at the trees, the fountains, the flowers; he had a strange sensation, as if everything had long been submerged and the flowing stream of time were passing over him with its clear and gentle waves, and the garden were lying deep beneath, bound by a magic spell and dreaming of a past existence.

He had not pressed far ahead when he heard the sounds of a lute, now louder, now echoing softly away in the splashing of the fountain. He stopped and listened; the tones came closer and closer, then suddenly into the silent arcade, out from among the trees, stepped a tall, slim woman of marvelous beauty, walking slowly, not raising her eyes. She carried on her arm a splendid lute embellished with golden designs, striking occasional chords upon it as if she were deeply immersed in thought. Her long golden hair fell in rich curls over her shoulders, almost pale in their gleaming whiteness, down over her back. Her long, wide sleeves, woven as if from the first snowy bloom of spring, were gathered with delicate golden clasps; her lovely body was enfolded in a sky-blue gown, its border embroidered all around with brightly shining colorful flowers, all marvelously intertwined. At that moment a bright burst of sunlight, falling through the opening of the arcade, passed quickly over her blossoming figure, bathing it in sharp, clear light. Florio shuddered—the features and the figure were unmistakably those of the beautiful statue of Venus he had seen the night before by the little lake. Oblivious of the stranger, she sang:

> Why, Spring, do you awaken me again?
> Let all the old desires arise once more?
> Send through the land this magic muffled roar
> That makes sweet shivers course through every vein?
>
> A thousand songs, fair Mother, hail thy reign,
> In bridal crown, more youthful than before,
> Streams whisper, voices fill the forest floor
> And naiads, singing, rise and sink again,
>
> I see the rose that rises from its cell
> Of green; the amorous winds caress it, while
> It meets the tepid air, with blushes burning.
> From quiet shelter you call me as well.
> And now I must, in spring, in sorrow, smile,
> Amid sweet sound and fragrance faint with yearning.

As she sang she walked along, sometimes disappearing in the greenery, then reappearing, but always farther away, until she was finally lost to sight in the vicinity of the palace. Now all was quiet once again, only the trees and the fountains murmured as before. Florio stood there, lost in the flowering world of his dreams; it seemed to him that he had long known the fair lutenist and had only forgotten her in the distractions of life, and so lost her; that now she was fading away in sorrow amid the murmuring of the fountains and calling to him incessantly to follow her. Deeply moved, he hurried farther on into the garden, toward the spot where she had disappeared. There, beneath ancient trees, he came upon ruined walls, along which at intervals beautifully carved designs were still half recognizable. At the foot of the wall, on shattered marble blocks and capitals, among which tall grasses and flowers grew luxuriantly, a man lay stretched out in sleep. Astonished, Florio recognized the knight Donati. But his features seemed strangely altered by sleep; he looked almost like someone dead. A suppressed shudder passed over Florio at the sight; he shook the sleeping man violently. Donati slowly opened his eyes; his first glance was so strange and glazed and wild that Florio was horrified. At the same time, half awake and half asleep, he muttered darkly some words Florio could not understand. When at last he had fully wakened he jumped up quickly and regarded Florio with what seemed to be great astonishment. "Where am I?" cried the latter in haste. "Who is that noble lady who lives in this lovely garden?" "How," Donati asked him in return, with great seriousness, "did you get into this garden?" Briefly, Florio recounted what had happened, leaving Donati deep in thought. Now the young man urgently repeated his previous questions and Donati replied absentmindedly, "The lady is a relative of mine, a person of wealth and power; her properties are widely scattered throughout the land. Sometimes you will find her in one place, sometimes in another. Occasionally she stays in the city, in Lucca." Florio's heart was strangely moved by these words tossed at him so casually, for now he was increasingly persuaded of something that earlier had barely touched his thoughts in passing, namely, that he had seen the lady before, somewhere, sometime when he was very young, without his being able to remember at all clearly.

Meanwhile, leaving in some haste, they had come, without his realizing it, to the gilded iron gate of the garden. It was not the same one through which Florio had previously entered. Surprised, he looked about the unfamiliar place. Far away, across the fields, the towers of the city lay serene in the light of the sun. Donati's horse stood by the gate, tethered, pawing the ground and snorting.

Shyly, Florio mentioned that he would like in future to see the beautiful mistress of the garden again. Donati had hitherto remained withdrawn, deep in thought, but at this he seemed suddenly to pull himself together. "The lady," he said, polite and circumspect as ever, "will be happy to make your acquaintance. Today, however, we should only be disturbing her, and I am myself called home by pressing business. Perhaps I can come by and pick you up tomorrow." And with this, speaking in well-turned phrases, he said farewell to the young man, mounted his horse, and was soon lost to sight among the hills.

For a long time Florio gazed after him; then, like a drunken man, he hurried off to the city. There the sultry heat held every living being prisoner behind the dark, cool shutters of the houses.

Streets and squares were all deserted and Fortunato too had not returned. Florio was too happy to feel other than confined in all this cheerless solitude. Quickly he mounted his horse and rode out again into the open countryside.

"Tomorrow, tomorrow!" The words rang without cease in his heart. He was happy beyond description. So the beautiful marble statue had become a living thing and had stepped down from its pedestal into the springtime. The quiet pond was suddenly transformed into an immeasurable landscape, its stars into flowers, and all of spring into an image of her beauty. And so he wandered for a long time through the beautiful valleys around Lucca, riding in turn past handsome country estates, past waterfalls and grottoes, until the waves of evening closed over him in his happiness.

The sky was already bright with stars as he passed slowly through the silent streets that led to his inn. In one of the lonely squares there stood a great, handsome house shining in the light of the moon. One of the upper windows was open. There, between flowers artfully trained on either side, he could see the figures of two women, apparently deep in lively conversation. To his amazement he heard his own name clearly mentioned, several times. In the brief, disjointed phrases brought to his ear by the wind he thought he recognized the voice of the wonderful singer with the lute. But the trembling of the leaves and flowers in the moonlight made it impossible to distinguish anything with certainty. He stopped, in the hope of hearing more. Then the two women noticed him and suddenly all was silent.

Unsatisfied, he rode on. Just as he was turning the corner, however, he saw one of the ladies, her eyes following him, lean out between the flowers and then quickly close the window.

The next morning, when he had shaken the dew of sleep from his lids and was looking happily out his window over the towers and domes of the city, sparkling in the morning sun, he was surprised to see Donati enter his room. The knight was dressed entirely in black and looked unusually agitated today, impatient and almost wild. Florio in fact trembled with joy to see him, for he thought at once of his lovely lady. "Am I to see her?" he cried out to him immediately. Donati shook his head in denial and, staring sadly at the floor in front of him, said, "Today is Sunday." Quickly gaining control of himself again, he continued, "But I did want to take you hunting with me." "Hunting?" replied Florio in great surprise. "Today, on the Sabbath?" With a foul and spiteful laugh the knight interrupted him. "Now really, don't tell me you're going to stroll off to church with your lover on your arm and kneel on the footstool in the corner and say 'God bless you' when the dear lady sneezes?" "I don't know what you mean," said Florio, "and you can laugh at me all you please, but there's no way I can go hunting today. Look out there and see how all the world is resting from its labors and all the forests and fields are as resplendent in God's praise as if angels were passing over them in the blue firmament—so silent, so solemn, so blessed a time." Donati stood by the window, deep in thought; watching him, Florio thought he noticed a secret tremor as Donati stood there looking out over the Sunday quiet of the fields.

Meanwhile the pealing of bells rose from the towers of the city and filled the bright air as with the sound of praying. Donati seemed to take fright; he reached for his hat and in near anxiety urged Florio to come with him, but Florio was insistent in his refusal. "Out, away from here!" came the voice of the knight, hardly audible, rising as if from the anxious depths of his heart. He pressed the astonished young man's hand and fled the house.

Florio's mind was put at ease again when shortly thereafter Fortunato, the bright and cheerful singer, stepped into his room like a harbinger of peace. He brought with him an invitation for the coming evening to a country estate not far from the city. "Be prepared," he added, "you are going to meet an old acquaintance there!" Florio was quite taken aback; he asked hastily, "Who is it?" But Fortunato gaily refused any explanation and soon left. "I wonder if it's the lovely singer," Florio thought to himself, and his heart was pounding.

He then went to church but he could not pray; he was too happy and distracted. He sauntered idly through the streets. Everything had such a clean and festive air: well-dressed gentlemen and ladies walked along, happy and resplendent, on their way to church. Alas, the fairest of all was not among them. He thought then of his adventure yesterday on his way home. He sought out the street and had soon found the great handsome house again. But strange! The door was locked, every window closed tight; it was as if no one lived there.

In vain he wandered about the neighborhood the rest of the

day, hoping to discover more about his unknown beloved or possibly even to see her once more. But the palace and the garden he had accidentally found that midday hour seemed to have vanished, nor was Donati anywhere to be seen. So that evening his heart beat with joy and expectation as, in accordance with his invitation, he at last rode out through the city gate to the country house with Fortunato, who was still playing the man of mystery.

By the time they reached their goal it was already pitch dark. A pretty villa with slender columns lay in what appeared to be the middle of a garden. Over the columns and rising from its parapet there was a second garden fragrant with oranges and flowers of all kinds. Tall chestnut trees stood round about and boldly stretched out to the night their giant arms, strangely illumined in the light that streamed from the windows. The singer and his friend were met at the door by the master of the house, a refined and cheerful man in his middle years, whom Florio could not remember having seen before. He welcomed them warmly and led them up the broad staircase into the ballroom.

The happy sound of dance music rang out; a large company of guests moved in bright and graceful turns under the glow of countless lights floating in crystal chandeliers above the merry throng, like stars in their constellations. Some were dancing, others happily engaged in animated conversation. Many were masked and their strange appearance often gave to these charming festivities a sudden and unintended air of deep, almost ominous meaning.

Florio stood dazzled and motionless, himself an image of grace among graceful flowing images. A pretty girl stepped up to him, her Grecian robes lightly draped, her beautiful hair wreathed in artful braids. A mask concealed half of her face, leaving the lower half all the more blushingly, charmingly visible. She made a fleeting bow, handed him a rose, and was quickly lost again in the moving crowd.

At the same moment he also noticed that the master of the house was standing close beside him, regarding him with a searching glance; but he quickly looked away when Florio turned toward him.

Puzzled, Florio now walked through the bustling crowd. What he had secretly hoped for he could find nowhere; he was on the

point of reproaching himself for having followed the merry Fortunato so frivolously out upon this sea of pleasures where he was
made to drift farther and farther from that other high and lonely
figure. Meanwhile the lax and carefree waves lapped over him as
he stood lost in reflection, teasing him, flattering him, until, imperceptibly, they worked a change in the very direction of his
thinking. Dance music, even if it does not stir and alter our inmost
being, casts a spell upon us much like spring, gentle and powerful.
Magically, its tones reach, like the first glances of summer light,
into the depths, wakening all the songs that sleep in bondage there,
and springs and flowers and ancient memories, the whole massive
weight of frozen, halting life becomes a clear, bright watercourse
bearing the heart with pennons flying happily back to long-aban-
doned desires. So the contagion of general pleasure had spread to
Florio as well; his spirit was quite unburdened, as if all the mys-
teries that weighed so oppressively upon him must surely be resolved.

His curiosity aroused, he now went looking for the pretty little
Grecian girl. He found her in animated conversation with other
masked figures, but he could clearly see that in the midst of their
conversation her eyes too were searching far afield and had already caught sight of him in the distance. He asked her to dance
with him. She made a friendly curtsy but her quick animation
seemed somehow to collapse as he touched her hand and held it
tight. She followed him quietly, her head bowed—whether
roguishly or sadly, one could not tell. The music commenced; he
could not for a moment stop gazing at the charming enchantress
who hovered close to him like the magic figures represented in
fabled pictures of olden times. "You know who I am," she whispered, in a barely audible voice, as for one fleeting moment during
the dance their lips almost touched.

The music suddenly stopped; the dance was over. Florio thought
he saw his lovely partner again, this time at the other end of the
room. The costume was the same, the colors of her dress and her
hairstyle the same. This beautiful apparition seemed to gaze over
at him with a fixed stare, ever unmoving in the now scattered
throng of dancers, like a serene constellation now receding, now
shining out in beauty again among the light and fleeting clouds.
Apparently the pretty Grecian girl did not notice the apparition,

or did not pay any attention to it; without a word she quickly left her partner, softly pressing his hand for a fleeting moment.

In the meanwhile the hall had for the most part emptied. Everyone thronged into the gardens below to stroll in the soft, warm air. The strange double had vanished as well. Florio followed the crowd and strolled under the high arching trees, deep in thought. The multitude of lights cast a magic glow on the trembling leaves. The maskers, wandering back and forth, their voices oddly different and sharp, their garb fantastic, stood out even more strangely, almost ghostlike, here in the unsteady light.

He had just drifted away a bit from the larger company, setting out, involuntarily, on a lonely path, when he heard in the bushes a lovely voice singing:

> Over there, from hilltops shining,
> Comes a distant sound of greeting.
> Treetops whisper, limbs inclining,
> As if they would kiss in meeting,
>
> He is fair and gentle surely!
> Voices passing in the night
> Sang his secret praise demurely—
> And I waken gay and bright.
>
> Quiet, fountains, still your chatter,
> Do not tell it to the morning!
> In the moonlit gentle water
> I shall drown my joys and yearning.

Florio followed the sound of the singing and came upon a circular open space in the lawn, with a fountain in its center, playing merrily with the sparkling moonlight. The Grecian girl sat like a fair naiad on the stone basin of the fountain. She had removed her mask and was toying pensively with a rose in the shining mirror surface of the water. In flattering caress, the moonlight moved up and down over her gleaming white shoulders. He could not see her face for she had her back turned toward him. When she heard the branches rustle behind her, the fair creature leaped up swiftly, put her mask before her face, and fled, fast as a startled deer, back to the assembled company.

Now Florio too joined in with the colorful procession of strolling people. Graceful words of love echoed softly in the warm breezes. The moonlight, with its invisible strands, had caught all these figures as if in a golden net of love, its meshes broken in comic gaps only by the uncouth parody of the masks. Fortunato in particular had changed disguises many times in this same evening and carried on a constant stream of strange and ever-changing, ingenious mummery. He was always in a different mask, never recognizable, often surprising himself by the audacity and deep meaning of his game, so that at times he turned suddenly silent with melancholy, even as the others seemed about to laugh themselves half to death.

The beautiful Grecian girl, however, was nowhere to be seen. She seemed intentionally to avoid any further encounter with Florio. The master of the house, by contrast, had laid full claim on him. Artfully and with great indirection he interrogated him extensively about his earlier life, his travels, his plans for the future. Florio was quite unable to confide in him, for Pietro, as he was called, had about him a constant air of surveillance, as if behind all his turns of phrase there lurked some special plan. In vain Florio tried to fathom the reason for this importunate curiosity.

Florio had just managed to break away and was turning aside at the end of one of the avenues, when he ran into several maskers, among whom, unexpectedly, he caught sight of his Grecian girl. The maskers were talking at length, in a strange and confused fashion. One voice seemed familiar, but he could not remember well enough to identify it. Soon one figure after another disappeared until at last, without truly realizing it, he found himself alone with the girl. She stood there hesitantly and looked at him for some time in silence. Her mask was off, but a short, snow-white veil, adorned with all manner of strange gold-embroidered designs, covered her little face. He was surprised that so shy a person as she would choose to remain alone with him.

"You were listening secretly to my singing," she said at last, in a friendly tone. They were the first words he had heard her speak, and the melodious sound of her voice filled his soul through and through, seeming to touch and stir in memory all the love and beauty and joy he had ever experienced in his life. He asked pardon for his presumption; he spoke confusedly of the sense of loneliness that had so carried him away, of his distraction, of the murmuring sound of the fountain. In the meantime the sound of voices drew near. The girl glanced shyly about and quickly withdrew deeper into the dark night. It seemed to please her that Florio followed.

Growing bold and more confident, he asked her to conceal herself no longer, or at least to tell him her name, so that her lovely vision would not be lost to him among the thousand confusing images of this day. "Don't ask that," she replied dreamily. "Take the flowers of life gladly as the moment offers them; don't ask questions about the roots beneath the ground because down there everything is cheerless and still." Florio looked at her in surprise. He was unable to understand how such puzzling words could come from the lips of so gentle a girl. At this moment the changing light of the moon, as it moved among the trees, fell upon her figure. It also seemed to him now as if she were taller, more slender, more dignified than before, at the dance or by the fountain.

By this time they had come to the entrance of the garden. No more lanterns were burning now. The only thing one could hear was an occasional voice echoing away in the distance. Beyond, the great encircling landscape rested in the glorious moonlight, still and solemn. On a meadow that lay before them Florio noticed a number of horses and people, moving about in confusion, only half recognizable in the dusk.

Here his companion suddenly stopped. "It will be my pleasure," she said, "to see you at my house sometime. Our friend will show you the way. Farewell!" With these words she lifted her veil and Florio drew back in surprise. It was the mysterious beauty whose singing he had overheard in the sultry noontime garden. But her face, brightly lit by the moon, seemed to him pale and immobile almost like the marble statue by the pond that night.

He watched her now as she crossed the meadow to be met by a number of servants in rich livery; there, quickly throwing a bright hunting jacket over her shoulders, she mounted a snow-white palfrey. He was as if spellbound with surprise, delight, and a secret inner dread that stole over him as he stood there, until horses, riders, the whole strange apparition, had disappeared into the night.

A shout from the garden finally roused him from his reverie. He recognized Fortunato's voice and hurried to catch up with his friend, who, having missed him for some time, had been trying in vain to find him. Fortunato had no sooner caught sight of him than he sang this song as he came to meet him:

Voice in air,
Rising, falling,
Fragrant, fair—
Lover calling.
Sweetheart strays,
High above her,
Starry maze
Hides her lover.
So she cries;
Heartsick, sighs.
Fragrance palls.
How time crawls!
Air in air—
Love and beloved the same everywhere!

"Now where have you been wandering off to? It's been a long time!" he said at last. Not for any price would Florio have revealed his secret. "A long time?" was his only reply, and he was himself surprised. For in fact the garden had in the meanwhile emptied completely, and almost all lights were now extinguished; only a few lanterns flickered uncertainly back and forth in the wind, like will-o'-the-wisps.

Fortunato did not press the young man further; in silence they climbed the stairs of the quiet house. "I shall now redeem my word," said Fortunato, as they reached the terrace above the roof of the villa. Here a small company was gathered under the clear starlit sky. Florio at once recognized several faces he had seen by the tents that first happy evening. In their midst he also caught sight, again, of his beautiful companion. But tonight the cheerful wreath of flowers was gone from her hair; without ribbons, without jewelry, her beautiful locks flowed softly about her little head and her pretty neck. He stood still, almost dazzled by the sight. The memory of that first evening came over him with a strangely melancholy power. It seemed to him as if all that were long, long ago, so completely had everything changed since then.

The girl, named Bianca, was introduced to Florio as Pietro's niece. She seemed quite abashed when he approached her, and barely dared look up to him. He expressed his surprise at not having seen her all evening. "You saw me several times," she said softly, and he thought he recognized her whispered voice. Meanwhile she had noticed on his breast the rose he had received from the Grecian girl, and she lowered her eyes, blushing. This did not escape Florio; indeed it made him recall how after the dance he had had a double vision of the Grecian girl. Good Lord, he thought to himself, confused, who was that?

She broke the silence, changing the subject. "It's very strange, suddenly to leave the noise of our party and come out into the open night. Look, the clouds change shape so frighteningly as they cross the sky—watching them too long would surely drive one mad. Sometimes they're like enormous moon mountains with dizzy precipices and terrible jagged peaks, really like great faces; other times like dragons, suddenly stretching out their long necks; and down below the river dashes along, mysteriously, through the darkness, like a golden serpent; and that white house over there looks like a still marble statue." "Where," cried Florio, roused from his thoughts and violently startled by her words. The girl looked at him in surprise and both were silent for a time. "You will be leaving Lucca?" she said at last, hesitantly and softly, as if she feared an answer. "No," replied Florio, absentmindedly, "or rather yes, yes, very soon indeed." She seemed about to say more, but suddenly turned her face away, into the darkness, holding back her words.

Finally he could stand the feeling of constraint no longer, his heart was so full and burdened down and yet so immoderately happy. He took his leave quickly, hurried down the stairs and rode back, without Fortunato or anyone else accompanying him, to the city.

The window of his room was open. He glanced out briefly once more. The landscape lay still and unrecognizable in the moonlight, like a curiously convoluted hieroglyph. He closed the window, almost in fear, and threw himself down on his couch, where, like a person in a fever, he sank into the strangest dreams.

Bianca, however, remained seated on the terrace for a long time. Everyone else had retired. Now and again a lark or two would awaken, to sweep high through the quiet air, singing tentatively. The treetops below began to stir. Pale glints of morning cast their flickering light over her wakeful face, framed in the careless waves of her loosely falling hair. It is said that, if a girl falls asleep wearing a garland woven of flowers of nine different kinds, her future bridegroom will appear to her in her dreams. After the evening by the tents Bianca had indeed dozed off in this fashion and in her dreams had seen Florio. Now it was all a delusion—he was so distracted, so cold and alien. She picked all the petals from her deceitful flowers, the flowers she had until now preserved like a bridal wreath. Then she leaned her forehead on the cold railing and cried her heart out.

Several days had passed and now Florio found himself one afternoon with Donati at his villa near the city. At a table set with fruits and refreshing wine they passed the sultry hours in pleasant conversation until the sun sank deep in the sky. Donati's servant meanwhile had been playing the guitar, an instrument from which he could draw forth the most charming tones. Great wide windows stood open and through them soft evening breezes wafted the fragrance of the many flowers in which the windows were framed. Beyond lay the city, in a colorful haze among gardens and vineyards, from which a murmur of happy sounds reached up to their window. Florio was deeply and inwardly content, for in the silence his thoughts and memories were constantly of his lovely lady.

From off in the distance, meanwhile, came the sound of hunting horns. Nearer now, then far away, endless and captivating, they answered one another. Donati stepped to the window. "That is your lady," he said, "the one you saw in the beautiful garden. She is coming back to her castle from the hunt." Florio looked out; down below he saw the lady riding across the fields on a handsome palfrey. A falcon, tied to her sash with a golden cord, sat on her hand; in the light of the evening sun a jewel on her breast cast long green-gold rays over the meadow. She gave a friendly nod in his direction.

"The lady is rarely at home," said Donati. "If you care to, we might still have time to visit her today." At these words Florio was pleasantly roused from the dreamy, contemplative state into which he had fallen. He was so happy he could have thrown his arms around Donati. Soon they were both outside, on horseback.

They had not ridden far when they saw the palace rising above them, serene in the splendor of its columns, surrounded by the beautiful garden as if by a happy garland of flowers. From time to time, jets of water from the many fountains rose as if in jubilation, high over the crowns of the bushes, and sparkled bright in the gold of evening. Florio wondered why he had never been able to find the garden again. His heart pounded with delight and anticipation when they finally reached the castle.

Several servants hurried up to them to take their horses. The castle was made of marble, strangely designed and built, almost like a pagan temple. The beautiful symmetry of all its parts, the columns, surging upward like the thoughts of youth, the artful ornamentation, depicting legends from a happy, long vanished world, and finally the beautiful marble statues of gods and goddesses, standing in the many niches round about—all this filled the soul with indescribable serenity. They now entered the spacious hall that traversed the entire castle. All along, between the airy columns, the garden cast its light and wafted its fragrance toward them.

On the broad, smoothly polished steps that led down into the garden they at last met the fair mistress of the palace, who welcomed them with grace and charm. She was resting, half recumbent, on a couch of costly fabric. She had taken off her hunting coat. A sky blue dress, fastened at the waist with a marvelously ornate sash, enclosed her beautiful figure. A girl who knelt at her side held out to her a richly decorated mirror, while several others were busy adorning their gracious lady with roses. At her feet, and disposed about the lawn, sat a circle of young women, singing in parts to the lute, in voices now carried away with joy, now soft and plaintive, the way nightingales make answer to one another on warm summer nights.

In the garden itself one could see everywhere a lively stirring and moving about. Gentlemen and ladies, all strangers to him, strolled up and down among the roses and fountains, in well-mannered conversation. Pages in rich livery passed around wine and flower-decked oranges and fruits, on serving plates of silver. Farther off in the distance, with the lute music and the lights of evening slipping across the fields of blossoms, beautiful girls rose from the flowers as if waking from midday dreams, shook their dark hair from their foreheads, bathed their eyes in the clear fountains, and joined the others, mingling with the happy throng.

Florio's eyes passed quickly from one brilliant image to the other, dazzled, but returned again and again, intoxicated anew, to the lovely mistress of the castle. As for her, she let nothing interrupt her pleasing occupation. Whether making some change in the arrangement of her dark, fragrant hair, or contemplating herself in the mirror, she kept up an unbroken conversation with young Florio, sweetly toying with matters of little moment, in graceful turns of phrase. At times she would suddenly turn and gaze at him from beneath her garland of roses with such indescribable charm as to touch his innermost soul.

Night, meanwhile, had already begun to cast its darkness among the flickering lights of evening, the merry echoes of the garden turned gradually to soft whispers of love, moonlight spread its magic over all the beautiful figures and images. Then the lady rose from her flowery couch and took Florio affectionately by the hand, to lead him into the interior of her castle, of which he had spoken admiringly. Many of the others followed. They went up and down a few flights of stairs, while the rest of the company dispersed merrily, laughing and joking, through the various colonnades. Donati too was lost in the crowd, and soon Florio found himself alone with the lady in one of the most splendid chambers of the castle.

Here his beautiful guide sank down upon silken cushions spread over the floor. As she did so, she cast her snow-white veil in all directions about her, in charming movements, at one moment revealing, at another loosely concealing ever lovelier glimpses of her figure. Florio gazed at her, his eyes burning. All at once a magically beautiful singing began in the garden outside. It was an old song of pious bent, one he had often heard in his childhood and had since nearly forgotten, with all the varied experiences and sights of his journey. He became quite distracted because at the same time it seemed to him as if it were the voice of Fortunato. "Do you know who is singing?" he quickly asked the lady. She seemed completely taken aback and in great confusion answered that she did not. Then she sat there for a long time, meditating in silence.

In the meantime Florio had the time and liberty to take exact note of the remarkable furnishings of the room. It was dimly lit by a few candles, held by two enormous arms protruding from the wall. Tall, exotic flowers, standing in ornate jars about the room, spread their intoxicating fragrance. Opposite him stood a row of marble statues, over which the wavering lights played voluptuously up and down.

The other walls were covered in costly tapestries depicting life-size narrative sequences of extraordinary freshness. In amazement Florio thought he could clearly recognize, in all the ladies depicted there, the beautiful mistress of the house. In one place she appeared, falcon in hand, as he had just now seen her, riding to the hunt with a young knight; in another she was represented in a splendid rose garden, a handsome page kneeling at her feet.

Then, as if from the sound of the song outside, there came to him the notion that he had often seen such a picture, at home, in his early childhood, a wondrously lovely lady in the very same dress, a knight at her feet; beyond, a garden with many fountains and avenues of artfully trimmed trees, looking precisely like the garden he had just seen out there. He also recalled having seen in it depictions of Lucca and other famous cities.

He told this, not without deep agitation, to his lady. "At that time," he said, lost in memory, "when I would stand, on sultry afternoons, in the lonely summer house of our garden, before those old pictures, contemplating the curious city towers, the bridges, and the streets, with splendid carriages driving along, and handsome cavaliers riding up to greet the ladies in the carriages—I had no idea then that all of that would come to life around me. At such times my father used to come over to join me and tell me amusing stories of things that had befallen him on his youthful campaigns in one or the other of the cities depicted there. Then, most often, he used to walk up and down in the garden for quite a long time, deep in thought. But I would throw myself down in the deepest grass for hours, watching clouds as they floated past over the sultry countryside. The grasses and flowers swayed softly back and forth above me as if to weave a fabric of strange dreams, and all the while bees buzzed away like summer, never stopping—

oh, all of that is like a great sea of silence where one's heart would gladly sink away and disappear in sadness."

"Forget all that," said his lady, as if her mind were on something else. "Every man thinks he has seen me before—I suppose an image of me is one of the things that rises dimly up and flowers in all the dreams of youth." As she spoke she soothed the young man's clear brow, stroking back his brown hair. But Florio got up, his heart was too full, too deeply moved; he stepped to the window. The trees rustled, here and there a nightingale sang; in the distance lightning flashed. Across the quiet garden the sound of singing still wafted along, like a clear, cool stream out of which rose his old dreams of youth. The power of those tones had plunged his whole spirit into deep meditation. He suddenly felt himself a stranger here, as if alienated from his own being. Even the lady's last words, which he could not rightly interpret, troubled him strangely. Then from the deepest depths of his soul he cried out softly, "Lord God, do not let me lose my way in this world!" Hardly had he uttered these fervent words when outside an oppressively heavy wind rose up, as if at the approach of a thunderstorm, blowing upon him confusingly. At the same time he noticed grass growing on the window ledge and little tufts of weed, as on some ancient wall. A snake slithered out with a hiss and threw itself, greenish gold tail writhing, down into the empty space below.

In his fright, Florio left the window and returned to the lady. She was sitting there motionless and silent as if she were listening to something. Then she rose quickly, went to the window, and in her charming voice spoke reproachfully out into the night. Florio could understand nothing, for the storm instantly swept her words away. The thundershower seemed meanwhile to draw ever nearer; the wind, interspersed with occasional notes of the singing that still floated heartrendingly up to him, whistled through the whole house, threatening to extinguish the wildly flickering candles. A long flash of lightning had just illumined the dusk-filled room; Florio suddenly drew back several paces, for it seemed to him that the lady stood stiff and motionless before him, her eyes closed, her face and arms completely white. Along with the fleeting glow of the lightning, however, this terrible vision also disappeared just as it had arisen. The old twilight filled the room again; his lady looked at him as before, smiling, but silently and sadly, as if she were holding back tears.

Stumbling back in his terror, Florio had collided with one of the stone images that lined the wall and at the same moment it began to move. The movement was soon communicated to the others, and before long all the statues were rising in fearful silence from their pedestals. Florio drew his sword and cast an uncertain glance toward the lady. He saw, however, that as the tones of singing rose from the garden, swelling ever more powerfully, she herself was turning paler and paler, like the vanishing glow of evening, and in this glow the stars of her eyes, lovely and twinkling, seemed at last to fade and set. He was seized with deathly horror. For the tall flowers in their containers began to writhe in unison, terrifyingly, like color-flecked snakes coiling to spring. Suddenly all the figures of knights in the wall hangings looked like him and leered sardonically at him. The two arms that held the candles struggled and stretched forward, longer and longer, as if some monster of a man were trying to work his way out of the wall. The hall kept filling, the flames of lightning cast a hideous light among the figures, in whose midst Florio saw the stone images surging forward at him with such force that it made his hair stand on end. Terror overpowered his senses. In confusion he rushed from the room, back down through the empty, echoing chambers and colonnades.

In the garden below and to the side lay the quiet pond he had seen that first night, with the marble statue of Venus. The singer Fortunato—or so it seemed to him—was standing in a boat in the middle of the lake, upright and tall, his back turned to Florio, still striking occasional chords on his guitar. But Florio took this vision as well to be a confusing delusion of the night, and hurried on and on, without looking back, until pond, garden, and palace had vanished from sight behind him. The city rested before him, bright in moonlight. Far off on the horizon there was only the echo of a slight thunderstorm; it was a splendidly clear summer night.

Isolated streaks of light flickered across the morning sky as he reached the city gates. Angrily, he sought out Donati's house, intending to call him to account for the events of this night. His country house lay on one of the highest spots around, with a view over the city and the entire surrounding area, so he was soon able to find the lovely spot again. But instead of the pretty villa in which he had been only yesterday, there was only a poor hut, completely overgrown with grapevines and enclosed by a small garden. Doves, playful in the first rays of morning, walked up and down the roof, cooing. A deep, serene sense of peace pervaded everything. A man with a spade on his shoulder was just coming out of the house, singing:

> Gone is the darkness of the night,
> The devil's tricks, his magic might,
> Work lies ahead this bright new day.
> Now honor God, awake, and pray!

He quickly broke off singing when he saw the stranger flying up, pale, his hair disheveled. In utter confusion Florio asked for Donati. The gardener did not know the name and seemed to take his interrogator for a madman. His daughter stood on the threshold, stretching in the cool morning air; fresh and clear as the dawn she looked at the stranger with great, astonished eyes. "Good Lord, where have I been all this long time?" said Florio to himself, half aloud; he fled in haste back through the city gate and the still empty streets, to the inn where he was staying.

Here he locked himself into his room and collapsed into glassy-eyed meditation. The indescribable beauty of the lady, the way she had slowly faded away before him, the way her lovely eyes had paled and closed, left behind in the deepest part of his heart such infinite sadness that he felt an irresistible longing to die on the spot.

This wretched brooding and dreaming did not leave him all that day or the night that followed.

The first light of dawn found him on horseback before the gates of the city. Thanks to the tireless urging of his loyal servant he had decided to leave this part of the world entirely. Slowly, his thoughts turned inward. He was now riding down the beautiful road leading from Lucca out into open country, between darkening rows of trees in which the birds were still sleeping. Not far from the city three other persons on horseback joined company with him. In one of them he recognized, not without a secret tremor, Fortunato. The second was Bianca's uncle, in whose country house he had danced that fateful evening; he in turn was accompanied by a boy who rode along beside him, saying nothing and rarely looking up. All three had resolved to travel together all through the fair land of Italy; they extended a friendly invitation to Florio to join them on their journey. However, he only bowed silently, neither agreeing nor refusing, and continued to take little part in their conversation.

The reddish glow of morning, meanwhile, rose higher and higher over the marvelously beautiful landscape before them. Then the cheerful Pietro said to Fortunato, "Look how strangely the half-light of dawn plays over the stonework of the old ruin on the hill up there. How often as a boy I used to climb around there, full of amazement, curiosity, and secret awe. You know so many old legends, can't you tell us something about the origins of the castle and how it became a ruin—there are so many curious rumors circulating about it."

Florio glanced toward the hill. In an area of great solitude lay the scattered remains of old crumbling walls, beautiful columns, half sunken in the ground, and artfully hewn blocks of stone, all overgrown with a rankly blooming wilderness of green intertwining hedges, vines, and tall weeds. A pond lay nearby; over its surface rose a partially ruined marble statue, brightly tinged by the morning. There was no doubt: it was the same area, the same spot, where he had seen the lovely garden and the lady. The sight of it made him shudder deep inside. Fortunato, however, said, "I know an old song about it, if that will satisfy you." Thereupon, without further reflection, he sang out into the serene morning air, his voice clear and happy:

> Bold, ancient works of wonder
> In row on ruined row;
> Above in fair disorder
> Luxuriant gardens grow.
>
> Long-buried worlds below me;
> Above, the skies I see
> Have other worlds to show me—
> For this is Italy.

Soft winds make sweet suggestion
Of spring on greening plain;
A gentle resurrection
Touches the vales again.

There comes a mighty stirring
In graves of gods long dead.
Its terror strikes unerring
In human heart and head.

Strange voices vaguely seeming
To move among the trees,
A longing and a dreaming,
Afloat on blue-green seas!

Whenever spring awakens,
Beneath its fragile veil,
The ancient magic quickens
And weaves its secret spell.

The lure's not lost on Venus—
Bird songs in chorus rise—
And she from flowered greenness
Springs up in glad surprise,

Seeks old familiar places,
Her temple, bright and fair.
Smiling in joy, she gazes
On waves of soft spring air.

But life has left these places,
Her temple, silent, bare;
Steps overgrown with grasses.
Only the wind moves there.

Her friends—where now their numbers?
In woods, Diana's bed;
In cool seas Neptune slumbers,
His palace still and dead.

Only a siren swimming,
At times, from seas below,
In troubled tones proclaiming
The very depths of woe.

Venus herself, in reverie,
Stands pale where spring light shone.
Her eyes fall back, and every
Lovely limb turns stone.

For now on land and waters
There shines, gentle and warm,
High where the rainbow glitters,
Another woman's form.

A wondrous mother holding
An infant at her side,
In heavenly grace enfolding
The whole world far and wide.

A child of earth awaking
In brighter regions now
Arises, quickly shaking
Bad dreams from troubled brow.

As larks to music warming
From haunted caverns flee,
Into the winds of morning
His spirit struggles free.

Listening to his song, they had all fallen silent. At last Pietro said, "So, if I've understood you rightly, that ruin must once have been a temple of Venus." "To be sure," replied Fortunato, "in so far as one can judge by the arrangement of the whole thing and by the decorations that still survive. People say, too, that the spirit of the beautiful pagan goddess never found peace. Every spring, again and again, the memories of earthly pleasure call her from the awful silence of the grave, to rise up into the green solitude of her ruined dwelling and to practice, with devilish deception, her old art of seduction, on young and carefree spirits who then, departed from this life, yet not admitted into the peace of the dead, wander about between wild pleasures and terrible repentance, lost in body and soul, their very beings consumed in the most horrible delusions. Often people claim to have felt the temptation of ghostly spirits there. Sometimes, they say, a marvelously beautiful lady or a group of fine cavaliers would appear and lead the passer-by into a phantom garden and palace conjured up before his eyes." "Have you ever been up there?" asked Florio in haste, awaking from his reverie. "Just night before last," replied Fortunato. "And didn't you see anything terrifying?" "Nothing," said the singer, "but the quiet pond and the mysterious white stones in the moonlight, and the wide, endless, starry sky above. I sang an old pious song, one of those ancient, original songs that resound in the paradise garden of our childhood, like memories and echoes of another world in which we were at home. Those songs are a true touchstone by which poetic souls recognize one another in later, more mature stages of life. Believe me, a true poet can venture a great deal; for his art, which is free of pride and free of sacrilege, can exorcise and tame the wild earth spirits that reach out from the depths to seize us."

All were silent. The sun was just rising before them, casting its sparkling light over the earth. Florio shook himself from head to foot, dashed on ahead of the others for some distance and sang in a bright, clear voice:

> Here, Lord, am I—and hail the light
> Whose power breaks the stillness
> And sets the turbid spirit right
> With all its bracing coolness!
>
> Now I am free! I almost fell
> And still cannot recover.
> But Father, now you know me well
> And will not give me over.

After every violent emotional upset that shakes the foundation of our being there comes upon our soul a still, clear serenity, just as fields green more freshly and breathe more deeply after a thunderstorm. So too Florio now felt inwardly revived. He glanced about in good spirits again and calmly waited for his companions, who came slowly along after him in the green landscape.

The pretty young fellow accompanying Pietro had now, like a flower in the first rays of morning, lifted his head. In astonishment Florio recognized Bianca. He was shocked to see how pale she looked in comparison to that evening when he had first seen her under the tent, in all her mischievous charm. In the midst of her carefree, childish games, the poor girl had been overcome by the power of first love. And then her dearly beloved Florio, following the powers of darkness, had become so estranged from her, had distanced himself more and more, until she was forced to give him up as lost. When that happened she fell into a deep melancholy, the secret cause of which she dared confide to no one. Wise Pietro, however, knew what was going on and had resolved to take his niece far away, to foreign parts and other climes, hoping if not to cure her at least to distract and save her. To be able to travel with less hindrance and at the same time to strip herself, as it were, of all her past, she had felt compelled to put on boy's clothing.

Florio's eyes dwelt with delight on her lovely form. A strange blindness had up to now held his vision enclosed in a magic haze. Now he was quite amazed to see how beautiful she was. Touched, and speaking with deep feeling, he talked with her about all manner of things. Surprised by her unexpected good fortune, humble in her joy, she rode along silently beside him with downcast eyes, as if she were undeserving of such grace. At times, though, she would look up at him from under her long, dark lashes, and her whole bright, clear soul lay in that glance, as if she wanted to say, imploring, "Do not deceive me again!"

Meanwhile they had reached a breezy hilltop; behind them the city of Lucca, with its dark towers, sank from sight in the shimmering haze. Florio turned to Bianca and said, "I am as if reborn. I feel as if everything will turn out all right, now that I have found you once more. I never want to part again, that is, if you agree."

Instead of answering, indeed rather as if asking a question, Bianca gazed at him in uncertain, half-suppressed joy, looking for all the world like a happy angel against the deep blue background of the morning sky. The sun, its long golden beams flying across the plain, shone directly toward them. The trees stood brightly touched by light; countless larks swirled and sang through the clear air. And so they journeyed happily through sun-drenched meadows down toward the flourishing city of Milan.

Translated by Frank G. Ryder

The Tale of the Myrtle-Girl

Clemens Brentano

In the sandy land, where not many plants grow, there dwelt some miles from the porcelain capital, where Prince Wetschwut resided, a potter and his wife, right in the middle of their clay field next to their potters' oven, childless and lonely. The surrounding countryside was as flat as a lake, not a single tree or bush was to be seen, and it was very sad and dull. Daily the good people prayed to heaven that they might be granted a child for company, but heaven did not grant their wishes. The potter adorned all his vessels with lovely angels' heads, and the potter's wife dreamt every night of green meadows and delightful bushes and trees where children were playing, for whatever the heart craves is always present before one's eyes.

The potter had once made two beautiful pieces for his wife's birthday, a wonderfully beautiful crib of the whitest clay, adorned all over with golden angels' heads and roses, and a large flowerpot of red clay, painted all round with multicolored butterflies and flowers. She made up a little bed in the crib and filled the flowerpot with the best soil, which she fetched herself from miles away, carrying it in her apron; then she placed the two gifts beside her bed, in constant hope heaven would grant her request; and so one evening she prayed with all her heart:

> O Lord! I pray on bended knee,
> Grant me a child, I beg you now,
> And I will rear it piously;
> If it's a girl, I'll teach her how
> To spin the purest thread that's spun

And pray and sweetly sing the while.
If by your grace it is a son,
I'll teach him to be free of guile,
Strong of will, in action fair,
In every word he utters, true,
An honored hero everywhere,
In combat and in council too.

O Lord! the crib is now prepared,
Give me a child, O say the word,
Ah! and should this never be,
Grant to me a single boon,
Were it but a little tree,
Which in the dear rays of the sun
I might grow and tend and rear
Until with my own husband dear,
In this self-cultivated shade
I may one day to rest be laid.

Thus weeping, the good woman prayed and went to bed. During the night a severe storm occurred; there was thunder and lightning, and once a bright light passed through the bedroom. Next morning the weather was perfect, a cool wind blew through the open window, and the good potter's wife lay in a sweet dream; she thought she was sitting with her dear husband under a beautiful myrtle tree. Then the foliage rustled around her and she awoke, and behold! a fresh young myrtle sprig lay beside her on her pillow and grazed her cheeks with its tender, wind-stirred leaves. Thereupon she delightedly woke her husband and showed it to him, and they both thanked God on their knees for giving them something live that they could see grow green and blossom. They planted the myrtle sprig with the greatest care in the beautiful flowerpot, and it was daily their dearest employment to water the young stem and set it in the sun and protect it from harsh frost and sharp winds. The myrtle sprig grew rapidly under their hands and its fragrance sent peace and joy into their hearts.

One day the ruler, Prince Wetschwut, came into this district with some scholars for some new porcelain clay, for so many houses were built of it in his capital, Porcelainia, that this clay had become scarce near town. When he entered the potter's dwelling to ask his advice, he was, on seeing the myrtle tree, so enraptured by its beauty that he forgot everything else and exclaimed in pure amazement, "O how lovely, how delightful this myrtle is! The sight of it refreshes my heart so, how I'd love to live all my life near this tree. I can't do without it, I *must* own it, were I to give one of my eyes for it."

After thus exclaiming, he immediately asked the potter and his wife what they wanted for the myrtle. The good folk explained in the most modest fashion that they were not prepared to sell the tree, and that it was the dearest thing they possessed on earth. "Ah," said the potter's wife, "I couldn't live, did I not see my myrtle before me, indeed, it's as dear to me as if it were my own child; I'd not even take a kingdom for this, my myrtle." When Prince Wetschwut heard this, he grew very sad and returned to his castle. His yearning for the myrtle grew so strong that he fell ill, and the whole realm was worried about him. Then envoys came to the potter and his wife and asked them to consign the myrtle to the prince, otherwise he would die of yearning. After long negotiations the woman said, "Unless he has the myrtle, he's bound to die, and unless we have the myrtle, we can't live; if then the prince wants the myrtle, he must also take us with it; we'll hand it over to him and beg him to take us into his castle as faithful servants so that we may see the beloved myrtle from time to time and delight in it." The envoys agreed; they immediately dispatched a horseman to town with the glad news that the prince was to take heart, the myrtle was on its way. The potter then placed the pot with the myrtle onto a stretcher, over which his wife had spread her finest silken cloths, and after they had locked up their cottage, the two of them, escorted by the envoys, carried the beloved tree to town. The prince came in person in a coach from town to meet them, bearing a little golden watering can, with which he watered the beloved myrtle, at the sight of which he rapidly recovered. Four maidens, dressed in white and festooned with roses, came with a red silk baldachin, under which the myrtle was carried to the castle. Children strewed flowers, and all the people were glad and threw their caps into the air. Only nine girls were not present at the general rejoicing; they wanted the myrtle to wither because the prince, before he saw the myrtle, had often come to visit them, and each of them had hoped to become queen one day of Porcelainia. But since people had started talking about the myrtle, he had not bothered about them any more, and so they had become so embittered towards the innocent tree that none of them showed themselves on this day of rejoicing. The prince arranged for the myrtle to be placed by the window of his room, and gave the potter and his wife a dwelling in the castle gardens, from the windows of which they could see the myrtle constantly, which satisfied the good folk.

The prince was soon completely recovered; he nurtured the tree with indescribable love and care; and the latter grew and spread to everyone's delight. One evening the prince happened to sit down on his couch by the tree. Everything was quiet in the castle, and, deep in thought, he fell asleep. When night had enveloped everything, he heard a wonderful rustling in his tree and awoke and listened; then he perceived a gentle motion around his room and a sweet scent diffused itself all around. He was still, quite still, and kept on listening; in the end, when he heard that wonderful rustling in the myrtle again, he began singing.

> What means this sweet rustling, say,
> My myrtle tree so wonderful!
> O my dear tree, for whom I glow?

Thereupon a lovely soft voice sang back.

> I seek your friendship to repay,
> My host so kind, so bountiful,
> My lord, for whom my blossoms blow!

The prince was enchanted by the voice more than words can tell; but soon his joy grew much greater still, for he noticed that someone sat down on the stool at his feet, and when he stretched his hand in that direction, a soft hand grasped his and took it to the lips of a mouth that said, "My dear lord and prince! Don't ask who I am, simply let me sit at your feet occasionally in the stillness of the night and thank you for looking after me so devotedly in the myrtle, for I am the inhabitant of this tree; but my gratitude for your affection has so grown that it had no more room in the tree, and so heaven has granted that I may sometimes approach you in human form." The prince was delighted at these words, and regarded himself as infinitely fortunate because of this gift of the gods. They conversed for some hours, and she spoke so wisely and sensibly that he burned with desire to see her face to face. The myrtle-girl said to him, however, "Let me first sing a little song, then you can see me," and she sang:

> Rustle, myrtle dear!
> The world is still—so soon,
> Across the heavens clear
> That shepherd of the stars, the moon,
> Drives the clouds, his sheep,
> Toward the other, sunrise shore,
> Sleep, my friend, oh sleep,
> Till I'm with you once more.

The myrtle rustled its accompaniment, the clouds drifted past so slowly in the sky, the fountains splashed so softly in the garden, and the song was so soft that the prince fell asleep, and when he was scarcely nodding, the myrtle-girl got up softly, softly from her stool and returned into the myrtle.

When the prince awoke next morning, he saw the empty stool at his feet, and did not know whether the myrtle-girl had really been with him or he had simply had a dream; but since he saw the little tree covered all over with blossoms that had opened during the night, he became more and more certain of the apparition. Never did anyone await the night with such longing; already towards evening he sat down on his couch and waited. At last the sun was down, it grew dusk, it became night. The myrtle rustled, and the myrtle-girl sat at his feet, and told him such beautiful things that he couldn't wait to hear more, and when he again asked her to be allowed to light the lamp, she again sang to him a little song.

> Rustle, my myrtle, O my dear!
> And dream away in starlight clear,
> The turtledove has cooed
> Deep into sleep her brood.

Soft the clouds, like sheep
Drift toward the sunrise shore
Sleep, my friend, oh sleep,
Till I'm with you once more.

Then the prince fell asleep again and awoke next morning with the same uncertainty, and awaited the night again with the same longing. But the same thing happened to him this time as in the first and second night: whenever he desired to see her she always sang him to sleep. For seven nights this went on, during which time she gave him such excellent advice concerning the art of ruling that his desire to see her grew even greater. Next day he therefore arranged for a silken net to be fixed to the ceiling of his room, which he could let down very gently, and thus he awaited night's arrival. When the myrtle-girl had sat at his feet again and had given him the most profound advice concerning the duties of a good prince, she was about to sing the lullaby again, but he said to her, "Today *I'll* sing," and after repeated requests she allowed him his wish. Thereupon he sang the following little song.

Do you hear the cricket chirping?
Do you hear the fountain sigh?
Quiet, quiet, let us hearken.
O, to dream and dreaming die!
O, to hear on soft clouds lying
Lullabies the old moon sings!
O, what joy to soar up flying
When your dreams can lend you wings
And to heaven's blue fields take you!
Pick a star just like a flower!
Sleep and dream and soar—I'll wake you,
Joy of mine, in morning hour.

And this little song had such an effect, because of the soft melody to which he sang it, that the myrtle-girl fell asleep at the feet of the prince. Then he let the net down over her and lit his lamp, and O heavens! what did he see? The most beautiful maid who ever lived, her face as mild and pure as the clear moon, curls like gold playing around her forehead, and on her head a little crown of myrtle; she wore a green dress, embroidered in silver, and her hands were crossed like a little angel. For a long time he looked at his friend and teacher in dumb amazement, then no longer able to contain his joy, he burst out into loud rejoicing, crying, "O virtue! O wisdom! how lovely is your form; who can live without you, once he's seen you." Then he caught her hand and put his signet ring onto her finger, saying, "Awake, o my sweet friend! Take my throne and my hand and never leave me again." Then the myrtle-girl awoke, and when she caught sight of the light, she blushed all over, and blew the lamp out. Then she lamented that he had taken her prisoner, saying that harm was bound to come of it; but the prince asked her for pardon so much that in the end she forgave him, promising to become the princess of his country, if her parents allowed. In the meantime, he was to make all the preparations for the marriage and then ask her parents; till then, however, he was not to see her again. The prince, agreeing to everything, asked her how he was to call her, when he had made all the arrangements, and she said, "Attach a small silver bell to the top of my little tree, and as soon as you ring, I'll appear." Then she tore the net, the tree rustled, and the myrtle-girl was gone.

Dawn had scarcely broken when the prince called together all his ministers and councillors and informed them that he intended marrying before long, and that they were to make all arrangements for the most magnificent wedding ever known in the land. The councillors were very glad at this and most humbly asked him the name of the bride, so that they might use it at the illuminations. Thereupon the prince said, "The first letter of her name is M, and at the celebrations myrtle sprigs are to be painted in every suitable place." The gentlemen were about to leave him when news suddenly arrived that a wild boar in the royal zoo had gone berserk and destroyed all the Chinese porcelain in the crystal summerhouse situated there; it was extremely urgent that it should be shot at once, lest it went round biting other pigs and making them mad, which then might easily throw the whole town of Porcelainia into confusion. The prince did not hesitate; he ordered his councillors to arrange the wedding in the meantime, and rode out with his huntsmen.

When the prince left the castle, the nine wicked girls who had

not joined in the rejoicing when the myrtle was brought so cere-
moniously into town lay, very beautifully adorned, in their windows, hoping the prince would notice and greet them; but, even
though they leaned out so far that they might easily have fallen
down into the street, it was all in vain: the prince gave no sign of
noticing them. Outraged at this, they met together and resolved to
take revenge. The rumor of the wild boar that had gone berserk
had been spread by them only to get the prince, who had stopped
appearing in public, to ride past; they had got their servants to
smash the Chinese porcelain in the summerhouse. When they were
thus assembled in their windows, the father of the eldest, who was
one of the ministers, entered and announced that they were to
prepare themselves for the wedding celebration; the prince was to
marry a certain Princess M, and there was talk of many myrtle
decorations at the illuminations. Scarcely were they alone again,
when they gave vent to all their wrath, for all nine of them had
calculated on ascending the porcelain throne. They commissioned
a mason to construct a subterranean passage right into the prince's
chamber, for they wanted to see whom he had locked up in there.
When the passage was finished, they persuaded a tenth young girl,
from whom they concealed their designs, to accompany them,
which she did, merely out of curiosity, however, and not out of
malice; but they only took her to leave her behind there, as if she
had done everything. Thereupon one night, provided with lanterns, they went through the passage into the prince's chamber
and rummaged through everything, very surprised to find nothing
special there, apart from the myrtle. They then vented all their
spite on it, tearing off its branches and leaves, and when they also
tore down the top, the little bell rang and the myrtle-girl, who
thought this was the sign for her wedding, suddenly stepped out
of the myrtle in the loveliest of wedding dresses. At first the wicked
creatures were full of consternation, but soon they agreed this must
be the future princess, and thereupon they set upon her, murdering her in the cruelest fashion by chopping up the poor myrtle-girl
into many little pieces with their knives. Each one of them took
away a finger from the poor myrtle-girl; only the tenth girl had
not joined in, but wept and wailed the whole time, for which they
then locked her in and escaped the way they had come.

When the prince's chamberlain, who had been ordered by the

former on pain of death to water the myrtle daily and tidy up the room, entered to perform his tasks, his horror was indescribable on seeing the myrtle-girl, all mangled, scattered about in blood on the ground and the myrtle tree broken and stripped. He did not know what the meaning of this might be, for he knew nothing of the myrtle-girl; then the young girl, who still sat crying in a corner, told him all. Weeping bitter tears, they gathered up all the limbs and bones of the hapless victim and buried them in the pot under the destroyed myrtle tree in such a way that it formed a small grave mound; then they washed the floor as clean as they could, and watered the tree with the water mixed with blood, tidied the chamber, locked it and fled in great fear. The girl, however, took away as a memento a lock of the unfortunate victim's hair.

Meanwhile the preparations for the wedding were almost finished, and the prince, who had hunted the wild boar without success, returned to the town. His first visit was to the good potter and his wife, to whom he told his story of the myrtle-girl, asking them for the hand of their daughter. The good people were almost beside themselves with joy when they learned that a daughter of their own had grown up in their myrtle tree, and now they knew why they had loved it so intensely. Joyfully they agreed to the prince's request and accompanied him to the castle to see their wonderfully beautiful daughter. When they entered the room where the myrtle stood, their eyes saw a sad spectacle: many bloodstains still on the floor, and their beloved tree stripped and wounded; next to it, a grave mound. The prince cried, the potter cried, the potter's wife exclaimed, "O my beloved bride! O my dear child! my one and only dear daughter! O where are you, show yourself to your unhappy parents!" But nothing stirred, and their despair was boundless. The three poor wretches then sat there for days at a time, watering the myrtle tree with their tears, and the whole country was dismayed and sad.

Thus suffering, the prince and the potter and his wife tended and watched over the sick myrtle tree in the most tender fashion, and it began to send out shoots again, which delighted them greatly, and soon it was fully restored, except for some leaves missing at the top, on the outer five shoots of its two main branches, and on the other four shoots, next to which the fifth was beginning to sprout. The prince observed this fifth shoot every day, and how delighted he was when he saw one morning this shoot fully grown and the ring which he had given the myrtle-girl fixed on it as on a finger. His delight was indescribable, for he now thought the myrtle-girl must still be alive. The next night he sat with the potter and the potter's wife by the tree, and they begged the myrtle so tenderly for a sign of life that the tree finally began to rustle, and sang the following words:

> Oh pity me!
> My hands, you see,
> Have had nine fingers torn away.
> But in your land, my prince and king,
> Nine new young myrtle branches spring;
> My very flesh and bone are they.
> Oh pity me
> And graciously
> Get my nine fingers back, I pray.

The prince and the parents were very touched by this sad song, and next day the prince published abroad in the whole land that whoever brought him the finest myrtle twigs he would reward with his royal hand. This came to the ears of the murderous women, who had so horribly tormented the poor myrtle, and they were highly delighted at it, for they had the nine fingers of the myrtle-girl, each one her own, buried in soil in a pot, and little myrtle shoots had grown out of them. They promptly put on their best clothes and, one after another, arrived at the castle with their myrtle twigs, for they thought that the prince's words meant he would marry the bearer of the most beautiful myrtle. The prince arranged for the myrtle twigs to be taken from them, and promised he would convey his answer to them in due course; they were, however, to prepare themselves for the festivities. When he now placed all nine twigs beside the large tree, a voice spoke out of it:

> Welcome, little twigs of mine!
> Welcome, little fingers nine!
> Flesh of my flesh, bone of my bone!
> Back into the pot—and welcome home!

Thereupon the prince buried the nine twigs and the nine fingers under the myrtle, which sent out the very same day the nine missing shoots. But now there came the youngest girl, who had only taken the lock of hair and left her the ringed finger, and threw herself at the prince's feet, saying, "My lord! I have no myrtle, nor did I want to have any; but I hand over this lock to you and crave your pardon." The prince granted it, and she told him how the whole murder had happened, and asked him to forgive the chamberlain who had fled, and marry her to him. So the prince gave her a pardon for him, and she ran to the forest, where he had hidden in a hollow tree, and she had daily brought him food. The chamberlain was highly delighted at his good fortune and returned with her to town. When, however, the prince had buried the lock of hair, the myrtle said:

> Now I'm once again restored
> To my old radiance,
> Go, fetch my bridal wreath, my lord,
> We'll foot a wedding dance.

Then the prince announced a great celebration for all the people in the castle gardens; when everybody had gathered, the myrtle-girl was set up under a baldachin, and the loveliest of floral wreaths, threaded with gold, was placed on her head by the potter and his wife. Scarcely was this completed, when the myrtle-girl, adorned as the most beautiful bride, stepped out of the tree and was warmly embraced, with tears of joy, by her parents, who had never seen her before, and then by the happy prince, as his bride. The nine murderous girls stood as if on coals of fire. The prince said, "What does that person deserve who has harmed this myrtle-girl?" And one after another of those present named a harsh punishment, and when the question was put to the nine girls they all said together, "That the earth should swallow him up and his hand grow out of the earth," and scarcely had they said this than the earth swallowed them up, and over them there grew up cinquefoil. Now the wedding was celebrated, and the chamberlain also celebrated his wedding with the youngest girl. Heaven soon presented the prince with a little myrtle-prince, who was rocked in the beautiful crib of the old potter, and the whole country was happy and glad.

The myrtle tree, however, soon grew so strong and big that it had to be planted out in the open country. Then Princess Myrtle desired it to be planted by her parents' former cottage; this was done, and the cottage was changed into a fine country house, and finally out of the myrtle tree there grew a myrtle forest, and the grandchildren of the potter and his wife played in it, and those two good people were buried under the myrtle tree, just as they desired. The prince and the myrtle-girl probably also rest there, if they are not, perchance, alive, which I tend to doubt, for this was all a very long time ago.

Translated by Derek Bowman

The Cold Heart

Wilhelm Hauff

Whoever travels through Swabia should not forget to take a brief look at the Black Forest, not on account of the trees, though one does not find everywhere such immeasurable stands of magnificent firs, but on account of the people, who are remarkably distinct from those who live in surrounding districts. They are taller than ordinary people, broad shouldered, strong limbed, and it is as though the invigorating breeze that wafts through the firs in the morning had endowed them from childhood with a freer breath, clearer eyes, and a firmer, if more rough-hewn spirit than the dwellers in the valleys and plains. And not only their bearing and stature, but also their customs and manner of dress form a marked contrast to those who live outside the forest. The costume of the inhabitants of that part of the Black Forest that lies in Baden is the handsomest. The men let their beards grow as nature will; their black jerkins, their tremendously full, close-pleated breeches, their red stockings, and peaked, broad-brimmed hats lend them a somewhat strange, but serious and venerable air. In this district the people are mostly glassmakers, but they also manufacture clocks and peddle them all over Europe.

On the other side of the forest dwells another branch of the same race, but their employment has given them other manners and customs than those of the glassmakers. They deal in their woodland: they fell and trim their firs, float them down the Nagold into the Neckar, and from the upper Neckar down the Rhine far into Holland; and on the shores of the Atlantic people know the men of the Black Forest and their long rafts. They touch at every town along the river, proudly waiting to see who will purchase their boards and beams; but the biggest and longest ones they sell for high sums to the Mynheers, the rich Dutch shipbuilders. These men are accustomed to a rough, nomadic life. Their delight is to float downstream on their rafts, their sorrow to have to return again on foot beside the river. Because of their trade, their dress is very different from the glassmakers. They wear dark linen jerkins, green suspenders a hand's breadth in width across their broad chests, and black leather breeches with a brass ruler sticking out of the pocket like a badge of honor. But their pride and joy are their boots, which are probably the biggest worn in any part of the world. They can be hitched up two spans above the knee, and in them the raftsmen can wade in three feet of water without getting their feet wet.

Until fairly recently the inhabitants of the Black Forest believed in spirits and gnomes that dwelt in their woodlands, and only latterly have they been dissuaded of this foolish superstition. The strange thing is, these legendary woodland spirits also dress according to the region to which they belong. Thus we are assured that the glassmanikin, a kindly gnome four and a half feet high, always appears wearing a peaked hat with a broad brim, a jerkin, great baggy breeches, and red stockings. Dutch Michael, on the other hand, who haunts the other side of the forest, is said to be a gigantic, broad shouldered fellow dressed like a raftsman, and a number of people who claim to have seen him vow they wouldn't like to have to pay for the calves whose skins went into the making of his boots. "They were so big," they say, "that a grown man could stand in them up to his neck, and that's no exaggeration."

It is these woodland spirits with whom a young Black Forester is said to have had a strange adventure, and this adventure is the theme of my tale.

In the Black Forest there once lived a widow, Dame Barbara Munk; her husband had been a charcoal burner, and after his death she kept urging her sixteen-year-old son to follow his father's trade. Young Peter Munk, a sly lad, since he had never seen his father do anything else, was satisfied to sit beside his smoking kiln all week long, or go into the towns, all black, and sooty enough to frighten one, to sell his charcoal. But a charcoal burner has a lot of time to think about himself and other people, and when Peter Munk sat beside his kiln, the dark trees and the deep forest stillness brought tears to his eyes and filled his heart with vague longings. Something saddened him, vexed him, he didn't rightly know what. Finally it came to him what it was: his station in life. "A lonely, sooty charcoal burner!" he said to himself; "what a miserable life. Just look how people respect the glassmakers, the clockmakers, even the musicians on Sunday evenings! But if Peter Munk, all washed and clean and in his best clothes, wearing his father's gala jerkin with the silver buttons and brand new red stockings, comes along, and someone is walking behind him and thinks, 'I wonder who that slender lad can be?' and admires my stockings and my elegant gait—why, when he goes past and looks around, he's bound to say, 'Bah, it's *only Peter Munk the charcoal burner.*' "

The raftsmen on the other side of the forest were also an object of his envy. When these forest giants came over to the glass- and clockmakers, handsomely dressed and wearing a half-hundred-weight of silver in buckles and chains, when they stood with their legs planted apart, watching the dance with an aloof air, cursing in Dutch, and smoking Cologne pipes an ell long, like the finest Mynheers, Peter thought he saw in them the perfect embodiment of human happiness. And when these lucky fellows would dive into their pocket, take out whole handfuls of big thalers and play dice at six bits a throw, five gulden this way, ten that, his head fairly swam and he would sadly steal away to his humble cottage. On some evenings he had seen one or the other of them lose more at dice than his father earned in a year.

There were three men in particular whom he admired and he couldn't say which he admired most. The first was a big fat man with a red face, considered the richest man in those parts. They called him Big Zeke. He traveled twice a year to Amsterdam with timber and was always fortunate enough to sell his load at a much higher price than the others, so that, while *they* went home on foot, *he* could ride back in a carriage. The second was the tallest and skinniest man in the whole Black Forest; they called him Long-Shanks Schlurker, and Munk envied him because of his astounding brazenness. He would contradict the most respectable people, and took up more room in a crowded tavern than three fat men, because he always sat with his elbows propped up on the table or pulled one of his long legs up on the bench; and yet no one dared oppose him, he had such an uncanny amount of money. The third was a handsome young man, the best dancer for miles around and therefore called the Dance King. He had been a poor hired man working for a wealthy timber merchant, but had suddenly become rich. Some said he had found a pot of gold beneath an old fir tree; others maintained that he had fished up a bundle with gold pieces in the Rhine not far from Bingen, using a long pike with which the raftsmen sometimes spear fish. The bundle, they said, was part of the great hoard of the Nibelungs that lies buried there. In short, he had suddenly grown rich, and young and old looked up to him as a prince.

Charcoal Peter often thought about these three men when he was sitting alone in the forest. To be sure, they all had one bad failing that made them generally detested, and this was their inhuman avarice and unfeeling conduct toward debtors and the poor, for the Black Foresters are a good-hearted people. But one knows how it is with such things: if they were disliked because of their avarice, they were nonetheless respected because of their wealth, for who could throw away thalers as they did, as though money grew on trees?

"It can't go on like this," said Peter to himself one day, painfully saddened. The day before had been a holiday and everyone had been at the tavern. "If I don't strike it lucky soon, I'll kill myself, that's what I'll do. If I were only rich and respected like Big Zeke, or bold and powerful like Long-Shanks Schlurker, or famous and could toss the musicians thalers instead of kreutzers, like the Dance King! Where in the deuce does that fellow get his money?" He thought of all kinds of ways of making money, but he did not like any of them. Finally he remembered the tales about people who, in times gone by, had become rich through Dutch Michael and the glassmanikin. When his father was still alive, other poor people often came to visit and there were long discussions about rich people and how they had become wealthy. In these conversations the glassmanikin often played a part; in fact, if Peter thought hard, he could almost recall the charm one had to recite on Fir Tree Knoll in the middle of the forest to make him appear. It began:

> Treasure keeper in the forest green,
> Many a century hast thou seen,
> Thine are all woods where fir trees stand—

But try as he might, he could not remember the last line. He often wondered whether he shouldn't ask some old man how it went, but a certain shyness always restrained him from revealing his thoughts. Also it seemed to him that the story about the glassmanikin must not be very widely known and that only a few would remember the charm by heart, for there weren't many rich people in the region, and—why hadn't his father and other poor people tried their luck? At last he asked his mother, but she only told him what he already knew and could recite only the first line of the charm, though she did finally tell him that the sprite appeared only to those born on Sunday between eleven and twelve o'clock. He himself, she said, if he only knew the charm, might well catch sight of the mannikin, for he himself was born on Sunday at twelve noon.

When Charcoal Peter heard this, he was beside himself with glee and eagerness to undertake this adventure. It seemed to him enough to know only part of the charm and be born on Sunday—the glassmanikin would be bound to appear. One day, then, when he had sold his charcoal, he did not light a fresh kiln but put on his father's best jerkin and new red stockings, set his Sunday hat on his head, took his five-foot blackthorn staff in his hand, and bade his mother adieu.

"I have to go to the city hall," he said; "we'll soon be drawing lots to see who's going to be a soldier, and I want to remind the magistrate once more that you are a widow and I am your only son."

His mother praised his resolution, but instead of going to the city hall, he headed for Fir Tree Knoll. This elevation lies at the highest point of the Black Forest and for a two hour walk in any direction there stood at that time no village, not even a hut, for the superstitious inhabitants considered the region unsafe. And tall and splendid as the fir trees stood there, they were reluctant to fell them, for it had not infrequently happened that the axes of woodmen working there flew from the handle and into their legs, or that the trees suddenly toppled, taking the men with them, injuring and even killing them. Besides, they could have used even the finest timber in that part of the forest only for firewood, for the timber merchants refused to incorporate a single log from Fir Tree Knoll into their rafts, because, so the story went, both men and timber would be lost if there was a log from the knoll in the raft. Thus it was that on Fir Tree Knoll the trees grew so dense and so high that even at midday it was almost like night, and Peter Munk felt a shudder run down his spine when he entered this part of the forest. He heard no voice, no step but his own, no ax; even the birds seemed to avoid this dense fir-tree darkness.

He had now reached the top of the knoll and was standing before a fir of immense girth, one the Dutch shipbuilders would have given many hundred guilders for, on the spot. "Here," he thought, "must be where the treasure keeper lives." He doffed his Sunday hat, bowed deeply before the tree, cleared his throat and said in an unsteady voice, "I wish you a blessed evening, Mr. Glassman." But there was no answer, everything was as still as before. "Maybe I have to say the charm," he thought and murmured:

> Treasure keeper in the forest green,
> Many a century hast thou seen,
> Thine are all woods where fir trees stand—

As he spoke these words, he saw to his great fright a very small, queer figure peering out from behind the giant fir. It seemed to him he had seen the glassmanikin, just as people described him: black jerkin, red stockings, little hat, everything just so. He even thought he had seen the pale, fine-featured, intelligent face that people spoke of. But alas! as quickly as he had peered forth, the glassmanikin no less quickly disappeared.

"Mr. Glassman," Peter Munk called out after some hesitation, "please don't take me for a fool. If you think I didn't see you, Mr. Glassman, you're much mistaken. I saw you peeking out from behind the tree."

Still no answer; only now and again Peter thought he heard a soft, hoarse chuckle behind the tree. Finally his impatience overcame his fear and he called out, "Just wait, you little rascal, I'll get you!" With a bound he was behind the great fir, but there was no treasure keeper in the forest green, only a little squirrel scampering up the tree.

Peter Munk shook his head. He realized that he had been partially successful in his conjuration and that perhaps he lacked only the final rhyme of the spell in order to be able to tempt forth Mr.

Glassman, but, wrack his brains as he might, he couldn't think of it. A squirrel showed itself on the lower branches of the fir as if encouraging him or mocking him. It cleaned its fur, curled up its bushy tail, and looked at him, bright-eyed, until Peter was almost afraid to be alone with it, for the squirrel first seemed to have a human face and to be wearing a three-cornered hat, then it was like any other squirrel, except that it had red stockings on its hind legs and was wearing black shoes. In short, it was a merry little beast, but Charcoal Peter still had the shudders: he was sure something uncanny was going on.

With more rapid steps than he had come Peter started on his way back. The darkness of the fir forest seemed to be growing blacker, the trees to be standing closer together; he felt such dread that he broke into a trot and his heart did not begin to beat more slowly until he at last heard in the distance the barking of dogs and soon afterwards glimpsed the smoke of a hut among the trees. But when he came nearer and saw the dress of the people near the hut, he realized that in his anxiety he had run in the wrong direction, and instead of reaching the glassmakers had come to the raftsmen. The people who lived in the hut were woodcutters—an old man, his son, evidently the head of the family, and several older grandchildren. They were glad to let Peter spend the night with them and asked neither his name nor his dwelling. They gave him apple wine to drink and for the evening meal served a large woodcock, the most delicious of all Black Forest dishes.

After supper the housewife and her daughters sat down with their distaffs around the big pine chip torch, which the boys kept supplying with fresh resin to make it burn brighter, while the grandfather, the guest, and the husband smoked their pipes and watched the women, and the boys busied themselves with carving wooden spoons and forks. Outside in the forest the wind was howling and raging in the firs; now and again one could hear a violent crash—it often seemed as though whole trees had been blown over. The boys wanted to rush out into the forest to watch this awesome spectacle, but their grandfather called them back with a stern glance and said, "I wouldn't advise anyone to step outside the door right now. He'd never come back again. Dutch Michael is cutting himself a new raft in the forest."

The boys stared at him wide-eyed. They had no doubt heard of

Dutch Michael, but now begged their grandfather to tell all about him for once, and not leave out anything. Peter Munk, who had heard only vague rumors about Dutch Michael on his side of the forest, also joined in, asking the old man who he might be and where he came from.

"He is the master of this forest, and to judge from the fact that at your age you still don't know that, you must live on the other side of Fir Tree Knoll or even farther away. Good, I'll tell you what I know about him and how the story goes. About a hundred years ago, at least that's what my grandfather used to say, there was no more honest folk in the world than the Black Foresters. Now, since there's so much money circulating in the region, people are dishonest and crooked. The young fellows dance and hoot on Sundays, and swear fit to frighten you. In those days it was different, and even if he were to look into the window this minute, I'd still say as I've said before: Dutch Michael is to blame for all this mischief. But, to get on with my story, a hundred years and more ago there lived a rich timber merchant who had many hired men; he traded far down the Rhine, and his business prospered, for he was a good, God-fearing man. One evening there comes to his door a man such as he had never seen before. His dress was like that of the Black Foresters, but he was a good head taller than the tallest man—you wouldn't have believed there could be such a giant. The fellow asks for work, and the timber merchant, seeing that he was strong and could carry great loads, proposed a wage and they shook on it. This Michael was a workman such as the timber merchant had never had. In felling trees he was worth three men, and if six were carrying one end of a log, he carried the other end alone. But after he had cut trees for a year, he goes up one day to the merchant and says, 'I've been cutting trees long enough, now I'd like to see where my logs go to. How about letting me steer a raft?'

"The timber merchant answered, 'I won't stand in your way, Michael, if you want to see a bit of the world, though I need strong chaps like you for felling trees; on the rafts, it's skill that counts, but try it once anyway.'

"And so the matter was settled. The raft that Michael was to take downstream had eight links, and in the last one were the largest timbers. But what happened? The evening before setting

192 · Wilhelm Hauff

off Michael brings eight more beams down to the water, thicker and longer than any you ever saw, and he's carrying them on his shoulder as though they were raft poles. No one could believe it. Where he cut them nobody knows to this day.

"The timber merchant was inwardly delighted when he thought of the price this lumber would fetch, but Michael said, 'There, I'll ride on these, I can't make any headway on those splinters.' His master wanted to give him a pair of raftsmen's boots out of gratitude, but he tossed them aside and produced a pair such as no man ever wore; my grandfather vowed they weighed a hundred pounds and were five feet high.

"The raft cast off, and if Michael had earlier amazed the woodcutters, it was now the turn of the raftsmen to be astonished, for instead of moving more slowly, as they had thought it would because of the enormous logs, the raft, as soon as it reached the Neckar, flew like an arrow. If the river made a bend where the raftsmen always had trouble holding into the current and not grounding on sand and gravel, Michael simply jumped into the water, gave the raft a tug to the left or right so that it easily slipped past, and when they came to a straight stretch, he ran forward onto the first link, made everyone set their poles beside the raft, stuck his great weaver's beam into the gravel, and with *one* shove they were flying downstream, fields and trees and villages flitting past their line of sight. In this way they arrived in half the usual time at Cologne on the Rhine, where they had always sold their timber. But now Michael said, 'You're fine merchants, you fellows! Use your heads! Do you think that in Cologne they want all this timber for their own use? No, they buy it from you for half what it's worth and then sell it at a high price in Holland. Let's sell the small stuff here and go on to Holland with the big stuff. What we take in above the going price in Cologne is just so much in our pockets.'

"So spoke cunning Michael, and the others fell in with his proposal, some because they wanted to see Holland, some because of the money. Only one man was honest enough to warn them against risking their master's property and cheating him of the higher price, but they wouldn't listen to him and soon forgot his words, all except Dutch Michael. So they sped down the Rhine with their load; Michael steered the raft and brought them safely to Rotterdam. There they were offered four times the usual price, and Michael's tremendous beams in particular brought an exorbitant sum. When the Black Foresters saw so much money, they could hardly contain themselves for joy. Michael divided their gains: one-third for the timber merchant, two-thirds for themselves. And now they trotted to the taverns and sat down with sailors and other disreputable characters, squandering their money on drink, women, and gaming. But the honest man, who had advised them against the course they took, Dutch Michael sold to a slave trader and he was never heard of again. From that time on Holland was paradise for the lads of the Black Forest, and Dutch Michael was their king. The timber merchants did not find out about these transactions for a long time, and before you knew it, money, cursing and swearing, bad morals, drunkenness, and gaming were introduced into this part of the world from Holland.

"When the news got about, Dutch Michael was nowhere to be found, but he's not dead either; for a hundred years he's been haunting our forest, and they say he's helped many a man to become rich, but—at the cost of their poor souls. I'll not say more. But this much is certain: on stormy nights like this one, he seeks out the finest trees on Fir Tree Knoll, where you're not supposed to cut timber—my father once saw him snap a trunk four feet thick as if it were a reed. These logs he gives to those who turn from the straight and narrow and follow him; then at midnight they bring them down to the river and steer for Holland. If I were king and ruled in Holland, I'd have him blasted with shot and shell, for any ship that has even *one* beam from one of Dutch Michael's rafts is bound to founder. That's why we hear of all these shipwrecks. How else could a great, strong ship, as big as a church, be lost at sea? And every stormy night, when Dutch Michael fells a fir in the Black Forest, one of the old timbers bursts from the side of a ship; the water pours in and crew and cargo must perish. That's the story of Dutch Michael, and it's true as can be that all the wickedness in the Black Forest is due to him. Oh, he can make you rich!" the old man added, mysteriously lowering his voice, "but *I* wouldn't want to be beholden to him. Not for the world would I be in the shoes of Big Zeke or Long-Shanks Schlurker. They say the Dance King is in league with him too!"

The storm had died down while the old man was telling his tale.

The girls shyly lit their lamps and went to bed, while the men laid a sackful of leaves on the bench near the stove as a pillow for Peter Munk and wished him good night.

Charcoal Peter had never had such disturbing dreams as those he dreamt this night. Now he thought that the sinister, gigantic figure of Dutch Michael was tearing open the window and holding out to him with his great long arm a bagful of gold pieces, shaking them and making them jingle sweet and clear; then again he saw friendly little Mr. Glassman riding about the room on a huge, green bottle and he was sure he heard his hoarse chuckle, as he had on Fir Tree Knoll; then again there was a humming noise in his left ear, which said:

> In Holland there's gold
> You can have, if you're bold,
> For a little 'tis sold,
> Gold, gold!

Then he would hear in his right ear the verse about the treasure-keeper in the forest green, and a soft voice would whisper, "Stupid Charcoal Peter, stupid Peter Munk, can't even think of a rhyme for *stand,* and yet you were born on Sunday at twelve noon. Rhyme, Peter, rhyme!"

He sighed and groaned in his sleep, he struggled to find a rhyme, but since in all his life he had never made one, his dream labor was in vain. When he awakened at the first light of dawn, his dream seemed to him strange indeed. He sat down at the table with folded arms and pondered the whisperings still sounding in his ears. "Rhyme, stupid Charcoal Peter, rhyme," he said to himself, tapping his forehead with his finger, but no rhyme would come. While he was still sitting there, staring blankly before him and trying to think of a rhyme for *stand,* three young woodmen passed by the house. As they walked by, one of them sang:

> On the hilltop I stand
> And gaze into the dale,
> She waves her dear hand
> And it makes my heart fail.

That shot through Peter like a bolt of lightning. He jerked himself up and dashed out of the house, thinking he hadn't heard right, ran after the three fellows and grabbed the singer roughly by the arm. "Hold on, friend," he cried, "what was that rhyme to *stand* just now? Do me a favor and recite what you sang."

"What's the matter with you, fellow?" answered the woodman; "I can sing what I like, and if you don't let go of my arm—"

"No, I tell you, recite what you sang!" yelled Peter, almost beside himself and grasping the other's arm still harder. When his companions saw this, they did not wait but fell upon poor Peter with stinging blows, giving him such a drubbing that he had to let go of the third man's sleeve, and sank to his knees, knocked out. "So, now you've had it," they said with a laugh, "and take note, you crazy fool, that you don't attack people like us on the open road."

"Oh, I'll take note," said Peter, moaning, "but since I've had my drubbing, please be kind enough to tell me exactly what he was singing."

They laughed again and made fun of him, but the singer recited the verse for him and they went their way, laughing and yodeling.

"Ah hah, *hand,*" said poor Peter, painfully struggling to his feet, "*hand, stand.* Now, Mr. Glassman, we'll have a further word with each other."

He went back into the hut, fetched his hat and long staff, took leave of his hosts and started out for Fir Tree Knoll. He walked slowly and pensively, for now he had to think of a verse; finally, when he was already in the vicinity of the knoll, and the firs were becoming denser and taller, he found his verse and jumped for joy. At that moment a gigantic figure dressed like a raftsman and carrying a pole as long as a ship's mast stepped from behind the trees. Peter Munk almost sank to his knees when he saw the giant walking slowly beside him, for he thought, "That's Dutch Michael and no mistake about it!" The fearsome figure still said nothing; Peter glanced at him fearfully out of the corner of his eye from time to time. He was at least a head taller than the tallest man Peter had ever seen; his face was no longer young, and yet it wasn't old, though furrowed with wrinkles. He was wearing a linen jerkin, and his tremendous boots, drawn up high on his legs, were well known to Peter from the tales he had heard.

"Peter Munk, what are you doing on Fir Tree Knoll?" asked the forest king at length in a deep, booming voice.

"Oh, good morning, countryman," answered Peter, trying to appear unafraid, though he was trembling like a leaf. "I'm just passing this way on the road home."

"Peter Munk," said the giant, with a fearsome, piercing look, "your road does not lie through this grove."

"Well, no, not exactly," said Peter, "but it's hot today and I thought it would be cooler here."

"Don't lie to me, Charcoal Peter!" Dutch Michael thundered, "or I'll knock you down with this pole. Do you think I didn't see you hanging around that dwarf?" he added, lowering his voice. "Come on, that was a stupid trick, and it's a good thing you didn't know the charm; he's a skinflint, the little chap, won't give you much, and those he does give something have no joy in it. Peter, you're a poor devil and I feel sorry for you. Such a lively, handsome lad—you could amount to something in the world—and to have to be a charcoal burner! While others are shaking thalers and ducats out of their sleeves, you've got scarcely two bits to spend. That's a miserable life."

"You're right there, no mistake—it's a miserable life."

"Well, that wouldn't make any difference to me," Michael went on. "I've helped many a good chap out of his misery, you wouldn't be the first. Tell me, how many hundred do you need, just for a start?"

He chinked the money in his enormous purse, and it sounded as it had in last night's dream. But Peter's heart trembled fearfully and painfully at these words, and he felt cold and hot by turns. Dutch Michael did not look like he was one to give away money just out of pity, without demanding something in return. He remembered the old man's mysterious words about those who had become rich, and, seized by inexplicable fear and anxiety, he cried out, "Thank you, sir! but I don't want anything to do with you. I know who you are," and he took to his heels as fast as he could go. But the forest king strode along beside him with huge steps, muttering in a hollow, menacing voice, "You'll regret it, Peter, it's written on your brow, I can read it in your eye. You won't escape me. Don't run so fast, listen to a word of reason, we're already at the boundary of my territory."

When Peter heard this and saw a narrow ditch not far ahead, he ran all the harder, in order to pass the boundary, while Michael pursued him cursing and threatening. With a desperate leap he cleared the ditch, for he saw that the giant had raised his pole and was about to smash him with it. He landed on the other side and the pole splintered in the air as though an invisible wall stood between them. A long piece fell at Peter's feet.

He picked it up exultantly, meaning to throw it back at brutal Michael, but at this instant he felt the length of wood moving in his hand and saw to his horror that he was holding a great serpent, which was already writhing up on him with slavering tongue and glittering eye. He tried to let go of it, but it had already wrapped itself about his arm and was coming nearer and nearer to his face with swaying head. At that moment a great woodcock came swooping down with a rush of wings, seized the serpent's head in its beak and bore it aloft, while Dutch Michael, who had observed all this from the other side of the ditch, howled and screamed and tore his hair to see the serpent overcome by a stronger foe.

Exhausted and shaking, Peter continued on his way. The path grew steeper, the region wilder, and he soon found himself beside the tremendous fir tree. He bowed to the invisible glassmanikin, as he had the day before, and then said:

> Treasure keeper in the forest green,
> Many a century hast thou seen,
> Thine are all woods where fir trees stand,
> Only Sunday's child can know thy hand.

"Not a very good last verse, Charcoal Peter, but since it's you, we'll let it pass," said a soft, gentle voice close beside him. He looked about him in astonishment. Beneath a beautiful fir sat a little old man in a black jerkin and red stockings with a big hat on his head. He had a delicate, friendly face and a beard as fine as cobwebs. He was smoking, strangely enough, a pipe made of glass, and when Peter came nearer, he was amazed to see that the little man's clothing, shoes, and hat were also made of colored glass, which was as pliable as though it were molten and conformed to every movement of the body like cloth.

198 · Wilhelm Hauff

"You met that oaf, Dutch Michael?" said the little man with an odd wheeze between each word. "He tried to give you a good scare, but I confiscated his fancy club, he'll never see that again."

"Yes, Mr. Treasurekeeper," Peter answered with a deep bow, "I was scared all right. I take it you must have been Sir Woodcock who bit the serpent dead? Thank you very much. I've come to you for advice. I'm not getting along well at all; a charcoal burner can't get anywhere in the world, and since I'm still young, I thought something worthwhile might yet become of me, especially when I see how other people often get so far in a short time; Big Zeke, for example, and the Dance King, they've got piles of money."

"Peter," said the little man in a solemn voice, blowing a puff of smoke into the air, "Peter, don't talk to me about *those* fellows. What good does it do them to be apparently happy for a few years and then afterwards to be all the more miserable? You must not despise your trade. Your father and your grandfather were honest men, and it was their trade too! I hope it's not just love of idleness that leads you to me."

Peter blushed, taken aback by the little man's seriousness. "No," he said, "I know, Mr. Treasurekeeper, that idleness is the source of all vice, but you can't blame me if I like another station in life better than my own. A charcoal burner is simply a nobody in this world—the glassmakers and raftsmen and clockmakers are all much more respected."

"Pride often comes before a fall," replied the little lord of the fir trees in a somewhat more friendly tone. "You're a strange race, you humans! Rarely is one of you satisfied with the condition in which he was born and bred, and I'll bet that if you were a glassmaker, you'd want to be a timber merchant, and if you were a timber merchant, you'd envy the forester or the magistrate—they get free housing. But so be it. If you'll promise me to work hard, I'll help you to improve your lot, Peter Munk. I make it a rule to grant every Sunday's child who finds the way to me three wishes. The first two I grant at once, but the third I can refuse, if it is foolish. So go ahead and wish for something. But, Peter, something good and useful."

"Hooray! You're a fine little glassman, and they're right to call you Treasurekeeper, you're really in charge of treasures. H-m-m, since I can now wish for whatever my heart desires, my first wish is to be able to dance better than the Dance King and always to have as much money in my pocket as Big Zeke."

"You fool!" said the little man wrathfully; "what a pitiable wish that is, to be able to dance well and have money for gambling! Aren't you ashamed, stupid Peter, to cheat yourself that way out of your happiness? What good will it do you and your poor mother if you can dance? What good is your money, if you only want to spend it in the tavern, which is where it will stay, like the miserable Dance King's? Then you'll be broke again in a week and be as poor as ever. You still have one more free wish, but see to it that it's a more sensible one."

Peter scratched his head and then said after some hesitation, "Well then, I wish for the finest and most productive glassworks in the whole Black Forest, with all the equipment and money to run it."

"Is that all?" asked the little man with a worried look. "Is that all, Peter?"

"H-m-m, well—you could add a horse and a cart—"

"Oh, you stupid Charcoal Peter!" cried the little man, throwing his glass pipe in disgust against a big tree and shattering it into a thousand pieces. "Horse? Cart? Understanding, I tell you, understanding, good common sense and insight, that's what you should have wished for, not for a horse and cart. Well, don't look so downcast, we'll see that you don't suffer for it; on the whole, your second wish wasn't so foolish. A good glassworks will make a living for man and master, but you still could have mentioned insight and understanding, then horses and carts would have followed of themselves."

"But Mr. Treasurekeeper," replied Peter, "I still have one wish left, so I could wish for understanding, if you feel it's so important."

"Nothing doing. You'll get into plenty of scrapes where you'll be glad to have a wish left. Now go home. Here are two thousand gulden," said the fir sprite, pulling a small purse out of his pocket, "and that's all you get. Don't come back asking for money, because I'd have to hang you to the highest tree. That's been my rule ever since I've been living in this forest. Three days ago old Winkfritz died. He owned the big glassworks in the lower valley. Go there tomorrow morning and make a fair offer for the business.

Stay out of trouble, work hard. I'll visit you now and then and give you some advice, seeing you failed to wish for understanding. But I'll tell you truly: your first wish was bad. Watch out about trotting to the tavern—that never did anyone any good for long."

While he was talking, the little man had pulled out a new pipe made of the most beautiful opalescent glass, filled it with dry fir cones, and stuck it into his toothless mouth. Then he produced an enormous burning glass, stepped into the sunlight, and lit his pipe. He then shook hands with Peter in a friendly fashion, offered him another piece or two of advice, meanwhile puffing faster and faster on his pipe, until he finally disappeared in a cloud of smoke that smelled like genuine Dutch tobacco and slowly curled away among the tops of the fir trees.

When Peter got home, he found his mother in great distress, for the good woman was sure her son had been drafted into the army. But he was in a merry mood and told her he had met a friend in the forest who had loaned him money to begin some other business besides charcoal burning. And although his mother had lived for thirty years in a charcoal burner's hut and was as used to the sight of a sooty man as a miller's wife is to her husband's flour-covered face, she was still vain enough, as soon as her Peter held out the prospect of a brighter future, to despise her former condition and to say, "Yes, as the mother of a man who owns a glassworks, I'll be something more than my neighbors Gretel and Beth and can sit in a front pew at church, like the important people."

Her son soon came to an agreement with the inheritors of the glass factory. He kept on the workmen who were already there and had them make glass day and night. At first he liked his trade very well. He would stroll leisurely through the factory with a dignified air, poking his nose in here and there and cracking some joke to make the workmen laugh. His greatest pleasure was to watch them blow glass, and he sometimes tried it himself, shaping strange figures out of the molten mass. But he soon tired of this and began to come to the factory first for only an hour a day, then every second day, finally only once a week, and his workmen did as they pleased. This was all due to his running to the tavern. The Sunday after he had come back from Fir Tree Knoll he went to the tavern, where the Dance King was already leaping about on the dance floor and Big Zeke was sitting behind a liter of beer, throwing dice for crown thalers. Peter immediately dived into his pocket to see if the glassmanikin had kept his word, and sure enough! his pocket was bulging with silver and gold. He also felt a twitching in his legs, as if they wanted to leap and dance, and when the first dance was over, he took his place with his partner at the head of the line next to the Dance King. If the Dance King leapt three feet, Peter bounded four, and if the Dance King executed elegant, exotic steps, Peter twisted and turned his legs in such a way that the onlookers gaped in amazement. When those at the dance heard that Peter had bought a glassworks, when they saw that he never danced by the musicians without tossing them four bits, their astonishment was boundless. Some thought he had found a treasure trove in the forest, some that he had inherited a fortune, but they all took him for a man of standing, just because he had so much money. That same evening he gambled away twenty gulden, and still his pocket chinked and jingled as if there were a hundred thalers in it.

When Peter saw how respected he was, he couldn't contain himself for pride and joy. He spent money with both hands and gave a lot to the poor, for he knew what it was to be poverty-stricken. The Dance King's skills were put to shame by the supernatural skills of the new dancer, and Peter was given the name of Dance Emperor. The most venturesome gamblers did not play for as high stakes as he, but they also did not lose as much. And yet the more he lost, the more he won. That was just what he had asked of the little glassman. He had wished always to have in his pocket as much as Big Zeke, and it was to Big Zeke that he lost his money. If he lost twenty, thirty gulden at a throw, he at once found them back in his pocket when Zeke scooped in his gains. Gradually he became more notorious for riotous living and gambling than the worst characters in the Black Forest, and people called him Gambling Pete more often than Dance Emperor, for he had begun to play on weekdays as well as Sundays. His glassworks now began to go downhill, and Peter's lack of common sense alone was to blame. He had made as much glass as possible, but with the factory he had not bought the secret of where he could best dispose of his glass. At last, he did not know what to do with all his wares and sold them at half price to peddlers, just to be able to pay his workmen.

One evening he was going home from the tavern consumed with

worry about the decline of his fortunes, in spite of all the wine he had drunk to cheer himself up. He suddenly noticed that someone was walking along beside him, and lo and behold! it was the glassmanikin. Peter became excited and angry and swore by high heaven that the little fellow was responsible for his bad luck.

"What am I supposed to do now with my horse and wagon?" he cried. "What good is my factory and all my glass? Even when I was still a miserable charcoal burner, I was happier than now. I had no worries. Now I don't know when the bailiff is going to come and assess my goods and distrain me for debt!"

"Is that the way it is?" replied the glassman. "I'm supposed to be to blame because you're in trouble? Is that the thanks for my kindness? Who told you to make such foolish wishes? You wanted to be a glassmaker and didn't know where to sell your glass. Didn't I tell you to be careful what you wished for? Understanding, Peter, common sense, that's what you lack."

"Understanding and common sense, indeed! I'm as smart as anyone and I'll prove it to you, Mr. Glassman," cried Peter, seizing the gnome roughly by the collar. "Have I got you now, Mr. Treasurekeeper in the forest green?" he shouted. "And now I'll make my third wish, and you'd better grant it. Right here on the spot I want twice one hundred thousand thalers in hard cash, and a house and—ouch!" He cried out, waving his hand in the air, for the gnome had transformed himself into molten glass that burned his hand like a furnace. The glassman himself, however, was nowhere to be seen.

For several days Peter's swollen hand reminded him of his folly and ingratitude. Then he drowned his conscience and said, "Suppose they do sell the glassworks and everything I own, I've still got Big Zeke. As long as he has money on Sundays, I can't lack any either."

And that's the way things were, until one day a strange kind of arithmetic changed things.

One Sunday Peter came driving up to the tavern, and people stuck their heads out of the window, one saying, "There comes Gambling Pete," and a second, "Yes, it's the Dance Emperor, the rich glassmaker," while a third shook his head and said, "With wealth like that he can do it, but they say he has all kinds of debts, and they even say it won't be long before he has the bailiff on his neck." Meanwhile, rich Peter gravely greeted those at the window, got down from his carriage, and called out to the tavern keeper, "Good afternoon, landlord! Is Big Zeke already there?" A deep voice replied, "Come on in, Peter! We've saved a place for you at the card table." Peter walked into the tavern parlor, reached into his pocket, and knew that Zeke must be well provided, for his own pocket was overflowing.

He sat down at the table with the others and began playing, now winning, now losing. They played until evening, when other honest people went home. Then they played by lamplight until two more said, "That's enough, we have to go home to our families." But Gambling Pete invited Big Zeke to stay on. At first, he was reluctant, but finally said, "Good. I'll count my money and then we'll shoot dice for five gulden a throw—anything less is just child's play." He pulled out his purse and counted his money. He found one hundred gulden in coin, and Gambling Pete now knew how much he himself had. But though Zeke had been winning before, he now began to lose one time after another, cursing frightfully all the while. If he threw a triplet, so did Peter, but always two points higher. Finally he laid his last five gulden on the table and cried, "One more time, and if I lose that, I'm still not stopping; you'll lend me some of your winnings, Peter, one honest man helps another!"

"As much as you want, even if it's a hundred," replied the Dance Emperor, tickled at his winnings. Big Zeke shook the dice and threw fifteen. "Triplet!" he cried; "now see if you can beat that." But Peter threw eighteen, and a familiar deep voice behind him said, "So, that does it."

He looked around, and there was Dutch Michael looming up behind him. Startled, he dropped the money he had just scooped in. But Big Zeke did not see the giant and asked Peter to lend him ten gulden. Peter reached into his pocket, but there was no money there; he felt in the other pocket—nothing there either; he turned his coat inside out and shook it, but not a red cent fell out, and now he recalled his first wish: to always have as much money as Big Zeke. Everything had disappeared like smoke.

Big Zeke and the landlord looked at him in astonishment, watching him search in vain for his money. They could not believe he didn't have any more; but when they finally searched his pock-

ets themselves, they became angry and swore that Peter was a wizard and had caused the money to fly to his house. Peter valiantly
denied it, but appearances were against him. Zeke said he would
spread this story all over the Black Forest, and the landlord promised him he would go into town the first thing in the morning and
denounce him to the magistrate for a wizard, and, he added, he
hoped he'd live to see him burned. They then fell upon him in a
rage, tore his shirt from his back, and threw him out of the door.

No star shone in the sky as Peter sadly stole home; nonetheless,
he could recognize a dark figure walking along beside him and
finally heard the words, "It's all over with you, Peter Munk, your
glory's past and gone. I could have told you that before, but you
wouldn't listen and ran to that stupid glass-dwarf. Now you see
what comes of it when you disregard my advice. Just give me a
chance, I have sympathy for your misfortunes. No one who turned
to me ever regretted it, and if you don't mind the walk, you can
find me tomorrow morning on Fir Tree Knoll—just let me know
you're there." Peter well knew who was talking to him like this,
and he was full of dread. He made no reply, but ran towards his
house.

When Peter went to his glassworks on Monday morning, not
only were his workmen there, but certain other people too, namely,
the magistrate and three of his beadles. The magistrate wished
Peter good morning, asked how he had slept, and then produced
a long list containing the names of Peter's creditors. "Can you pay
or not?" the magistrate asked sternly. "Make it short, I haven't
any time to waste and it's a good three hours to the debtors'
prison." Peter was in despair; he confessed he had no more money
and left it to the magistrate to appraise his house, glassworks,
barn, horses, and wagons; but while the magistrate and his men
were going around inspecting and estimating the value of his
property, Peter was thinking, "It's not so far to Fir Tree Knoll;
since the *dwarf* didn't help me, I'll give the *giant* a chance," and
he headed for the knoll as fast as if the bailiff were already at his
heels. As he ran by the place where he had first spoken to the
glassmanikin, it seemed to him as though he were being restrained
by an invisible hand, but he tore himself loose and ran on to the
boundary he had taken note of before, and no sooner had he
breathlessly called out "Dutch Michael! Dutch Michael!" than the
gigantic raftsman stood before him, his great pole on his shoulder.

"So you did come," said Dutch Michael with a laugh. "Did they try to skin you and sell your hide to your creditors? Well, just take it easy; as I told you before, your trouble's all due to the glassman, that sanctimonious separatist. When you give someone something, you've got to really give it, not just halfway, like that stingy runt. Come along," he continued, turning toward the forest, "follow me to my house and we'll see if we can't strike a bargain."

"Strike a bargain?" thought Peter. "What can he want from me, what have I got to trade him? Am I supposed to become his servant or something?" They climbed a steep forest path and suddenly found themselves beside a dark, deep, precipitous chasm. Dutch Michael leapt down the cliff as though it were an easy flight of stairs, but Peter almost fainted, for Michael, when he arrived at the bottom, made himself as tall as a church steeple and extended an arm as long as a weaver's beam, with a hand on it as broad as a tavern table, and cried up to Peter in a voice like a funeral bell, "Just sit down on my hand and grab my fingers, then you won't fall." Trembling, Peter did as he was told, sat down on the hand, and grasped the giant's thumb.

It was a long, long way down, but to Peter's surprise it didn't get darker in the depths; on the contrary, the daylight seemed to grow brighter in the chasm, so bright it hurt his eyes. As Peter was descending, Dutch Michael had made himself smaller again and now stood in his former shape before a modest, well-built house, such as those of the rich peasants in the Black Forest. The room into which he led Peter was in no way different from that of other people, except that it seemed deserted.

The wooden clock on the wall, the enormous tiled stove, the wide settles, the utensils on the windowsills, all were here as they were everywhere. Michael showed him a seat behind a large table, then went and fetched a pitcher of wine and glasses. He poured a drink and they chatted. Dutch Michael told him about the pleasures of the world, about foreign lands, beautiful cities and rivers, so that in the end Peter was overcome with longing to see these things and frankly admitted as much to the Dutchman.

"When you had courage and bodily strength and could undertake anything you liked, a couple of beats of that stupid heart of yours could make you tremble; and then there was wounded pride, honor, your misfortunes—why should a sensible fellow need to bother about such things? Did you feel it in your head the last time someone called you a cheat and a liar? Did you get a stomachache when the magistrate came to throw you out of your house? Tell me, what was it that hurt?"

"My heart," said Peter, pressing his hand to his breast, for it seemed to him that his heart was jumping with anxiety.

"If you don't mind my saying so, you've thrown away hundreds of gulden on lousy beggars and other riffraff. What good did it do you? Oh yes, they blessed you and wished you health, but were you any healthier for that? For half the price you could have retained a private physician. Blessing indeed—that's a fine blessing, to be dispossessed! And what was it made you reach into your pocket every time a ragged beggar held out his greasy hat? Your heart, my friend, nothing but your heart, not your eyes, nor your tongue, your arms, your legs, but your heart. As the saying goes, you took it too much to heart."

"But how can a person get used to not acting that way? Right now, though I'm trying as hard as I can to suppress it, my heart's pounding and paining me."

"*You*, of course," said Michael with a laugh, "can't do anything about it, poor wretch that you are. But give me that gently throbbing organ, and you'll soon see how well off you are."

"Give you my heart?" cried Peter, horrified. "Why, I'd die on the spot! No, never!"

"Yes, if one of your fine surgeons were to cut it out of your breast, you'd die, no doubt about it. But with me it's different. Just come into the next room and see for yourself."

Michael got up and opened the door to an adjoining room and led Peter in. His heart contracted painfully as he crossed the threshold, but he paid no attention, for the sight that met his eyes was strange and surprising. On several wooden shelves there stood glasses full of a transparent liquid, and in each glass there lay a heart. Peter read the labels pasted on the glasses with eager curiosity. There was the heart of the magistrate in F., there the heart of Big Zeke, the heart of the Dance King, the heart of the head forester; there were six hearts of grain speculators, eight of recruiting officers, and three of usurers: in short, it was a collection of the most respected hearts within a radius of twenty miles.

"You see," said Dutch Michael, "all these have cast aside life's woes and worries; not one of these hearts now beats careworn with anxiety, and the former owners are glad to be rid of the restless guest."

"But what do they now have in their breast instead?" asked Peter, who felt faint from all he had seen.

"This," replied Michael. He reached into a drawer and took out—*a stone heart.*

"That?" said Peter, who could not help shuddering. "A heart of marble? But listen, Mr. Dutch Michael, that must feel mighty cold in one's breast."

"No, just pleasantly cool. Why should a heart be warm? In the winter its warmth does you no good, a good shot of brandy is better than a warm heart, and in the summer, when it's hot and sultry—why, you can't imagine how a heart like this keeps you cool. And as I said, neither fear nor worry, neither silly pity nor any other kind of distress can move such a heart."

"And is that all you can offer me?" asked Peter, more than a bit disappointed. "I was hoping for money, and you want to give me a stone!"

"Well, I should imagine a hundred thousand gulden should be enough for the time being. If you invest it cleverly, you can soon be a millionaire."

"A hundred thousand!" cried poor Peter Charcoal Burner, beside himself with joy. "Now, don't throb so mightily in my breast, we'll soon be quit of each other. It's a deal, Michael; give me the stone and the money, and you can remove this restless inmate from its house."

"I thought you were a sensible chap," answered the Dutchman with a friendly smile. "Come on, let's have another drink, then I'll pay you the money."

They sat down again in the living room to their wine, drank, and then drank some more, until Peter fell into a deep sleep.

Charcoal Peter awoke to the merry notes of a post horn, and lo and behold! he was sitting in a fine carriage driving along a broad highway. When he leaned out of the window, he could see the Black Forest behind him in the blue distance. At first he could not believe that it was he himself riding in the carriage. His clothes were no longer the same as those he had worn yesterday; nonetheless, he could recall every detail about himself quite clearly, so he finally gave up puzzling and cried, "Charcoal Peter I must be, that's for sure, and no one else."

He was surprised that he could feel no touch of melancholy at leaving, for the first time, his homeland and its quiet forests, where he had lived so long. Not even when he thought of his mother, whom he was probably leaving behind helpless and destitute, could he shed a tear or heave a sigh—he was indifferent to everything. "Of course," he said, "tears and sighs, homesickness and longing all come from the heart and thanks to Dutch Michael mine is cold and made of stone."

He laid his hand on his breast. All was quiet there, nothing pulsed. "If he kept his word about the hundred thousand as well as he did about the heart, I'll be satisfied," he said, and he began to search about in the carriage. He found clothing of all kinds, anything he could possibly need, but no money. Finally he came across a purse with many thousand thalers in gold and notes drawn on banking houses in all the large cities. "Now I've got what I want," he thought, settled back in the corner of the carriage, and let himself be driven into the wide, wide world.

For two years he traveled about the world, looking up out of his carriage at the houses on the left and right, yet seeing nothing but the sign of the tavern where he meant to spend the night, running about the towns in which he stopped and having himself shown the local sights. But nothing gave him any pleasure, no picture gallery, no building, no music, no dance; nothing could move his heart of stone, and his eyes and ears were insensitive to all beauty. Nothing remained but the pleasure of eating, drinking, and sleeping, and thus did he live, traveling about the world without purpose, eating for amusement and sleeping out of boredom. Now and then, to be sure, he remembered that he had been happier and more cheerful when he was still poor and had had to work for a living. Then every distant view into the valley, all music and song had delighted him, then he had looked forward for hours to the simple meal his mother would bring out to him at the kiln. When he thought back on his past, it seemed to him very strange that now he could not even laugh, though he had once laughed at the slightest joke. Now, when others were mirthful, he screwed up his mouth out of politeness—but his heart could not smile. He felt that he was indeed perfectly calm, but he still did not feel content. It was not homesickness or melancholy, but emptiness, boredom, a joyless existence that finally drove him home again.

When he was driving eastward from Strasbourg and caught sight of the dark forests of his homeland, when he first saw again the sturdy figures and friendly, good-natured faces of the Black Foresters, when he heard the sounds of his native speech, ringing, deep, melodious, he quickly laid his hand to his heart, for his blood seemed to flow faster and he thought he ought to rejoice and weep at the same time, but—how could he be so foolish—he had a heart of stone. And stones are dead; they neither smile nor weep.

When he got home, he immediately went to see Dutch Michael, who received him with his old friendliness. "Michael," he said, "I've been on my travels and seen everything, but it's all stupid stuff. I was only bored. It's true, that stone thing of yours that I carry in my bosom shields me from many ills. I never get angry, I am never sad, but I'm also never happy. It's as if I were only half alive. Can't you liven my stone heart up a bit? Or, even better, give me back my old heart. I had gotten used to it after twenty-five years, and even if it played a stupid trick on me now and then, still it was a merry, inoffensive heart."

The forest giant gave a fierce, bitter laugh. "When you're dead, Peter Munk," he replied, "then you'll get everything you want, then you'll get your old tender, sensitive heart back again, and you'll feel whatever is in store for you, joy or sorrow. But in this life, my friend, it can never again be yours! Oh yes, Peter Munk, you've traveled all right, but the way you had to live it could do you no good. Now settle down somewhere in the forest, build yourself a house, get married, invest your capital. Your trouble was that you had no work. Because you were idle, you were bored, and now you blame everything on that innocent heart."

Peter realized that Michael was right so far as too much leisure was concerned and determined to become richer and richer. The Dutchman gave him another hundred thousand gulden and they parted good friends.

Word soon got around in the Black Forest that Charcoal Peter was back again, richer than ever. Things were now no different than before: when he had been reduced to beggary, they had thrown him out of the tavern, but now, when he made his first entry there one Sunday afternoon, they shook his hand, praised his horse, asked about his travels, and, when he again gambled with Big Zeke, his reputation was as exalted as ever. He was no longer engaged in glassmaking, but had become a timber merchant, though only for the sake of appearances. His real businesses were trading in grain and usury. Half the Black Forest was soon in debt to him; he lent money only at ten percent, or sold grain to the poor, when they could not pay immediately, for three times the market price. He was now a close friend of the magistrate, and if someone did not pay Peter Munk on the dot, the magistrate rode out with his officers, appraised the property, sold it up at once, and drove father, mother, and children into the forest. At first, this made rich Peter a bit uncomfortable, for the dispossessed people besieged his house, the men pleading for forbearance, the women trying to move his stone heart with their pleas, the children whining for a piece of bread. But after he had got himself a pair of huge mastiffs, this yowling, as he called it, soon stopped. He would whistle to his dogs, sic them on, and the crowd of beggars would take to their heels screaming.

It was an old woman who caused him the most trouble. She was none other than Dame Barbara Munk, Peter's mother. She had been reduced to utter poverty when they sold her house, and her rich son, when he returned, did not even go to see her. She appeared at his door now and then, aged, weak, and trembling, supporting herself with a cane. She did not dare come in, for he had once chased her away, but it pained her to have to live from the kindness of others when her own son could have so abundantly provided for her old age. But the cold heart remained untouched by the sight of her pale, familiar features, her pleading looks, her withered outstretched hand, and her infirm body. When she knocked at his door on Saturday evenings, he ill-humoredly produced a small coin, wrapped it in a piece of paper, and had it handed to her by a servant. He heard her quaking voice, thanking him and wishing him well on earth, he heard her turn, wheezing, from his door, but all he thought was that he had again thrown away his money.

Finally it occurred to him that he ought to get married. He knew that every father in the Black Forest would gladly give him his daughter's hand, but he was fussy about his choice, for he wanted people also to envy his good fortune and praise his wisdom in such a matter. For this reason he rode around everywhere in the region, searching here and there, but none of the Black Forest maidens seemed to him beautiful enough. After vainly going to all the dances, looking for the prize beauty, he at length heard that the most beautiful and virtuous girl in the whole Black Forest was the daughter of a poor woodcutter. She lived in seclusion, diligently keeping house for her father, and never went to dances, not even at Whitsuntide or fair time. When Peter heard of this local marvel, he determined to ask for her hand, and rode out to the woodcutter's hut. Lisbeth's father was astonished to see the fine gentleman, and he was even more astonished when he heard that rich Mr. Peter wanted to become his son-in-law. He did not hesitate long, for he thought that now all his worries were over; he accepted the offer without asking beautiful Lisbeth, and she, in her goodness, obediently gave Peter her hand.

But things did not go as well for the poor girl as she had dreamed. She thought she knew how to run a house, but nothing she did pleased Mr. Peter. She felt pity for the poor, and since her husband was rich, she thought there could be no harm in giving a wretched beggar a bit of money or in offering an old man a glass of schnaps; but when Mr. Peter found out about this one day, he scolded her fiercely: "Why are you squandering my money on tramps and beggars? Did you contribute anything to our marriage that you can give away? Your father's poverty wouldn't warm a pot of soup, and you throw away money like a princess. Let me catch you again and you'll find out what my hand feels like!"

Beautiful Lisbeth shut herself in her bedroom and wept at her husband's harshness, wishing she were back home in her father's lowly hut rather than living with this rich, stingy, hardhearted man. Alas! if she had only known that he had a heart of marble and could love neither her nor anyone else, she would not have been so surprised. Now, whenever she was sitting on her doorstep and a beggar came by, doffed his hat, and began his speech, she shut her eyes, in order not to have to look at his misery, and clenched her fists to keep herself from involuntarily reaching into her pocket for a coin. Thus it came to pass that beautiful Lisbeth got a bad reputation in the whole region, and people said she was even stingier than Peter Munk. One day she was sitting before her door spinning and humming a tune; she felt cheerful because of the lovely weather and because Mr. Peter had ridden away on an errand. A little old man came along carrying a great, heavy sack; Lisbeth heard him gasping for breath even at a distance. She looked at him sympathetically and thought, "A little old man like that shouldn't have to carry such a heavy burden."

Meanwhile the little man came panting and staggering towards her, and when he arrived in front of her, he almost collapsed beneath his load. "Oh, ma'm, please be so kind as to give me a drink of water," he gasped. "I can't go any farther, I'm dying of thirst."

"At your age you shouldn't be carrying a load like that," said Dame Lisbeth.

"You're right, but I have to work, I'm poor and must earn a living," he answered. "Oh, a rich lady like you doesn't know how oppressive poverty can be and how good a drink of fresh water tastes in this heat."

When she heard this, she hastened into the house, took a jug from the shelf and filled it with cold water; but when she returned and saw how miserable and downcast the little man was, sitting there on his sack, she felt deep pity for him, and, remembering that her husband was not at home, she set down the jug of water, fetched a cup and filled it with wine, placed a good piece of rye bread on top of it, and offered it to the old man. "Here, a sip of wine will do an elderly person like you more good than water," she said, "but don't drink it too fast, and eat the bread with it."

The little man looked at her in astonishment, and great tears stood in his old eyes. He drank and then said, "I've grown old, but I've not seen many people as kindly as you. You extend your gifts from the heart, Dame Lisbeth. In return, it will go well with you on this earth; such a heart must have its reward."

"That's right, and she'll have her reward on the spot," cried a terrible voice, and when they turned around, there stood Mr. Peter, his face crimson with rage.

"So you even pour my best wine for beggars and let tramps drink out of my private cup? Take that for your reward!"

Lisbeth fell at his feet, imploring forgiveness, but the stone heart knew no pity. Reversing the whip he was carrying, her husband struck her such a blow on the temple with the ivory handle that she sank lifeless into the old man's arms. When Peter saw this, he seemed immediately to regret his deed; he bent down to see if she was still breathing, but the little man said in a familiar voice, "Don't bother, Charcoal Peter. She was the loveliest flower in the Black Forest, but you have trod her into the ground, she will never bloom again."

Peter blanched. "So it's you, Mr. Treasurekeeper," he said. "Well, what's done is done. I suppose it had to be. I hope you're not going to report me to the police for murder."

"You wretch!" cried the glassman, "what would it avail me to deliver your mortal body to the gallows? It is not an earthly judgment you have to fear, but another and sterner one, for you have sold your soul to the Evil One."

"If I have sold my heart," shrieked Peter, "you are the one who is to blame, you and your deceptive treasures. It was you, you malicious sprite, who brought about my ruin and drove me to seek help from the other one—you alone are responsible."

No sooner had he uttered these words than the glassman began to grow and swell, becoming tall and broad; his eyes, they say, were as big as soup plates, his mouth was like a flaming furnace. Peter fell to his knees, his stone heart could not keep him from trembling like a leaf. The wood spirit seized him by the neck with claws of steel, turned him about like a dry leaf in a whirlwind, then threw him to the ground so hard that his ribs cracked. "You worm!" he cried in a voice of thunder, "I could smash you to pieces if I wanted to, for you have sinned against the lord of the forest. But for the sake of this dead woman, who gave me food and drink, I will grant you one week's grace. If in that time you don't mend your ways, I'll break every bone in your body and let you go to hell with all your sins on your head!"

It was already dusk when some men who were passing by saw rich Peter Munk lying there on the ground. They turned him over and sought to determine whether he was still breathing; for a time it seemed he was not. At last one of them went into the house, fetched a pail of water, and dashed it in his face. Peter drew a deep breath, groaned and opened his eyes, looked around him, and then asked about Dame Lisbeth, but no one had seen her. He thanked the men for their help, stole into his house, and looked for her everywhere, but she was neither in the cellar nor the attic, and what he had thought was a terrible dream turned out to be bitter reality. Now that he was quite alone, strange thoughts came to him. He feared nothing, for his heart was cold, but when he thought of his wife's death, he also thought about his own and how he would have to die burdened with the tears and thousand-fold curses of the poor, who had been unable to move his heart; burdened with the misery of the wretches he had chased from his door with his dogs; burdened with his mother's quiet despair and with the blood of beautiful, kind Lisbeth. And if he would not even be able to account to her father, if he should come and ask, "Where is my daughter?" what was he going to say to Him to whom belong all forests and seas, all mountains and the lives of men?

At night, in dreams, he was also tortured. A soft voice kept saying to him, "Peter, get yourself a warmer heart!" And when he awakened, he quickly closed his eyes again, for the voice could only be that of Lisbeth, who was warning him. The next day he went to the tavern to distract himself, and there he met Big Zeke. He sat down with him and they talked of various things, the fine weather, the war, taxes, until at last they fell to talking about death and the way every now and then someone dies so suddenly. Then Peter asked Zeke what he thought about death and what comes afterwards. Zeke said, "They bury the body, and the soul goes either to heaven or to hell."

"They also bury the heart, do they?" asked Peter tensely.

"Yes, of course, they bury it too."

"But suppose someone no longer has a heart?"

Zeke gave him a searching look. "What do you mean by that? Are you trying to make a fool of me? Do you think *I* don't have a heart?"

"Oh sure, you've got a heart all right, firm as a rock," replied Peter.

Zeke looked at him in surprise, glanced about to see if anyone was listening, and then said, "How did *you* find out about it? Or doesn't your own beat any more either?"

"It doesn't beat any more, at least not here in my breast!" said Peter Munk. "But tell me, now that we know each other's secret, what *will* become of our hearts?"

"What difference does it make, friend?" said Zeke with a laugh. "You've got all you want on this earth and that's enough. That's the nice thing about our cold hearts—we don't have to fear such thoughts."

"True enough, and yet a person thinks about it, for though I have no more fears, I can remember how much I feared hell when I was a boy and still innocent."

"Well—we won't exactly have a jolly time of it," said Zeke. "I once asked a schoolmaster about it and he told me that after death all hearts are weighed to see how heavy their sins are. The light ones rise up and the heavy ones sink down. And I think these stones of ours are going to weigh a bit."

"No doubt of that," replied Peter, "and sometimes I feel rather uncomfortable because my heart is so unsympathetic and indifferent—that is, if I think of such things."

Thus ran their conversation. The next night he again heard the well-known voice whispering in his ear a number of times, "Get yourself a warmer heart, Peter!" He felt no remorse at having killed his wife, but when he told the servants that she had gone on a trip, he wondered to himself, "Where can she have gone to?" For six days he went on in this way, and at night he kept hearing the voice and thought of the wood spirit and his terrible threat. On the seventh morning he leaped out of bed and cried, "Very well, then, I'm going to see if I can't get myself a warmer heart, this unfeeling stone in my breast is making life too dreary to bear!" He quickly donned his Sunday best, mounted his horse, and set off for Fir Tree Knoll.

Upon reaching the dense stand of trees on the knoll, he dismounted, tied up his horse, and hastened to the top of the hill. When he was standing before the great fir, he recited the charm:

> Treasure keeper in the forest green,
> Many a century hast thou seen,
> Thine are all woods where fir trees stand,
> Only Sunday's child can know thy hand.

Thereupon the glassmanikin came forth, not with a kind and friendly mien as before, but sad-looking and gloomy. He had on a coat made of dark glass, and a long, black crepe ribbon trailed down from his hat. Peter well knew for whom he was in mourning.

"What do you want from me, Peter Munk?" he asked in a hollow voice.

"I still have one more wish, Mr. Treasurekeeper," Peter answered with downcast eyes.

"Can hearts of stone still wish for anything?" asked the glassman. "You have everything your evil mind can need; I doubt that I shall be able to grant your wish."

"But you promised me three wishes, and I still have one left."

"I can refuse to grant it if it is foolish," returned the wood spirit; "but go on, let's hear what you want."

"Take this lifeless stone out of my breast and give me back my living heart," said Peter.

"Am *I* the one who struck the bargain with you?" asked the glassmanikin. "Am I Dutch Michael, who gives away riches and cold hearts? He's the one you have to ask if you want your heart back."

"He'll never give it to me," answered Peter sadly.

"Bad as you are, I'm sorry for you," said the little man, after reflecting a bit. "And since your wish isn't foolish, I cannot refuse my help. You can be sure you'll never retrieve your heart by force; perhaps, though, through cunning. In fact, it may not be too difficult, for stupid Michael will always be stupid Michael, even if he thinks he's unusually clever. So go straight to him and do exactly what I tell you." He gave Peter precise instructions and presented him with a little cross made of crystal.

"He cannot harm you and he will have to let you go if you hold this before him and say a prayer. When you have gotten what you want, come back to me here."

Peter took the little cross, and impressing the glassman's words firmly on his memory, proceeded to Dutch Michael's dwelling. He called out his name three times and the giant at once appeared.

"So you slew your wife, did you?" he said with a horrible laugh. "Just what I would have done; she was squandering your wealth on beggars. But you'll have to leave the country for a while, there'll be a big stink about this if they don't find her. I suppose you've come to me for more money?"

"You guessed it," replied Peter, "and I'll need a lot this time—America is a long way off."

Michael led him into his house, opened a chest brimming with gold, and took out large handfuls of the shining metal. While he was counting it out on the table, Peter said, "You played fast and loose with me, Michael. You lied to me when you said I had a stone in my breast and you had my heart!"

"Why, isn't that the way it is?" asked Michael in astonishment. "Do you feel your heart? Isn't it cold as ice? Have you any griefs or fears, do you feel remorse?"

"You merely brought my heart to a standstill; I've still got it in my breast just as always and so has Big Zeke—he was the one who told me you'd tricked us. You're not clever enough to take someone's heart out of his breast without endangering his life: you'd have to be a wizard."

"But I can assure you," cried Michael, much offended, "that you and Big Zeke and all the rich people who have come to me have cold hearts like yours, and that their own hearts are standing there in the next room."

"Oh, you've got a glib tongue, all right!" laughed Peter. "Tell that to someone else. Don't you think I saw tricks like that by the dozen on my travels? Those are wax hearts you've got in there. You're rich, that's for sure, but you're no magician."

The giant became furious and tore open the door to the adjoining room. "Just come in here and read the labels. That one there, see, is Peter Munk's heart. Do you see how it's throbbing? Can anybody make a heart like that out of wax?"

"Just the same," said Peter, "it *is* wax. A real heart doesn't beat like that. I still have mine in my breast. No, you're not a magician!"

"I'll prove it to you!" Michael shouted angrily. "You're going to feel for yourself that this is your heart."

He took the heart out of its glass, tore open Peter's jerkin, removed the stone from his breast, and showed it to him. Then he took the heart, breathed on it, and carefully put it back in its rightful place. Peter at once felt it beating, and he was again able to rejoice that it did.

"How does that feel?" asked Michael, grinning.

"I have to admit you were right," said Peter, cautiously pulling the little cross out of his pocket. "I wouldn't have believed such a thing was possible!"

"See? I *am* a magician. Now I'll just put this stone back in your breast."

"Take it easy, Mr. Michael!" cried Peter, retreating a pace and holding the cross before him. "You can catch mice with bacon, and this time I think you're the mouse!" And he at once began to recite the first prayer that came into his head.

At this, Michael began to grow smaller and smaller; he fell to the floor, writhing like a worm, groaning and moaning, and all the hearts standing on the shelves began to beat and throb, so that it sounded like a watchmaker's shop. Peter was afraid; all this gave him a very uncanny feeling. He ran out of the room and out of the house, and, driven by his fear, climbed the high wall of the chasm, for behind him he could hear Michael pulling himself together, stomping and raging and cursing fearfully. When he reached the top, he ran towards Fir Tree Knoll. A terrible storm was rising, bolts of lightning were falling to the right and left, striking the trees beside him, but he finally arrived safely in the glassman's territory.

His heart was pounding for joy, only *because* it pounded. Then he looked back on his life, horrified. He thought about Lisbeth, his beautiful, kindly wife, whom he had murdered out of avarice, and he seemed to himself the lowest specimen of humanity. He was weeping bitterly when he came to the glassman's mound.

The treasurekeeper was sitting beneath a fir tree smoking his pipe. He looked more cheerful than before. "Why are you weeping, Charcoal Peter?" he asked. "Didn't you get back your heart? Is the cold one still lying in your breast?"

"Oh sir!" sighed Peter, "when I was still carrying that stone heart around in me, I never wept, my eyes were as dry as the fields in midsummer. Now my old heart is about to break for what I have done! I have driven my debtors to poverty and ruin, I have chased the poor and the sick from my door, and you know yourself how I struck Lisbeth's lovely brow with my whip!"

"Peter, you have sinned greatly," said the gnome. "Money and idleness were your downfall; then your heart turned to stone and no longer knew either joy or sorrow, remorse or pity. But repentance can reconcile, and if I were only sure that you truly repent, I could still do something for you."

"I want nothing more," answered Peter with drooping head. "It's all up with me; I can never be happy again. What am I to do all alone in the world? My mother will never forgive me for what I have done to her—perhaps I've even brought her to her grave, monster that I am! And my wife Lisbeth! Go on and strike me dead, Mr. Treasurekeeper, put an end to my miserable existence once and for all."

"Very well," answered the glassmanikin, "if that's the way you want it; I've got my ax right here." He calmly took his pipe from his mouth, knocked it out, and put it in his pocket. Then he slowly stood up and went behind the fir trees. Peter sank down weeping on the grass; his life meant nothing to him any longer. Patiently he awaited the fatal blow. After a time he heard light steps behind him and thought, "Now he's coming!"

"Turn your head, Peter Munk!" cried the gnome. Peter wiped the tears from his eyes, looked around him, and saw his mother and his wife Lisbeth, gazing at him with friendly faces. He jumped up joyously. "You aren't dead, Lisbeth? And you are here too, mother, and have forgiven me?"

"They are willing to forgive you," said the glassmanikin; "because you feel true repentance, everything shall be forgotten. Now go home to your father's hut and be a charcoal burner, as you were before. If you're upright and good, you'll be an honor to your trade, and your neighbors will love and respect you more than if you had ten tons of gold." Thus spoke the glassmanikin and bade them adieu.

All three thanked him and blessed him and turned their steps homeward.

The splendid house Peter had built when he was rich was no longer standing. Lightning had struck it and burned it to the ground with all its treasures. But his paternal hut was not far and toward it they now took their way, little concerned about their heavy loss.

Yet what was their wonder upon reaching the hut! It had become a fine farmhouse, simply but neatly furnished.

"That's the hand of our good glassmanikin!" cried Peter.

"How beautiful!" said Lisbeth. "I'll feel much more at home here than in the big house with all those servants!"

From this day on, Peter Munk was an honest, diligent man. He was satisfied with what he had and carried on his trade uncomplainingly. Thus it came to pass that by his own powers he became well-to-do and respected and well liked in the whole Black Forest. He never again quarrelled with his wife; he honored his mother and gave alms to the poor who knocked at his door. When Lisbeth gave birth to a fine boy after a year and a day, Peter went up to Fir Tree Knoll and recited his charm. But the glassmanikin did not appear. "Mr. Treasurekeeper!" he called, "listen to me, I only want to ask you to become the godfather of my little boy!" But there was no answer; only a gust of wind rushed through the firs and blew some cones down into the grass. "I'll take these as a memento, since you won't show yourself," called Peter, stuck the fir cones in his pocket, and went home. But when he got to his house and took off his Sunday jerkin and his mother turned the pockets inside out to lay it away in the clothespress, four large rolls of money fell out. When they opened them, they found beautiful bright new Baden thalers, with not a single counterfeit among them. That was the godfather's present to his godson, Peter's little boy.

Thus they lived on in peace and contentment, and often afterwards, when Peter Munk's hair was already gray, he would say, "It's better to be satisfied with a little than to have gold and goods and a cold heart!"

Translated by Robert M. Browning

Translator's note: A number of phrases in this translation are adapted from the lively but erratic translation by Percy E. Pinkerton in *Little Mook and Other Fairy Tales by W. Hauff* (New York: G. P. Putnam's Sons, 1881, pp. 196–269).

The Story of Beautiful Lau

Eduard Mörike

The Blue Pot is the large, round basin of a miraculous spring by a steep rock face, immediately behind the monastery. To the east it sends out a brook, the Blau, which issues into the Danube. This pool narrows down in the shape of a deep funnel; its water is pure blue in color, quite magnificent, indeed beggaring description; when you scoop it up, however, it looks perfectly clear inside its container.

Once upon a time a water sprite with long, flowing hair used to sit at the bottom of the pool. Her body was exactly like that of a beautiful, real woman but for one thing: between her fingers and toes she had webbed skin, which was shining white and finer than any poppy petal. In the town nearby there still stands an old building, originally a convent, later made into a large inn, and therefore called The Nuns' Inn. There sixty years ago a picture of the naiad still hung, its colors still recognizable in spite of smoke and age. In it she had her hands crossed upon her breast, her face looked pallid, her hair black; but her eyes, which were very large, were blue. The common folk called the picture "Naughty Lau in the Pot," or sometimes "Beautiful Lau." The naiad was now bad, now good to human beings. Sometimes, when she made the pot overflow, the town and monastery were endangered; then the citizenry in a solemn procession would often bring her gifts to placate her, such as gold- and silverware, goblets, bowls, little knives, and such like. The honest monks inveighed against this practice as paganism and idolatry, and it was finally abolished completely. However hostile the naiad was towards the monastery because of this, it occurred by no means infrequently that, whenever Father

221

Emeran played the organ and no one was in the vicinity, she would emerge in broad daylight, exposing her body down to the waist, and listen; on such occasions she would sometimes wear a chaplet of broad leaves on her head, and something similar round her neck.

Once an impudent shepherd boy, observing her from some bushes, called out, "Hey there, tree frog! Are we goin' to get good weather?" Swifter than lightning, and more venomously than a viper, she leaped out, grabbed the lad by his hair, and dragged him down with her into one of her wet chambers, where she intended to allow the boy, who'd fainted, to perish and rot away miserably. He soon recovered consciousness, however, found a door, and, by means of steps and passages, traversing many chambers, he at last entered a beautiful hall. Here it was lovely and warm even in the depth of winter. In one corner of the room, where Lau and her retinue were already sleeping, there burned a night-light, a lamp set upon a tall candelabra adorned with golden birds'-feet. Many precious things stood round the walls, which were, like the floor, decorated with tapestries in all colors. The lad quickly took the light down from its stand, and, looking round hurriedly for anything he might purloin, snatched something out of a cupboard; it was a bag and weighed so much he thought it must contain gold. Then, running, he came to a little bronze door that was probably a good two fists thick, pushed back the bolt, and climbed a staircase of stone steps, up many flights, now left, now right, certainly four hundred steps in all, until they finally stopped, and he was met by boundless chasms. He then had to leave the light behind, and thus, in mortal peril, he climbed about in the dark for an hour, only suddenly to thrust his head up out of the ground. It was dead of night and thick forest all around. After wandering about for a long time, he finally, at first light, hit upon beaten tracks, and, standing on a rock, caught sight of the little town below. He desired to see by daylight what was in his bag and discovered there was nothing but a cob of lead, a heavy cone as long as a handsbreadth, with an eye at its upper end, and white with age. Angrily he threw this trash down into the valley, and afterwards told no one of the theft because he was ashamed of it. But it was from him that people first learned about the naiad's dwelling.

Now it should be known that this was not the home of beautiful Lau. No, as a prince's daughter, indeed on her mother's side of half-human origin, she was married to an old Danube water sprite down by the Black Sea. Since all her children had been still-born, her husband banished her. But that was because she was always sad, though for no particular reason. Her mother-in-law had prophesied to her that she would not bear a live child until she had laughed heartily five times. The fifth time something was bound to happen, but what, she was not allowed to know, nor the old water sprite. But no luck ever came of it, however hard her servants tried on her account; finally the old king refused to keep her any longer at his court, and sent her to this place near the Upper Danube, where his sister lived. The mother-in-law had provided her with some chambermaids and maids to wait on her and divert her, as cheerful and capable girls as ever walked on webbed feet (for those who belong to the common stock of water sprites have fully webbed feet). Six times a day, out of sheer boredom, they would give her a change of clothing—because out of the water she went about in fine clothes, although barefoot—tell her old stories and tales, make music, and dance and disport themselves before her. Adjoining that hall, in which the shepherd boy had been, was the princess's chamber or bedroom, from which a flight of steps went into the Blue Pot. There she lay many a fine day and many a summer's night to cool herself. She also had all sorts of jolly animals, such as birds, rabbits, and monkeys, but above all a merry dwarf, thanks to whom an uncle of the princess had once been released from similar sadness. Every evening she would play draughts, chess, or "sheep and wolf" with him; every time she made a poor move he would pull such odd faces, each one different, making them worse and worse, till even wise Solomon could not have helped laughing, never mind the chambermaids, or you, dear reader, had you been present. Nothing, however, touched beautiful Lau; seldom did she betray even the ghost of a smile.

Every year at the beginning of winter there came messengers from back home, who would knock with a hammer on the hall doors, whereupon the chambermaids would ask:

Who's that making such a din?

And the former would say:

> The king commands,
> Let his heralds in!
> Deliver to the royal ear
> The good you've done this yesteryear.

And they would say:

> Oh! you should have heard us sing!
> We've danced our dances, had our fling,
> We almost made it, masters dear!
> See you in another year.

Then the men returned home. Before the arrival of the embassy, however, and after, the naiad was always twice as sad.

In The Nuns' Inn there dwelt a fat hostess, Mistress Betha Seysolffin, a good, cheerful woman, Christian, affable, kind; she displayed her qualities as a real landlady, especially to poor journeymen. Her eldest son, Stephan, who was married, ran the place for the most part; another, Xaver, was convent-cook, and there were two daughters. She had a small kitchen-garden outside town, by the Pot. Once, when she was there on the first warm day in spring, working away at her patch, sowing cabbage and lettuce, putting in beans and onions, she happened to look delightedly once more at the beautiful blue water over the fence and then disgustedly at the old pile of rubbish near it that spoiled the whole spot; so as soon as she had finished her work and closed the little garden gate behind her, she took up her hoe once more, pulled out the rankest weeds, and, selecting a few pumpkin seeds from the seed basket, stuck them in different places in the pile. (The abbot of the convent, who thought the landlord's wife a fine, upstanding woman, just then happened to be standing at an upstairs window, and called across to her, meanwhile wagging his finger, as if she were on the side of his adversary.)

The waste patch bloomed the whole summer through—it was a joy to see—till in autumn the great yellow pumpkins hung down the slope to the pool.

Now one day the landlady's daughter, Jutta, happened to go

down to the cellar, where from time immemorial there had been an open well set in a stone. By the light of her lamp, horrified, she saw beautiful Lau floating up to her breast in the water; full of fear, she dashed off and told her mother. The latter, undaunted, descended alone, nor would she let her son follow her for protection, because the woman was naked.

The strange guest pronounced this greeting:

> The water sprite has come,
> Has crawled along and swum,
> Through ways all stony, wild,
> To the convent hostess mild.
> Because she bent and worked the soil,
> Adorned my Pot, thanks to her toil,
> With fruit and tendrils copiously,
> I duly thank her courteously.

She had a spinning-top of water-bright stone in her hand, which she gave to the landlady, saying, "Take this toy, dear lady, to remember me by. It will come in very handy. For only just recently I heard you in your garden, complaining to your neighbor that you'd been afraid to go to the fair because burghers and peasants were always squabbling and you dreaded murder and manslaughter. Well, dear lady, whenever drunken guests again start arguing during dances or over drinks, take the top into your hand, stand out in the hall, spin it outside the door of the room, and then you'll hear such a mighty, such a splendid sound ring through the whole establishment that all the company will lower their fists on the spot and be well disposed one to another, because in a flash everyone will have sobered up. That done, throw your apron over the top and it will immediately wrap itself up and lie still."

Thus spoke the water sprite. Mistress Betha gladly took the treasure with the golden cord and the ebony handle, called her daughter Jutta to her (she happened to be standing behind the sauerkraut tub by the stone steps), showed her the gift, thanked the lady, and kindly invited her, whenever she felt bored, to pay her a further visit; whereupon the water sprite went down and disappeared.

It was not long before it became clear what a treasure the house had in the top, for not only did it, thanks to its power and high virtue, unfailingly calm any unpleasant rows in a trice, it also soon brought the inn remarkable patronage. It was the goal of whosoever came into that area, whether commoner or nobleman; in particular the Count of Helfenstein came soon, also the Count of Wirtemberg and a number of great prelates. Indeed a famous Duke of Lombardy, who had been a guest of the Duke of Bavaria and happened to be traveling through these parts to France, offered a lot of money for the toy, if the landlady would only part with it. Certainly there was nothing like it to be seen or heard in any other country. At first, when it began to turn, it gave a soft hum, then it sounded louder and louder, both in the high and low registers, and more and more splendidly, as if the sound came from many pipes, streaming forth and rising through every story right up to the rafters and down into the cellar, so that, resounding and swelling, all the walls, floors, pillars, and landings seemed to be full of it. Whenever the cloth was thrown over it and it lay powerless, the music did not cease immediately, rather the torrent of sound, once let loose, moved about, accompanied by a powerful ringing, booming, humming for well nigh a quarter of an hour.

In Swabia we generally call a wooden top like that a "hummer"; Frau Betha's was, according to its chief property, generally called "the peasant-quieter." It was made of a large amethyst, whose name means "against drunkenness," because it rapidly expels heavy wine fumes from the head, indeed from the very start prevents a drinker from falling too much under the influence; accordingly both laity and clerics used to wear an amethyst on their fingers.

The water sprite came once a month, also at unexpected times, on which account the landlady fixed up a bell in the house with a wire that went down the wall by the well, so that the naiad could advertise her presence right away. In time she came to be more and more obliging to the good women, the mother as well as the daughters and the daughter-in-law.

One afternoon in summer, when there happened to be no guests, and the son had gone out haymaking with the laborers and servant girls, Frau Betha was drawing wine with her eldest daughter in the cellar. Lau was in the fountain amusing herself watching this activity, and the women were having a little chat with her, when the landlady asked, "How would you like to have a look round my house and garden? Jutta here could give you some clothes; you're both the same size."

"Yes," Lau said, "for a long time now I've been wanting to see inside human dwellings, and the activities, the spinning and weaving that go on there, also the way your daughters celebrate weddings and rock their babies in the cradle."

Thereupon the daughter gladly dashed upstairs to fetch a clean sheet, brought it and helped her to climb out of her well, a feat she managed easily, smiling all the while. Instantly the girl wrapped the sheet round her and led her by the hand up a narrow staircase in the furthermost corner of the cellar, whence there was access by means of a trapdoor into the daughter's room. There, sitting on a chair, she allowed herself to be dried, Jutta toweling her feet. When the latter came to her soles, Lau started back, giggling.

"Wasn't that laughter?" she promptly asked. "What else?" cried Jutta delightedly. "Blest be the day! That's one success!" The landlady in the kitchen heard the laughter and merriment and entered the room, eager to learn what had happened. When she heard the reason she thought, "You poor dear, that will hardly count!" But she kept her doubts to herself, and Jutta took a number of things from the cupboard, the best she had, to clothe this family friend of theirs. "See," said the mother, "it looks as if she wants to make a fashion model out of you." "No," cried Lau delightedly, "let me be the Cinderella in your fairy tale!" So saying, she took up a plain circular pleated skirt and jacket; neither shoes nor stockings would she wear on her feet, and her hair hung unplaited down to her ankles. And thus she went over the house from top to bottom—the kitchen, the parlor, even the bedrooms. She was amazed at the most ordinary of utensils, and inspected everything: the bar, which had been swept clean; above it, in long rows, the pewter tankards and glasses, all upside down, their lids hanging; the copper rinsing tub with its brush; and, in the middle of the room, hanging from the ceiling in its little glass box, the insignia of the weavers' guild, adorned with silken cords and silver wire. It so chanced that she glimpsed her own reflection in a mirror; she stood quite a while in front of it, taken aback, and when the daughter-in-law took her along to her room and presented her with a little mirror worth threepence, she was overcome with gratitude for the gift, considering it to be the pearl of all her treasures.

But before she took her leave, she happened to look behind the curtains of the alcove, where stood the bed of the young woman and her husband, as well as that of the children. There sat a little grandchild, his cheeks flushed from sleep, with an apple in his hand, upon a little round chair of good Ulm ware, glazed green. The guest was exceedingly pleased with it; she called it a most charming seat; suddenly, however, she twitched her nose, and when the three women turned away to laugh, she noticed something was afoot and also began laughing heartily, and the good landlady split her sides with laughter, saying, "*This* time it's worked! God send you as bonny a lad as my Hans there!"

The night this happened beautiful Lau went to bed easier and more contented than she had for many a long year, down at the bottom of the Blue Pot. She promptly fell asleep, and soon she dreamed a crazy dream.

She thought it was the hour after noon, when in the hot season folk are out in the meadows mowing, while monks take a snooze in their cool cells; hence it was doubly quiet in the whole monastery. Before long, however, the abbot ventured forth to see if the landlady happened to be in her garden. The latter, however, was sitting in the guise of a fat, long-haired water sprite in the Pot, where the abbot soon discovered and greeted her, and gave her a kiss so resounding that it echoed from the little monastery tower, and the tower told it to the refectory, that told it to the church, and it told it to the stable and it told it to the fish shed, and it told it to the washhouse, and in the washhouse the tubs and pails shouted it to one another. The abbot was startled at such a noise; while he was bending over the landlady, his skullcap fell into the Blue Pot; she quickly returned it to him and he rapidly waddled off.

But just then the Lord God came forth out of the monastery to see what was going on. He wore a long, white beard and a red coat. He asked the abbot, who bumped straight into him:

Lord abbot, how did you get your skullcap so wet?

And the abbot answered:

I met a boar in the wood today,
And from the beast I ran away;

I ran so hard, raised such a sweat,
I think that's why my skullcap's wet.

Thereupon the Lord God, indignant at this lie, raised his finger, and, beckoning to him, led the way to the monastery. The abbot looked surreptitiously back at the landlady, and the latter cried, "My goodness me! my goodness me! Now the kind old gentleman's going to jail!"

That was beautiful Lau's dream. But on waking she knew and still felt in her heart that she had laughed heartily in her sleep and, even awake, her heart still danced so much that the Blue Pot made rings on top.

Because it had been very sultry during the day there was now lightning at night. It lit up the Blue Pot, and Lau could feel from the bottom that there was thunder in the distance. So she calmly stayed put for a while, her head resting in her hand, and looked at the flashes of lightning. Then she went up to see if dawn was coming, but it wasn't yet much after midnight. The moon stood smooth and fair over Rusen Castle, and the air was full of the spring smell of mown hay.

She almost thought she would not have the patience to wait for the time when she might proclaim her new good fortune; indeed she very nearly got up in the middle of the night and went to Jutta's door, but she changed her mind and went at a more opportune moment.

Mistress Betha good-naturedly listened to her dream, even though it did seem to her a bit defamatory. But then she said dubiously, "Don't trust any laughter that occurs during sleep; the devil's a joker. If you were to send back messengers with good tidings on the strength of such delusions, and the future were to prove you wrong, it could go ill for you at home."

Beautiful Lau's mouth dropped at this speech of hers, and she said, "The lady's annoyed with the dream!" She left shamefacedly and dived down.

It was almost noon when the sacristan called out vehemently to the cellarer in the monastery, "I notice the pool's upset. It looks as if the witch is once again trying to teach your barrels to swim. Close your shutters quickly, make everything fast!"

Now the monastery cook, the landlady's son, was a jolly man, and well liked by Lady Lau. He thought he'd soothe her anger with a practical joke, ran to his room, stripped his bedstead of its laths, and stuck them into the lawn by the Blue Pot where the water tended to overflow, and pretended with words and gestures that he was a most devoted servant who was very afraid his mistress would fall out of bed and hurt herself. When she saw the laths so carefully set up and straddling the brook, in the midst of her anger she began laughing, and she laughed so excessively that the noise could be heard in the monastery garden.

When she then came to see the women that evening, they had already learned the news from the cook and wished her all the joy in the world. The landlady said, "From his earliest years our Xaver's been a proper joker; now at least his tomfoolery has been of some use."

Now, however, one month followed another, and no third or fourth time seemed likely to occur. Martinmas had already gone; a few more weeks and the messengers would be back. Even the good folk at the inn began to doubt whether anything would happen that year and they all had their work cut out consoling their lady. The greater her fear, the less hope there was.

So that she might forget her troubles sooner, Mistress Betha invited a spinning party to join her; after supper half a dozen lively lasses and wives, all related, were in the habit of meeting, with their distaffs, in a secluded room. Lady Lau came every evening in Jutta's old skirt and smock and sat down on the floor in the corner away from the warm stove and listened to the gossip, at first as a silent guest, but soon she became friendly and familiar to them all. For her sake Mistress Betha one evening set about constructing a little Christmas crib in good time for her grandchildren: the madonna and child in the stable, with her the three magi from the East, each one with his camel, on which he had ridden hither, bringing his gifts. In order to deck it all out and glue whatever happened to be loose, the landlady, with her glasses on, sat at the table in the lamplight, and the water sprite watched her with great delight. She loved to listen to all the holy stories that were told her then, even though she did not understand them properly or take them to heart, however much the landlady might have liked her to.

Mistress Betha knew many instructive fables and proverbs as

well as subtle questions and riddles. Being in charge of the pro-
ceedings, she posed a whole series of them, because the water sprite
had from her earliest years loved such things particularly, and always seemed very pleased whenever she happened to hit on the
answer (something, however, that didn't happen all that easily).
One of them especially appealed to her, and without a moment's
thought she gave the answer:

> Here I am, a spindly queen,
> And on my head I wear a crown,
> And those who serve me loyally,
> Gain affluence and high renown.
>
> My maids must coif me carefully,
> And ceaseless stories they do tell,
> However much they pluck me bare,
> You've never seen me without hair.
>
> I often go out for a drive,
> And whirl about along my way;
> And yet I never move an inch.
> Say, what am I, good people, say?

In this regard she said rather more cheerfully than before, "When
I'm back one day in my homeland, and a Swabian, especially one
from your town, rides out to war or on some other quest through
Walachian country to our shores, then he's to call me by name,
where the Danube at its widest enters the Black Sea—for my husband's kingdom extends ten miles into this sea, as far as the fresh-
water colors it—and I'll come to that stranger's aid. But so that
he may be sure it's me and not someone else who might harm
him, he's to ask this riddle. No one of our family but me will
answer him, for in those parts such distaffs and spinning wheels
as you use in Swabia are not to be seen, nor do they know your
language there; and so this may serve as a password."

Another evening the story was told of Doctor Veylland and Sir
Conrad of Wirtemberg, the old count of the region, in whose days
the town called Stuttgart did not yet exist. In the grassy valley,
where it arose later, all that stood at that time was a splendid

castle with a moat and drawbridge, built by Bruno, the Canon of Speyer, Conrad's uncle, and, not very far away, a tall stone house. In it there lived alone with an old servant an eccentric, who was very learned in natural lore and medicine. With his lord, the count, he had traveled far and wide in hot lands, whence he had brought back to Swabia many a strange animal, many kinds of plants, and wonders of the sea. In his hall you could see a lot of strange things hanging round the walls—a crocodile's skin, as well as snakes and flying fish. The count visited him almost every week; he cultivated little acquaintance with other folk. It was rumored he was an alchemist. This much, at any rate, is certain: he could make himself invisible, because he kept amongst his possessions a kraken tooth. Once, when he let down his plumb line into the Red Sea in order to sound its depths, there was such a jerk underwater the line almost snapped. A kraken had sunk its teeth into the lead, and two of the fangs got stuck in it. They are as sharp and shiny black as a shoemaker's awl. One stuck quite fast, the other could be pulled out easily. Now since such a tooth, mounted in, say, silver or gold, and worn on one's person, was supposed to possess great power and is counted amongst the very greatest possessions—so great that one cannot buy it with money—and since the doctor thought such a gift suited no one better than a wise and benevolent lord, so that he might everywhere keep his ears and eyes open to all that went on in his own and in foreign countries, he gave one of these teeth to his count (as indeed he was probably obliged to do anyway), at the same time indicating its secret power, of which his lord knew nothing. From that day on the count was more gracious to the doctor than to all his nobles or councillors, treating him as his dear friend, gladly letting him keep the plumb in which the other tooth was stuck, though only after performing a vow not to use it unnecessarily, and, before he died, to bequeath it either to him, the count, or somehow to remove it from the world. The noble count, however, died two years earlier than Dr. Veylland and did not leave the treasure to his sons: it is thought that out of piety and wise prudence he took it to the grave with him, or else hid it.

When the doctor too was on his deathbed he called his faithful servant, Curt, to him and said, "Dear Curt, I feel I shall die to-night, I therefore wish to thank you for your loyal service and give a few orders. There by the books in the bottom drawer in the corner is a purse containing a hundred imperials. Take it, and you'll never go short your whole life long. Second, burn that old manuscript in the little chest, here in the chimney before my very eyes. Third, you'll find a plumb line there. Take it and hide it amongst your things, and when you leave this household and return home to Blaubeuren, the first thing you must do is throw it into the Blue Pot." He was thus concerned that it should in perpetuity never come into human hands without God's special dispensation. For at that time Lady Lau had never yet revealed herself in the Blue Pot, and it was held to be unfathomable anyway.

After the faithful servant had arranged all these things, partly there and then, partly by promises, with tears in his eyes he took his leave of the doctor, who departed this life before dawn.

When the bailiff and his man came and sought out and sealed everything down to the smallest trifle, Curt, not being the most astute of men, had set aside the plumb line, but had not hidden the purse, and had to leave it behind, nor did he ever after catch a glimpse of even a farthing: indeed, the base heirs scarcely paid him his annuity.

He already had a presentiment of such a misfortune when, depressed enough even without such worries, he entered his hometown, his bundle on his shoulder. Now his only thought was to carry out his master's orders. Because he had not been here for twenty-three years, he did not know the people he ran across, and even though he bade one or another good evening, no one returned his greeting. When he passed, the people at the doors of their houses looked round in astonishment to see who might have been greeting them, for they could see no one. This was because the plumb in his bundle hung on the left side; when, however, he carried it on the right, he was seen by everyone. But all he said to himself was, "In my day the Blaubeuren folk were not as rude!"

Arriving at the Blue Pot, he found his cousin, the master ropemaker, busy with his lad, going backwards along the monastery wall, paying out tow from his apron while the boy passed the string over his wheel. "Good day to you, cousin ropemaker!" called Curt, clapping him on the shoulder. The master looked round, paled, dropped his work, and ran off as fast as his legs could carry him. Then the other laughed, saying, "Bless my soul, he thinks I'm a ghost! The folks here are no doubt saying it's me who's died and not my master—the idea!"

He now went to the pool, untied his bundle and pulled out the plumb. Then it occurred to him that he would like to find out if it was true that the pool had no bottom to it (he himself had ambitions to be a bit of a Paul Pry, like his master before him), and because he had just seen three big, strong coils of rope in the ropemaker's basket, he fetched them out and tied the plumb to one. There happened to be many freshly bored pipes in the water stretching out right up to the middle of the Pot, on which he could take up his position, and so he lowered the weight by measuring off a length of cord against his outstretched arm, reckoning three such lengths to a fathom, and counting out, "one fathom, two fathoms, three, four, five, six, seven, eight, nine, ten." The first ball of string ran out and he had to tie the second to its end, measuring it off in its turn and counting up to twenty. Then the other ball of string was used up—"Cripes, *is* it deep!" murmured Curt—and, tying on the third one, he continued his count: "twenty-one, twenty-two, twenty-three, twenty-four—crikey, my arm's giving out—twenty-five, twenty-six, twenty-seven, twenty-eight, twenty-nine, thirty—That's it, mate, no more measuring there! Whoosh! No end to it!" He wound the cord, before he pulled it up, around the wooden pipe on which he stood, in order to get his breath back, and remarked to himself, "That Pot's definitely bottomless."

While one of the spinning-women was telling this comical tale, the landlady shot a sly glance at Lau, who was smiling, for she of course knew best what had happened as regards all this measuring; but the two of them said nothing. It will now be revealed, however, to the reader.

Beautiful Lau lay that afternoon on the sand down in the depths, and at her feet a lady-in-waiting, Aleila, who was her favorite, was cutting her toenails in a leisurely fashion with a golden pair of scissors, as happened from time to time.

Then slowly from the clear upper world there descended a black object like a skittle, at which the two of them were at first very amazed, until they recognized what it was. As the plumb touched the bottom, ninety feet down, the merry lady-in-waiting seized the string and gently pulled it with both hands, pulled and pulled until it would not yield any more. Then she quickly took the scissors and cut off the plumb, took a fat onion that had fallen into the Pot only yesterday and was almost as big as a child's head, and tied it by its green top to the string to give the man a surprise when he found a different plumb from the one he'd thrown out. Meanwhile beautiful Lady Lau had, to her joy and amazement, discovered the kraken's tooth in the lead. She knew its power very well, and, although naiads do not go after such things very much for themselves, they begrudge human beings such a big advantage, especially as they have from time immemorial regarded the sea and all that is in it as their lease and fief. Accordingly, beautiful Lau hoped to receive praise from the old water sprite, her husband, when she came home with this unexpected booty. But she didn't want to leave the man above without compensation, so she took everything that she happend to be wearing, such as the beautiful necklace of pearls around her neck, and wound it round the big onion just as it was going up; and as if that was not enough, she even hung the golden scissors on it too, and watched, bright-eyed, as the weight was pulled up. The lady-in-waiting, however, inquisitive as to how the human being would react, went up after the plumb and, resting two spans below the surface, feasted her eyes on the old man's fright and confusion. Finally she waved her two raised hands four times in the air, spreading her white fingers into a fan. But, roused by the ropemaker's cries, many people had come from town; they stood round the Blue Pot, observing the goings-on up to the point when the gruesome hands appeared, then suddenly scattered and ran off.

From that moment, however, the old servant was quite addled in the head for a whole week and did not look at Lau's presents, but sat with his cousin by the stove, murmuring to himself a good hundred times a day an old proverb, concerning which no scholar in the whole of Swabia can give any information as to whence and how or when it first originated. For the old man did not make it up; long before his time children were asked in jest—as they still are nowadays—which of them could repeat it most often very fast without making a mistake. It goes:

A cob of lead lies hard by Blaubeuren,
Hard by Blaubeuren lies a cob of lead.

The landlady pronounced it to be pure gibberish, saying, "Who on earth would be so foolish as to look for even a glimmer of sense in it, never mind a prophecy!"

But when a week later Curt finally came to his senses and his cousin showed him the valuable things that were his lawful property, he grinned, put them into safe custody, and consulted the ropemaker as to what to do with them. They all thought it best that he take the pearls and scissors to Stuttgart, where Count Ludwig happened to have his court, and offer to sell them to him. And so he did. Now this lord, not being stingy, was immediately prepared to acquire such precious things for his wife, paying according to an expert's valuation. Only when he heard from the old man how he had come by them did he start up and irately spin round on his heels at the thought of losing the miraculous tooth. He had heard about it before, and soon after his father, Lord Conrad, had died, he had pressed the doctor for it, but in vain.

Now this was the story the spinning-women were then talking about. But they were ignorant of the best part of it. An old grannie who was sitting amongst them with her distaff would dearly loved to have heard whether beautiful Lau still had the plumb, and what she was doing with it, and kept on making hints about it. Thereupon Frau Betha gave Lau one of her little digs, saying, "Aye, go on, make yourself invisible for a spell, eh? Visit people's homes, look into the women's pots and see what they're cooking for dinner. A plumb like that's just the thing for Nosy Parkers!"

Meanwhile one of the girls began murmuring the foolish adage; the others copied her, each one vying with the other, and not one managed to say it three or four times without stumbling; this caused much laughter. Finally beautiful Lau had to try, Jutta simply would not leave her in peace. She blushed to the roots of her hair; nevertheless she started to recite very slowly, "A cob of lead lies hard by Blaubeuren."

The landlady called to her that there was no skill in that, it had to trip off the tongue! So she launched boldly into it, but before she knew where she was, she was in a jam, a real pickle. Now, as you can well imagine, there were gales of laughter, and in the midst of it all came ringing out beautiful Lau's own laughter, as bright as her teeth, for all the world to hear!

Then unexpectedly in the midst of all this fun and jollity something frightful happened. The son of the house, the landlord (he had just come home by horse and cart from Sonderbuch and found the laborers asleep in the stable), came racing up the steps, called his mother to come outside, saying loud enough for all to hear, "For goodness sake, send Lady Lau home! Don't you hear the noise in town? The Blue Pot's emptying, the lower street's already under water, and there's such a roaring and a rolling from the hill by the pool, it's as if the Flood was coming!" While he was saying this, Lau gave a shout inside. "It's the king, my husband, and I'm not at home!" Thereupon she fell to the ground, unconscious, causing the room to shake. The son had disappeared, the spinning-women ran home, moaning, with their distaffs; the others, however, didn't know what they should do with poor Lady Lau, who lay there like a corpse. One of them loosened her clothes, another rubbed her, a third flung the windows open, but it was all to no avail.

Then the jolly cook thrust his head unexpectedly in at the door, saying, "I *thought* she was with you! But I can see the situation's not good. Just get the duck into the water, and she'll swim!" "It's all right for you!" said his mother, trembling, "but even if you *get* her in the cellar and into the well, won't she go and break her neck in all the crevices?" "What do you mean by cellar?" cried the son. "Or the well? That's impossible. You leave it to me! Needs must when the devil drives—I'll carry her to the Blue Pot." Thereupon, like the stout fellow he was, he took up the naiad. "Come on, Jutta, don't cry! You lead the way with your lantern." "For goodness sake!" said the landlady, "take the back path round through the gardens; the street's thronged with people and torches." "This fish isn't exactly light!" he said, descending the steps with firm tread, then proceeding across the yard, this way and that between hedges and fences.

At the pool they found the water level already fallen appreciably, but they did not notice Lau's three ladies-in-waiting, their heads close to the surface, swimming anxiously to and fro, on the lookout for their mistress. Jutta set down the lantern, and the cook put down his burden by leaning his back carefully against the pumpkin mound. Then his own private imp whispered in his ear, "If you kissed her, you'd be glad your whole life long, and you could say you'd once kissed a water sprite." And before he knew where he was, it had happened. Then a wave from the pot suddenly dowsed the light, making everything pitch black, and then it sounded as if a good half dozen wet hands were slapping a couple of chubby cheeks. Jutta called out, "What's the matter?" "A good walloping, we call it round here!" he said. "I'd no idea they also knew such things down by the Black Sea!" With these words he began to steal away hurriedly, but because the noise of slaps came ringing, echoing from the monastery walls and roofs, he stood nonplussed, not knowing what to do, thinking danger was threatening him on every side. (Such a warning was necessary so that he would be too afraid to boast about the mouth he had kissed; he himself was ignorant that he had *had* to do it for the benefit of the beautiful Lau.)

In the midst of this terrible racket the princess could be heard laughing as heartily in her unconscious state as she had that time during her dream when she saw the abbot jump. The cook heard it from a long way away, and even though he thought he was the object of the laughter—and rightly so—he was glad to deduce from it that the sprite's problems were solved once and for all.

Soon Jutta returned home with good news, carrying the clothes, the skirt and bodice that beautiful Lau had worn today for the last time. From her ladies-in-waiting, who had received her in the Pot in the girl's presence, she had learned, to her great relief, that the king had not yet come, but he would not be long now—the great waterway had already filled up. This was a wide, high, rocky course, far below human dwellings, beautifully straight and level right through the middle of the mountain, two miles long from there to the Danube, where the old water goblin's sister had her royal seat. Many rivers, streams, and springs of this region were subject to her; when the summons went out to them, they swelled the said watercourse in a very short time so high with their waters that it could be conveniently used by all sea creatures, sea horses and carriages. This sometimes occurred on festive occasions, to the accompaniment of many torches and music from horn and drum, providing a magnificent display.

The ladies-in-waiting, accompanied by their mistress, now dashed to the attiring room to anoint her, plait her hair, and dress her splendidly, which she gladly permitted, indeed assisted in, for in her heart she felt everything had now been fulfilled, and she awaited the result of having laughed five times, which the old goblin and she were not allowed to know.

About three hours after the watchman had called out "Midnight," when everyone was already asleep in The Nun's Inn, the cellar bell gave two tremendous clangs as a sign that the matter was urgent, and the wives and daughters quickly assembled there.

Lady Lau greeted them as usual from the well, only now her face was made beautiful by joy, and her eyes shone as they never had before. She said, "Hark! My husband came at midnight. My mother-in-law had prophesied to him not long ago that my fortune should be granted tonight, whereupon he left without delay with a retinue of princes, his uncle and my brother Synd, and many lords. Tomorrow we journey forth. The king is as kind and gracious to me as if I had become his spouse only today. They will rise from the meal as soon as they have drunk the toast. I slipped to my chamber and then came here in order once more to greet and embrace my old friends. I thank you, lady, dear Jutta, you, daughter-in-law, and you, the youngest. Greet those who are not present, men and maids. Every third year you'll hear from me; and it may happen that I come sooner myself; then I'll fetch along in these, my arms, living evidence that Lady Lau laughed with you. My people want you to live in happy memory of this, as I do myself. Therefore, dear landlady, my will is now to provide a blessing on this house for many of its guests. I've often seen the way you do a kindness to poor wandering journeymen by giving them free board and lodging. So that you may continue lending a helping hand to them, you'll find by the well here a stone jar, full of good silver groats. Give them out as you think fit, and I'll refill the vessel before the last coin's spent. I also institute as well five lucky days (for this is my lucky number) every century, with different gifts, such that, whoever of the journeymen crosses your threshold first on the day that brought me my first laugh, will receive from your hand or that of your children the best of all the five. Everyone who receives this prize must promise not to betray either the place or the time of this presentation. Such gifts you'll always find here by the well. This endowment I solemnly bestow for all time, as long as a branch of your family is in charge of the hostelry."

After these words she quietly talked over a lot of things with the hostess, finally saying, "Don't forget the plumb! The little shoemaker* must never get it." Then kissing everyone, she took her leave. The two women and the girls wept copiously. Lau placed a ring of green enamelwork onto Jutta's finger, saying, "Adieu, Jutta! We were so fond of each other. This must continue!" Then with a wave she dived and disappeared.

In a niche behind the well there indeed was the jar with the promised gifts. There was a hole in the wall, provided with a little iron door. No one had ever known where it led. Now it stood open, and beyond could be seen many gifts: a dice box of dragon's skin, furnished with golden bosses; a dagger with a precious inlaid handle; an ivory weaver's shuttle; a fair cloth woven abroad; and more of the like. But separate from these lay a cooking spoon of rosewood, with a long handle, beautifully painted and gilded from top to bottom; this the landlady was instructed to give the merry cook as a memento. Nor were any of the others overlooked.

Mistress Betha religiously observed kind Lau's instructions, and her descendants no less. As to the lady's paying a subsequent visit with her child to The Nuns' Inn, of this there is no mention in the old book; nevertheless, I think it likely.

Translated by Derek Bowman

Translator's note: The translator wishes to express his gratitude for help with finer points to Karin Donhauser of Passau University.

---

* Reference to the "Stuttgarter Hutzelmännlein," a folk figure involved in the main story by the same name from which the story of Beautiful Lau is taken. (*Translator's note.*)

Hinzelmeier.
A Thoughtful Story

Theodor Storm

The White Wall

In a spacious old house lived Herr Hinzelmeier and his beautiful wife Abel. They had been married for eleven years; in fact, the people of the town reckoned that the two of them were carrying around the combined weight of almost eighty years, and yet they were still young and handsome, not a wrinkle on their foreheads, not a crow's foot by their eyes. It was obvious enough that something funny was going on, and when the talk at coffee clatches got around to the subject of the Hinzelmeiers, the town gossips would drink three more cups than they did the first Sunday afternoon of Easter. One would say, "They've got a fountain of youth in the backyard." Another would agree. "Not just a fountain of youths, either; girls too—it's a mill of maidens." A third would add, "Their boy, little Hinzelmeier, was born with a lucky caul and now his parents take turns wearing it, one night one of them, the next night the other." Of course, little Hinzelmeier had no such thoughts; on the contrary it seemed quite natural to him that his parents were forever young and beautiful. But all the same he was to get his own little mystery to solve and he couldn't crack it.

One fall afternoon, toward dusk, he was sitting in the long hall of the top story of his house, playing hermit. Normally he would have been giving lessons to the silver gray house cat, but she had just crept out into the garden to check on the finches, so for the rest of the day he was compelled to give up playing professor.

Now he was sitting in a corner, being a hermit, and wondering about all sorts of things, such as where birds flew to, and what the world out there looked like, and even more profound matters; for he intended to give the cat a lecture on these subjects the next day, when he saw his mother, beautiful Frau Abel, walk past him. "Hey, Mother," he called, but she did not hear him. She walked on with rapid steps to the end of the hall; there she stopped and struck the white wall three times with her handkerchief. Hinzelmeier counted in his mind, and hardly had he gotten to three when the wall opened without a sound and he saw his mother disappear through it. The tip of her handkerchief barely had time to slip through after her when the whole thing closed shut with a soft clap and our hermit was left with much more to wonder about, namely, where in the world his mother went when she went through the wall. While he was thus occupied, it gradually grew darker and the dusk in his corner became so thick that it swallowed him up completely. At this point there came, as before, a soft clap and lovely Frau Abel stepped out of the wall again, into the hall. As she brushed past him, the fragrance of roses reached the boy. "Mother, Mother," he called, but she would not stop; he heard her walk down the stairs and into his father's room, where, that same morning, he had tied his hobbyhorse to the brass knob on the stove. Now he could contain himself no longer; he ran through the hall and rode like the wind down the banister. When he entered the room it was full of the smell of roses and it almost seemed to him that his mother was a rose herself, such was the glow on her face. It made Hinzelmeier very thoughtful.

"Mother dear," he said finally, "why do you always go through the wall?"

And when this caused Frau Abel to fall silent, his father said, "Well, after all, my son, because other people always go through the door."

That made sense to Hinzelmeier; but soon he wanted to know more.

"Where do you go when you go through the wall?" he went on, "and where are those roses?"

But before he knew it his father had turned him head over heels and plopped him on his hobbyhorse and his mother was singing a beautiful song:

Hatto of Mainz and Poppo of Trier
Rode together from Luenebier.
Hippity Hatto, a-trotting we go,
Hoppity Poppo, galloping so!

One, two, three!
Past Zelle with me;
One, two, three, four!
Now we're at our own front door.

"Untie him, untie him!" cried Hinzelmeier, and his father loosened the reins of the little horse from the knob of the stove, and his mother sang her song, and the rider rode up and down and had soon forgotten all the roses and white walls in the whole world.

The Tip of the Handkerchief

Many years went by without a repetition of the miraculous event Hinzelmeier had witnessed. So he no longer thought about it all the time, though his parents remained as young and beautiful as they had always been, and even in winter were often surrounded by the fragrance of roses.

Hinzelmeier was rarely to be found in the lonely corridor of the top story now, for the cat had died of old age and his school had consequently folded for lack of pupils.

About this time he began to think that his beard ought to start growing in a few years. One day he went up again into the old hallway to take a look at the white walls, because he planned that evening to do a production of the famous shadow play "Nebuchadnezzar and his Nutcracker." With this in mind he had come to the end of the corridor and was looking up and down the opposite wall when to his astonishment he saw the tip of a handkerchief hanging out of it. He bent down to look at it more closely: the corner bore the initials A.H. That could only mean Abel Hinzelmeier; it was his mother's handkerchief. Now the wheels in his head began to turn and his thoughts worked backward, farther and farther, until they came to a sudden stop at the first chapter of this story. At this point he tried to pull the handkerchief out of the wall and, fortunately, after some rather painful experimentation, succeeded. Then, like the lovely Frau Abel before him, he struck the piece of cloth against the wall three times, and "one—two—three" it parted silently. Hinzelmeier slipped through and found himself—the last place he thought he would be—in the attic. No doubt about it: there stood his great-grandmother's wardrobe with its wobbly pagoda towers on top, next to it his own cradle, and beyond that his hobbyhorse, things that had served their purpose and been discarded, all of them. Under the rafters, on rows of iron hooks, hung his father's long coats and traveling capes, as they always had, turning slowly whenever there was a draft of air from the open dormers. "Strange," said Hinzelmeier. "Why in the world did mother always go through that wall?" However, unable to discern anything besides the objects he was familiar with, he thought he would go back down through the attic door into the house. But the door was not there. He was momentarily taken aback and at first thought that he had simply got lost, having come up from a different direction than usual. He therefore turned and walked through the coats and capes to the old wardrobe in order to get his bearings again and, sure enough, there was the door. He could not imagine how he had overlooked it. But when he went up to it, everything suddenly seemed strange once more, so that he began to doubt whether he was at the right door. As far as he knew, however, there was no other. What confused him most was the fact that the iron latch was missing, and also that the key, which was always in the lock, had been removed. He therefore put his eye to the keyhole, hoping to catch sight of someone on the stairs, or on the landing, who might let him out. To his amazement, however, he was not looking down the dark stairs but into a bright, spacious room, the existence of which he had never suspected.

In the middle of it he could make out a pyramidal shrine-like cabinet, closed off with glittering gold doors and adorned with curious carving. Hinzelmeier couldn't tell whether the narrow keyhole was distorting his vision, but it almost seemed as if the figures of snakes and lizards in the brown leaves festooning the corners were rustling up and down and occasionally even stretching their supple heads over the gold background of the door. All this had so occupied the boy's attention that it was some time before he noticed his lovely mother and her husband, kneeling before the shrine with their heads bowed. Involuntarily he held his breath so as not to be discovered, and heard his parents' voices, softly singing:

> Ring around the roses shine
> Open, open, golden shrine,
> Open up to me and mine!
> Ring around the roses shine.

During their singing all the reptilian life in the fretwork foliage ceased. The golden doors opened slowly and revealed in the interior of the cabinet a crystal chalice in which a half-opened rose stood upon its slender stem. Gradually the calyx opened, farther and farther, until one of the shimmering petals became detached and fell between the kneeling couple. But before it had reached the ground it dissolved in the air with a sound like the ringing of bells and filled the room with a rosy-red mist.

The powerful fragrance of roses poured through the keyhole. The boy pressed his eye to the opening but saw nothing except an occasional luminescence that ascended in the reddish half-light and vanished again. After a time he heard steps at the door; he was about to leap up but a violent pain in his forehead robbed him of consciousness.

The Rose

When Hinzelmeier awoke from his swoon, he was lying in his bed. Frau Abel sat beside him, holding his hand in hers. She smiled when he opened his eyes and looked at her, and the reflected glow of the rose was on her face. "You've heard too much to stop part way; there's more you must know," she said. "Only you have to stay in bed the rest of the day; but meanwhile I'll tell you the secret of your family. You're old enough now to know."

"Please tell me, mother," said Hinzelmeier, and laid his head back on his pillow. Then Frau Abel told her story. "Far from this little town lies the old, old rose garden, which legend says was one of the things made on the sixth day of Creation. Inside its walls are a thousand red rosebushes that never stop blooming, and every time a child is born to our family (which is now spread through all the lands of the world, in many branches) a new bud springs from the leaves. Each bud has a maiden assigned to tend it, and she may not leave the garden until the rose has been picked by the one whose birth caused it to bud. Such a rose, which you just saw, has the power to keep its owner young and beautiful for life, so no one would lightly miss the chance to get his rose. It's only a question of finding the right way, because the entrances are many and often strange. One may lead through a thickly overgrown fence, another through a narrow, hidden door, and sometimes"—with mischievous eyes Frau Abel looked at her husband, who was just entering the room "—sometimes through the window, too."

Herr Hinzelmeier smiled and sat down by his son's bed.

Frau Abel went on with her story. "Most of the young maidens are released from their imprisonment in this fashion, and each leaves the garden with the owner of her rose. Your mother was a rose maiden too and for sixteen years tended your father's rose. But if the man in question passes the garden without entering he can never return. Only the Maid of the Rose is allowed, after three times three years, to go out in the world and look for her Lord of the Rose, and not until another three times three years have passed may she repeat the attempt. Few, however, risk the first trip and almost no one risks the second. For the Rose Maidens are fearful of the world and if in fact they go forth in their white robes they go with downcast eyes and trembling footsteps. Still, for every hundred such brave women, hardly a one has ever found her wandering Lord of the Rose. As far as *he* is concerned, however, the rose is lost, and while the maiden returns to everlasting imprisonment he has forfeited the grace of his birth, and, pitifully, like ordinary human beings, he must age and die. You too, my son, are one of the Lords of the Roses and when you enter the world out there, don't forget the Rose Garden."

Herr Hinzelmeier bent down and kissed Frau Abel's silken hair. Then, taking the boy's other hand in his friendly grasp, he said, "You are big enough now. Would you like to go out into the world and master some art?"

"Yes," said Hinzelmeier, "but it would have to be a great art, the kind no one ever was able to master before."

Frau Abel shook her head in distress; but his father said, "I will take you to a wise teacher who lives in a large city many miles from here; then you can choose the art you want."

Hinzelmeier was satisfied with that.

A few days later Frau Abel packed a great trunk with innumerable clothes, and Hinzelmeier himself put in a razor so that whenever his beard came he could shave it off again right away. Then one day the coach pulled up before the door and, as his mother embraced him in farewell, she said to her son, through her tears, "Don't forget the Rose!"

Crohirius

After Hinzelmeier had lived with his wise mentor for a year he wrote to his parents to tell them that he had now chosen the art he would master: he was going to seek the Philosophers' Stone. In two years his teacher would dismiss him and he would then set out on his travels as a journeyman and not return until he had found the stone. This was the kind of art no one had ever before acquired, for even his master was really just a senior journeyman; he had never come close to discovering the Stone.

When lovely Frau Abel had read this letter she folded her hands, fingers intertwined, and cried, "Oh, he will never reach the Rose Garden. The same thing will happen to him that happened to our neighbor's boy Caspar, who went away twenty years ago and never came home again."

Herr Hinzelmeier, however, kissed his lovely wife and said, "He had to go his own way. I too wanted to look for the Philosophers' Stone once; instead I found the Rose."

So young Hinzelmeier stayed with his wise master and time slowly ran its course.

It was late at night. Hinzelmeier sat before a smoky lamp, bent over a folio volume. But he could make no progress today; he felt his veins pounding and swirling, he was overcome by an anxious feeling that he might forever lose his comprehension for the deep wisdom of the formulas and incantations preserved in the ancient book.

Occasionally he would turn his pale face to look back into the room, staring vacantly at the corner and at the cheerless figure of his master puttering about before a low hearth among glowing retorts and crucibles. At times, when the bats swept past the windowpanes, he would look longingly out into the moonlit night, which lay like a magic spell over the fields. At the master's side, on the floor, crouched the herb lady. She had the gray house cat on her lap and was gently stroking the sparks out of his fur. Sometimes, when there was a nice comforting crackle and the beast meowed with a pleasant shudder, the master would reach back to pat him and would say, with a cough, "The cat is the philosopher's companion."

Suddenly there came from outside, from the ridge of the roof that ran beneath the window, a long drawn out sound of yearning, such as only the cat, among all animals, is capable of, and then only in spring. The tomcat straightened up and dug his claws into the old lady's apron. Another cry from outside, and the creature sprang with a vigorous leap to the floor and over Hinzelmeier's shoulder through the windowpane and into the open, so that the slivers of glass sprayed out behind him with a sound like the ringing of bells.

A sweet smell of primroses swept into the room on the draft of air. Hinzelmeier sprang up. "It's spring, master!" he cried and threw back his chair.

The old man buried his nose deeper in the crucible. Hinzelmeier went over to him and took him by the shoulder. "Don't you hear, master?"

The master ran his hand through his grey-dappled beard and stared dully at the young man through his green spectacles.

"The ice is breaking up!" cried Hinzelmeier. "There's a ringing in the air!"

The master seized him by the wrist and began to count his pulse. "Ninety-six," he said gravely, but Hinzelmeier paid no attention to that, rather he requested permission to leave that very hour. The master told him to take up his walking stick and his knapsack; he walked with him to the door, where they could look far out into the countryside. The boundless plains lay at their feet, in the bright moonlight. They stood there quietly. The master's face was furrowed with a thousand wrinkles, his back was bent, his beard hung down deep over his brown robe; he looked inexpressibly old. Hinzelmeier's face was pale too, but his eyes shone. His master spoke to him: "Your time is over. Kneel down so that you may receive permission to go." Then he drew a little white rod from his sleeve and, as Hinzelmeier knelt there, touched him on the back of the neck three times, saying:

> The Word's in the keeping
> Of spirits; the faster
> You rouse it from sleeping,
> The sooner you're master.
> It's found in no kingdom, grown in no clime
> It's partly a name, an aura in part;
> To find and create at the very same time
> That is the art!

Then he bade him stand up. A shiver coursed through the youth's body as he gazed into the grizzled, solemn face of his master. He took up his walking stick and knapsack and was about to leave when the master called, "Don't forget the raven!" He stuck his bony fist into his beard and pulled out a black hair. He blew it through his fingers and it rose into the air as a raven.

Now he swung his staff in a circle about his head and the raven circled after. Then he stretched out his arm and the bird settled on his fist. He lifted his green spectacles from his nose and, clamping them on the raven's beak, he spoke:

> Show the way, that's what you'll do;
> Crohirius is the name for you.

Then the raven cried, "Crohiro, crohiro!" and with outstretched wings hopped onto Hinzelmeier's shoulder. The master, in turn, said to Hinzelmeier:

> Journeyman's book and journeyman's rhyme,
> Now you have both—and now it is time!

With his finger he pointed down into the valley, where an endless road ran across the plain, and as Hinzelmeier, waving his traveling cap in farewell, walked out into the spring night, Crohirius took off and flew overhead.

The Entrance to the Rose Garden

The sun was already high in the sky. Hinzelmeier had set out on a straight path over a field of green winter grain that spread without limit before him. At the end of it the footpath led out through an opening in the wall to a spacious enclosure, and Hinzelmeier found himself before the buildings of a large farm estate. It had been raining, and the thatched roofs were steaming in the crisp spring sun. He stuck his journeyman's staff into the ground and gazed up at the ridgepole of the farmhouse, where crowds of sparrows were carrying on. Suddenly, from one of the two chimneys, he saw a shining disc rise into the air, turn slowly in the sunshine, and then fall back again, down the chimney.

Hinzelmeier pulled out his pocket watch. "It's noon," he said, "they are baking egg pancakes." A lovely fragrance spread all about; another egg pancake rose into the sunshine and after a brief time sank back into the chimney.

Hunger asserted itself. Hinzelmeier stepped into the house and, crossing a broad hallway, reached a high, spacious kitchen, like those commonly found in larger farmhouses. At the hearth, with its bright fire of brush and twigs, stood a sturdy farm woman, pouring the batter into the sizzling pan.

Crohirius, who had silently flown in behind Hinzelmeier, lit on the mantel over the hearth, while Hinzelmeier asked if he might get a meal here in exchange for money and kind words.

"This is no inn," said the woman and swung her pan so that the pancake rose with a sizzle up the black flue and plopped down again, right side up in the pan, but only after a considerable time.

Hinzelmeier reached for his stick, which he had leaned against the door as he entered. The old lady, however, ran her fork into the pancake and flipped it quickly onto a plate. "Well, all right," she said, "I wasn't serious. Go ahead and sit down. Here's one that's ready." Then she shoved a wooden chair up to the kitchen table for him and set the steaming pancake in front of him, along with bread and a mug of new local wine.

Hinzelmeier accepted it all gladly and had soon consumed the hearty food and a considerable part of the firm rye bread. He then put the mug to his mouth and took a good draft of it to the old lady's health, and then a good many more to his own. This made him so happy that he began to sing just because he felt like it. "You're a cheerful fellow," cried the old lady from her hearth. Hinzelmeier nodded. Suddenly he found himself reminded of all the songs he had heard long ago in his parents' house, sung by his lovely mother. Now he sang them, one after the other:

> It's all because the nightingale sang,
> Sang all the livelong night;
> The song was sweet, its echo rang,
> And that is why the roses sprang
> Into bloom and bright.

> Once the most carefree maid of all,
> She walks, perplexed and blue,
> In the summer sun, no shade at all,
> Forgets she has her parasol
> And can't think what to do.

> It's all because the nightingale sang,
> Sang all the livelong night.

In the wall opposite the hearth, beneath the rows of shiny pewter plates, a small sliding window opened and a pretty blond girl, perhaps the farm owner's daughter, stuck her head into the kitchen, with a curious look on her face.

Hinzelmeier, who had heard the rattling of panes in the window, stopped his singing and let his eyes wander over the walls of the kitchen, over the butter tub and the shiny cheese vats, and over the old woman's broad back to the open window, where they came to rest on another pair of youthful eyes.

The girl blushed. "You sing nicely, young man," she said at last.

"It just came over me," Hinzelmeier replied. "I don't usually sing at all."

Then they were both silent for a time, and all one could hear was the sizzling of the pan and the crackle of the pancakes.

"Caspar sings well too," the girl spoke up again.

"No doubt he does," agreed Hinzelmeier.

"Yes," said the girl, "but not as nicely as you do. Where did you ever learn that beautiful song?"

Hinzelmeier did not answer; he stepped up on an overturned tub that stood under the sliding window and looked past the girl into the room beyond. It was full of sunshine. On the red tiles of the floor lay the shadows of carnations and roses, doubtless from bushes growing to the side and in front of a window somewhere. Suddenly toward the back of the room a door opened. The spring wind swept in and lifted a blue silk ribbon from the girl's bonnet, blew it through the sliding window, and bore its prize about the kitchen in circles; but Hinzelmeier threw his cap after it and caught it as one catches a summer bird.

He was about to hand the ribbon up to the girl, but found the window was a bit high. She bent out toward him, and their two heads bumped together with a crack. The girl cried out, the pewter plates rattled. Hinzelmeier became totally confused.

"You have a good solid head, young man," said the girl and with her hand wiped away the tears from her cheek. Hinzelmeier pushed his hair back from his forehead and with a friendly smile looked her in the face, and when he did so she cast her eyes down and asked, "You didn't hurt yourself, did you?"

Hinzelmeier laughed. "No, miss," he cried, and then suddenly asked, although he couldn't figure out why this should occur to him, "Don't be offended, but I suppose you already have a sweetheart?"

She put her fist under her chin and tried to look defiantly at him, but her eyes remained fixed on his. "You must be imagining things," she said softly.

Hinzelmeier shook his head; not a word passed between them.

"Young lady," Hinzelmeier said after a time, "I'd like to bring the ribbon to you, in your room."

The girl nodded.

"But how do I get there?"

Words echoed in his ears: "Sometimes through the window!" It was his mother's voice. He saw her as she sat by his bed, he saw her smile; suddenly it seemed to him as if he were standing in a rosy cloud that was floating through the open panel window into the kitchen. He got up on the tub again and put his arms around the girl's neck. Through the open door of the room he could look out into a garden where rosebushes bloomed like a sea of red, and in the distance he heard the crystal voices of girls singing:

> Ring around the roses shine,
> Open up for me and mine!

Hinzelmeier pushed the girl gently back into the room and braced his hands on the windowsill, ready to swing himself up and in with a single leap. Then he heard a whirring over his head and a "Crohiro, crohiro!" and before he knew it the raven had dropped the green spectacles from the air right onto his nose. He saw the girl stretch out her arms toward him, but it was only as if in a dream; then everything disappeared before his eyes. In the far distance, however, he could see, through the green spectacles, a dark figure in a deep, rocky crevasse, apparently engaged in busily probing the ground with a long crowbar.

A Master Shot

"He is looking for the Philosophers' Stone!" thought Hinzelmeier, and his cheeks began to burn. He strode off vigorously toward the figure but it was farther away than it had looked through the lenses of his spectacles. He called out to the raven and had it fan his temples with its wings. It was hours before he reached the floor of the ravine. Before him he saw a coarse, black figure with two horns on its forehead and a long tail, which it draped down over the rock. On Hinzelmeier's arrival it took the crowbar between its teeth and greeted him with the most deferential bow of its head, while it used the tuft of its tail to sweep up the debris from the boring. Hinzelmeier was quite at a loss for the proper form of address, so each time he bowed back with equal deference, with the result that this exchange of compliments lasted for some time. Finally the other one asked, "I assume you do not know who I am?"

"No," said Hinzelmeier. "Are you perhaps a master pumpman?"

"Yes," said the other, "something like that; I am the Devil."

Hinzelmeier was not prepared to believe that, but the Devil looked at him with two eyes so owlish that he was at last thoroughly convinced and said meekly, "Might I be permitted to ask whether you mean to use this enormous hole for an experiment in physics?"

"Are you familiar with the *ultima ratio regum?*" the devil asked.

"No," said Hinzelmeier. "The *ratio regum* has nothing to do with my art."

The Devil scratched himself behind the ears with his horse's hoof and said, in a condescending tone of voice, "My son, do you know what a cannon is?"

"Naturally," said Hinzelmeier with a smile, for he saw in his imagination the whole wooden arsenal of his boyhood propped up before him.

The devil was so pleased he clapped his tail on the rock cliff. "Three pounds of gunpowder, a spark of hell's fire, and then—!" At this point he stuck one paw in the bore-hole and, laying the other on Hinzelmeier's shoulder, said confidentially, "The world has gotten out of control. I'm going to blow it up."

"Good grief," cried Hinzelmeier, "that certainly is radical therapy; that's real horse medicine."

"Yes," said the Devil, *"ultima ratio regum*—I assure you, it takes a superhuman disposition to stand this sort of thing. But now you must pardon me for a while, I have to do a bit of inspecting." With these words he tucked his tail in between his thighs and leaped down the bore-hole. Suddenly Hinzelmeier was seized with courage quite beyond the ordinary and decided he might as well shoot the Devil right out of the world. With a firm hand he drew his tinderbox from his pocket, struck a spark from it, and threw it into the bore-hole. Then he counted, "one—two—," but he hadn't gotten to three yet when this bottomless pistol discharged its shot along with its priming. The earth executed a terrifying sidewise leap through the sky. Hinzelmeier fell to his knees. The Devil, however, flew through the air like a bombshell, from one solar system to another, where the gravitational pull of our earth could no longer reach him. Hinzelmeier followed him with his eyes for a while, but when he kept flying farther and farther off, seemingly never to stop, Hinzelmeier couldn't hold back his tears.

As soon as the earth had quieted down enough to permit standing on it with both feet, he leaped up and looked around him. At his feet, the black and burnt-out mortar barrel yawned up at him. From time to time a cloud of brownish smoke puffed out from it and moved lazily along the cliffs. But the sun was already breaking through the haze and touching the tips of all the rocks with gold. Hinzelmeier took his tobacco pipe from his pocket and, blowing clouds of blue smoke before him, cried out in triumph, "I've shot Mr. Sulfurous Brimstone right out of this world; the Philosophers' Stone isn't going to get away from me. Let's be on our way!"

So he continued his journey, with Crohirius flying overhead.

The Rose Maiden

He journeyed back and forth, first this way, then that. He grew more and more weary, his back became bent, but he still did not find the Philosophers' Stone. Nine years had passed in this way when one evening he stopped at an inn situated at the entrance to a large city. Crohirius took off his spectacles with his claw and cleaned them on his wings, then put them back on and hopped into the kitchen. When the people who worked there saw him they laughed at his spectacles, called him Professor, and threw him the fattest scraps of food.

"If you are the owner of this bird," said the innkeeper to Hinzelmeier, "then someone has been asking about you."

"As a matter of fact I am," said Hinzelmeier.

"And what is your name?"

"My name is Hinzelmeier."

"Ah ha," said the innkeeper. "I am very well acquainted with your son, the husband of beautiful Frau Abel."

"That's my father," said Hinzelmeier with annoyance, "and beautiful Frau Abel is my mother."

The people laughed when they heard this and said that he was an extraordinarily funny fellow. Hinzelmeier, however, stared angrily into a shiny pot.

A gloomy face stared back at him, full of wrinkles and crow's feet, and now he could see clearly that he had grown disgustingly old.

"Yes, yes!" he cried, and shook himself as if he were emerging with difficulty from a deep dream. "Where was it anyway? I was very close." Then he asked the innkeeper who had inquired about him.

"It was only a poor serving girl," said the innkeeper. "She was wearing a white dress and walking around barefoot."

"That was the Rose Maiden!" cried Hinzelmeier.

"Yes," replied the innkeeper, "it may well have been a flower girl, but she had only one rose left in her basket."

"Where did she go?" cried Hinzelmeier.

"If you feel you have to talk to her," said the innkeeper, "you'll surely be able to find her on some street corner in the city."

When Hinzelmeier heard that, he strode quickly out of the house and into town. Crohirius, the spectacles on his nose, flew after him, cawing. Their way took them from one street to another, and on the curb at every corner stood flower girls, but they wore big, shapeless buckled shoes and cried their wares with shrill voices. Those were no Rose Maidens. At last, when the sun had already set behind the buildings, Hinzelmeier came to an old house; from the open door a delicate light shone forth onto the street. Crohirius threw his head back and beat his wings anxiously, but Hinzelmeier paid no attention; he stepped over the threshold into a broad entrance hall, filled with a red glow. He could see, far in the background, sitting on the lowest step of a spiral staircase, a pale young woman. On her lap she held a basket and in the basket lay a red rose, the chalice of which was the source of that delicate light. The girl seemed tired; she was just taking her lips from an earthenware water pitcher, which a little boy was holding out to her in both his hands. A large dog lay beside her on the stair; like the boy, he seemed to be a part of the household. He had put his head on her white dress and was licking her bare feet.

"That's her," said Hinzelmeier, and his steps were unsteady with hope and expectation. And when the girl lifted up her face to look at him, it was as if scales fell from his eyes: he suddenly recognized the girl from the farm kitchen, only today she was not wearing the colorful blouse, and the red of her cheeks was only the reflection of the light from the rose.

"There you are," cried Hinzelmeier, "now everything is going to be all right, everything."

She stretched her arms out to him; she tried to smile, but tears sprang to her eyes. "Where in all the world have you been, wandering around so long?" she said.

And when he looked into her eyes, he was taken aback for pure joy, because there was his own image, not the image that had glowered at him moments ago from the copper kettle. No, it was a face so young and fresh and cheerful that he could not help shouting for happiness. He could not give this up for anything in the world.——

Then, from the street, a crowd of people poured into the house, shouting and waving their arms. "Here's the bird's master," cried a stocky little man. Then everyone surged down upon Hinzelmeier.

Hinzelmeier seized the girl's hand and asked, "What's the raven done?"

"What's it done?" said the fat man; "it has stolen the mayor's wig!"

"Right!, right!" they all cried, "and now it's sitting up there on the eaves-trough, the monster, with the wig in its claws, staring at His Excellency through those green glasses."

Hinzelmeier was about to say something, but they surrounded him and pushed him toward the door. Horrified, he felt the Rose Maiden's hand slip from his. Thus he found himself on the street.

The raven was still sitting high on the eaves-trough of the house, looking down with its black eyes on the people as they came out of the house. Suddenly it opened its claws, and, while the townspeople jabbed around in the air with their canes and umbrellas, trying to catch their mayor's wig, Hinzelmeier heard over his head the whirring sound of "Crohiro, crohiro" and at the same moment the green spectacles were on his nose again.

Then suddenly the city disappeared before his eyes; through the spectacles he saw beneath him a green valley full of dairy farms and villages. Sun-drenched meadows extended all around, and through the grass walked barefoot girls with shiny milk pails, while far in the distance young lads swung their scythes. What caught and held Hinzelmeier's eye, however, was the figure of a man in a red and white smock, with a pointed cap on his head. He seemed to be sitting on a rock in the middle of a field, in a thoughtful attitude.

Caspar, the Neighbor's Boy

Hinzelmeier thought, "That's the Philosophers' Stone!" and headed straight toward him. The man, however, did not stir from his thoughtful pose; the only thing he did, to Hinzelmeier's amazement, was pull his great nose down over his chin, like a piece of rubber.

"I say, sir, what are you doing there?" cried Hinzelmeier.

"I don't know," the man said, "but I have this cursed bell on my cap that makes it abominably hard for me to think."

"But why are you pulling at your nose in such a dreadful way?"

"Oh," said the man and let go the tip of his nose, causing it to fly back with a snap into its original shape. "I beg your pardon there, but I often suffer from thoughts, since I'm seeking the Philosophers' Stone."

"My Lord," said Hinzelmeier, "then you must be our neighbor's boy Caspar, who never came back home!"

"Yes," said the man, extending his hand to Hinzelmeier, "that's who I am."

"And I am Hinzelmeier from next door to you, and I am looking for the Philosophers' Stone as well."

At this they put out their hands to one another again and in so doing crossed their fingers in a certain way so that each knew the other was one of the initiates. Then Caspar said, "But now I'm not looking for the Philosophers' Stone anymore."

"Then perhaps you're on your way to the Rose Garden," cried Hinzelmeier.

"No," said Caspar, "the reason I'm not looking for the Stone is because I've already found it."

At this Hinzelmeier fell silent for quite some time. Finally he folded his hands reverentially and said in a solemn voice, "It had to happen this way, I knew it did; because nine years ago I shot the Devil right out of the world."

"That must have been his son," said the other. "I met the old Devil just the day before yesterday."

"No," said Hinzelmeier, "it was the old Devil, because he had horns on his forehead and a tail with a black tuft at the end. But tell me how you found the Stone."

"That's simple," said Caspar. "All the people down there in the village are really stupid; they associate with no one but sheep and cows. They didn't know what a treasure they had. I found it in an old cellar and paid three half-shillings a pound for it. And ever since yesterday I've been trying to think what it's good for, and I probably would have figured out the answer if this cursed bell hadn't made it so hard for me to think."

"My dear colleague," said Hinzelmeier, "that is a most crucial question, one that surely no man *before* you ever thought about! But where are you keeping the Stone?"

"I'm sitting on it," said Caspar and, getting up, pointed out to Hinzelmeier the round, waxy yellow object he had previously been perched on.

"Yes," said Hinzelmeier, "no doubt about it, you have really found it, but now let's try to think what it's good for."

Thereupon they sat down on the ground, facing each other, placed the stone between them, and propped their elbows on their knees.

So they sat and sat. The sun set, the moon rose, and still they had found no answer. Now and again one of them would ask, "Have you got it?" but the other would always shake his head and say, "No, not me; how about you?"; to which the first would answer, "I haven't either."

Crohirius walked happily up and down in the grass, catching frogs. Caspar was tugging at his big, beautiful nose again. Then the moon set and the sun came up, and Hinzelmeier asked once more, "Have you got it?" and Caspar shook his head again and said, "No, not me; how about you?"; and Hinzelmeier answered gloomily, "I haven't either."

Then they thought hard again for quite a while, and finally Hinzelmeier said, "We'll have to polish our spectacles first, then we'll soon see what it's good for." And scarcely had Hinzelmeier taken off his spectacles when he let them drop into the grass in astonishment. "I've got it! Dear colleague, we must *eat* it! Just take your spectacles off your handsome nose, if you don't mind."

Then Caspar took his spectacles off too and, after contemplating his stone for a time, said, "This is what is called a leather cheese, and it must be eaten with God's help. Have some, dear colleague!"

And now the two took their knives from their pockets and made a healthy stab at the cheese. Crohirius came over on the wing and, after gathering up the spectacles from the grass and clamping them on his beak, sat down comfortably between the two diners and snapped at the pieces of rind.

"I don't know," said Hinzelmeier, after the cheese was eaten up, "I am open to contradiction but I feel as if I have gotten substantially closer to the Philosophers' Stone."

"My esteemed colleague," replied Caspar, "you speak after my own heart. Let us therefore continue our journey without delay."

After these words they embraced. Caspar went to the west; Hinzelmeier to the east, and overhead, with the spectacles on his beak, flew Crohirius.

The Philosophers' Stone

Hinzelmeier journeyed back and forth, first this way, then that; his hair grew gray, his legs became unsteady; leaning on his staff he walked from land to land and still he did not find the Philosophers' Stone. In this fashion another nine years had passed, when one evening, as was his custom, he entered an inn. Crohirius as usual polished his spectacles and then hopped into the kitchen to beg for his supper. Hinzelmeier entered the room and leaned his staff in the corner by the tile stove. Then he sat down, silent and weary, in the great armchair. The innkeeper placed a jug of wine before him and said in a friendly way, "You seem tired, my dear sir; drink, it will give you strength."

"Yes," said Hinzelmeier and took the jug in both his hands, "very tired; I have had a long journey, a very long one." Then he closed his eyes and took a thirsty draught from the wine jug.

"If you are the bird's master, I'm almost sure someone inquired about you," said the innkeeper. "What is your name, my dear sir?"

"My name is Hinzelmeier."

"Well," said the innkeeper, "your grandson, the husband of beautiful Frau Abel, is someone I know very well."

"That's my father," said Hinzelmeier, "and beautiful Frau Abel is my mother."

The innkeeper shrugged his shoulders, and turning back to his bar he said to himself, "The poor old man is in his second childhood."

Hinzelmeier let his head sink on his chest and asked who had inquired about him.

"It was only a poor servant girl," said the innkeeper. "She wore a white dress and was barefoot." Hinzelmeier smiled and said softly, "That was the Rose Maiden; now everything will be all right. Where did she go?"

"She did seem to be a flower girl," said the innkeeper. "If you want to talk with her, you'll have no trouble finding her; she'll be on the street corners."

"I must sleep for a while," said Hinzelmeier. "Give me a room and when the cock crows, knock on my door."

So the innkeeper gave him a room and Hinzelmeier went to sleep. He dreamed of his beautiful mother speaking to him. Then Crohirius flew through the open window and lit at the head of his bed. He ruffled his black feathers and snatched the spectacles from his beak with his claw. Then he stood motionless on one leg and looked down at the sleeper. The latter went on dreaming, and his mother said, "Don't forget the rose!" The sleeper nodded his head softly, and the raven opened its claw and dropped the spectacles on his nose.

His dreams changed; his sunken cheeks began to tremble, he stretched out to his full length and moaned. And so the night passed.

When the cock crowed in the dim light of dawn the innkeeper knocked on the door of his room. Crohirius stretched his wings and shook out his feathers. Then he cried, "Crohiro, crohiro!" Hinzelmeier pulled himself up with a great effort and stared about. Through the spectacles, which were still fixed on his nose, he looked out through the door of his room, over a wide, desolate field, then beyond to a slowly rising hill. On the hill, under the stump of an old willow, lay a flat gray stone. The area round about was lonely, not a human being in sight.

"That's the Philosophers' Stone!" said Hinzelmeier to himself. "At last, at last it's going to be mine after all!"

Hastily he threw on his clothes, took his staff and knapsack, and strode out the door. Crohirius flew overhead, making clicking noises with his beak, and turned somersaults in the air as he flew. In this fashion they journeyed for many hours. At last they seemed to be approaching their goal, but Hinzelmeier was exhausted, his chest heaved, the sweat dripped from his white hair. He stopped and stood there, supporting himself on his staff. Then there came from the distance, behind him, almost like a dream, the sound of singing:

> Ring around where roses shone.
> Do not leave him here alone!
> Hold him fast and bring him home,
> Ring around where roses shone.

The sound was like a golden net woven about him; he let his head drop to his chest; but Crohirius cried, "Crohiro! crohiro!" and the song fell silent. When Hinzelmeier opened his eyes again he was standing at the foot of the hill.

"Only a little bit longer," he said to himself, and made his tired feet take up their journey once more. But when, after a time, he saw the great, broad stone close at hand, he thought, "You'll never lift that."

At last they had reached the high point. Crohirius flew on ahead with outspread wings and settled on the tree trunk. Hinzelmeier stumbled along behind, trembling. But when he had reached the tree, he collapsed. His staff slipped from his hand, his head sank back upon the stone, and the spectacles slipped from his nose. Far on the horizon, at the edge of the desolate plain he had crossed, he saw the white figure of the Rose Maiden, and once again he heard from a great distance:

> Ring—around—the roses shine.

He tried to rise, but he no longer could. He stretched his arms out, but a cold shiver coursed through his limbs. The sky turned grayer and grayer, the snow began to fall; it glistened and danced and drew veils of white between him and the hazy figure in the distance. He dropped his arms, his eyes were sunken, his breath stopped. On the willow stump, by his head, the raven put its beak under its wing, to sleep. The snow fell over both of them.

The night came and then the morning, and with the morning the sun; it melted the snow away. And with the sun came the Rose Maiden. She loosened her braids and knelt by the dead man, her blond hair covering his pale face, and she wept until the end of day. But when the sun faded, the raven gurgled softly in his sleep and rustled his feathers. Then the slim young figure of the Rose Maiden drew itself up from the ground. With her white hand the girl seized the raven by its wings and hurled it into the air, so that it flew off croaking into the gray sky. She planted the red rose by the stone and as she did so she sang:

> Let your little roots run deep,
> Cast your petals on his sleep.
> The wind will sing at break of night,
> But you must speak to set it right
> With "Ring around a rosy light."

Then she tore her white dress asunder from hem to waist and went back into the Rose Garden to be a prisoner forever.

Translated by Frank G. Ryder

Bulemann's House

Theodor Storm

I n a North German coastal city, on Darkling Street, as it is called,
there stands an old, dilapidated house. It is quite narrow, but
four stories high. In the middle, from the ground to the eaves of
the gable, the wall projects to form an alcovelike structure, which
is provided in front and on the sides with windows, so that on
bright nights the moon can shine through.

Within living memory no one has entered this house and no one
has come out of it; the heavy brass knocker is almost black with
verdigris, and between the cracks of the stone steps grass grows
year in and year out. When a stranger asks, "What sort of house
is that anyway?" he is sure to receive the answer, "That's Bulemann's house." And if he then asks, "Who lives in it?" the answer
is equally certain: "No one lives in it." The children in the streets
and the nurse beside the cradle sing:

> In Bulemann's house,
> In Bulemann's house,
> From the windows there peeks
> Many a mouse.

And, in fact, some roistering companions, coming past on their
nocturnal carousings, claim to have heard the squeaking of innumerable mice behind the dark windows. One of them, who was
bold enough to raise the brass knocker and slam it against the
door, in order to hear the echo resounding through the deserted
rooms, even maintains that he distinctly heard the leaping of large
animals inside on the stairway. "It almost sounded," he would

add when told the story, "like the leaps of those great beasts of prey they showed in the menagerie in the marketplace."

The house that stands opposite is one story lower, so that at night the moonlight can fall directly into the upper windows of the old house. Of such a night the night watchman also has a tale to tell, but it was only the face of a little old man in a brightly colored stocking cap that he claims to have seen up behind the bow windows. The neighbors say, however, that the night watchman was merely drunk again; for their part, they had never seen anything resembling a human soul.

An old man living in a distant quarter of town, who was organist at St. Magdalene's years ago, seems to be able to furnish the most information. "I well remember," he stated, when once asked about the matter, "a gaunt man who used to live in that house with his elderly housekeeper when I was a boy. For some years he conducted a lot of business with my father, who was a second-hand dealer, and I was often sent to him to make arrangements. I also remember that I didn't like to go on such errands and tried to find all sorts of excuses, for even by day I was afraid to climb the dark narrow stairs up to Herr Bulemann's room on the fourth floor. People called him the 'soul trader' and the very name aroused my fears, especially since all kinds of other uncanny rumors were circulating about him. Before he had moved into the old house after the death of his father, he had sailed for many years as a supercargo to the West Indies. There he was said to have married a black woman, but when he came home again people waited in vain for his wife to arrive one day with dark-skinned offspring in tow. Soon it was said that on the return voyage he had met a slaver and had sold the captain of that ship his own flesh and blood together with their mother for filthy lucre. The truth about all this I don't know," the old man would add, "for I don't want to speak ill of the dead, but this much is certain: he was a miserly character who shunned human companionship, and his eyes also looked as though they had beheld evil deeds. No unfortunate and no one seeking help dared cross his threshold, and whenever I went there, the iron chain was always fastened inside the door. After I had knocked several times with the brass knocker, I usually heard the master's impatient voice shouting down from the top of the uppermost stairs, 'Frau Anken! Frau Anken! Are you deaf?

Someone's knocking!' I would then immediately hear the steps of the old woman shuffling through the back hallway and along the corridor. Before she opened up, she would ask in a wheezing voice, 'Who's there?' and only when I had replied, 'It's Leberecht!' would she remove the chain. After I had then hastily climbed the seventy-seven steps—I counted them once—I would see Herr Bulemann waiting for me in the narrow, dark hallway in front of his room. The room itself I was never permitted to enter. I still see him standing there before me in his yellow flowered dressing gown and peaked stocking cap, one hand behind him holding the door handle of his room. While I explained my errand, he would look at me impatiently with his round, piercing eyes and then send me away with harsh, curt words. What most attracted my attention at that time was a pair of enormous cats, one yellow and one black, which sometimes squeezed behind him out of his room and rubbed their heads against his knees. After a few years he stopped dealing with my father and I never went back there. All this was more than seventy years ago, and Herr Bulemann must have long since been carried to the place from whence no one returns."—— The man was mistaken when he said this. Herr Bulemann was not carried out of his house; he lives there to this day. This is how it happened.

Before Herr Bulemann, in the days when men still wore pigtails and bagwigs, there lived in that house a pawnbroker, an ancient, bent man of small stature. Since he had plied his trade with circumspection for more than five decades and had lived frugally with a woman who kept house for him after the death of his wife, he had finally become a rich man. His wealth, however, consisted mainly in an almost unsurveyable quantity of precious objects, various utensils, and rare antiques, which he had taken as pledges for loans to spendthrifts and persons in dire straits in the course of the years and which then, since they had not been redeemed, had remained in his possession. Since he would have been compelled upon selling these objects—which had to be done through the court—to return the amount exceeding the loan and the interest to the rightful owners, he preferred to pile them up in great walnut cabinets acquired for that purpose, and with these the rooms on the second and finally on the third floor had gradually become crowded. But at night, when Frau Anken was snoring soundly in her lonely little room at the back of the house and the heavy chain was securely fastened on the front door, he often stole up and down the stairs with light tread. Buttoned into his fitted pike grey dressing gown, a lamp in one hand and a bunch of keys in the other, he would open the rooms and the cabinets, now on the second, now on the third floor, taking here a gold watch, there an enamelled snuffbox out of its hiding place and reckoning to himself the number of years it had been in his possession and whether the original owners might be dead or missing and forgotten or whether they might one day return with the money in their hands and demand their property.

The pawnbroker had finally died in extreme old age, leaving his treasures behind, and had had to leave his house together with its packed cabinets to his sole son, whom he had craftily managed to keep at a distance during his lifetime.

This son, who had just returned to his native city from a voyage to foreign parts, was the supercargo so feared by little Leberecht. After his father's burial he gave up his former occupation and moved into his father's rooms on the fourth floor of the old house with the bay windows, where now, instead of the bent, old man in the pike grey gown, there paced up and down a gaunt figure in a yellow flowered one with a colorful stocking cap on his head, or stood reckoning at the dead man's desk. But Herr Bulemann had not inherited the old pawnbroker's fondness for the precious objects the latter had collected. After he had examined behind locked doors the contents of the great walnut cabinets, he considered whether he should venture to sell these things, which were still the property of others, and on which he had a claim only in the amount of the inherited loan, which, as the books showed, was usually quite trifling. But Herr Bulemann was not a man of indecision. In a few days he had already struck up a business relationship with a secondhand dealer who lived at the edge of town, and, after some pledges from recent years had been set aside, the motley contents of the walnut cabinets were secretly and cautiously transformed into sterling silver. That was the time when the boy Leberecht used to go to the house. The money he had realized Herr Bulemann stored in big ironbound chests and had these placed beside each other in his bedroom, for, considering the illegality of his wealth, he did not dare to buy up mortgages with it or otherwise openly invest it.

When everything was sold, he set about calculating all imaginable expenses he might incur for the presumable length of his life. Assuming he would live to ninety, he divided his money into separate packets, each calculated for one week, then added an extra packet for each quarter to cover unforeseen expenditures. This money he stacked in a special box that stood in the adjoining living room, and every Saturday morning Frau Anken, the old housekeeper whom he had taken over from his father's estate, would appear to receive a new packet and to render an account of how the last one had been expended.

As we have said, Herr Bulemann had not brought his wife and children with him; however, on the day after the old pawnbroker's funeral, a sailor brought two cats of remarkable size, a yellow one and a black one, into the house from shipboard in a securely tied sack. The animals soon became the sole companions of their master. At midday they got their own platter, which Frau Anken, with suppressed resentment, had to prepare for them day in and day out. After the meal, while Herr Bulemann took his noon nap, they sat beside him, well satisfied, on the sofa, letting a tip of tongue hang out of their mouths and blinking at him sleepily with their green eyes. If they had been in the lower rooms of the house hunting mice, which always earned them a clandestine kick from the old housekeeper, they were sure to carry any mice they had caught to their master and show them to him before creeping under the sofa to devour them. When night had fallen and Herr Bulemann had exchanged his brightly colored stocking cap for a white one, he climbed into the big curtained bed in the adjoining alcove with his two cats and let himself be lulled to sleep by the regular purring of the beasts curled up at his feet.

This peaceable existence had not, however, remained undisturbed. In the course of the first years a few owners of pledges had come and demanded the return of their valuables upon payment of the slight sum they had received as a loan. And Herr Bulemann, being afraid of a trial, which could have made his misconduct public, reached into his strong box and bought the silence of the borrowers with a larger or smaller cash settlement. This made him all the more inimical and sullen toward his fellowmen. His commerce with the old secondhand dealer had ceased long ago. He now sat alone in his room with the bay windows engaged upon a problem he had often attempted to solve: the calculation of a surefire lottery winning, by means of which he hoped one day to increase his wealth immeasurably. Grabs and Schnores, the two great tomcats, now had to suffer his ill humor. One minute he might scratch them with his long fingers and the next, if his figuring wouldn't work out, throw the paperweight or the shears at them, making them limp howling into the corner.

Herr Bulemann had a relative, a half-sister from his mother's first marriage, who, however, had been awarded her inheritance upon her mother's death and thus had no further claim on the money he had fallen heir to. But he paid no attention to this half-sister, although she lived in a suburban quarter of town in the most impoverished circumstances; for even less than intercourse with other people did Herr Bulemann care for intercourse with poverty-stricken relatives. Only once, when, after the death of her husband, she had given birth to a sickly child, had she come to him seeking help. Frau Anken, who had let her in, had sat down on the stairs below to eavesdrop. She soon heard her master's sharp voice above; finally the door was flung open and the woman came down the stairs in tears. That same evening Frau Anken was given strict orders not to remove the chain from the door, in case Christine should ever come back again.

The old woman began to be more and more afraid of the hooked nose and piercing owlish eyes of her master. When he called out her name from the top of the stairs or, as he was accustomed to do on shipboard, merely stuck his fingers in his mouth and gave a shrill whistle, she was sure to come hastily crawling out of any corner where she had been sitting and climb the narrow stairs with a groan, muttering imprecations and lamentations under her breath.

But just as Herr Bulemann had on the fourth floor, so had Frau Anken in the lower rooms hoarded her likewise not quite legally gained treasures.——

In the very first years of working for her master she had been seized by a kind of childish anxiety that Herr Bulemann might take over the dispensing of the household funds himself and she would then have to suffer want in her old age because of his miserliness. In order to avoid this, she had lied to him and said the price of wheat had gone up and then asked for more money to buy bread. The supercargo, who had just begun the calculation of his lifetime expenditures, had torn up his figures with a curse and then begun anew, adding the sum demanded to the weekly cash ration. But Frau Anken, her purpose achieved, in order to ease her conscience and mindful of the proverb, "Sampling's not stealing," had not stashed away the extra shillings she received, but rather the loaves of bread she regularly bought with them, and with these, since Herr Bulemann never entered the lower rooms of the house, she gradually filled the big walnut cabinets that had been robbed of their valuable contents.

Thus perhaps ten years went by. Herr Bulemann became ever gaunter and grayer, his yellow flowered dressing gown ever more threadbare. For days at a time he did not open his lips to say a word, for he saw no living creature except his two cats and his old housekeeper. Only occasionally, when he heard the neighbors' children playing horsey on the curbstones in front of the house, would he stick his head out of the window a little and yell down into the street in his piercing voice. "The soul trader, the soul trader!" the children would shout, fleeing in all directions. But Herr Bulemann only cursed and scolded all the more fiercely, until he finally slammed shut the window and took out his spite on Grabs and Schnores.

In order to avoid any contact with the neighbors, Frau Anken had for some time been compelled to do her shopping in a distant part of town. She was permitted to go out only after dusk and had to lock the front door behind her.

About a week before Christmas the old woman had again left the house to go shopping. In spite of her usual carefulness she must this time have been guilty of neglect. For just as Herr Bulemann had lighted his tallow candle with a sulphur match, he was surprised to hear a noise on the stairs, and when he stepped out into the hall holding the candle in front of him, he saw his half-sister standing before him, a pale boy at her side.

"How did you two get in?" he barked, after staring at them for a moment in fierce astonishment.

"The front door was open," the woman said shyly.

He cursed the housekeeper under his breath. "What is it you want?" he asked.

"Please don't be so harsh, brother," the woman pleaded, "or I won't have the courage to speak to you."

"I can't imagine what you have to say to me. You've got your share, we're through with each other."

The sister remained silent, vainly searching for the right words. Inside the room a persistent scratching at the door was audible. Herr Bulemann reached behind him and opened the door; the two cats bounded into the hallway and began to twist and purr about the pale boy, who fearfully retreated to the wall. Their master looked with impatience at the woman still standing silently in front of him. "Well, are you going to talk?" he demanded.

"I wanted to ask you for something, Daniel," she said at last. "A few years before his death your father, at a time when I was in bitter need, took a silver cup from me as a pledge."

"My father took it from you?" said Herr Bulemann.

"Yes, Daniel, your father, the husband of our mother. Here's the pawn ticket. He didn't lend me very much on it."

"Go on!" said Herr Bulemann, quickly examining his sister's empty hands.

"Some time ago," she continued hesitantly, "I dreamed that I was walking in the graveyard with my ailing child. When we came to the grave of our mother, she was sitting on her tombstone beneath a bush of white roses in full bloom. She had the little silver cup in her hand that I once received as a present from her as a child. When we came closer, she put it to her lips, smiling at my boy, and I clearly heard her say, 'To your health!' It was her gentle voice, Daniel, just as in life, and this dream I dreamed three nights in a row."

"What are you getting at?" demanded Herr Bulemann.

"Give me back the cup, brother! Christmas is near—I'll put it on my sick child's empty Christmas plate!"

The gaunt man in his yellow flowered dressing gown stood motionless and observed her with his piercing, round eyes. "Have you got the money with you?" he asked. "You can't redeem pledges with dreams."

"O Daniel!" she cried, "believe our mother. He'll get well if he drinks from the little cup. Be merciful. After all, he's your blood too!"

She had stretched out her hands to him, but he retreated a step. "Don't come near me," he said. Then he called his cats. "Grabs, you old beast! Schnores, my boy!" And the great yellow tomcat bounded with a leap onto its master's shoulder and sunk its claws in his brightly colored stocking cap, while the black one pawed at his knees, mewing.

The sickly boy had stolen closer. "Mother," he said, pulling hard at her dress, "is that the bad uncle that sold his black children?"

Herr Bulemann threw the cat down from his shoulder and seized the arm of the boy, who began to scream. "Damned little beggar," he shouted, "are you singing that crazy song too?"

"Brother, brother!" moaned the woman. But the boy already lay whimpering on the landing. The mother sprang to him and gently took him in her arms; then she raised herself to her full height and, pressing the boy's bleeding head to her breast, shook her clenched fist at her brother, who was standing between his purring cats on the landing.

"Wicked, evil man!" she cried. "I hope you perish here with your beasts!"

"Curse as much as you like," the brother answered, "but see to it that you leave this house!"

Then, while the woman descended the dark stairs with the weeping child, he called his cats and smartly closed the door of his room behind him.——He did not give thought that the curses of the poor are dangerous when the hardheartedness of the rich has called them forth.

A few days later Frau Anken came as always into her master's room with the midday meal. But today she was pursing her thin lips more than usual, and her small, weak eyes were gleaming with pleasure. For she had not forgotten the harsh words she had had to put up with some evenings before and now intended to repay them with interest.

"Did you hear the bell of St. Magdalene's tolling?" she asked.

"No," replied Herr Bulemann curtly. He was sitting over his table of figures.

"Do you know who it was tolling for?" the old woman persisted.

"Stupid talk! I don't pay attention to that bim bam!"

"It was for your nephew!"

Herr Bulemann put down his pen. "What's that you're saying, old woman?"

"I'm saying," she replied, "that they've just buried little Christoph."

Herr Bulemann had already returned to his figures. "Why tell me that? What do I care about the boy?"

"Well, I just thought you might be interested. People do spread the news when something happens about town."——

When she had left the room, Herr Bulemann again laid down his pen and for a long time paced up and down the room with his hands behind his back. Whenever he heard a noise in the street, he would hastily step to the window as though he expected to see the bailiff arriving to cite him for mistreatment of a minor. Black Grabs, who was yowling and demanding his part of the meal that had been served, got a kick that sent him flying into the corner. But, whether it was hunger or whether the usually subservient nature of the animal had changed, the cat turned against its master and attacked him, spitting and fuming. Herr Bulemann gave it another kick. "Eat," he said, "you don't need to wait for me."

With a bound the two cats were at the full dish, which he had set on the floor for them.

Then something strange took place.

As yellow Schnores, who had finished first, was standing in the middle of the room stretching himself and arching his back, Herr Bulemann suddenly paused in front of him. Then he walked around the animal and looked at it from all sides. "Schnores, you old rascal, what is this anyway?" he said, scratching the tomcat's head. "You've grown in your old age!" At this moment the other cat leaped forward. It ruffled up its shiny pelt and stretched up on its black legs. Herr Bulemann pushed his stocking cap from his brow. "And so has he!" he murmured. "Strange, it must be the breed."

Meanwhile dusk had fallen, and since no one came in to disturb him, he sat down to the dishes standing on the table. Finally he even began to look at his great cats, which were sitting next to him on the sofa, with a certain satisfaction. "A couple of handsome chaps, you are!" he said, nodding to them. "And that old woman downstairs is not going to poison your rats any more, either!" But when he later retired to his bedroom, he did not, as he ordinarily did, let the cats come in with him. And in the night, when he heard their scratching and yowling at the door, he pulled the bedclothes over both ears and thought, "Go on and yowl, I saw your claws."

The next day at noon, the same thing happened as the day before. The two cats sprang with a heavy bound from their emptied platter into the middle of the room and stretched themselves. When Herr Bulemann, who was again sitting over his figures, cast a glance in their direction, he shoved back his revolving chair in horror and stood gazing with outstretched neck. There were Grabs and Schnores, whining softly, as though something unpleasant had happened to them, their tails curled and trembling, their hair on end. He saw it clearly: they were getting longer, they were getting bigger and bigger.

For a moment he stood there grasping the table; then he suddenly strode past the animals and tore open the door of his room. "Frau Anken, Frau Anken!" he called, and, since she did not seem to hear him, he whistled on his fingers. Soon the old woman shuffled out of the back of the house and slowly ascended the three flights of stairs, gasping for breath.

"Just take a look at the cats!" he cried, when she had come into the room.

"I've seen them lots of times, Herr Bulemann."

"Don't you see anything special about them?"

"Not that I know of, Herr Bulemann," she said, squinting about her with weak eyes.

"What kind of animals are they anyway? Those are no longer cats!" He grabbed the old woman by the arms and pushed her against the wall. "You red-eyed witch!" he shouted, "tell me what kind of spell you've put on my cats!"

The woman clasped her bony hands together and began to babble incomprehensible prayers. But the terrible cats bounded from the right and left onto their master's shoulders and licked him in the face with their rough tongues. He had to let go of the old woman.

Still babbling and wheezing, she stole out of the room and crept down the stairs. She was confused, and she was afraid, whether more of her master or of the great cats, she herself did not know. She went to her room in the back of the house. With trembling hands she pulled a woolen sock filled with money out from beneath her mattress; then she took out of a drawer a number of old skirts and rags and wrapped them around her hoard, finally making a large bundle. For she meant to leave at all costs. She remembered her master's poor half-sister at the edge of town; she had always been friendly to her—she would go to her. To be sure, it was a long way, through many streets, across many narrow and long bridges that led over dark ditches and canals, and outside the winter evening was already growing dusk. Nevertheless, she had to go. Without thinking of the thousands of loaves of bread she had piled up with childish concern in the big walnut cabinets, she stepped out of the house with her heavy bundle on her back. With a big, large-bitted key she carefully locked the heavy oak door, then stuck the key in her leather satchel, and went, gasping and wheezing, out into the dark streets.——

Frau Anken has never returned, and the door of Bulemann's house has never again been unlocked. On the same day that she left, however, a young lad who was running around in the houses playing Knecht Ruprecht* laughingly told his comrades that as he was crossing the Crescentius bridge in his shaggy furs he had frightened an old woman so violently that she had jumped down into the black waters with her bundle as though she had lost her mind. And it is true that on the morning of the next day at the far edge of town the body of an old woman, bound to a large bundle, was fished out of the water by the watchmen and soon afterwards, since no one identified her, buried in a flat coffin in the potter's field of the local graveyard.

The next day was Christmas Eve. Herr Bulemann had had a bad night. The scratching and pawing of the animals at his bedroom door had kept him awake; only toward morning had he fallen into a long, leaden sleep. When he finally stuck his stocking-capped head into his living room, he saw the two cats restlessly circling about each other, purring loudly. It was already after midday; the clock on the wall pointed to one. "No doubt they're hungry, the beasts," he muttered. Then he opened the door to the hallway and whistled for the old woman. At the same time, the cats shoved past him and ran down the stairs. He soon heard the sound of

* Figure who accompanies St. Nicholas inquiring about the behavior of children.

leaping and the rattling of plates from the kitchen, and thought they must have jumped up on the cupboard where Frau Anken set aside the food for the next day.

Herr Bulemann stood at the top of the stairs and shouted loudly and peevishly for the old woman. But only silence answered him or, from below out of the corners of the old house, a faint echo. He was just wrapping the skirts of his flowered dressing gown about him and was about to go down to see for himself, when there was a thumping on the stairs and the two cats came running up again. But they were no longer cats; they were two fearsome, unidentifiable beasts of prey. They took their stand opposite him, glaring at him with their glittering eyes and emitting hoarse growls. He tried to get past them, but a blow of the paw that tore a piece out of his dressing gown drove him back. He ran into his room; he tried to open a window and shout to someone in the street, but the cats bounded after him and prevented him. Fiercely purring, with raised tails, they paced up and down before the windows. Herr Bulemann ran out into the hall, slamming the door of his room behind him, but the cats struck the door handle with their paws and in an instant were standing before him on the stairs. Again he fled into his room and again the cats were there.

Daylight was already fading and darkness was creeping into all the corners. Far below in the street he heard singing. Boys and girls were going from house to house caroling for Christmas. They stopped at every door; he stood and listened. Wouldn't anyone come to his door? But he knew, of course: he had driven them away himself. No one knocked, no one rattled the locked front door. They went by, and it gradually grew still in the street, still as death. Once more he sought to escape. He resorted to force and wrestled with the animals; blood ran down his hands and face. Then he tried a ruse. He called them by their old pet names, he stroked sparks from their fur, and even ventured to scratch their flat heads armed with great, flashing teeth. They threw themselves at his feet and rolled over purring, but when he thought the moment had come and tried to slip out the door, they sprang up and stood before him, growling hoarsely. Thus the night passed and the day came, and he was still running back and forth between the head of the stairs and the windows of his room, wringing his hands, panting, his gray hair disheveled.

Twice more night followed day; then he at last threw himself onto the sofa, completely exhausted, twitching in every limb. The cats sat down before him and blinked at him sleepily out of their half-closed eyes. Gradually the heaving of his body subsided and finally ceased altogether. A sallow pallor spread over his face beneath the stubble of his gray beard. With one last sigh he stretched out his arms and spread his long fingers over his knees; then he did not move again.

But downstairs in the deserted rooms it had not been quiet. Outside, at the back door of the house, which looks on the narrow courtyard, a busy gnawing and chewing was in progress. At last an opening became visible above the threshold. It grew larger and larger, and a gray mouse shoved its way through; then came another and another and soon a whole horde of mice was flitting through the hallway and up the stairs to the second floor. Here they began to work again at the door of the room, and when this had been gnawed through, it was the turn of the large cabinets in which Frau Anken had stored the treasures she left behind. That was paradise for the mice; whoever wanted to get through, had to eat his way through. The mice filled their bellies, and when they could eat no more, they curled up their tails and took a nap in the hollowed-out loaves. At night they came out, darted across the floor or sat licking their paws before the window and, when the moon shone, looking out on the street with their little bright eyes.

But this pleasant life was soon to come to an end. On the third night, when upstairs Herr Bulemann had just closed his eyes, there was a thumping out on the stairs. The great cats came bounding down, opened the door with a blow of the paw, and began their hunt. The old happy life was over. Squeaking and piping, the fat mice scurried about, desperately trying to climb the walls. All in vain; they fell silent one after the other between the crunching jaws of the two beasts of prey.

Then it grew quiet and soon nothing was audible in the whole house but the soft purring of the great cats, who were lying with outstretched paws upstairs before their master's room, licking the blood from their whiskers.

Downstairs the lock began to rust in the front door, the brass knocker became covered with verdigris, and between the stone steps the grass started to grow.

Outside, the world went its way uncaring. When summer had come, there stood in bloom on little Christoph's grave in the churchyard of St. Magdalene's a white rosebush. Soon there was a memorial stone lying beneath it. The rosebush his mother had planted; the stone, to be sure, she had not been able to afford. But Christoph had had a friend; he was a young musician, the son of a secondhand dealer who lived in the house across the street. At first, Christoph used to slip under his window when the musician was sitting inside at the piano; later, the latter had sometimes taken him along to St. Magdalene's, where he practiced the organ. There the pale boy would sit at his feet, leaning his head against the organ bench and watching the sunbeams play through the church window. When the young musician, carried away by his theme, would let the mighty, deep registers roar through the vaulted building, or when he sometimes pulled out the tremulo and the tones flooded forth as though trembling before God's majesty, then it might happen that the boy would break out in quiet sobs and his friend would have difficulty calming him. Once he said pleadingly, "It hurts, Leberecht; don't play so loud!"

The organist at once replaced the deep registers with the flute and other gentler stops, and the boy's favorite chorale, "Commit thou all thy griefs," swelled sweetly and movingly through the silent church. Softly, he began to sing along in his weak voice. "I want to learn to play too," he said, when the organ had fallen silent. "Will you teach me, Leberecht?"

The young musician let his hand rest on the boy's head and said, patting his yellow hair, "Get good and well first, Christoph, then I'll be glad to teach you."

But Christoph did not get well. Beside the boy's mother, the young organist followed the small casket to the graveyard. Here they spoke together for the first time. The mother told the organist her thrice-dreamt dream of the little silver cup.

"The cup," said Leberecht, "I could have given you. My father, who acquired it years ago, together with many other things, from your brother, gave it to me once for Christmas."

The woman broke out in bitter lamentations. "Oh," she cried again and again, "he would have surely gotten well!"

The young man walked for a while at her side without speaking. "Our Christoph shall still have the cup," he said at last.

And so it happened. A few days later he sold the cup to a collector of such precious objects for a good price; from the proceeds he had a memorial stone made for Christoph. He had a marble tablet inlaid in the stone and on this was hewn an image of the cup. Beneath it stood the words, To your health!

For many years following, whether snow lay on the grave or whether the rosebush stood in full bloom in the June sun, a pale woman would often come and reverently and thoughtfully read the three words on the gravestone. Then one summer she came no more, but the world went its way uncaring.

Only one time, many years later, did a very old man visit the grave. He looked at the small memorial stone and picked a white rose from the old rosebush. It was the retired organist of St. Magdalene's.

But we must now leave the child's peaceful grave and, so this tale can be brought to a conclusion, cast one more glance at the old house with the bay windows over in Darkling Street.

It still stood locked and silent. While life outside flowed by incessantly, inside in the closed-up rooms mould was growing rankly between the floorboards, the plaster on the ceilings was loosening and falling down, chasing on lonely nights an uncanny echo along the hallway and staircase. The children who had sung in the streets on that distant Christmas Eve were elderly people or had already put life aside and died. The people who now walked the street wore different clothes, and in the graveyard at the far edge of town the black numeral post marking Frau Anken's nameless grave had long since rotted away. Then one night the full moon shone again, as it had so often, over the house across the way into the bow window on the fourth story and painted the little round panes on the floor with its bluish light. The room was empty except for a tiny figure the size of a one-year-old child which sat crouched on the sofa, but its face was old and bearded and its thin nose was disproportionately long. It wore a stocking cap that fell far down over its ears and a long dressing gown obviously meant for a grown man. Its feet were pulled up onto the skirt of the gown.

The figure was Herr Bulemann. He had not starved to death, but lack of nourishment had made his body dry up and shrink, so that in the course of years he had grown smaller and smaller. Now and then, on nights with a full moon like this one, he awakened and attempted, though with ever failing strength, to escape his captors. When he would sink back on the sofa or, finally, crawl back onto it, exhausted by his efforts, then Grabs and Schnores would stretch out at the head of the stairs, beating the floor with their tails and listening to hear whether Frau Anken's treasure trove had attracted a new migration of mice into the house.

Tonight it was different; the cats were neither in the room nor out in the hallway. As the moonlight falling through the window and across the floor gradually crept up on the tiny figure, it began to stir; the great, round eyes opened and Herr Bulemann stared out into the empty room. After a while he slid down from the sofa, laboriously folding back the long sleeves of his gown, and stepped slowly towards the door, the wide skirts of his garment dragging along behind him. Grasping the handle on tiptoes, he managed to open the door and get as far as the railing of the stairs outside. For a moment he stood gasping for breath, then he stretched out his neck and attempted to call. "Frau Anken, Frau Anken!" But his voice was like the whisper of a sick child. "Frau Anken, I'm hungry. Listen to me!"

All remained silent; only the mice began to squeak shrilly in the lower rooms. Then he grew angry. "Damned witch, what are you whistling for?" And a stream of unintelligibly whispered oaths poured forth from his mouth until a choking fit stopped his tongue.

Outside, down at the front door, the heavy brass knocker banged, sending an echo to the very rafters. Perhaps it was the nocturnal carouser we mentioned at the beginning of our story.

Herr Bulemann had regained his breath. "Go on, open up!" he whispered. "It's the boy, Christoph; he's come to fetch the cup."

Suddenly, from downstairs, amidst the squealing of the mice, the leaps and growls of the great cats could be heard. Herr Bulemann realized that for the first time when he was awake the cats had quitted the top floor and left him to his own devices. Hurriedly, dragging the long gown behind him, he trudged back into the room.

Outside, from the street below, he heard the night watchman calling. "A human being, a human being," Herr Bulemann murmured; "the night is so long and I have woken up so often and yet the moon's still shining."

He climbed up onto the armchair that stood beside the window. His tiny withered hands worked busily at the window catch, for down in the moonlit street he had seen the watchman standing. But the catch was rusted tight; he labored in vain to open it. Then he saw the man, who had stared up at the house for a while, step back into the shadow of the houses.

A weak cry broke from his mouth; trembling, with clenched fists, he struck at the panes, but he had not the strength to smash them. Now he began to whisper confused pleas and promises; gradually, as the figure of the man walking along the street grew more distant, his whispering became a choked, hoarse croaking; he promised to share his treasures with him, if he would only listen; he could take everything; he wanted nothing for himself, not a single thing, only the cup that belonged to little Christoph.

But the man below went his way and soon disappeared into a side street. Of all the words Herr Bulemann spoke that night not one was heard by a human soul.

Finally, after all this vain effort, the tiny figure crouched down in the armchair, straightened its stocking cap and gazed up into the empty sky, murmuring unintelligibly.

And so he sits to this day, awaiting God's mercy.

Translated by Robert M. Browning

The Tale of the 672nd Night

Hugo von Hofmannsthal

I

A merchant's son, who was young and handsome and whose father and mother were no longer living, found himself, shortly after his twenty-fifth year, tired of social life and entertaining. He closed off most of the rooms of his house and dismissed all of his servants with the exception of four, whose devotion and general demeanor pleased him. Since his friends were of no great importance to him and since he was not so captivated by the beauty of any woman as to imagine it desirable or even tolerable to have her always around him, he grew more and more accustomed to a rather solitary life, one which seemed most appropriate to his cast of mind. However, he was by no means averse to human contact; on the contrary, he enjoyed walking in the streets and public gardens and contemplating the faces of men and women. Nor did he neglect either the care of his body and his beautiful hands or the decorating of his apartments. Indeed, the beauty of carpets, tapestries, and silks, of panelled walls, candelabras, and metal bowls, of vessels of glass and earthenware became more important to him than he could ever have imagined. Gradually his eyes were opened to the fact that all the shapes and colors of the world were embodied in the things of his household. In the intertwining of decorative forms he came to recognize an enchanted image of the interlocking wonders of the world. He discovered the figures of beasts and flowers and the transition of flowers into animals; the dolphins, the lions, and the tulips, the pearls and the acanthus; he discovered the tension between the burden of pillars and the resistance of solid ground, and the will of all water to move upward and then downward again. He discovered the bliss of motion, the sublimity of rest, dancing, and being dead; he discovered the colors of flowers and leaves, the colors of the coats of wild beasts and of the faces of nations, the color of jewels, the color of the stormy sea and the quietly shining sea; yes, he discovered the moon and the stars, the mystic sphere, the mystic rings and firmly rooted upon them the wings of the seraphim. For a long time he was intoxicated by his great, profound beauty that belonged to him, and all his days moved more beautifully and less emptily in the company of these household things, which were no longer anything dead or commonplace but a great heritage, the divine work of all the generations.

Yet he felt the emptiness of all these things as well as their beauty. Never did the thought of death leave him for long; often it came over him when he was in the company of laughing, noisy people, often at night, often as he ate.

Since there was no sickness in him, however, the thought was not terrifying; it had about it, rather, something of solemnity, of splendor, and was at its most intense precisely when he was intoxicated with thinking of beauty, the beauty of his own youth and solitude. For the merchant's son often drew great pride from his mirror, from the verses of poets, from his wealth and intelligence, and dark maxims did not weigh on his soul. He said, "Wherever you are meant to die, there your feet will carry you," and he pictured himself, handsome, like a king lost on a hunt, walking in an unknown wood under strange trees toward an alien, wondrous fate. He said, "When the dwelling place is finished, death will come," and he saw death coming slowly, up over the bridge, the bridge borne on winged lions and leading to the palace, the finished dwelling, filled with the wonderful booty of life.

He thought he would now be living in solitude, but his four servants circled him like dogs, and although he spoke little with them he still felt somehow that they were incessantly thinking how best to serve him. For his part, too, he began to reflect now and then upon them.

The housekeeper was an old woman; her daughter, now dead, had been the nurse of the merchant's son; all her other children had also died. She was very quiet, and the chill of age emanated from her white face and her white hands. But he liked her because she had always been in the house and because she carried about with her the memory of his own mother's voice and of his child-hood, which he loved with a great longing.

With his permission she had taken into the house a distant rel-ative, a girl scarcely fifteen years old, extremely withdrawn. The girl was harsh with herself and hard to understand. Once in a sudden, dark impulse of her angry soul she threw herself out of a window and into the courtyard but fell with her childlike body into some garden soil that happened to be piled up there, so that all she broke was a collarbone, and that only because at this spot there had been a rock in the dirt. After she was put to bed the merchant's son sent his physician to see her. In the evening, how-ever, he came himself and wanted to see how she was getting along. She kept her eyes closed; for the first time he looked at her long and quietly and was amazed at the strange and precocious charm of her face. Only her lips were very thin, and there was something disturbing and unattractive in this. Suddenly she opened her eyes, looked at him in icy hostility and, with her lips clenched in anger, overcoming her pain, turned toward the wall, so that she lay on her injured side. At this instant her deathly pale face turned color, becoming greenish white; she fainted and fell back into her former position, as if dead.

For a long time after her recovery the merchant's son did not speak to her when they met. Once or twice he asked the old lady whether the girl did not resent being in his house but she always denied it. The only servant whom he had decided to retain in his house was a man he had once come to know when he was dining with the ambassador assigned to this city by the king of Persia. This man had served him on that occasion and was so accommo-dating and circumspect and seemed at the same time to be so very retiring and modest that the merchant's son had discovered more pleasure in observing him than in listening to what the other guests were saying. His joy was all the greater, therefore, when many months later this servant stepped up to him on the street, greeted him with the same deep earnestness as on that previous evening, and, without a trace of importuning, offered him his services. The merchant's son recognized him immediately by his somber, mul-berry-hued face and by his good breeding. He employed him instantly and dismissed two young servants whom he still had with him, and from that moment on would let himself be served at meals and other times only by this earnest and reserved person. The man had permission to leave the house during the evening hours but almost never took advantage of it. He displayed a rare attachment to his master, whose wishes he anticipated and whose likes and dislikes he sensed instinctively, so that the latter in turn took an ever greater liking to him.

Although he allowed only this person to serve him as he ate, there was still a maid who brought in the dishes with fruit and sweet pastries, a young girl but still two or three years older than the youngest. This girl was one of those who, seen from afar or stepping forth as dancers by the light of torches, would scarcely pass for very beautiful, because at such times the refinement of their features is lost. But seeing her close to him and every day, he was seized by the incomparable beauty of her eyelids and her lips; and the languid, joyless movements of her beautiful body were to him the puzzling language of a self-enclosed and wondrous world.

It was a time when, in the city, the heat of summer was very great and its dull incandescence hovered along the line of houses, and in the sultry, heavy nights of the full moon, the wind drove white clouds of dust down the empty streets. At this time the merchant's son traveled with his four servants to a country house he owned in the mountains, in a narrow valley surrounded by dark hills, the site of many such country estates of the wealthy. From both sides waterfalls descended into the gorges, cooling the air. The moon was almost always hidden on the far side of the mountains, but great white clouds rose behind the black walls, floated solemnly across the darkly glowing sky, and disappeared on the other side. Here the merchant's son lived his accustomed life, in a house whose wooden walls were constantly penetrated by the cool fragrance of the gardens and the many waterfalls. In the afternoon, until the time when the sun fell beyond the hills, he sat in his garden, most often reading a book in which were recorded the wars of a very great king of the past. Sometimes, in the midst of a passage describing how thousands of cavalrymen of the enemy kings turned their horses, shouting, or how their chariots were dragged down the steep bank of a river, he was compelled to stop suddenly, for he felt, without looking up, that the eyes of his four servants were fixed on him. He knew, without lifting his head, that they were looking at him, each from a different room. He knew them so well. He felt them living, more strongly, more forcefully than he felt himself live. Concerning himself he sensed on occasion a slight shock of emotion or surprise, but also on this account a puzzling fear. He felt, with the clarity of a nightmare, how the two old people were moving along toward death, with every hour, with the inescapable, slow altering of their features and their gestures, which he knew so well; and how the two girls were making their way into that life, barren and airless, as it were. Like the terror and the mortal bitterness of a fearful dream, forgotten on awakening, the heavy weight of their lives, of which they themselves knew nothing, lay upon his limbs.

Sometimes he had to rise and walk about, lest he succumb to his anxiety. But while he gazed at the bright gravel before his feet and observed with great concentration how, from the cool fragrance of grass and earth, the fragrance of carnations welled up toward him in bright, sharp breaths and, intermittently, in warmish, excessively sweet clouds, the fragrance of heliotropes, he felt their eyes and could think of nothing else. Without raising his head, he knew that the old woman was sitting by her window, her bloodless hands on the sun-drenched sill, the bloodless mask of her face an ever more terrible setting for her helpless, black eyes, which could not die. Without raising his head he could sense when his servant stepped back from the window, for a matter only of minutes, to busy himself with one of the wardrobes; without looking up he waited in secret fear for the moment when he would return. While his two hands were letting supple branches close behind him, so that he might crawl away and disappear in the most overgrown corner of his garden, and while all his thoughts were bent on the beauty of the sky that fell from above through the dark net of branches and vines, in little gleaming bits of turquoise, the one thing that seized hold of his blood and all his thinking was that he knew the eyes of the two girls were fixed on him; those of the taller languid and sad, filled with a vague challenge that tormented him, those of the little one with an impatient, then again a mocking attentiveness that tormented him even more. And still he never had the idea that they were looking at him directly, in the act of his walking about with lowered head, or kneeling by a carnation to tie it with twine, or leaning down beneath boughs. Rather it seemed to him that they were contemplating his entire life, his deepest being, his secret human inadequacy.

A terrible oppression came over him, a mortal fear in face of the inescapability of life. More terrible than their incessantly watching him was the fact that they forced him to think of himself in such a fruitless and exhausting fashion. And the garden was much too small to permit his escaping them. However, when he was very close to them, his fear paled so completely that he almost forgot the past. Then he was capable of ignoring them totally, or of calmly observing their movements, which were so familiar that he felt an unceasing, as it were a physical sense of identification with their lives.

The little girl crossed his path only now and then, on the stairway or in the front part of the house. The three others, however, were frequently in the same room with him. Once he caught sight of the taller one in a slanting mirror; she was passing through an adjoining room set at a higher level; in the mirror, however, she approached him from below. She walked slowly and with effort but fully erect; she carried in each arm the heavy, gaunt figure, in dark bronze, of an Indian deity. The ornate feet of the figurines rested in the hollows of her hands; the dark goddesses reached from her hips to her temples, leaning their dead weight on her slender living shoulders, but their dark heads, with their angry serpents' mouths, their brows above three wild eyes apiece, the mysterious jewels in their cold, hard hair, moved alongside breathing cheeks and brushed her lovely temples in time with her measured steps. In fact, however, the true burden she bore with such solemnity seemed not so much the goddesses as the beauty of her own head with its heavy ornaments of dark and living gold, the hair curled in two great arching spirals at either side of her bright brow, like a queen at war. He was seized by her great beauty but at the same time realized clearly that to hold her in his arms would mean nothing to him. For he well knew that the beauty of his maidservant filled him with longing but not with desire; hence he did not rest his eyes long upon her but stepped out of the room, out to the street in fact, and walked on in strange unrest between the houses and gardens in the narrow shadows. Finally he passed along the banks of the river where the gardeners and flower sellers lived; there for a long while he sought—knowing that he would seek in vain—a flower whose form and fragrance, a spice whose fading breath could grant him for one moment of calm possession precisely that same sweet charm as lay, confusing and disconcerting, in the beauty of his maidservant. And as he peered about in the gloom of the greenhouses or bent over the long beds in the open air, with darkness already falling, his mind repeated, over and over, involuntarily, tormentedly and against his will, the words of the poet: "In the stems of carnations, swaying, in the smell of ripe grain you awakened my longing; but when I found you, you were not the one I was seeking, but the sisters of your soul."

II

During this time there came a letter that rather upset him. The letter was unsigned. In vague terms the writer accused the young man's servant of having committed, while he was in the household of his previous master, the Persian ambassador, some sort of repugnant crime. The unknown correspondent appeared to be consumed with violent hatred of the servant and accompanied his letter with a number of threats; in addressing the merchant's son himself he also assumed a discourteous, almost threatening, tone. But there was no way of guessing what crime was alluded to or what purpose this letter might serve for the writer, who neither gave his name nor demanded anything. The merchant's son read the letter several times and was forced to admit that the thought of losing his servant in such a disagreeable manner caused him a strong feeling of anxiety. The more he thought it over the more agitated he became and the less he could bear the idea of losing any one of these persons to whom he had grown so completely attached, through habit and through mysterious forces.

He paced up and down and became so heated in his angry agitation that he cast aside his cloak and his sash and kicked them with his feet. It seemed to him as if someone were insulting and threatening the things that were most deeply his, and were trying to force him to desert himself and to deny what was dear to him. He was sorry for himself and, as always at such moments, felt like a child. He pictured his four servants torn from his house and felt as if the whole content of his life were being drawn out of him, all the bittersweet memories, all the half-unconscious hopes, everything that transcended words, only to be cast out somewhere and declared worthless, like a bunch of seaweed. For the first time he understood something that had always irritated and angered him as a boy: the anxious love with which his father clung to what he had acquired, the riches of his vaulted warehouse, the lovely, unfeeling children of his hopes and fears, the mysterious progeny of the dimly apprehended, deepest wishes of his life. He came to understand that the great king of the past would surely have died if his lands had been taken from him, lands he had traversed and conquered, from the sea in the west to the sea in the east, and dreamed of ruling, yet lands of such boundless extent that he had no power over them and received no tribute from them, other than the thought that he had subjugated them, that no other than he was their king.

He determined to do everything he could to put to rest this thing that caused him such anxiety. Without saying a word to his servant about the letter, he set out and traveled to the city alone. There he determined first of all to seek out the house occupied by the ambassador of the king of Persia, for he had a vague hope of finding some kind of clue there.

When he arrived, however, it was late afternoon and no one was at home, neither the ambassador nor a single one of the young people of his entourage. Only the cook and a lowly old scribe were sitting in the gateway in the cool semi-darkness. But they were so ugly and answered him in such a short and sullen manner that he turned his back on them impatiently and decided to return the following day at a better time.

Since his own house was shut and locked—for he had left no servants back in town—he was compelled to think of some place to stay for the night. Curiously, like a stranger, he walked through the familiar streets and came at last to the banks of a little river, which at this time of year was virtually dry. From here, lost in thought, he followed a shabby street inhabited by a large number of prostitutes. Without paying much attention to where he was going, he then turned to the right and entered a completely deserted, deathly still cul-de-sac, which ended in a steep stairway almost as tall as a tower. On this stairway he stopped and looked back on the way he had taken. He could see into the yards of the little houses; here and there were red curtains and ugly, dried-out flowers; there was a deathly sadness about the broad, dry bed of the stream. He climbed higher and at the top entered a quarter of the city that he could not recall having seen before. Nonetheless, an intersection of low-lying streets suddenly struck him with dreamlike familiarity. He walked on and came to a jeweler's shop. It was a very shabby little shop, befitting this part of the city, and its show window was filled with the kind of worthless finery one can buy from pawnbrokers and receivers of stolen goods. The merchant's son, who was an expert in jewels, could scarcely find a halfway beautiful stone in the lot.

Suddenly his glance fell on an old-fashioned piece of jewelry, made of thin gold and embellished with a piece of beryl, reminding him somehow of the old woman. Probably he had once seen in her possession a similar piece obtained in her youth. Also, the pale, rather melancholy stone seemed in a strange way to fit in with her age and appearance; the old-fashioned setting had the same quality of sadness about it. So he stepped into the low ceilinged shop to buy the piece. The jeweler was greatly pleased to have such a well-dressed customer drop in, and wanted to show him his more valuable stones as well, those that he did not put in his window. Out of courtesy he let the old man show him a number of things but he had no desire to buy more, nor, given his solitary life, would he have had any use for such gifts. Finally he grew impatient and at the same time embarrassed, for he wanted to get away and yet not hurt the old man's feelings. He decided to buy something else, a trifle, and leave immediately thereafter. Absentmindedly, looking over the jeweler's shoulder, he gazed at a small silver hand mirror, half coated over. In an inner mirror an image came to him of the maid servant with the bronze goddesses at either side; he had a passing sense that a great deal of her charm lay in the way her neck and shoulders bore, in unassuming, childlike grace, the beauty of her head, the head of a young queen. And in passing he thought it pretty to see around this same neck a thin, gold chain, in many loops, childlike, yet reminiscent of armor. And he asked to see such chains. The old man opened a door and invited him to step into a second room, a low ceilinged parlor where numerous pieces of jewelry were on display, in glass cases and on open racks. Here he soon found a chain to his liking and asked the jeweler to tell him the price of the two ornaments. The jeweler asked him also to inspect the remarkable metalwork of some old saddles, set with semiprecious stones; he replied, however, that as the son of a merchant he never had anything to do with horses, in fact did not even know how to ride and found no pleasure in old saddles or in new. He took out a gold piece and some silver coins to pay for what he had bought, and gave some indication of being impatient to leave the store. The old man, without saying another word, picked out a piece of fine silk paper and wrapped the chain and the beryl, each separately; while he was doing so the merchant's son, by chance, stepped over to the low latticed window and looked out. He caught sight of a very well-kept vegetable garden, obviously belonging to the neighboring house, framed against a background of two glass greenhouses and a high wall. He was struck by an immediate desire to see these greenhouses and asked the jeweler if he could tell him how to get there. The jeweler handed him his two packages and led him through an adjoining room into the courtyard, which was connected to the neighboring garden by a lattice gate. Here the jeweler stopped and struck the gate with an iron clapper. Since, however, there was no sound from the garden and no sign of movement in the neighboring house, he urged the merchant's son simply to go ahead and inspect the forcing beds and, in the event that anyone should bother him, to say that he had his, the jeweler's, permission, for he was well acquainted with the owner. Then he opened the door for him by reaching through the bars of the latticework. The merchant's son immediately walked along the wall to the nearer of the two greenhouses, stepped in, and found such a profusion of rare and remarkable narcissus and anemones and such strange, leafy plants, quite unfamiliar to him, that he kept looking at them for a long time, never feeling he had seen enough. At last he looked up and saw that the sun had set behind the houses. It was not his wish to remain in a strange, unattended garden any longer but rather simply to cast a glance through the panes of the second forcing shed and then leave. As he walked slowly past this second shed, peeking in, he was suddenly struck with great fear and drew back. For someone had his face against the panes and was looking out at him. After a moment he calmed down and became aware that it was a child, a little girl of no more than four years, whose white dress and pale face were pressed to the windowpanes. But now when he looked more closely, he was again struck with fear, and felt in the back of his neck an unpleasant sensation of dread and a slight constriction in his throat and deeper down in his chest. For the child, who stared at him with a fixed and angry look, resembled in a way he could not fathom the fifteen-year-old girl he had in his own house. Everything was the same, the pale eyebrows, the fine, trembling nostrils, the thin lips; like her counterpart this child also held one of her shoulders a bit higher than the other. Everything was the same, except that in the child all of this resulted in an expression that was terrifying to him. He did not know what it was that caused him such nameless fright. He knew only that he would not be able to bear turning around, knowing that this face was staring at him through the glass.

In his fear he walked quickly up to the door of the greenhouse, in order to go in. The door was shut, bolted from the outside; in his haste he bent down to reach the bolt, which was very low, and shoved it back so violently that he painfully dislocated one of the joints of his little finger, and headed for the child, almost at a run. The child came toward him and, not saying a word, braced itself against his knees, trying with its weak little hands to push him out. It was hard for him to avoid stepping on her. But now that he was close, his fear abated. He bent down over the face of the child, who was very pale and whose eyes trembled with anger and hatred, while the little teeth of its lower jaw pressed with unnerving fury into its upper lip. His fear disappeared for a moment as he stroked the girl's short, fine hair. But instantly he was reminded of the girl who lived in his house and whose hair he had once touched as she lay in her bed, deathly pale, her eyes closed; and immediately a shiver ran down his spine and his hands drew back. She had given up trying to push him away. She stepped back a few paces and looked straight ahead. It grew almost unbearable to him, the sight of this frail doll-like body in its little white dress, this contemptuous, fearfully pale child's face. He was so filled with dread that he felt a twinge of pain in his temples and in his throat as his hand touched something cold in his pocket. It was a couple of silver coins. He took them out, bent down to the child, and gave them to her, because they shone and jingled. The child took them and let them drop in front of his feet, so that they disappeared in a crack of the floor where it rested on a grating of wood. Then she turned her back on him and walked slowly away. For a time he stood motionless, his heart pounding with fear lest she return and look at him from outside, through the panes. He would have preferred to leave immediately but it was better to let some time pass, so that the child might leave the garden. By now it was no longer fully light in the glasshouse and the shapes of the plants took on a strange appearance. Some distance away, black, absurdly threatening branches protruded disagreeably from the semi-darkness, and behind them was a glimmer of white, as if the child were standing there. On a board stood a row of clay pots with wax flowers. To deaden the passage of a few moments he counted the blossoms, which, in their rigidity, bore little resemblance to living flowers and were rather like masks, treacherous masks with their eye sockets grown shut. When he had finished he went to the door, thinking to leave. The door did not budge; the child had bolted it from the outside. He wanted to scream but he was afraid of the sound of his own voice. He beat his fists against the panes. The garden and the house remained as still as death, except that behind him something was gliding through the shrubbery with a rustling sound. He told himself it was the sound of leaves that had loosened in the shattering of the sultry air and were falling to the ground. Still, he stopped his pounding and peered through the half-dark maze of trees and vines. Then he saw in the dusk of the far wall something that looked like a rectangle of dark lines. He crawled toward it, by now unconcerned that he was knocking over and breaking many of the clay flowerpots, that the tall, thin stalks and rustling fronds, as they fell, were closing over and behind him in a ghostly fashion. The rectangle of dark lines was the opening of a door; he pushed and it gave way. The open air passed over his face; behind him he heard the broken stalks and crushed leaves rise with a soft rustling sound as if after a storm.

He stood in a narrow walled passageway; above him the open sky looked down and the wall on either side was barely taller than a man. However, after a distance of fifteen paces, roughly speaking, the passage was walled up once more, and he started imagining himself a prisoner for the second time. Hesitantly he moved ahead; here on the right an opening in the wall had been broken through as wide as a man, and from this opening a board extended through empty space to a platform located opposite him; on the near side of it there was a low iron grating closing it off. On the other two sides were the backs of tall houses with people living in them. Where the board rested, like a gangplank, on the edge of the platform, the grating had a little door.

So very impatient was the merchant's son to escape the confines of his fear that he immediately set one foot, then the other, on the board and, keeping his glance firmly fixed on the opposite shore, started to cross over. Unfortunately, however, he became aware that he was suspended over a walled moat several stories deep; in the soles of his feet and the hollow of his knees he felt fear and helplessness, in the dizziness of his whole body the nearness of death. He knelt down and closed his eyes; then his arms, groping forward, encountered the bars of the grating. He clutched them; they gave way, and with a slow, soft rasping sound that cut through his body like the exhalation of death the door on which he was hanging opened toward him, toward the abyss. With a sense of his inner weariness and great despondency, he felt in anticipation how the smooth iron bars would slip from his fingers, which seemed to him like the fingers of a child, and how he would plunge downward and be dashed to bits along the wall. But the slow, soft opening of the door ceased before he lost his footing on the board, and with a swing he threw his trembling body in through the opening and onto the hard floor.

He was incapable of rejoicing; without looking around, with a dull feeling of something like hate for the absurdity of these torments, he walked into one of the houses and down the dilapidated staircase and stepped out again into an alleyway that was ugly and ordinary. But he was already very sad and tired and could not think of anything that seemed worth being happy about. In a strange way, everything had fallen away from him; empty and deserted by life itself he walked through this alley, and the next, and the next. He went along in a direction he knew would bring him back to the part of the city where the rich people lived and where he could look for lodging for the night. For he felt a great desire for a bed. With childlike longing he remembered the beauty of his own wide bed and he recalled, too, the beds that the great king of the past had erected for himself and his companions when they married the daughters of the kings they had conquered: a bed of gold for himself, of silver for the others, borne by griffins and winged bulls. Meantime he had come to the low-set houses where the soldiers lived. He paid no attention to them. At a latticed window sat a couple of soldiers with yellowish faces and sad eyes; they shouted something at him. He raised his head and breathed the musty smell that came from the room, a particularly oppressive smell. But he did not understand what they wanted of him. However, they had startled him out of his blank and aimless wandering, so now he looked into the courtyard as he passed the gate. The yard was very large and sad, and because the sun was just setting it seemed even larger and sadder. There were very few people in it and the houses that surrounded it were low and of a dirty yellow color. This made it even larger and more desolate. At one spot roughly twenty horses were tethered in a straight line; in front of each one there knelt a soldier in a stable smock of dirty twill, washing its hooves. Far in the distance, out of a gate, came many others in similar outfits of twill, two by two. They walked slowly, with dragging steps, and carried heavy sacks on their shoulders. Only when they came closer did he see that the open sacks they lugged along in silence had bread in them. He watched as they disappeared in a gateway, wandering on as if under the weight of some ugly, treacherous burden, carrying their bread in the same kind of sacks as clothed the sadness of their bodies.

Then he went over to the ones who were on their knees before their horses, washing their hooves. Here, too, each looked like the other and they all resembled the ones at the window and those who were carrying the bread. They must have come from neighboring villages. They too spoke hardly a word to one another. Since it was very hard for them to hold the horses' front feet, their heads swayed and their tired, yellowish faces moved up and down as if in a strong wind. The heads of most of the horses were ugly and had a look of malice about them, with their laid-back ears and their raised upper lips exposing the corner teeth of their upper jaws. For the most part they also had angry, rolling eyes and a strange way of expelling the air impatiently and contemptuously from curled-back nostrils. The last horse in line was particularly powerful and ugly. With its great teeth it tried to bite the shoulder of the man kneeling before it, drying its washed hoof. The man had such hollow cheeks and in his weary eyes such a deathly sad expression that the merchant's son was overcome by deep and bitter compassion. He wanted to give the wretched fellow a present, to cheer him up if only for a moment, and reached into his pocket for silver coins. He found none and remembered that he had tried to give the last ones to the child in the greenhouse, who had scattered them at his feet with such an angry look. He started to look for a gold coin, for he had put seven or eight into his pocket for his journey.

At that moment the horse turned its head and looked at him with ears treacherously laid back and rolling eyes that looked even more angry and wild because of a scar running straight across its ugly head just at the level of its eyes. At this ugly sight he was struck with a lightning-like memory of a long forgotten human face. However hard he might have tried, he would never have been capable of summoning up the features of this person's face; but now, there they were. However, the memory that came with the face was not so clear. He knew only that it came from the time when he was twelve years old, from a time the memory of which was associated somehow with the fragrance of sweet, warm, shelled almonds.

And he knew that it was the contorted face of an ugly poor man whom he had seen a single time in his father's store. And that his face was contorted with fear, because people were threatening him because he had a large gold piece and would not say where he had gotten it.

While the face dissolved again, his fingers searched the folds of his clothes; and when a sudden, vague thought restrained him, he drew out his hand hesitantly and in doing so cast the piece of jewelry with the beryl, wrapped in the silk paper, under the horse's feet. He bent down; the horse, kicking sideways with all its force, drove its hoof into his loins, and he fell over backward. He moaned aloud, his kees were drawn up, and he kept beating his heels on the ground. A couple of the soldiers rose and picked him up by the shoulders and under his knees. He sensed the smell of their clothes, the same musty, hopeless smell that earlier had come out of the room and onto the street, and he tried to recall where it was he had breathed it before, long, long ago; with this he lost consciousness. They carried him away over a low stairway, through a long, half-darkened passageway into one of their rooms, and laid him on a low iron bed. Then they searched his clothing, took the little chain and the seven gold pieces, and finally, taking pity on his incessant moaning, they went to get one of their surgeons.

After a time he opened his eyes and became conscious of his tormenting pain. What caused him even greater terror and fear, however, was to be alone in this desolate room. With effort he turned his eyes in their aching sockets, and, looking toward the wall, caught sight of three loaves of the kind of bread they had been carrying across the courtyard.

Otherwise there was nothing in the room but hard low beds and the smell of the dried rushes with which the beds were stuffed, and that other musty, desolate smell.

For a while the only things that occupied him were his pain and his suffocating, mortal fear, compared to which the pain was a relief. Then for a moment he was able to forget his mortal fear and wonder how all this had come to pass.

Then he felt another kind of fear, a piercing, less oppressive one, a fear he was not feeling for the first time; but now he felt it as something he had to overcome. And he clenched his fists and cursed his servants, who had driven him to his death, one to the city, the old woman into the jeweler's shop, the girl into the back room, the child, through the treacherous likeness of her counterpart, into the greenhouse, from which he saw himself reel dizzily over dreadful stairs and bridges, until he lay beneath the horse's hoof. Then he fell back into great, dull fear. He whimpered like a child, not from pain but from misery, and his teeth were chattering.

With a great feeling of bitterness he stared back into his life and denied everything that had been dear to him. He hated his premature death so much that he hated his life because it had led him there. This wild inner raging consumed his last strength. He was dizzy and for a time he slept a groggy, restless sleep. Then he awoke and felt like screaming because he was still alone, but his voice failed. Finally he vomited bile, then blood, and died with his features contorted, his lips so torn that his teeth and gums were laid bare, giving him an alien, threatening expression.

Translated by Frank G. Ryder

Jackals and Arabs

Franz Kafka

We were camping in the oasis. My companions were asleep. The tall, white figure of an Arab passed by; he had been seeing to the camels and was on his way to his own sleeping place.

I threw myself on my back in the grass. I tried to fall asleep; I could not; a jackal howled in the distance; I sat up again. And what had been so far away was all at once quite near. Jackals were swarming round me, eyes gleaming dull gold and vanishing again, lithe bodies moving nimbly and rhythmically, as if at the crack of a whip.

One jackal came from behind me, nudging right under my arm, pressing against me, as if he needed my warmth, and then stood before me and spoke to me almost eye to eye.

"I am the oldest jackal far and wide. I am delighted to have met you here at last. I had almost given up hope, since we have been waiting endless years for you; my mother waited for you, and her mother, and all our foremothers right back to the first mother of all the jackals. It is true, believe me!"

"That is surprising," said I, forgetting to kindle the pile of firewood that lay ready to smoke away jackals, "that is very surprising for me to hear. It is by pure chance that I have come here from the Far North, and I am making only a short tour of your country. What do you jackals want, then?"

As if emboldened by this perhaps too friendly enquiry the ring of jackals closed in on me; all were panting and open-mouthed.

"We know," began the eldest, "that you have come from the North, that is just what we base our hopes on. You Northerners have the kind of understanding that is not to be found among

Arabs. Not a spark of understanding, let me tell you, can be struck from their cold arrogance. They kill animals for food, and carrion they despise."

"Not so loud," said I, "there are Arabs sleeping near by."

"You are indeed a stranger here," said the jackal, "or you would know that never in the history of the world has any jackal been afraid of an Arab. Why should we fear them? Is it not misfortune enough for us to be exiled among such creatures?"

"Maybe, maybe," said I; "matters so far outside my province I am not competent to judge. It seems to me a very old quarrel; I suppose it's in the blood, and perhaps will only end with it."

"You are very clever," said the old jackal; and they all began to pant more quickly. The air pumped out of their lungs although they were standing still; a rank smell, which at times I had to set my teeth to endure, streamed from their open jaws. "You are very clever; what you have just said agrees with our old tradition. So we shall draw blood from them and the quarrel will be over."

"Oh!" said I, more vehemently than I intended, "they'll defend themselves; they'll shoot you down in dozens with their muskets."

"You misunderstand us," said he, "a human failing which persists apparently even in the Far North. We're not proposing to kill them. All the water in the Nile couldn't cleanse us of that. Why, the mere sight of their living flesh makes us turn tail and flee into cleaner air, into the desert, which for that very reason is our home."

And all the jackals around, including many newcomers from farther away, dropped their muzzles between their forelegs and wiped them with their paws; it was as if they were trying to conceal a disgust so overpowering that I felt like leaping over their heads to get away.

"Then what are you proposing to do?" I asked, trying to rise to my feet. But I could not get up; two young beasts behind me had locked their teeth through my coat and shirt; I had to go on sitting. "These are your trainbearers," explained the old jackal, quite seriously, "a mark of honor." "They must let go!" I cried, turning now to the old jackal, now to the youngsters. "They will, of course," said the old one, "since that is your wish. But it will take a little time, for they have got their teeth well in, as is our custom, and must first loosen their jaws bit by bit. Meanwhile, give ear to our petition." "Your conduct hasn't exactly inclined me to grant it," said I. "Don't hold it against us that we are clumsy," said he, and now for the first time had recourse to the natural plaintiveness of his voice; "we are poor creatures, we have nothing but our teeth; whatever we want to do, good or bad, we can tackle it only with our teeth." "Well, what do you want?" I asked, not much mollified.

"Sir," he cried, and all the jackals howled together; very remotely it seemed to resemble a melody. "Sir, we want you to end this quarrel that divides the world. You are exactly the man whom our ancestors foretold as born to do it. We want to be troubled no more by Arabs. We want room to breathe; a skyline cleansed of them; no more bleating of sheep knifed by an Arab; every beast to die a natural death; no interference till we have drained the carcass empty and picked its bones clean. A clean life, nothing but cleanliness is what we want"—and now they were all lamenting and sobbing—"How can you bear to live in such a world, O noble heart and kindly bowels? Filth is their white; filth is their black; their beards are a horror; the very sight of their eye sockets makes one want to spit; and when they lift an arm, the murk of hell yawns in the armpit. And so, sir, and so, dear sir, by means of your all-powerful hands slit their throats through with these scissors!" And in answer to a jerk of his head a jackal came trotting up with a small pair of sewing scissors, covered in ancient rust, dangling from an eyetooth.

"Well, here's the scissors at last, and high time to stop!" cried the Arab leader of our caravan, who had crept upwind towards us and now cracked his great whip.

The jackals fled in haste, but at some little distance rallied in a close huddle, all the brutes so tightly packed and rigid that they looked as if penned in a small fold girt by flickering will-o'-the-wisps.

"So you've been treated to this entertainment too, sir," said the Arab, laughing as gaily as the reserve of his race permitted. "You know, then, what the brutes are after?" I asked. "Of course," said he, "it's common knowledge; so long as Arabs exist, that pair of scissors goes wandering through the desert and will wander with us to the end of our days. Every European is offered it for the great work; every European is just the man that fate has chosen for them. They have the most lunatic hopes, these beasts; they're just fools, utter fools. That's why we like them; they are our dogs; finer dogs than any of yours. Watch this, now, a camel died last night and I have had it brought here."

Four men came up with the heavy carcass and threw it down before us. It had hardly touched the ground before the jackals lifted up their voices. As if irresistibly drawn by cords each of them began to waver forward, crawling on his belly. They had forgotten the Arabs, forgotten their hatred; the all-obliterating immediate presence of the stinking carrion bewitched them. One was already at the camel's throat, sinking his teeth straight into an artery. Like a vehement small pump endeavoring with as much determination as hopefulness to extinguish some raging fire, every muscle in his body twitched and labored at the task. In a trice they were all on top of the carcass, laboring in common, piled mountain high.

And now the caravan leader lashed his cutting whip crisscross over their backs. They lifted their heads, half swooning in ecstasy, and saw the Arabs standing before them. When they felt the sting of the whip on their muzzles, they leaped and ran backwards a stretch. But the camel's blood was already lying in pools, reeking to heaven; the carcass was torn wide open in many places. They could not resist it; they were back again; once more the leader lifted his whip. I stayed his arm.

"You are right, sir," said he, "we'll leave them to their business; besides, it's time to break camp. Well, you've seen them. Marvelous creatures, aren't they? And how they hate us!"

Translated by Willa and Edwin Muir

Biographical Notes

These tales are arranged almost exactly in their chronological order, giving a sense of the evolution and persistence of the *Märchen* tradition in literature—at the cost, to be sure, of obscuring one or two connections of importance. Novalis, for example, intended his "Klingsohr" as a response to Goethe's "Märchen."

The writers are without exception of prime rank. Goethe (1749–1832), Germany's greatest, worked in every literary form from the semi-autobiographical novel to classical drama, from operetta to the vast pageant of *Faust*. He was artist and scientist, director and actor, writer and civil servant—indeed for years he served as the Duke of Weimar's minister of practically everything, from roads and mines to higher education. At the same time he was building a corpus of writing that fills about 150 volumes. Much of the lasting force of German literature derives from his major works: *Werther, Egmont, Iphigenia, Torquato Tasso, Wilhelm Meister, Poetry and Truth,* and the vast body of incomparable lyric poetry. In later years his writing turned often to the symbolic and to the concentrated paradigmatic statement possible in epigram, masque, novella—and fairy tale.

The Romantics rejected what they saw as the excessive concentration of the eighteenth century on reason and intellect, perfectibility and progress. Belief in the mysterious, non-rational forces of nature and their counterparts in human life, in the unity of dream and reality, in the interpenetration of all aspects of existence, made the fairy tale one of their favorite modes of expression. The Grimms, who collected folktales (and, more than we realize, remodeled them) were their friends and contemporaries. Tieck

(1773–1853) was one of the first to make writing his profession and one of the most prolific of the Romantics: in drama, novels, tales, translations, in editing and criticism. His psychological insights served as models for the Freudians. Wackenroder (1773–1798), for a time Tieck's closest friend, was supposed to become a lawyer but turned instead to music, art, and art criticism, some of the latter published jointly with Tieck. Our story is in fact set in the context of his *Fantasies on Art*. His critical and philosophical work is practically a manifesto of Romanticism.

Novalis (Friedrich, Baron von Hardenberg; 1772–1801) wrote in his brief lifetime some of the classics of Romantic poetry, among them the *Hymns to the Night*. His novel *Heinrich von Ofterdingen*, with its famous Blue Flower, symbol of the magic ideal, is also the source of our two tales—not surprisingly, for the Romantics also believed in the unity (and the unifying) of all art forms.

Ernst Theodor Amadeus Hoffmann (1776–1822)—the Amadeus from his beloved Mozart—is the Romantic master of the supernatural and fantastic. Artist, musician and composer, lawyer and judge, he was to become the director, orchestra conductor, and stage designer for the theater in Bamberg and later a high civil servant in Berlin. His odd appearance and eccentric personality seem to reappear in the remarkable characters of his stories: mad musicians, ghosts, doubles, and living marionettes. The French loved his works—witness Offenbach's "Tales of Hoffmann." Poe learned from him. Thackeray's remarkable translation shows him in his best humor.

Joseph, Freiherr von Eichendorff (1788–1857), of the nobility like Novalis, a civil servant like Hoffmann, Catholic like—or more so than—most Romantics, ranks as one of the great German lyricists, a master of simple and moving verse, extolling the "folk," nature, love and longing. His finest stories, "The Marble Statue" and "The Life of a Ne'er-do-well," exhibit a greater sense of psychological peril than is commonly conceded. But innocence, love, and faith prevail.

The last of our real Romantics is Clemens Brentano (1778–1842), an earlier associate of both Tieck and Eichendorff. The great collection of German folksongs, *Des Knaben Wunderhorn*, is in large part his work—he was wealthy enough to afford an independent career of writing and collecting—and many of his own stories bear clear resemblance to folktales. In the novel and drama his work was too amorphous for his contemporaries—or for posterity. His poetry, however, is of remarkable sophistication and musicality. And one or two of his stories are classics.

Wilhelm Hauff (1802–1827) is perhaps the least familiar writer in our volume—he has no European reputation—and his entire literary career spanned barely three years of a short life. Yet his historical novel *Lichtenstein* is not unworthy of its models in Sir Walter Scott, while our story "The Cold Heart" is one of the single most popular adaptations of the fairy tale form with moralistic tendencies. He stands as a successor to the Romantics and a precursor of the Poetic Realists.

Of the latter, Theodor Storm (1817–1888) is one of the greatest. (Gottfried Keller, with whom he corresponded extensively, is another—and another of the many Realists for whom the fairy tale, despite its obvious Romantic affinities, was an appealing and stimulating form; see his "Mirror the Cat" in *Gottfried Keller: Stories,* volume 46 in THE GERMAN LIBRARY.) A lawyer and civil servant like Hoffmann and Eichendorff, Storm wrote dozens of novellas focussing on the everyday life of the sea provinces of Northern Germany, but his best characters and situations are always endowed with a symbolic dimension that transcends ordinary Realism—and often with a melancholy or bittersweet or tragic sense of fatedness.

Eduard Mörike (1804–1875) stands rather apart from the other Realists; indeed Romantic elements, balanced by almost classical perfection of form, characterize his poetry. Vicar and pastor, he lived a life of relative isolation. Indeed, he devoted himself so wholeheartedly to writing that he neglected his parish duties and was encouraged to retire. His oeuvre is small but of extraordinary quality. His story "Mozart on the Way to Prague" is a classic, as is his autobiographical novel *Maler Nolten.*

Austrian aristocrat and European intellectual, Hugo von Hofmannsthal (1874–1929) is probably best known to the English-speaking world as Richard Strauss's collaborator (libretti for the "Rosenkavalier" and five other operas), and as co-founder with Max Reinhardt of the Salzburg Festival. But he is also one of the greatest of twentieth-century writers of stories and essays, plays (*Everyman, Der Schwierige, Death and the Fool,* and many others), and lyrics (where he counts as one of German literature's most polished, articulate, and subtle artists—even though he ceased writing poetry when he was barely twenty). Some of his stories anticipate Kafka, with their exploration, in natural, realistic style, of the frightening depths of human existence. *The Thousand and One Nights* had an obvious appeal to him—he wrote a sensitive general introduction to an edition in German—but none bears any literal resemblance to *his,* despite its name and number!

We end with Franz Kafka (1883–1924), though he is by no means the last among German writers for whom the folk and fairy tale had lasting appeal. In a sense all of Kafka's work is part of this long tradition, for it is a parabolic statement, through "fantastic" events and characters, of truths which may be elusive but which strike us as internally consistent and externally—in terms of the human condition—shockingly, comically, or terrifyingly valid. This is true of the great stories such as the "Metamorphosis" (man as insect) or the "Judgment," equally true of the famous novels *The Trial* and *The Castle.* His work is not simply an end point of the traditional literary imagination but one of the few truly seminal forces in a new literature.

FRANK G. RYDER

ACKNOWLEDGMENTS

All reasonable efforts have been made to locate the parties who hold rights to previously published translations reprinted here. We gratefully acknowledge permission to reprint the following material:

"Jackals and Arabs," from Franz Kafka, *The Penal Colony*, translated by Willa and Edwin Muir. Copyright © 1948, 1975 by Schocken Books Inc. Reprinted by permission of Schocken Books Inc.